Episodes

Also by Christopher Priest from Gollancz:

Episodes
Short stories

Christopher Priest

GOLLANCZ

LONDON

First published in Great Britain in 2019 by Gollancz
an imprint of The Orion Publishing Group Ltd
Carmelite House, 50 Victoria Embankment
London EC4Y 0DZ

An Hachette UK Company

1 3 5 7 9 10 8 6 4 2

A CIP catalogue record for this book is
available from the British Library.

ISBN (Hardback) 978 1 473 22600 5
ISBN (Export Trade Paperback) 978 1 473 20062 3
ISBN (eBook) 978 1 473 20064 7

Typeset by Input Data Services Ltd, Somerset

Printed and bound in Great Britain by Clays Ltd, Elcograf S.p.A.

www.gollancz.co.uk

For Nina

Contents

First

This is a book of episodes, short and long stories, each uncon-nected with the others except by way of authorship. Most of the stories have never been collected in volume before, but two of them appeared in an earlier book, published four decades ago, another in a long-forgotten story collection, even earlier, in 1972. They were indicators of the direction in which my writing was then developing. Because the stories in this book have been chosen to represent the range of what I have been doing for most of my time as a writer, all three of them should be here.

They and the others are unchanged from when they were first published, but because everything in life moves on and develops, not least of which for a writer is an interest in and knowledge of language and style, I have done a little polishing here and there. I hope it will be invisible, and not indicative of some motive to make the stories seem better than they were at the time.

Each story is presented in three sections. The story itself sits in the middle, but there is a *Before* section, which describes informally how the story came to be written, in some cases noting circumstances that were relevant, and what I had in mind as I was working out what to do with the story. Then there is the *After* section, perhaps even more informal in manner, and this describes how the writing of the story went, where it was published, what if anything happened as a result of it.

The intention is to try to convey an insight into the writing of short stories, the context from which they have arisen. I usually write short stories when I'm between novels, although in one needlessly disruptive case, described when its turn comes, I had to break off from a novel in progress to write a story.

Novels are of course a long haul. I need a basic minimum of six months of concentrated work to complete a novel, but have managed that only occasionally. Most of them have taken much longer. *The Prestige* and *The Separation* were both endurance tests – the former because I had a pre-school family, the latter because of the amount of research that was necessary. For a large part of the time while writing a novel the outcome is never certain, and there is an ever-present danger of something going wrong – sometimes it can be a failure of nerve, but most often the taking of a misguided direction with the story or the characters.

Short stories have the advantage to a writer of seeming doable within a manageable period of time – even if they have to be abandoned or put aside for any reason, the loss, the sacrifice, is of a few days or weeks of work, rather than several months.

Even so, at least one of the stories here took longer to write than at least one of my published novels. No generalization about writing is ever completely true.

These stories are, for want of a better word (and I have searched for a better one), *fantastic* in kind. That is to say they do not deal with the normal, the familiar, the daily grind, the historical, but take that for granted and stretch credulity, test the reader's assumptions about what is real or experiential. I make no apology for this, because for half a century I have been putting into practice the belief that the fantastic is a crucial if often misunderstood element of literature.

The various images and situations of the fantastic, of science fiction, are now so widespread as to seem banal. Science fiction has become huge in Hollywood, for instance. It's hardly worth mentioning that some of the biggest box office successes in the last three or four decades have been recognizably science fiction in type (Hollywoodistas call it 'sci-fi'): the *Star Wars* and *Star Trek* franchises, for obvious examples, but those are just the most famous. The world of movies has been fascinated by spaceships, alien invaders, monsters, robots, etc., for most of its existence. One of the first feature films ever made, Georges Méliès' *Le Voyage dans la Lune* (1902), mixed surrealism, special effects and science fiction. Computer gaming draws heavily on the presumed images and clichés. Superheroes in comic books go in for extreme versions of the standard science-fiction tropes. Advertising, television shows, computer software, consumer electronics, internet graphics, industrial design, architecture, magazine illustrations – the visual and metaphorical references to the fantastic are endless.

Oddly, though, one thing has not changed at all in that half century, my half century of writing. Fantastic literature itself is still largely unappreciated beyond a small but consistently intelligent readership. Criticism from outside is usually general, based on perceptions of the form rather than what it should be: an assessment of particular titles or, more importantly, the work of individual authors. Because of this inexactitude it is therefore treated as a genre with its own self-enclosed rules, assumed to be subject to special standards that do not apply to general literature, thought to be aimed at an audience of nerds or computer geeks or sensation seekers.

I have always hoped this would change, but it never has. The inference of sameness is patently flawed, because it lumps the good work with the bad and does not recognize the middle ground. Literature is the product of individuals, almost always working alone. Those who speak up against the generalization therefore find themselves in the wrong argument, because a defence of the whole has to include a defence of the mundane and the frankly indefensible.

Fantastic literature is therefore regarded as genre fiction. The OED usefully provides two definitions of the word in its non-French usage.

The first says that a 'genre' is a style or a category, a kind of art, music or literature. Use of the word in this sense makes identification easy but also implies a taxonomy, a summing up of what it is without going into particulars. The label is handy. It is thought to serve, Janus-like, a dual role – an encouragement to those who like to read it, but also a warning off to those who do not wish to know.

But the OED offers a second definition: 'genre', as a modifier, denotes a term for paintings of a certain type, that of scenes from ordinary life, typically domestic or realistic.

As has been pointed out by Ursula K. Le Guin, a supreme writer of the fantastic, the phrase 'realistic scenes of ordinary life' neatly describes the subject matter of the realistic or general literary novel.

Paradoxically, when 'genre' started being used in the critical lexicon of literature, it was applied to certain types of fiction at a slight remove from absolute reality: detective stories, spy thrillers, romances, Westerns, sea stories, and so on, were all called genre fiction.

Because these categories actually do have clear boundaries, they are limited by them. If a gunman in the Old West sees the error of his ways and becomes a social reformer in the slums of

Chicago, the book is no longer a Western; if Hornblower falls overboard and drowns it is no longer a sea story; if a doctor and nurse spend long hours of overtime in A&E it is not a romance.

The fantastic is different. It is indefinable and free of boundaries, with no restrictions on place or time – it can be located in the realist here and now if needs be, but also anywhere in the world or universe, real or imagined, past, present or future. There are no expectations about style and internal rules are few. The fantastic includes shallow and meretricious hackwork, but also the work of fine literary writers – Ursula K. Le Guin, Octavia E. Butler, J. G. Ballard. Margaret Atwood, winner of multiple awards, has not only written several fantastic novels, but a book about science fiction. The culminating works of Doris Lessing, Nobel Laureate in Literature, were resolutely fantastic in nature. Kazuo Ishiguro, another Nobel Laureate, has written at least two fantastic novels, and has fantastic elements in others.

All the best literature exists and survives outside definitions. That which is uncategorizable, unrepeatable, inimitable, will break all the rules but outlive its contemporaries forever. Regard such twentieth-century fiction as *Dubliners*, *Cold Comfort Farm*, *Catch-22*, *The Prime of Miss Jean Brodie*, *L'étranger*, *Animal Farm*, *The Catcher in the Rye*.

I make no such high claim for the stories in this book, but from reading them you will probably discern that very few of them conform to the standard expectations of science fiction. Looking over them, I think only two of them come close to what many people think of as SF: 'An Infinite Summer' has people from the future taking an advanced kind of photograph, and in 'Palely Loitering' there is talk of a starship – but both of those stories are wistful love stories in romanticized settings, and the gimmick is in the background. One other story is a sort of extended gag about science-fiction gadgets. The rest are what I prefer to think of as speculative fiction, where strangeness is something that is perceived or encountered or imagined, and is not set off by aliens invading in UFOs or mad professors building super-weapons. None of that is interesting to me, not back then when I began writing, or now, while I continue.

One of the under-regarded strengths of the science-fiction idiom, something almost unknown in the larger literary world, is that it has always been an active market for the writing, selling and publishing of short stories. When I began trying to sell stories professionally, there were three regularly published magazines that specialized in science fiction or fantasy – they were sold on ordinary bookstands. I first discovered them displayed in a WH Smith branch in an Underground station in London.

Although soon after I started writing the three were reduced to two, the lost one was in effect replaced by a series of anthologies of previously unpublished fiction: four a year from a major paperback publisher, with national distribution. All these markets for short stories operated what is called these days an 'open submission' system, which meant that anyone who cared to could submit material. That is how I began: typing out my faltering first efforts, putting them in envelopes and sending them in. Most came back after an agonizing delay – one or two did not. I was paid eight guineas for my first story (which in fact was at the time more than my weekly wage).

All those magazines and anthologies, long ago, have of course ceased to exist, but they were replaced by others, and they in their turn have come and gone. At the time of writing there are two regularly published print magazines of fantastic fiction in the UK, which will accept stories from new or unknown writers, as well as printing material from established writers. *Interzone* and *Black Static* are not easily found on bookstalls, but they are regularly published and distributed, they accept subscriptions and can be located online. Both magazines are superbly printed on good-quality paper, with an emphasis on striking design and beautifully executed commercial art. They run a range of intelligent essays, reviews and features as well as several stories, in every issue.

Nor are these alone. In the *Before* and *After* essays about each of the stories you will notice a recurring theme: which is that several of the first story appearances were in anthologies of original fiction. In most cases, my own involvement came about because the editor or publisher invited me to submit, but as far as I know none of these books was a closed shop for established writers. The intention to publish an anthology, and its progress as work goes along, is almost always reported online, in blogs and social media – any new writer seeking a market, and who is prepared to carry out a little online legwork, will find several markets open for submissions.

Here then are some episodes arising from and between the work of a novelist.

Christopher Priest

Isle of Bute, 2018

Before – 'The Head and the Hand'

Although the stories in this book are not intended to be samples from a retrospective album, 'The Head and the Hand' is one of the earliest stories here. I wrote it at the end of the 1960s when I was in my twenties – even noting that makes me now drift mentally back fifty years, a distance that still astonishes me when I have to realize how long I have been a writer.

Like all the others here, this story has another story behind it – not a great revelatory exposition, but a mix of personal recollections. I look back on old relationships, the place I was living in, the almost invariable struggles with the difficulty of staying financially afloat. I am of course intermittently nostalgic for the youthfulness now lost, and glad I came through the problems associated with that. In every case I recall memories of my concerns with the art and craft of writing, as those have always involved me. They are reflected in the title I gave the story.

The story behind 'The Head and the Hand' is this. In the late 1960s I moved to a rented ground-floor apartment in a beautiful Victorian villa on the edge of the village of Harrow on the Hill. (The suburban town of the same name was just up the road.) Perched high on the eponymous hill, Harrow School dominated the area – the house itself, at the bottom of the hill, was almost entirely surrounded by the wide expanse of playing fields belonging to the school. A small gate at the end of the back garden opened into the fields, and we who lived there were permitted to stroll across the peaceful sward, provided none of the pupils was actually out there at the time. The grounds were surrounded by mature trees, many of which shielded the area from the main road that ran along one side,

9

making it into a huge and almost unknown island of greenery in a busy London suburb. It was large enough for several cricket pitches to be marked out. It soon became for me the place where I could think hardest and most creatively, where I could stride around unseen, talk to myself without being overheard, work out ideas for stories.

This almost idyllic writerly existence had, of course, a few snags attached to it, and in the case of the apartment the main disadvantage was that the elderly landlady, and her only slightly less ancient siblings, lived in the upper floors of the same building. They had old-fashioned ideas about the status and social undesirability of tenants, whom they clearly saw as representatives of an underclass. Naturally, I was deemed to be one. Perhaps it was the long hours of typewriting I went in for, or that I had a car I parked in their drive, or most of all the fact that I had long hair, but I became a target for snooty comments and general condescension. I wanted only to have a home where I could be private and secure, and concentrate on my work.

One day during the summer of 1969, working in my office at the back of the house, I became aware of a sporadic loud screeching from outside, interspersed with shouting voices and crashing noises. After a while I went out to the front to see what was going on. It turned out the landlady had employed a team of tree surgeons to pollard the two large lime trees that stood next to the drive. As the branches came away they were tossed deliberately in the direction of my car, which by the time I arrived was half-buried under the mass of leaves and branches, with several scratch marks plainly visible. I found the man in charge of the team – he told me that they were waiting for their truck to turn up and had been instructed by the landlady that in the meantime they should throw everything over my car. 'She told us it shouldn't be parked there,' he said, sounding half apologetic, half amused. 'We thought it was a bit odd, but she insisted.'

After that he and the other tree surgeons aimed the branches away from my car, but many dents and scratches had been made on the bodywork. After the men had left, and for the weeks that followed, the shorn stumps of the trees stood starkly outside the house, and to me they somehow seemed symbolic of an uncaring wish to control the natural environment for particular and (as I saw them) vengeful reasons.

Of course, the trees quickly regenerated and looked much healthier, and I later realized that mature trees benefit from being pollarded from time to time, however drastic and extreme the immediate results appear to be.

The incident gave rise to a series of reflections about trying to shape the world as you wished it to be rather than as it really was, and eventually, by way of the usual convoluted thought process, the horror story that is 'The Head and the Hand' was the result.

The Head and the Hand

On that special morning at Racine House we were taking exercise in the grounds. There had been a frost overnight and the grass lay white and brittle. The sky was unclouded, and the sun threw long blue shadows. Our breath cast clouds of vapour behind us. There was no sound, no wind, no movement. The park was ours and we were alone.

Our walks in the mornings had a clearly defined route, and as we came to the eastern end of the path at the bottom of the long sloping lawn I prepared for the turn, pressing down hard on the controlling handles at the back of the carriage. I am a large man, and well-muscled, but the combined weight of the invalid carriage and the master was almost beyond the limit of my strength.

That day the master was in a difficult mood. Though before we set out he had clearly instructed me to wheel him as far as the disused summer lodge, when I tried to lift him around he waved his head from side to side.

'No, Lasken!' he said irritably. 'To the lake today. I want to see the swans.'

I said to him: 'Of course, sir.'

I swung the carriage back into the direction in which we had been travelling and continued with our walk. I waited for him to say something to me, because it was unusual that he would give me untempered instructions without qualifying them a few moments later with a more intimate remark. Our relationship was a formal one, but memories of what had once existed between us still had an influence on our behaviour and attitudes. Though we were of a similar age and social background, Todd's career had affected us considerably. Never again could there be any kind of equality between us.

I waited for his mood to change.

In the end he turned his head and said: 'The park is beautiful today, Edward. This afternoon we must ride through it with Elizabeth before the weather gets any warmer. The trees are so stark, so black.'

'Yes sir,' I said, glancing at the woods to our right. When he bought the house, the first action he had taken was to have all the evergreen trees felled, and the remainder sprayed so that their greenery would be inhibited. With the passage of years they had regained their growth, and now the master would spend the summer months inside the house, the windows shuttered and the curtains drawn. Only with the coming of autumn would he return to the open air, obsessively watching the orange and brown leaves dropping to the ground and swirling across the lawns.

The lake appeared before us as we rounded the edge of the wood. The grounds dropped down to it in a shallow and undulating incline from the house, which was above us and to our left.

When we were about a hundred metres from the water's edge I turned and looked towards the house and saw the tall figure of Elizabeth moving down towards us, her long maroon dress sweeping across the grass.

Knowing he would not see her, I said nothing to Todd.

We stopped at the edge of the lake. In the night a crust of ice had formed on its surface.

'The swans, Edward. Where are they?'

He moved his head to the right and placed his lips on one of the switches there. At once, the batteries built into the base of the carriage turned the motors of the servos, and the back-rest slid upwards, bringing him into a position that was almost upright.

He moved his head from side to side, a frown creasing his eyebrow-less face.

'Go and find their nests, Lasken. I must see them today.'

'It's the ice, sir,' I said. 'It has probably driven them from the water.'

I heard the rustle of silk on frosted grass, and turned. Elizabeth stood a few yards behind us, holding an envelope in her hands.

She held it up, looking at me with her eyebrows raised. I nodded silently: that is the one.

She smiled at me quickly. The master would not yet know that she was there. The outer membrane of his ears had been removed, rendering his hearing unfocused and undirectional.

She swept past me in the peremptory manner she knew he approved of, and stood before him. He appeared unsurprised to see her.

'There's a letter, Todd,' she said.

'Later,' he said without looking at it. 'Lasken can deal with it. I have no time now.'

'It's from Gaston I think. It looks like his stationery.'

'Read it to me.'

He swung his head backwards sharply. It was his instruction to me: move out of earshot. Obediently I stepped away to a place where I knew he could not see me or hear me.

Elizabeth bent down and kissed him on his lips.

'Todd, whatever it is, please don't do it.'

'Read it to me,' he said again.

She slitted the envelope with her thumb and pulled out a sheet of thin white paper, folded in three. I knew what the letter contained – Gaston had read it to me over the telephone the day before. He and I had arranged the details. We both knew that no higher price could be obtained, even for Todd. There had been difficulties with the television and other media concessions, and for a while it had looked as if the French government was going to intervene.

Gaston's letter was a short one. It said that Todd's popularity had never been higher, and that the Théâtre Alhambra and its consortium had offered eight million euros for another appearance. I listened to Elizabeth's voice as she read, marvelling at the emotionless monotone of her articulation. She had warned me earlier that she did not think she was going to be able to read the letter to him without breaking down.

When she had finished, Todd asked her to read it again. She did this, then placed the open letter in front of him, brushed her lips against his face and walked away from him. As she passed me she laid a hand on my arm for a moment, then continued on up towards the house. I watched her for a few seconds, seeing her slim beauty accentuated by the sunlight falling sideways across her face, and strands of her hair blown behind by the wind.

The master waved his head from side to side.

'Lasken! Lasken!'

I went back to him.

'Do you see this?'

I picked it up and glanced at it.

'I shall write to him of course,' I said. 'It is out of the question.'

'No, no, I must consider. We must always consider. I have so much at stake.'

I kept my expression steady.

'But it is impossible. You cannot imagine granting any more performances.'

'There is a way, Edward,' he said, in as gentle a voice as I had ever heard him use. 'I must find that way.'

I caught sight of a waterfowl a few yards from us, in the reeds at the edge of the lake. It waddled out on to the ice, confused by the frozen surface. I took one of the long poles from the side of the carriage and broke a section of the ice. The bird slithered across the ice and flew away, terrified by the noise.

I walked back to Todd.

'There. If there is some open water, the swans will return.'

The expression on his face was agitated.

'The Théâtre Alhambra,' he said. 'What shall we do?'

'I will speak to your solicitor. It is an outrage that the theatre should approach you. They know that you cannot go back.'

'But eight million euros.'

'The money does not matter. You said that yourself once.'

'No, it is not the money. Nor the public. It is everything.'

We waited by the lake for the swans as the sun rose higher in the sky. I was exhilarated by the pale colours of the park, by the quiet and the calm. It was an aesthetic, sterile reaction, for the house and its grounds had oppressed me from the start. Only the transient beauty of the morning – a frozen, fragile countenance – stirred something in me.

The master had lapsed into silence, and had returned the backrest to the horizontal position he found most relaxing. Though his eyes were closed I knew he would not be asleep.

I walked away from him so that I was again beyond his hearing, and strolled around the perimeter of the lake, always keeping a watch for movement on the carriage. I wondered if he would be able to resist the offer from the Théâtre Alhambra, fearing that if he did there would never be a greater attraction.

The time was right – he had not been seen in public for nearly four and a half years. The mood of the public was right – for the media had recently shown their old interest in his exploits, criticizing his many imitators and demanding his return. None of this was lost on the master. There was only one master, one Todd Alborne – only he could have gone so far. No one could compete with him. Everything was right and only the participation of the master was needed to complete it.

The electric klaxon I had fitted to the carriage sounded. Looking back at him across the ice I saw that he had moved his face to the switch. I turned back and went to him.

'I want to see Elizabeth,' he said.

'You know what she will say.'

'Yes. But I must speak to her.'

I turned the carriage round and began the long and difficult return up the slope to the house.

As we left the side of the lake I saw large, white birds flying low in the distance, headed away from the house. I hoped that Todd had not seen them.

He looked from side to side as we moved past the wood. I saw on the branches the new buds that would burst in the next few weeks. I think he saw only the bare black twigs, the stark geometry of the naked trees.

In the house I took him to his study and lifted his body from the carriage he used for outside expeditions, switching to the motorized one in which he moved about the house. He spent the rest of the day with Elizabeth. I saw her only when she came down to collect the meals I prepared for him. In those moments we had time only to exchange glances, to intertwine fingers, to kiss lightly. She would reveal nothing of what he was saying or thinking.

He retired early and Elizabeth with him, going to the room next to his, sleeping alone as she had done for five years.

When she was sure he was asleep she left her bed and came to mine. We made love at once. Afterwards we lay together in the dark, our hands clasped possessively. Only then would she tell me what she thought his decision would be.

'He's going to do it,' she said. 'I haven't seen him as excited as this for years.'

I have been connected with Todd Alborne since we were both eighteen, casual friends at first, then closer, then competitors, rivals, friends again. We took our knocks against each other, some from sport, some from occasional skirmishes, but mostly mental or emotional confrontations. We met during a European holiday – our parents had known one another and chance brought us together one year while were in the south of France. Though we did not become close friends immediately, I found his company fascinating and on our return to England we stayed in touch with each other.

The fascination he held over me was not one I admired, but neither could I resist it: he possessed a fanatical and passionate dedication to whatever he was doing, and once started he would be deterred by nothing. He conducted several disastrous love affairs, and twice lost most of his money in unsuccessful business ventures. He had a general aimlessness that disturbed me – I always believed that once he was somehow channelled into a direction he could control, he would be able to exploit his unusual talents.

It was his sudden rise to unexpected fame that separated us. No one had anticipated it, least of all Todd. Yet when he recognized its potential, he embraced it readily.

I was not with him when it began, although I saw him soon

after. He told me what happened and though it differs from the popular version, still repeated in the tabloids and on television, I believe it.

He was drinking in a bar in a bad part of town with some friends. An accident with an illegally carried knife occurred. They were passing it around, pretending to attack and foil with it. One of his companions had been cut badly and had fainted. During the commotion that followed, a stranger made a wager with Todd that he would not voluntarily inflict a wound on his own body.

Todd slashed the skin of his forearm and collected his money. The stranger offered to double the stake if Todd would amputate a finger.

Placing his left hand on the table in front of him, Todd removed his index finger. A few minutes later, with no further encouragement from the stranger – who by this time had left the place – Todd cut off a second finger. He went to the hospital with his injured companion, and both fingers were sewn back into place. The following day a television company picked up the story and Todd was invited to the studio to relate what had happened. His hand and forearm were swathed in bandages. It was a live current events show. Against the wishes of the interviewer, Todd repeated the operation, crudely manipulating a razor-sharp knife with his bandaged hand, slashing at the fingers of the other.

He was rushed to hospital – a second operation to restore his fingers was carried out.

It was the reaction to this first broadcast – a wave of prurient shock from the public, and an hysterical condemnation in the media – that perversely suggested to Todd the potential in such displays of self-mutilation.

Finding a promoter he commenced a tour of Europe,

performing his act to paying audiences only. As several of his extremities were sliced away, others were slowly healing. Bandages, plaster casts, slings and, later, crutches, became part of his recognized image.

It was around this time – as I began to find out about his arrangements for publicity, and as I learned about the extravagant sums of money he was confident of earning – that I became alienated from him. I deliberately isolated myself from news of his exploits and tried to ignore the constant reports of the various stunts he was performing in public.

The horrendous self-mutilation alone was appalling to try to understand, but as he developed what he called a performance act an element of ritual steadily began to take over. That sickened me, and his native flair for showmanship only made him all the more offensive to me.

It was a year after this alienation that we met again. It was he who approached me. I resisted him at first, but I was unable to keep it up.

I learned that in the time we had been out of contact he had married.

At first I was repelled by Elizabeth because I thought that she loved Todd for his obsession, in the way the blood hungry public loved him. But as I grew to know her better I realized that she saw herself playing some messianic role. I soon understood that she was as vulnerable as Todd, though in an entirely different way. I found myself agreeing to work for Todd and to do for him whatever he requested. At first I refused to assist him with the mutilations, but later did as he asked. I changed my mind about this because of Elizabeth.

The condition of his body when I started to work for him was desperate. So horrific were his self-inflicted wounds that he was almost entirely crippled. From the start he had sought expensive medical and surgical help to try to keep his body repaired, but the human body has limits of repair and regeneration, and it was not long before regrafting extremities or parts of limbs was no longer effective. Where repair surgery succeeded, distortions and abnormalities sprouted. Healing after a performance took longer, sometimes causing a break of several weeks or months before he could agree to another show. These were the worst times for Todd, because whenever he had to deny himself exposure to an audience, he felt his admirers were falling away.

But the limits were becoming traumatic. His left arm below the elbow had been removed; his left leg was almost intact beyond the two removed toes. His right leg was intact. One of his ears had been removed, and he had been scalped. All fingers but the thumb and index on his right hand had been removed.

As a result of these injuries he was incapable of administering any more amputations himself, and in addition to the various assistants he employed for his act he required me to operate the mutilating apparatus during the actual performances.

He attested disclaimer forms at every performance, protecting me against any consequence of the physical injuries I caused him, and his career continued.

And it went on, between spells for recovery, for another two years. In spite of the apparent contempt he had for his body, Todd bought the most expensive medical supervision he could find, and the recovery from each amputation was strictly observed before another performance.

But his eventual retirement was inevitable.

At his final performance, his genital organs were removed amid the greatest storm of publicity and outrage he had known. Afterwards, he made no further public appearance, and spent a long spell of convalescence in a private nursing home. Elizabeth and I stayed with him, and when he bought Racine House fifty kilometres from Paris, we went there with him.

From that day we had played out the masque, each pretending to the others that his career had reached its climax, each knowing that inside the limbless, earless, hairless, castrated man there was a flame burning still to finally be extinguished.

And outside the gates of Racine House, Todd's private world waited for him. And he knew they waited, and Elizabeth and I knew they waited.

Meanwhile our life went on, and he was the master.

After I had confirmed to Gaston that Todd was to make another appearance, three weeks went by before the night of the performance. There was much that Elizabeth and I had to do.

While we left the publicity arrangements to Gaston, Todd and I began the job of designing and building the equipment for the show. This was a process that in the past had been one I had always found unpleasant. It created tension between Elizabeth and myself, because she never wanted to know about the equipment, and would not let me talk about what I was building.

This time, though, there was no such problem. Halfway through the work she asked me about the apparatus, and that night, after Todd was asleep, I took her down to the workshop. For ten minutes she walked from one instrument to another, testing the smoothness of the mechanism and the sharpness of the blades.

Finally, she looked at me without expression, then nodded.

I contacted Todd's former assistants, and confirmed with them that they would be present at the performance. Once or twice I telephoned Gaston, and learned of the wave of intense speculation about Todd's comeback.

As for the master himself, he was taken with a burst of energy and excitement that stretched to its limits the prosthetic machinery which surrounded him. He seemed unable to sleep and several nights would call for Elizabeth. For this period she did not come to my room, though I often visited her for an hour or two. One night Todd called her while I was there, and I lay in bed listening to him talk to her, his voice unnaturally high-pitched, though never uncontrolled or overexcited.

When the day of the performance arrived I asked him if he wanted to drive to the Alhambra in our specially built car, or to use the carriage and horses that I knew he preferred for public appearances. He chose the latter.

We departed early, knowing that in addition to the distance we had to cover there would be several delays caused by admirers.

We placed Todd at the front of the carriage, next to the driver, sitting him up in the seat I had built for him. Elizabeth and I sat behind, her hand resting lightly on my leg. Every so often, Todd would half turn his head and speak to us. On these occasions, either she or I would lean forward to acknowledge him and reply.

Once we were on the main road into Paris we encountered many large groups of admirers. Some cheered or called, some stood in silence. Todd acknowledged them all, but when one woman tried to scramble up into the carriage he became agitated and nervous and screamed at me to get her away from him.

The only place where he came into close contact with any of his admirers was during our stop to change horses. Then he spoke volubly and amiably, though afterwards he was obviously tired.

Our arrival at the Théâtre Alhambra had been planned in great detail, and the police had cordoned off the crowd. There was a broad channel left free through which Todd could be wheeled. As the carriage halted, the crowd began to cheer, and the horses became nervous.

I wheeled Todd in through the stage door, reacting in spite of myself to the hysteria of the crowds. Elizabeth was close behind us. Todd took the reception well and professionally, smiling round from side to side, unable to acknowledge the acclaim in any other way. He appeared not to notice the small but determined and vociferous section of the crowd chanting the slogans that they bore on placards.

Once we were safely inside his dressing room we were able to relax for a while. The show was not scheduled to start for another two and a half hours. After a short nap, Todd was bathed by Elizabeth, and then dressed in his stage costume.

Twenty minutes before he was due to give his performance, one of the female staff of the theatre came to the dressing room and presented him with a bouquet of flowers. Elizabeth took them from the woman and laid them uncertainly before him, knowing well his dislike of flowers.

'Thank you,' he said to the woman. 'Flowers. What beautiful colours.'

Gaston came in fifteen minutes later, accompanied by the manager of the Alhambra. Both men shook hands with me, Gaston kissed Elizabeth on her cheek and the manager tried to strike up a conversation with Todd. Todd did not reply, and a little later I noticed that the manager was weeping silently. Todd stared at us all.

It had been decided by Todd that there was to be no special ceremony surrounding this performance. There were to be no speeches, no public remarks from Todd. No interviews to be granted. The act on the stage would follow carefully the instructions he had dictated to me, and the rehearsals that the other assistants had been following for the last week.

He turned to Elizabeth and put his face up towards her. She kissed him tenderly and I turned away.

After nearly a minute he said: 'All right, Lasken. I'm ready.'

I took the handle of his carriage and wheeled him out of the dressing room and down the corridor towards the wings of the stage.

We heard a man's voice talking in French of Todd and a tremendous roar of applause from the audience. The muscles of my stomach contracted. The expression on Todd's face did not change.

Two of the assistants came forward and lifted Todd into his harness. This was connected by two thin wires to a pulley in the flies. When it was operated by one of the assistants in the wings Todd would be lifted and moved around the stage. When he was secure, his four false limbs were strapped in place.

He nodded to me and I prepared myself. For a second, I saw the expression in Elizabeth's eyes. Todd was not looking in our direction, but I made no response to her.

I stepped on to the stage. A woman screamed, then the whole audience rose to its feet. My heart raced.

The equipment was already on the stage, covered with heavy velvet curtains. I walked to the centre of the stage and bowed to the audience. Then I walked from one piece of apparatus to another, removing the curtains.

As each piece was revealed the audience roared its approval. The voice of the manager crackled over the PA system, imploring them to return to their seats. As I had done at so many earlier performances I stood still until the audience was seated once more. Each movement I made was provocative.

I finished revealing the equipment. To my eye it was ugly

and utilitarian but the audience relished the appearance of the razor-sharp blades.

I walked to the footlights.

'Mesdames. Messieurs.' Silence fell abruptly. *'Le maître.'*

I moved downstage, holding out my hand in the direction of Todd. I tried purposely to disregard the audience. I could see Todd in the wings, hanging in his harness beside Elizabeth. He was not talking to her or looking at her. His head was bent forward as he concentrated on the sound from the audience.

They were still in silence – the anticipatory motionlessness of the voyeur.

Seconds passed and still Todd waited. Somewhere in the audience a voice spoke quietly. Abruptly, the audience roared.

It was Todd's moment. He nodded to the assistant, who wound the pulley ropes and propelled Todd out on the stage.

The movement was eerie and unnatural. He floated on the wire so that his false legs just scraped the canvas of the stage. His false arms hung limply at his side. Only his head was alert, greeting and acknowledging the audience.

I had expected them to applaud, but at his appearance they subsided again into silence. I had forgotten about that in the intervening years. It was the silences that had always appalled me.

The pulley assistant propelled Todd to a couch standing to downstage right. I helped him lie down on it. Another assistant – a qualified medical doctor – came on the stage and carried out a brief examination.

He wrote something on a piece of paper and handed it to me. Then he went to the front of the stage and made his statement to the audience.

I have examined the master. He is fit. He is sane. He is in full possession of his senses, and knows what he is about to undertake. I have signed a statement to this effect.

The pulley assistant raised Todd once more and propelled him around the stage, from one piece of equipment to another. When he had inspected them all he nodded his agreement.

At the front of the stage, in the centre, I unstrapped his false legs. As they fell away from his body, one or two men in the audience gasped.

Todd's arm was removed.

I then pulled forward one of the pieces of equipment: a long, white-covered table with a large mirror above it.

I swung Todd's torso on to the table then removed the harness and signalled for it to be lifted away. I positioned Todd so that he was lying with his head towards the audience, and with his whole body visible to them in the mirror. I was working in silence. I did not look towards the audience. I did not look towards the wings. I was sweating. Todd said nothing to me.

When Todd was in the position he required he nodded to me and I turned towards the audience, bowing and indicating that the performance was about to commence. There was a ripple of applause, soon finished.

I stood back and watched Todd without reaction. He was re-acting again to the audience. In a performance consisting of one solitary action, and a mute one at that, for best effect his timing had to be accurate. There was only one piece of apparatus on the stage which was to be used this evening; the others were there for the effect of their presence.

Todd and I both knew which one it was to be: I would wheel it over at the appropriate time.

The audience was silent again, but restless. I felt that the crowd was poised critically. One movement would explode everyone into reaction. Todd nodded to me.

27

I walked again from one piece of apparatus to the next. On each one I put my hand to the blade, as if feeling its sharpness. By the time I had been to each one, the audience was ready. I could feel it, and I knew Todd could.

I went back to the apparatus Todd had selected: a guillotine made from tubular aluminium and with a blade of finest stainless steel. I trundled it over to his table and connected it with the brackets for that purpose. I tested its solidity and made a visual check that the release mechanism would work properly.

Todd was positioned now so that his head overhung the edge of the table, and was directly beneath the blade. The guillotine was so constructed that it did not obscure the view of his body in the mirror.

I removed his costume.

He was naked. The audience gasped when they saw his scars, but returned to silence.

I took the wire loop of the release mechanism and, as Todd had instructed me, tied it tightly around the thick meat of his tongue. I heard him gagging, but we had rehearsed this at home and he had instructed me to ignore it.

To take up the slack of the wire I adjusted it at the side of the apparatus.

I leaned over him, and asked if he was ready. He nodded.

'Edward,' he said indistinctly. 'Come closer.'

I leaned forward so that my face was near his. To do this I had to pass my own neck under the guillotine blade. The audience approved of this action.

'What is it?' I said.

'I know, Edward. About you and Elizabeth.'

I looked into the wings, where she was still standing.

I said: 'And you still want to . . . ?'

He nodded again, this time more violently. The wire release on his tongue tightened and the mechanism clicked open. He nearly caught me in the apparatus. I jumped away as the blade plummeted down. I turned from him, looking desperately into the wings at Elizabeth as the first screams from the audience filled the theatre.

Elizabeth stepped out on to the stage. She was looking at Todd. I went to her.

Todd's torso lay on the table. His heart was still beating, for blood spurted rhythmically in thick gouts from his severed neck. His hairless head swung from the apparatus. Where the wire gripped his tongue, it had wrenched it nearly from his throat. His eyes were still open.

We turned and faced the audience. The change that had come over them was complete. In under five seconds they had panicked. A few people had fainted, the rest were standing, lurching, waving their arms, holding their heads. The noise of their shouting was unbelievable. They moved towards the doors. None looked at the stage. One man swung his fist at another, but immediately was himself knocked down from behind. A woman was having hysterics, tearing at her clothes. No one paid her any attention. I heard a shot and ducked instinctively, pulling Elizabeth down with me. Women screamed and men shouted. I heard the PA click on, but no voice came through. Abruptly, the doors of the auditorium swung open simultaneously on all sides, and armed riot police burst in. It had been prepared carefully. As the police attacked them the crowd fought back. I heard another shot, then several more in rapid succession.

I took Elizabeth by the hand, and rushed her from the stage.

In the dressing room we watched through a window as the

police attacked the crowds in the street. Many people were shot. Tear gas was released, helicopters hovered overhead.

We stood together in silence, Elizabeth crying. We were kept within the safety of the theatre building for another twelve hours.

The next day we returned to Racine House and the first leaves were spreading.

After – 'The Head and the Hand'

The title was derived from a remark by John Ruskin. I intended the story to be about a form of art, a negative and self-destructive art, but even so. Seeking a title, I looked around for an unusual definition of art and discovered an appropriate one from Ruskin: *Fine art is that in which the hand, the head, and the heart of man go together.*

With the pollarding of the trees still fresh in my memory I wrote the story in the early weeks of 1970. I received an offer straight away from Kenneth Bulmer, who was editing the *New Writings* books. This was the series of regular anthologies I mentioned in the introduction. The series was always given prominence in the publisher's catalogues, and was distributed nationally. The quality of work was high but the market was difficult. The series was eventually discontinued by the publisher, and when it happened Ken Bulmer kindly passed my story across to Michael Moorcock, editor of *New Worlds*.

Moorcock said he would publish it but suggested the story could be made a little longer. He offered a few detailed comments. For instance, I had called the building in the story 'Rimbaud House', but Moorcock said he felt Rimbaud had been done to death recently – I was not sure if that was a joke, but I changed it to 'Racine House' anyway.

The new version is the one here, and is about two thousand words longer than the original. It was not the first short story I sold to *New Worlds*, but it was the last.

My early writing career shadowed what are now seen by some as the mythic years of *New Worlds*, and the period of the British 'new wave' of science fiction (1964 to about 1970). So long ago, yet still a crucial period for those who went through it. I had stories published in both *New Worlds* and the sister magazine *Impulse*.

I usually say of the new wave that I was of it but not in it. As a young and raw writer I loved the propaganda from Mike Moorcock and his followers about doing your own thing, casting off the clichés of the past, taking inspiration not from the American science-fiction tradition but from poetry, rock music, painting, cinema, and much more. But I was also a prickly young man, determined to find my own way. The new wave idiom quickly became an orthodoxy of radical mannerism, a set of values which were deemed OK for a kind of sainted inner circle based around *New Worlds*, but which made everything else not-OK.

An extra problem was that although in those days Mike Moorcock and I always got along well in person, I did not admire what he wrote. He was a quick and clever writer, but his shallow and superficial skill won out every time over depth of feeling, an authentic voice, an opening up of heart. For me, it was the fatal flaw that tended to undermine the propaganda, and underlined my dislike of the new wave orthodoxy. However, Mike did occasionally buy a story from me, and I was always impressed by his editorial percipience, his loyalty to the writers around him. Grateful too.

I later included 'The Head and the Hand' in my early collection *Real-Time World*. It was reprinted in *Penthouse*, but soon after that it had run its course and it has not been in print for more than forty years.

Looking back to those years, I am surprised by the story's ruthlessness but not particularly shocked. The period in which I wrote it is often misremembered as a time of peace and love, but this was a fallacy peddled by the media, and in particular by the tabloid press. There were social and political upheavals going on in several parts of the world, many of them violent and destructive. The war in Vietnam was at its height. In the UK, some of the performing arts liberated themselves to the point where they became confrontational and sometimes intrusive to audiences, and in the world of rock music the American musician Alice Cooper had a stage act that included scenes of mock suicide, involving a guillotine, an electric chair and a noose. I did not find out about the Alice Cooper act until after the story was published, but at the time it all seemed to confirm the darker side of the zeitgeist.

Horrifyingly, perhaps, a film version of 'The Head and the Hand' was planned by Amicus Productions. It was destined never to get very far, as I discovered when they commissioned me to write a treatment based on the story.

Because the story itself is concerned with a single violent act, it clearly had to be expanded and developed: it needed much more character involvement, a plausible environment, early incidents leading to the climax, deeper personal relationships, and so on. I knew that Mick Jagger had started to drift away from the Rolling Stones and was making films. The Stones were not then the force of nature they later became. Mick Jagger had recently starred in the films *Ned Kelly* and *Performance*, and was rumoured to be looking around for other roles. Because by then I knew of the Alice Cooper act, it struck me that Todd Alborne could well be portrayed as a leading member of a heavy rock band in decline, looking for a new gimmick to spice things up a bit.

At a script meeting soon after, the producer, a mild-mannered and expatriate American gentleman, asked me if I had any ideas about the direction in which the film could go. Without naming Mr Jagger I described the grungy rock ambience I had in mind, and the sort of dark society of the near future, all chaos, riots and bread-and-circuses. This obviously sparked a response

33

because the producer looked inspired. 'Do you have a rock band in mind?' he said. I opened my mouth to suggest Mick Jagger and the Stones, but he went on: 'I know exactly how we could do this. Do you know a band called The Temptations?'

I did, and I also knew from that moment the project would be doomed. Although I went ahead and wrote the treatment, the film was never made.

Before – 'A Dying Fall'

'Your story has to be set in Belgium,' Jean-Claude said. 'It must mention our monarch, King Albert II. And *of course* it must mention Brussels sprouts! Other than that you are free to write anything you like.'

Jean-Claude Vantroyen, a long-term friend and colleague, was literary editor of the French language newspaper, *Le Soir*, published in Brussels. I had met him several times in the past at conventions in France, and also during a visit to the Belgian capital in 2000. At the time he phoned me I was not sure what the occasion was, but he was suddenly in a position to commission some short stories for the newspaper, and he offered me the chance to write one of them.

The story became a speculative one – that is, there is no scientific or even logical rationale for what happens, but neither is it fantastical. 'A Dying Fall' is a meditation on death, or at least on the moments of life when death becomes inevitable. I saw it as an optimistic story.

Although I managed to find a way to mention both the king and the vegetable in the original, published in the Brussels newspaper, I later removed them for English-language publication – the story is still set largely in Belgium, though.

A Dying Fall

You are about to die. What will be the last thought to flash through your mind?

When his own final moment came to him, Marcus Birch realized at once what was happening. There was no doubt about it. Death was about to strike him unavoidably, an appalling accident with an inevitable outcome. There was no time for fear or regrets or avoiding action or last-minute farewells. He simply experienced a feeling of disbelief and terror, and a total involvement with the accident.

You cannot prepare for death. That was the first thing Birch learned. It strikes without warning, a double blow – death and its accompaniment.

Death was to be expected, but it did not come alone. It brought with it one great and last illuminating thought, a vision of life, a summation and consummation. Birch had read of people who survived near-death experiences, speaking of the way their whole lives had seemed to run before them.

That was not what he experienced, on the day of his death, that last hour, that final minute, that culminating split second. But a last thought did burst upon him. His vision consisted of a stretch of straight road glimpsed through the windshield of a car, the land bright with sunlight, traffic roaring along, beside him and in front of him. Although there were almost no identifying marks, Birch knew at once that he was in Belgium, driving at speed along a modern highway. The mystery of the memory flooded into him.

Why should *this* be the last thought of his lifetime?

Why Belgium? When was this? Why should Birch, an Englishman living in London, think of Belgium?

How was he so sure? It was urgent that he understood.

Time slowed, time halted. The split second expanded like a bloom flowering in the sunlight. The memory flashed in, came to rest, stayed there at the forefront of his mind and communicated the knowledge.

'This is it. This is the end. This is what you will take to your grave, the climactic moment of your life.'

In that instant of frozen introspection he was drawn irrevocably to the image that had appeared in his mind. He understood it, realized that it was like a single frame of film taken from a whole story. But the meaning of the story was a mystery! Birch hardly knew Belgium, had visited the country only once, then just passing through, as now in this flash of memory he was passing through. Why should his life close with thoughts of a place he barely knew?

We are none of us ready to die, but even so we spend our lives knowing that the moment of dreaded departure will come. Most of the time we try not to think about it. We shrink from contemplating death, what it will mean. Death is the great blackness, and the only experience you take into death is the moment of dying.

Of course, death comes to us all in the end, the huge inescapable fact. Shakespeare died, Beethoven died, Einstein died, Rembrandt died, Jeanne d'Arc died. Their immortal abilities, their lasting influence on the world, were no use to them as a way of warding off the moment of passing. Death does not discriminate with its horrors.

But did these great people think mysteriously of another country, as they breathed their last? Did Rembrandt dream inexplicably of Spain as he died, as Marcus Birch dreamed of Belgium? Did Shakespeare, without warning, suddenly think of Italy?

Birch was not a great man, and he harboured no illusions that he might be. However, as his life went on he too would from time to time wonder more prosaically about what his fate was going to be. It seemed to him that some kinds of death were more likely or predictable than others — a car accident, a heart attack, pneumonia, old age, all these were familiar ways of dying, ones that could strike Birch as they struck most other people.

Other fates were more personal, the ones that everyone in a sense designs for himself. We all make choices, and avoid others. Birch was no different.

He discounted many possibilities. He felt it unlikely, for instance, that he would die in the frozen catastrophe of an ava-lanche, or under the lava flow from a volcano, or in a hail of machine-gun bullets in a gangland shooting, or from the bite of a rabid animal, or in the clutching hands of a strangler. Or in many other exotic or unusual ends. His life as a middle-aged Londoner did not expose him to those dangers.

But respiratory illness: now that was a possibility. Birch suf-fered from bronchitis when he was child, he took up smoking when he was a teenager and he had smoked for years before finally quitting. So what kind of mortal ending would that lead him to?

He imagined himself dying in his own bed, struggling for

breath, his heart labouring, his thoughts becoming vague, while anxious relatives surrounded him. In this fanciful end his pallid hands would lie on the starched sheets, while his frail head would be propped on linen pillows. He would be old, of course, exceedingly old, so old that life would no longer matter to him. If images of Belgium loomed in the last moment, he would barely notice.

Other illnesses would be similar. Hospital beds, sickbeds, visitors, the physical degradations of terminal disease. All of these he could imagine and even expect. None of them seemed likely to include a motorway in Belgium.

Perhaps instead he would choke on food – he always talked too much when he was eating, and his wife said he ate too fast anyway. He imagined a half-chewed morsel of steak lodging in his windpipe, a piece of pasta, a lump of cheese, a crust of bread. Choking, he would fall to the floor, struggle pitifully for a while, then expire.

Or drink. How much alcohol had he drunk in his life? And how much more was there to come (because he had no intention of giving it up)? He wondered about cirrhosis, pancreatitis, dementia, kidney disease, heart failure. He disliked the prospect of all of them, although there was always the saving thought, or perhaps it was a delusion, that terminal agonies might be cushioned by a bottle or two in the last hour.

Transport accidents: he drove his car several times a week, he was often on trains, he flew four or five times a year. Anything was possible.

But a traffic accident on a Belgian freeway? Was that what was coming?

Then there was his own particular danger-of-choice: Birch had taken up free-fall parachuting when he was twenty and still unmarried.

For about two decades afterwards he gave up all his spare time to this expensive hobby. Every spring, summer and fall he spent most weekends taking headlong leaps from high flying aircraft, plummeting towards the map-like ground so far below. It was an exhilarating pastime, addictive, endlessly exciting and rewarding.

Dangerous too. He often heard of accidents happening to other parachutists, a fact that gave an undoubted extra thrill to every jump. Although there was little risk of harm so long as you fell freely through the sky, there always came the moment when it was necessary to tug on the ripcord and trust to the saving billow of the parachute, cracking open in the air above you, slowing your mad dive, lowering you in a more controlled way towards the ground.

Perhaps once he might have wondered if that strenuous, thrilling hobby might signal the personal fate awaiting him, but in the end this too became less and less possible. By the time Birch reached the age of forty his children were in secondary school and his wife had not been in full-time employment since before they were born. Marcus Birch was the sole breadwinner and there was no family money to spare. Free-fall parachuting was a luxury he could no longer afford, and since his mid-thirties he had visited the parachute club in rural Essex with increasing irregularity.

In the end it stopped altogether. Parachuting went out of his life as easily as it had arrived. It might once have been a risk to him, but it was no more.

Not one of these deaths was to happen to him. It appeared to involve Belgium. Inescapably, illogically.

So Marcus Birch lived his ordinary life, whose outer appearance was no different from that of any other man, until he was forty-eight. He was early middle-aged, his hair was starting to go grey (but only a few strands), and his stomach was a little plumper than he would have liked (but nothing that could not be swiftly slimmed down by sensible eating and exercise). His general health was good, his work and home life were stable and contented. He loved his wife. His children, now in their late teens, had settled down at their universities. He was free of worries.

One evening in this unconcerned life he was standing on the platform of an Underground station, deep beneath the centre of London. He was about to cross from one side of town to the other. He was keeping a mental distance from the pressing crowds by listening on his iPod to Clara Haskil, the Romanian-born concert pianist, playing Mozart's 20th piano concerto. It was by modern standards an old performance, before cassette tapes, before CDs, before downloads. Haskil had recorded the concerto in 1960, the same year of her sudden death. In spite of its age the transfer was perfect, and it was a sensitive, atmospheric rendition, a personal favourite of his.

But Haskil's playing was not at the forefront of his mind. As he waited for the next train to pull in he was thinking about the meeting he was heading for, unworried about the future. It was a warm evening, the meeting would be short, he would be seeing some friends for a drink afterwards. The train was signalled to arrive within a minute.

While he waited he looked along the railway lines, staring down at the shallow channel that had been created between the rails and beneath the sleepers. As in every Underground station in London, this trench, an emergency measure to help protect anyone who fell or leaped from the platform, was littered with rubbish – plastic bottles and cardboard cartons and loose papers.

The second movement of the concerto ended. Clara Haskil

fingered the first notes of Mozart's finale, the *Rondo*. The familiar refrain swelled in his earphones. He felt the customary rush of warm air belching out of the tunnel into the station, as the train approached from the distant darkness. The litter between the rails moved with the wind. The great rumbling of the wheels grew louder.

He glanced towards the opening of the tunnel, saw the front of the train rushing alongside the platform, heard the rising screech of brakes and wheels as the train slowed down to pick up the waiting passengers.

Behind him someone moved suddenly, pushing against Birch's lower back, and catching him off balance. He turned, trying to steady himself, but his foot slipped. He began to topple to the side.

The motion had spun him around so that he was facing the oncoming train. He was tipping over as he fell, away from the platform, stiff with fear above the rails, angling down, unstoppably tumbling.

He could see the train, five metres away, three metres away. Clara Haskil played on as if nothing had changed. Over the orchestra and piano, Birch could hear the screaming of the train. The driver was at the controls, one arm thrown up above his eyes, the other pressing frantically against something on the panel in front of him, trying to ward off the sight of the man toppling before him, trying to stop the train in the impossibly short distance that remained.

Then, in the final split second before the train struck him, Marcus Birch saw a vision of Belgium.

He was in Belgium. He was on a divided highway, inside a car, driving at high speed. A sign went by, indicating Bruxelles and Liège, and Brussel and Luik, and other places whose names he either did not recognize or did not have time to read. Everything had two names.

The experience of the vision was a shock – shockingly real, clear, actual, immediate. Brilliant, hot sunshine, the roar of the traffic outside, the passing trees and the fleeting glimpses of fields and houses.

Birch allowed the vision to continue, trying to understand what he was seeing or what he might be doing. He looked around at where he was sitting. Yes, he was in a car. It was his own car, a Renault, one he had owned many years before. He remembered that Renault well. He remembered buying it, using it for three or four years, selling it when it was time for another.

He stayed with the memory, the image of the memory, letting it flow seamlessly around him. He wondered how long this final remaining fragment of his life might last. Would it be possible to sit here forever, watching the Belgian highway unfurling before him, endlessly putting off the moment when he would have to let himself go back to the Tube station in London, back to be crushed by the train?

Time appeared to be frozen, so the frozen time gave him long enough to think.

This, he knew now, was based on a memory, a fleeting, distant memory of a visit he had made a quarter of a century before. He was in his early twenties and was driving down to southern Germany, where he was planning to visit some friends. His route from Dunquerque led him down the west side and through the south of Belgium: Bruxelles, Liège, Verviers, across the Ardennes.

That thought made the image change, in a flash of different light and scenery. The road still lay ahead, but now it was narrower and the traffic noise was less. To his right and left were tree-covered hills. The lush Ardennes landscape rolled away endlessly on either side. He saw a road sign to Spa, and another to Malmédy. The border with Germany was not much further ahead. The road signs were in French alone.

The vision changed again, with another jolt of shifting perspective. Now he was on a country road, with tall trees planted along each side, farmland spreading away. A town lay ahead: he could see houses, a church spire, small businesses beside the road. Cars were moving slowly, as was his – he saw people riding bicycles.

A sign said the place was called Saint-Vith.

Instantly, he recognized and remembered the name. Instantly, the memory changed again.

Now he was out of the car, standing on a grassy slope. He was in a forest clearing, with trees growing on all sides. He was not alone.

He looked around at the scene. There were about a dozen other young men and women, standing in an orderly semi-circle, watching him. A harness was tied around his chest, running up behind his shoulders, and with broad leather straps looped between his thighs to support his weight. He glanced upwards. A gantry built of dull grey tubular steel supported the pulleys for the harness. The two ropes were taut, but not restraining him.

There was a young, fierce-looking man standing beside him, his arms and legs braced aggressively.

'This is how to fall!' he shouted at Birch.

He was some kind of trainer, instructor. He was wearing grey camouflage pants and shirt, which fit him like well-cut military fatigues. He stepped away from Birch, half-turned, then fell suddenly to the ground. His body rolled easily and smoothly, like that of a trained athlete. Immediately he was on his feet again, springing upright, standing in front of Birch, exactly as he had been before. It was like a loop of film, replaying.

'This is how to fall!' the instructor shouted, facing Birch but making sure everyone else was paying attention. 'Loosen the muscles of your arms and legs! Let the momentum take you as you hit the ground!'

The instructor turned away and fell swiftly to the ground, his body rolling easily on the rough turf. With the same lithe movement as before, he came springing upright and stood beside Birch.

'This is how to fall!' he shouted again. 'Relax your muscles, but prepare for the impact!'

He turned away to demonstrate once more, dropping athletically to the ground, breaking his fall, spreading the impact, then leaping to his feet with an easy strength.

'That is how to fall!' he shouted at Birch again. 'Now you try it!'

The instructor signalled to someone standing next to the gantry. To Birch's amazement the harness tightened around him and he was swept two or three metres into the air. Dangling on the ropes he swung to and fro, spinning slowly.

Remembering, remembering . . .

This was a course in parachuting in which he had enrolled when he first became interested in free-falling. He had made it part of his trip to Germany, all those years ago. He had interrupted his journey at Saint-Vith to spend three days in a training camp in this forest clearing, situated in the hills outside the town. In the world of parachuting the Saint-Vith course was considered the best. Every free-fall parachutist he met told him to train there if he possibly could. He had come to Belgium to learn the technical skill of landing on the ground at the end of a parachute descent without breaking any bones.

So he remembered.

The gantry released him. He crashed to the ground. His supple body took the impact, while the momentum rolled him across the grassy floor of the clearing.

'This is how to fall!' the instructor shouted at him again, as the memory looped. The harness raised him, spinning him in the air. He was released. His body fell rapidly to the earth. In a reflex he loosened his body, raised his knees to take the first shock of impact, let his limbs relax. He clouted the ground, but rolled easily and painlessly across the uneven turf.

'This is how to fall!' the instructor barked at him again and again. Birch landed repeatedly on the hard ground, rolling easily with his limbs relaxed, never hurting himself.

The memory went no further. He was hoisted into the air, he swung around, he plummeted to the ground, he landed and rolled, leapt again to his feet.

He believed he could spend eternity in that rondo, replaying the memory with its subtle variations, the frozen image that came to him in the split second before he was killed.

He was terrified of the alternative, the reality behind this false image, this hopeless, despairing glimpse of memory, clinging to life. So he swung and fell and landed and rolled, then swung again, fell again, landed and rolled, putting off the moment of dying . . .

Then he was back in grim reality, falling again, swinging out from the edge of the railway platform deep beneath the streets of London. His body was stiff and defensive, braced against the imminent pain, toppling out over the electrified track, in front of the rushing train, his arm raised uselessly to try to break the impact.

The train, brakes screeching, hammered unstoppably towards him.

Remembering, he relaxed his outstretched arm, loosened the muscles of his back, let his legs become pliable. The direction of his fall altered immediately. Instead of swinging out stiffly like a pole across the metal tracks, he dropped more directly downwards, vertically, a much quicker fall.

He landed heavily against one of the rails, felt agonizing pain as his head crashed against it. One of the front wheels, locked solid in a spasm of emergency braking, was slewing towards him with white-hot sparks flying around it.

He thumped down, a pliant body, rolling with the momentum into the emergency trench beneath the rails. The train roared over him, a hell of shattering noise and vibration. He was in total darkness, his entire body paralysed by pain.

There it ended for him as blackness swooped down on him.

There in the clearing in the Belgian forest it had also ended, many years ago, but with a broken ankle and a sarcastic instructor, unsympathetically yelling at the next trainee to put on the harness. Marcus Birch lay on the uneven ground, both hands reaching down to grip the agony of his ankle, his face and arms pale and strained, trying to look as if it didn't matter, in front of the other men and women, under the harsh manner of the instructor.

Someone eventually called for an ambulance and in the hospital he was treated well and efficiently. He travelled home from Belgium by train a few days later, hobbling on crutches, full of regrets and the humiliated anger of having had to abandon the course before it properly started. The face of the instructor, his expression hard and his eyes narrowed with impatience, haunted him for days. The plaster did not come off for several weeks, and that ankle was weaker than the other for the next two years.

47

★

The blackness was brief. It swooped away as swiftly as it had swooped down. Birch huddled in the littered, filthy space between the rails as the train came to a final halt. Somewhere out there in the main part of the station there was a racket of shouting voices, warnings, yelled instructions, people screaming, footsteps running away. Closer in, around him in the darkness beneath the train, was a deep silence. Even closer, pressed into his right ear, was the remaining earpiece. The iPod was still working.

He was not dead, but later they said at the hospital that he came as close to it as anyone they had ever seen. Serious injuries to his head. His left hand had been severed by the train's wheel. A hip was broken, also his pelvis. There were cuts, grazes and bruises all over him. He was in pain so deep and extensive that he simply lacked the words to describe what he felt – in any event, he was sedated for many days and remembered almost nothing of his first period of slow recovery.

The iPod was still working, one remaining earphone clinging on somehow. In the years ahead he often played again the final movement of that Mozart concerto, the *Rondo*. The familiar refrain, endlessly repeated, was a way of holding on to his moment of saved life, the postponement of the inevitable. He loved Clara Haskil's interpretation, her delicate musician's touch, the sublimely fluid notes of the concerto, the reworked phrases, the repetitions, the subtle variations, her dying fall.

After – 'A Dying Fall'

A few months before Jean-Claude Vantroyen phoned me with the invitation to write a story for his newspaper I had in fact been driving across Belgium on the A10 freeway. We went past Bruxelles, past Luik, down through the Ardennes forest towards the border with Germany. Afterwards I did not remember much about the physical environment of the long motorway, except that it was an unscenic, dull journey. When we started crossing the Eifel Mountains the lush scenery was a relief. We stopped for lunch in Saint-Vith, a pretty town in the forested hills.

This much was my recent memory of Belgium, and when I started thinking about the story the boring image of the motorway came clearly to mind.

I have, though, never parachuted, free fall or otherwise.

Clara Haskil was one of the most accomplished classical pianists of the twentieth century, particularly noted for her interpretations of Mozart and Beethoven. Her recordings are still available. I chose to put her music on Marcus Birch's iPod more or less at random, but I knew her interpretation of the final movement, the *Rondo*, of Mozart's 20th Piano Concerto was widely regarded as sensitive and subtle.

Then, when I was working on the final draft of the story, I discovered the circumstances of Clara Haskil's death. The way the poor woman died, and where she was when it happened, came to me as a shocking coincidence, one of those occasional moments in a writer's life when you can't help wondering where the material you thought you had made up really comes from.

Before – 'I, Haruspex'

The novels I have written have without exception been self-generating: none has been written on request, or in response to some kind of editorial demand. The opposite is true of my shorter work. Almost every story in this collection was at least started because of an invitation, or a suggestion, or even a kind of challenge. Once kickstarted like that, though, the result has always been something of my own, something that grew from personal instincts.

'I, Haruspex' is a case in point. Attracted by the offer of a fairly substantial fee, I was in indirect contact with a software games company who were looking for original short stories that might provide the background for new programs. The basis, considered loosely, was the Cthulhu Mythos of H. P. Lovecraft. My familiarity with Mr Lovecraft's work was taken for granted, or at least I was not questioned about it. It was also assumed, I believe, that I already knew, or fully understood, the kind of scenarios that gamer writers liked to use as a basis for developing their work. I could not make the same assumptions about my suitability for the job. Lovecraft's work was in fact terra incognita to me, and I was not a gamer.

I settled down to work, and this extraordinarily nasty story soon emerged. Once I had the title (if you don't know what a haruspex is, or more likely was, a dictionary will of course inform you) the sheer pleasure of delving into bottomless foulness had me in its grip. It truly is a horror story.

I, Haruspex

The morning of that January day was icy cold with bright but slanting sunlight, the blue sky lending an electric radiance to the hoar frost that lay sharply on the grass and shrubs of the Abbey grounds. Earlier I had taken a brief walk across the Long Lawn, but the predawn chill had driven me indoors again after a few minutes. Now I waited in the draughty main entrance hall of the Abbey, behind the closed double doors, listening for the sound of tyres on the gravel drive outside.

The car sent by the solicitor arrived punctually, only a few seconds after the clock in the stairwell had finished chiming nine o'clock. I snatched the doors open as soon as I heard the car come to a halt. The frozen air swirled in and around me.

The simple formality began.

The chauffeur climbed out of the driver's seat, lowering his head to one side to avoid dislodging his cap, then straightened his full-buttoned jacket with a jerking motion at the hem. He stood erect. Without looking in my direction he walked smartly to the rear compartment of the car, and held the door open. He stared into the distance. Miss Wilkins stepped down: a brief vision of silken stockings, a tight black skirt, glossy shoes, mousquetaire gloves, a discreet hat with a wide brim and a veil. She was clutching the small, box-shaped parcel I was expecting.

As she climbed the double flight of steps towards the main door, the chauffeur followed. He stood protectively behind her as she confronted me. As usual she did not look directly at me but held out the package for me to take. She was looking down at the steps, a parody of demureness. Intoxicating waves of her civet-based perfume drifted across to me, and I could not suppress a relishing sniff.

I took the package from her, and also the release form that required my signature, but now I had the parcel in my hands I was no longer in any hurry.

I shook the package beside my ear, listening to the satisfying, provocative sound of the hard little pellets rattling around inside. All that potential locked within! I stared directly at Miss Wilkins, challenging her to look back at me, but her expression remained frightened and evasive. She could not leave without my signature on the release, so naturally I made her wait. I like to see fear in another person's face, and in spite of her seeming composure, and her deliberate avoidance of my gaze, Miss Wilkins could hide her apprehension no better than she could conceal her youthful allure.

She was trembling, a hint of convulsive movement that induced a terrible bodily craving in me. As usual, she had gone to manifest efforts to make herself unattractive to me. The jacket and skirt of her suit, made of heavy, businesslike serge, and of forbidding stiffness, for me only served to emphasize the hint of feminine ripeness that lay beneath. The delay I was causing interested me, the fear in the young woman stimulated me, and her scents were all but irresistible.

I said softly: 'Will you enter my house, Miss Wilkins?'

Beneath the veil, her steadfast gaze at the ground was briefly interrupted; I saw her long lashes flicker.

'I dare not,' she said, in a whisper.

'Then—'

The moment was interrupted by the chauffeur, who shifted his weight in an impatient, threatening manner.

'Just sign the receipt, Mr Owsley,' he said.

I did not mind him intervening, although I resented the sense of intimidation. He had his job to do. I expected only that he should do it civilly. I gave the young woman an appreciative smile for bringing me my pellets, hoping to excite another response, perhaps even a glimpse of her eyes, but during the many brief visits she had made in the last few months she had never once looked straight at me.

I fussed with my pen, making it seem that it was unexpectedly dry of ink, but I must have tried this once before in the past. Miss Wilkins had another pen at the ready, concealed in her gloved hand, and she moved deftly to provide me with it. I took it from her, contriving to brush my fingers against the soft fabric covering the palm of her hand, but once I had the thing in my hand there were no more excuses for delay. I signed the receipt for the package, and Miss Wilkins seized it from me with a fearful sweep of her hand.

There was a momentary unavoidable collision of her fingers with mine, but she turned back to the steps and at once hurried down them to the car. The chauffeur strode beside her. Her last scents briefly swirled around me and I darted my face through them, sniffing them up – not every aroma exuded by her flesh was concealed by the bottled perfume.

I went to the parapet to watch her, again admiring her silk-clad legs as she climbed elegantly into the rear compartment of the limousine. Although blinds obscured most of the windows I could make out her head and shoulders as she settled back into the seat. I could not fail to notice the shudder that convulsed her when the chauffeur closed the door on her. He hurried to his cab, climbed stiffly inside, and started the engine at once. Neither of them glanced back at me or the Abbey. Miss Wilkins lowered her face, brought a folded white handkerchief to her eyes, held it there.

The silver-grey Bentley Providence swung around the ornamental sundial, then accelerated down the drive towards the gates. Gravel flew behind it. I could hear the sound of the tyres long after the car had passed behind St Matrey's Stump and out of my sight.

Aware of the importance to me of the day, Mrs Stragg had arrived at work early that morning and was already in the kitchen, waiting for me to bring the pellets to her. What she did not know was that I had mystical evaluations of the pellets to perform first.

I hurried as quietly as I could to the conservatory at the far end of the East Wing and locked the connecting door behind me. I glanced in all directions from the windows to make sure I was unobserved.

Across the Long Lawn, in the hollow beyond the trees, morning mist hung in an evil shroud above the Beckon Slough. I stared across at it for a moment, trying to detect any sign of movement from within the cover of thick trees. It was a windless day and the mist was persisting well into the morning, the sunlight as yet too weak to disperse it. I shivered, knowing that I would soon have to venture that way.

I was in the cooler part of the conservatory, the one that faced down towards the Slough. In the normal course, tropical plants could be expected to thrive in a glass enclosure on the south face of any house in this part of England, but here on the Beckon Slough side the air was inexplicably chilly and condensation usually clung to the panes. No specimens from the equatorial rainforests would grow in the mysterious dankness, so here were kept the pots of common ivy, the thick-leaved ficus, the fatsia japonica in its huge cauldron. Even hardy plants like these had to struggle to maintain life.

I squatted on the floor beneath the fatsia, first checking the most basic of facts, that no error had been made and that the package was appropriately addressed to me: *Mr James Owsley, Beckon Abbey, Beckonfield, Suffolk*. Of course it was correct – who else would receive such a package? But like everyone else I had my fantasies.

Inside, as I rocked the parcel to and fro, I could feel the loose movement of the pellets, their deadly weights knocking about in their separate protective compartments. The medical staff at the Trust had for some reason sealed up today's consignment more securely than usual, itself an intriguing augury. I was forced to tear at the stiff brown sealing tape, accidentally bending back the nail of my middle finger as I did so. Sucking at it to try to assuage the pain, I got the lid open and shot a glance inside to be certain as quickly as possible that everything was in order and as I required.

A faint chemical smell, with its hint of preservatives masking the truer stench, drifted promisingly around my nostrils. Beneath it, the darker, headier fragrance of putrid organics. The muscles of my throat tightened in a gagging reflex, and I felt the familiar conflict of terror against rapture, both hinting at different kinds of oblivion.

The sixteen compartments on the top layer, four by four, each contained a pellet, brown-red or grey-pink, the exact shade indicating to me from which part of the source it had been removed. Every pellet had undergone primary compression by the Trust staff, bringing it down to the approximate size of a large horse-chestnut, but their methods had not yet become systematized or a matter of routine and the results were uneven in shape and size.

I knew that the compression was one of the means by which the staff tried to distance themselves from their work, but I cared only about the vital essence. Each pellet was the result of individual sacrifice and surgical endeavour.

Satisfied already with the contents of the package, I pushed my fingers down the sides of the box and with immense care lifted away the top layer. I placed it gingerly aside on the stone flagged conservatory floor. Underneath was the carton's second level, also arranged four by four, and here the pellets were less well formed than the ones on the top, closer in shape to their clinical origins. Rapture and terror again took hold of me. I touched one of the pellets at random and found it bewitchingly hard and resilient to my touch, as if it had been allowed to dehydrate.

I picked it up and pressed it gently beneath my nostril, inhaling its subtle fragrance. The hardening process had made the release of its essence more reluctant, but even so I could sense the death of the person who had grown the pellet for me. I knew that this pellet had struggled for months in the silent but unceasing contest of decay, and as a consequence it was empowered with the ineluctable life-rage of the dying.

I returned the pellet to its tiny compartment, then lifted aside the second layer. Two more layers were below, also arranged in sixteen square compartments. All of them were filled. For once the Trust had sent me not only quality and diversity, but quantity too. Sixty-four pellets were more than enough to get me through the week that lay ahead. A new and surprising sense of optimism surged through me.

I wondered: could this be the time I had been waiting for? If I regulated my appetites, partook steadily of the pellets, varied my intake? I could start with the most powerful to make up for the unsatisfactory week I had recently endured, then gradually moderate my intake. I would use only the grey slices of tissue until I had the pit under control, then could take the rest in a rush, dosing myself until insensate on the most potent of the reddish ones . . . ?

Would the nightmare then reach the end that until now had eluded me?

This sudden rush of optimism came because I knew my strength was starting to decline. I could not continue to struggle alone much longer.

Many aspects of my life were a source of consternation to me.

My father, who as a young man had been employed as a sin eater in the six parishes in the vicinity of the Abbey, often spoke of his wish for me to follow his way, while warning me of the attendant dangers. As he saw me growing up with a greater haruspical power than his own I knew he realized that I was overtaking him. The conflict of parental hope against fear helped destroy him, and in his last years he slumped into hopelessness and melancholy. In the final twelvemonth of his life his madness took hold completely and he taunted me with grotesque descriptions of what befell those who perceived the powers of entrails in their efforts to control past and future. That I was already one such was a fact he could never entirely accept.

He had had his own arcane methods – I had mine. It was the duty and curse of the male line of our family to stand on the brink of the abyss and repel the incursion from hell. When he perforce abandoned the struggle, I took his place.

I remain in that rôle, following my ancestors, until someone else replaces me. There is no alternative, no end to the struggle.

I was brought out of my reverie by a staccato rapping sound on the glazed door that led back into the house. Mrs Stragg was standing beyond it, her hand raised, the bulging signet ring she had used to rap on the glass glinting in the daylight. I moved my chest and arms around to shield what I had been doing and quickly returned the trays of pellets to their carton.

I stood up and unlocked the door.

'Mr Owsley, I must speak to—'

'I have obtained some more supplies, as expected,' I said, walking through and closing the conservatory door behind me. I proffered the parcel of pellets to her. 'You know what to do with them. The rest may be kept in the cold store until later.'

'Mr Owsley. James—'

'Yes?'

'Whatever you instruct, of course,' she said. She glanced at the parcel in her hands, and I heard a deep intake of breath. 'I am ready for that. Also, should you—'

Our eyes met and her unspoken meaning was clear. The arrival of the packages from the Trust often had a disturbing effect on us both, and sometimes, unpredictably to outsiders had they been there to see it, but memorably for us both, alone together in the house, violent sexual coupling would follow in the minutes after I received the pellets.

Our physical encounters were so spontaneous that they often occurred wherever we happened to be. Once it was against a bookcase in my library, another time on the snooker table in the Great Hall, actually beneath the eye of the hagioscope hidden there.

We rarely alluded explicitly to the darker side of our relationship, so this morning's invitation from her was a novelty. Normally, we played the roles of master and servant, she with an undercurrent of resentment I was never quite sure was genuine or assumed, I with a lofty disdain that sometimes I truly felt, sometimes I put on for her benefit or mine. It was my place to make the first move, but today I was full of haruspical hope, not bodily lust.

'No, Patricia,' I said as gently and quietly as I could. 'Not today.'

Anger briefly flared in her eyes; I knew she hated sexual rejection. But I was feeling calm and positive, excited by the realization of what the new pellets would mean for my destiny.

'Then allow me to cook for you . . . sir.'

'If you would.'

'Do you have a preference today?'

'A ragout,' I said, having already considered the various choices. 'Do you have a suitable recipe?'

'Mr Owsley,' she said. 'Don't you recall the stew I cooked for you last week?'

'I do,' I said, for it had been a memorable experience. 'I do not wish you to try that recipe again.'

'It was not the method but the ingredients.'

'But it is the ingredients I must consume,' I said. 'No matter what your damned method might be, I require the pellets to be appetizingly prepared.'

She walked away from me with bad grace.

At times like this I cared little for her feelings, because I knew she was being well remunerated under the terms of the Trust. The mortgage on her house had been repaid in full to the loan corporation. Invalid John Stragg, her husband, whose health had been ruined during his service in the Great War, was more comfortable than he could ever once have dreamed of. I was the greatest good fortune to the family Stragg. In this light the additional pleasures I took with her were a small price for her to pay. None the less, she continued to resent me. My father once told me that he and my mother had also had problems with servants, until they found the remedy.

With the domestic arrangements taken care of for the remainder of the day – indeed, for the rest of the week – I was
determined that my optimistic mood should not be broken.
I felt that if I could not confront the mystery of the Beckon
Slough on a morning like today, then I might never in any
conscience be able to again. I found my warmest coat, and left
directly.

The day was bright, icy and shimmering with the promise
of deeper winter weather to come. The frosted grass crunched
enticingly under my shoes as I strode down the slope of the
Long Lawn. I knew I was counting on the buoyancy of a passing mood to bear me through the dread of what lay ahead. As I
passed from the blue-white, winter-sunlit slopes of frosted grass
close to the house, and went along the cinder track that led into
the dark wood, the cooler fears of my mystical calling returned.
My pace slowed.

Soon the first tendrils of mist were reaching out above my
head. Around my ankles eddies of whiteness dashed like slink-
ing fish. The temperature had dropped ten or fifteen degrees
since I left the house. Above, in the gaunt branches of the trees,
rooks cawed their melancholy warnings.

The slope was steeper now and where the path lay in permanent shadow the frozen soil was slippery and treacherous.
Brambles grew thickly on each side, the dormant shoots lying
across the path, their buds and thorns already worn away in
several places by my frequent passing.

The Beckon Slough was ahead.

I smelt it before I could see it, a dull stench drifting out with
the mist, a dim reminder of the pellets' own putrid reek. Then I
could see it, the dark stretch of mud and water, overgrown with
reeds and rushes, and the mosses and fungi that surrounded it.

Life clung torpidly and uselessly to the shifting impermanence of the bog. Saplings grew further back around the edge of the marsh, although even here the ground was too sodden to hold the weight of full-grown trees. The young shoots never grew to more than twelve or fifteen feet before they tipped horribly into the muck below. Roots and branches protruded muddily all around the periphery of the consuming quagmire, along with the sheets of broken ice, slanting up at crazy angles, broken by the sheer weight of the intrusion from above, the machine that had descended so catastrophically into the vegetating depths.

It remained in place, an enigma that fate had selected me to unravel.

About a third of the way across the Slough were the remains of the crashing German aircraft. Now it rested, frozen in time. It was painted in mottled shades of dark brown and green. After its first shattering impact it had been immobilized as it rebounded. Plumes of icy spray rose from the frozen muck. The plane's back had broken, but because the process of disintegration had still been taking place it remained recognizable. A few seconds into the future the plane would inevitably become a heap of twisted, burning wreckage among the trees, but because it had been immobilized in some fantastic way it was for the moment apparently whole.

The wing closer to me had broken where it entered the fuselage. It and its engine would soon cartwheel dangerously into the trees as the terrible stresses of the crash continued. The propeller of this engine was already broken: it had two blades instead of three, the missing one apparently trapped somewhere in the mud, but the spindle was still rotating with sufficient speed that the remaining two blades were throwing a spray of mud in a soaring vane through the mist above.

The other wing was out of sight, below the surface, its

presence evinced by a swollen bulge of water, about to break out in an explosion of filthy spray.

The perspex panes of the cockpit cover were starred where machine-gun bullets had left their trail across the upper fuselage. Mud had already sprayed across what was left of the canopy. Inside, horribly and inexplicably, crouched the figure of the man who waved to me.

He waved again now.

I stared, I raised one hand. I raised another. Uncertainty froze me. What would a wave from me mean? What would it imply?

I briefly averted my gaze and lowered my arms, embarrassed by my weakness of will. When I looked back the man inside the aircraft waved again, pointing up at the perspex canopy with his other hand.

I had been visiting the scene of this frozen crash for several weeks and by careful measurement and reckoning had worked out roughly where the plane's final resting place was likely to be. Every day the tableau I saw had moved forward a few more instants of time, heading for its final surcease. Throughout the gradual process the man remained in the cockpit, signalling to me. His face was distorted, but whether it was with pain, or anger, or fear, or all three, I could not tell. All I knew was that he was imploring me to help him in some way.

But how? And who was he? For some reason he was standing in the cramped cockpit, not in one of the two seats where the pilot and another crewman would normally be positioned. I knew he was not one of them, because I could also see their bodies, strapped into the seats, their heads slumped forward.

The tail of the aircraft was intact, painted dark green with paler speckles, and bearing a geometrical device that already had such profound terror and significance that I could only stare at it in awe. It was the sign of the swastika, the broken four-legged cross, once a symbol of prosperity and creativity, Celtic, Buddhist, Hindu, revered by ancient peoples of all kinds, but recently suborned by the vile National Socialists in Germany and made a token of suppression, brutality and tyranny.

It was an aircraft of the German Air Force, the *Luftwaffe*, the Air Weapon, that was crashing here. It was rising out of Beckon Slough, immobilized by my attention to it. Somehow, my interest in it held it here. Soon, if I were to release it, presumably by inattention, the plane would conclude its crash – the broken wing would cartwheel into the woods, the fuselage would complete its rebounding lurch into the air before sinking finally beneath the filthy mud, and the spilling aviation spirit would explode in a deadly ball of white flame, detonating the hidden load of bombs that were carried aboard.

But not yet. I had its mysteries to fathom first.

They were focused on the presence of the man who watched me from the damaged cockpit, signalling desperately to me.

How could I reach him? Did he expect me to walk across the wreckage, in hazard to myself, to free him? There was a violent dynamic in the plane: to try to enter it might embroil me in its destructive end. The only logical way for me to scramble across to the cockpit would be along the unbroken wing, but this, as I have said, was half-submerged in the frozen slime.

I felt no urgency to respond to the man's pleas. Anyway, there was a larger mystery.

Five weeks earlier I had spotted what I thought must be a serial number stencilled on the side of the plane's fin, beneath the swastika. I had since spent many hours in my library, and in correspondence with other scholars and investigators, some of them abroad, and had established beyond doubt that such a plane with such a registration number did not exist! Indeed, the Heinkel company, whose serial number sequence it turned out to be, was at present several hundred units short of such a number.

Moreover, it was self-evidently a warplane, apparently shot down while flying over Britain, and therefore in itself a riddle. No state of war existed. Peace remained in this year 1937, fragile and tentative, but peace none the less.

The inexplicable German warplane was moving through time in diverse directions. Forward, at fractional speed, into its own oblivion, throwing up the sludge of the marsh in a fountain of vile spray, killing the occupants, detonating the store of bombs it carried in its bay and felling a giant swathe of Beckon Wood as it did so.

But it had also moved *back* through time, perplexingly, impossibly. Europe was at peace, Chancellor Hitler's armies of workers, thugs and soldiers were not as yet on the march, the boot of the tyrant was still at rest within the borders of the old Reich. The Nazi cry was for *Lebensraum*, living space for the German race, and a deadly spreading of the nationalist poison through Europe must inevitably follow. Total war against Germany might indeed lie somewhere ahead, as some of the politicians warned, inevitably, devastatingly.

As yet, though, in the quiet time in which I lived, Britain and Germany and much of Europe clung to peace, brittle but miraculously persisting.

Out of that future, floating back to its own destructive destiny in the wood that grew in the grounds of my family's house, came this German bomber, victim of a machine-gun attack. By British defenders? How could I possibly tell? But it had fallen into my terrible domain, and consequently I had inadvertently sealed it in my present, slowing the plunge into its own final future.

I was a man of certainties: good and bad, order and chaos,

liberty and death. These were my concerns. I cared not for enigmas, even though this one could exert a deadly fascination over me.

I could feel the haruspical strength in me waning and knew I must hurry back to the house for Patricia Stragg's meal. In recent days a demon in me had sometimes urged me to delay while I regarded the German bomber. As the essential power of the pellets faded – my last meal had been eaten more than twelve hours before – so my ability to halt or reverse time failed in me. I knew that if I were simply to stand here at the fringe of Beckon Slough for the rest of the afternoon I would likely see the final destructive moments of the aircraft enacted before my eyes. The prospect of such a spectacle was undeniably tempting.

I had other masters, though.

I turned and walked back through the trees towards the house. At the point where the track curved to the right, taking me out of sight of the plane, I turned to look back. The man in the cockpit was waving frantically at me, apparently urging me not to leave. I pondered his plight again for a few moments – nothing ever occurred in my life without mystical significance – but then continued on towards the house.

Mrs Stragg's cooking was sufficient, but only just. Today she had soaked the pellets in a dark brown gravy, rather lumpy for my taste but otherwise acceptable. She was employed to provide me with food that gave nourishment, not pleasure. When I had prepared myself in the Great Hall she brought me the dish under its silver chafing lid, placed it before my seat at the long table and then hovered expectantly.

'Will there be anything else, Mr Owsley?'

'Not, I think, at present.'

'A little later, perhaps?'

Her gaze was steady, determined. I said: 'I don't know, Patricia. I have to work. If you could stay late this evening, maybe when I have finished . . . ?'

Again, I knew I was hurtfully rejecting an overt offer, but now she had laid the pellets before me I was single-minded, as she must have known.

'Whatever pleases you, sir.'

She left. I followed her to the double doors, trying to seem courteous, and closed them behind her.

I listened for the sound of her steps receding along the uncarpeted corridor, then I locked the doors and bolted them top and bottom. I gave them a forceful testing shake to be certain they were securely closed against her or anyone else who tried to interrupt what I was about to do. I put in place my secret anti-tamper seals, then returned to the dish waiting for me at the table.

I quickly removed the chafing cover and seasoned the food with several vigorous shakes of the pepper pot, and three long scoops with the knife into the mustard jar. With one last glance behind me to make certain I was not being observed, I picked up the plate, dropped a knife and fork into my breast pocket, and went to the raised dais at the gallery end of the Hall. I worked the mechanism of the concealed door in the panelling of the wall and passed through into the hagioscope that lay behind. I took up my position.

From here I was afforded a double view: the cell was a squint, to use the term that the original masons themselves would have employed. On one side of me, through a slit cunningly contrived in the stone wall and the wooden panelling, was a narrow, restricted view back into the Great Hall I had left moments before. It was only through this narrow aperture that the dim ambient light inside the hagioscope arose. On the other side, through a much larger gap, a mere turn of the head away, was a glimpse into hell.

There was no light down there, in the great abyss lying beneath the Abbey. I could see nothing in the impenetrable black, nor was I intended to see. Whatever inhabited that sunken void required no light to give itself life. It, they, existed in a dark of such profundity that all human feeling or emotion was extinguished too.

However, my presence in the hagioscope enabled me, Janus-like, to sit at the gateway between past and present, guarding the way. Behind me, the present world. Before me, the denizens of an ancient past and a deplorable future. I was suspended in time, like the dying aircraft that even now was arrested in the mire of Beckon Slough.

I was still cradling the plate of cooked meat. I knew that it was cooling quickly. Difficult to eat even when hot and freshly served, the pellets were nauseating if they were allowed to cool down. I retrieved the knife and fork from my pocket and began to eat the ragout as quickly as possible.

With Mrs Stragg's artful culinary techniques, and the more brutal coverings of spices I had latterly applied, the food was just about edible. Even so, it required an inhuman will to be able to put the pellets in my mouth. Instinctively, for there were still vestiges of the human in me, I looked first for the smaller pieces, the ones most likely to have had their fibres cooked down into masticable form, or the ones which would yield easiest to the knife, or the ones which I could see had received the greatest share of the pepper.

While I chewed steadily through the stuff, feeling the sense of evil power growing in me, I tried to distract myself with childish mnemonics – old nursery rhymes, playground chants – in a vain attempt to postpone the imminent confrontation, distract myself not only from the knowledge of what I was putting into my mouth, but also from the growing malignity that took shape whenever I ate.

I could unerringly sense the fiends of the nether world, rousing themselves for our fray, in the same way as I had to relish the rubbery gristle of the pellets and the vile flavours of death that were released with their juices.

Even so, I could take comfort from the consequence of the grotesque meal. I had the transcendent knowledge that time was being reversed by my actions, that evil was being repulsed and that the lurkers of the pit were being held back. On the colossal scale of the vast death-universe, the delay was breathtakingly short, but enough, enough, all I could do. I alone, haruspex against evil.

Continuing life was my reward. Life denied would be my punishment.

As I worked the meat between my jaws I began to sense action and reaction below. I heard discarnate screams, the fury of the frustrated malignity of evil embodied, of the dashing of whatever hopes such monstrous skulkers could entertain, as their slow attempts to claw their way up and out of the pit towards the surface of the world were suddenly thwarted. Most of the meal would be used up pushing them back down to the level at which I had left them the day before, but with this new potency I believed there would be enough energy to force larger reversals on them.

I chewed steadily, drawing every iota of flavour from the pellets, returning the beings whence they had come. Every time I swallowed I felt the peristaltic thrust of my oesophagus, forcing down the meat. My mind's eye glimpsed in fitful bursts the outlines of their noisome forms as they surrendered to the release of the death force I was sucking from the pellets.

Their calling threats, echoing hoarsely around the slime-caked walls of the pit, gave aural shape to their forms!

They were low, flat, many-legged beings, each forelimb and hindlimb jointed at horrible double knees, like immense arthropods. Their limbs extruded to small claws, with which they flailed at the rubbery walls, trying to gain purchase. Each one of the beings was more than two metres in length, far too large for reason! I shuddered to perceive them!

Their heads, sunk low towards the part that could only be the abdomen, were wreathed in cilia, flailing as the angry brows swung from side to side. They had deep mandibles, their maws perpetually slack-jawed and drooling, emitting their beastly howls of anger, vengeance and threat. And the rattling! How they clattered! Some large part of their arthropodic bodies was chitinous, perhaps a loosely connected cuticle or carapace, so that each thrusting step produced a loud, ghastly clicking as they moved their ill-formed frames. It was the cacophony of sticks, of staves flailed against each other, of bones breaking in a yard.

And their relentless, ineluctable climbing would bring them, if not halted or at least given pause, into the world of men, women and children. I and only I stood before these denizens of the pit, barring their way, reversing their quest for escape.

Into this, my long-suffered private world of struggle with stasis, had come by some freakish chance a modern-day in-trusion. It was itself as baffling as the creeping horrors I was doomed to obstruct. Somehow, from a militarized future, had appeared a German warplane. This, shot down and crashing into the Beckon Slough, had become frozen by the same distortions of time that I, haruspical mystic, used to repel the underworld invaders. What was the link?

Because I could never see the dwellers of the world beneath

me, inevitably I often wondered whether my loathsome toil might be the product of delusion. Only I, aberrant haruspex from an ancient family of mystics, scholars, clairvoyants, contemplatives, could deal with the threat they presented, but equally it was only my family who had divined their presence.

The crashing German warplane was the first evidence of third-party recognition, incomprehensible though it might be. The plane must have come to Beckon Abbey either because I was in it, or because the pit was to be found beneath it. Now, whether or not this was the intention, it was held frozen in time not unlike the way the repugnant dwellers of the pit were halted.

Furthermore, I knew, as I chewed stoically on the pellets, that not only were the malignant beasts being forced back into their abyss, so the warplane too would at this moment be inching back in time, plotting a reversal of its catastrophic arrival. First it would sink briefly but necessarily into the mud, where its broken components would start to reassemble, then there would come an abrupt and cataclysmic reverse lifting out of the mud, and it would begin the long backwards tracing of its crash from the sky.

Seven days before, while cheerlessly consuming the pellets of last week's inferior consignment, I had found entirely by chance a uniquely potent example. In devouring it I recognized that the disturbing potency within was having a powerful effect on the arthropodous horrors inside the pit. The moment the eating ritual had been completed I rushed down to the Slough to see for myself. I found I had managed to reverse the bomber's path so far that the doomed machine was actually hovering briefly in the air above the mire, returning for an inert instant to its rôle as a dweller of the skies. Both of its propellers were intact at this moment before final impact (and to my perception

71

slowly turning), but from the nacelle of the engine on my side was streaming some kind of transparent liquid, presumably the fuel, and behind that a searing whiteness of flame, and flowing behind that was a long trail of black smoke. This traced the aircraft's final path: an almost straight line backwards and up at an angle of some forty-five degrees to the horizontal, past the treetops, into the blue sky, into the unseen flying formation of its fellow bombers, and, for all I knew, back thence into the heart of the German nation.

It was this action of mine that had alerted the man in the cockpit. He had been invisible to me until that day, presumably crouching or lying on the floor, but in some amazing way he had become aware of my actions. Ever since then, his signalling for help had been distraught and constant.

As the days passed, and I eked out my supply of pellets, the Heinkel had gradually returned to its inexorable collision with the bog, while the man within gestured towards me with increasing consternation. Soon the plane had reached the position in which I had seen it this morning, not more than a second or two from its final destruction.

For the first time I had a kind of yardstick to judge my progress. It had seemed to me until today that if I allowed the aircraft to continue on into oblivion the other struggle too would end, but in that case with the catastrophic escape of the horrors into the world. This was the true significance to me of the new consignment of pellets.

I was saving the largest, juiciest, most deadly pellet to last. Earlier in the meal, as I began eating, I had sensuously stroked the cutting edge of my knife across it and nothing of its sinewy texture had succumbed. It was tough, perfectly shaped! A streak of gristle, unreduced by Mrs Stragg's cooking, ran through it from side to side. When I finally took the pellet into my mouth, whole, as it had been found, it was the gristle that produced the tensile strength. It stayed stubbornly in my mouth, distending and bulging while I chewed, but retaining its overall shape. Juices in it were nevertheless released, and as I worked horribly at my task I could taste their exotic menace as they flowed over my tongue.

The final pellet at last produced a reaction from one of my enemies lurking in the dark. In my mind, a dread familiar voice:

'Owsley, Owsley, abandon this work and surrender to the pit!'

'Leave me!' I cried aloud.

'You can never prevail,' came the mentally perceived tones of my accuser. 'Flesh is weak, life is short, we are forever! Tighten your gut muscles, Owsley!'

'I shall not!'

'Do you not feel the nausea creeping within you? Do you not taste the fleshly residues of what you have consumed? Are they not churning within you, indigestible, disgusting, sickening, wrenching your gut into coils of vomitory? Puke up the cancers, Owsley! Vomit them up!'

I lurched back from the gap that led to hell. I could hardly breathe and nausea had me in its grip. If I stayed where I was I would doubtless spew up everything I had eaten, as often before I had found myself doing. But if I did eject the half-digested tumours all my work would be undone. This my hellish interlocuter knew full well. He came for me on most days, but always when my haruspical work was being most effective. If I were to vomit up the epitheliomata of the meal I would lose almost everything I had just achieved.

So I retreated. The only way I could ignore the terrible voice was to leave the hagioscope, and this I did.

Once I had regained the comparative normality of the Great

Hall, it was not difficult to regain control over the feelings of nausea. After I had taken several deep breaths I made sure that the concealed door had closed firmly behind me, and also that no one had entered the Great Hall while I had been in the hagioscope. I lit a candle and hurried to the main door to check the locks, then examined my secretly placed seals, a disturbance to which would reveal if someone had tried to force their way in. Of course, only Mrs Stragg was generally with me at the house, and she could probably be trusted, but the way time was dilated by my struggles inside the hagioscope meant I had to be sure. Hours of subjective time could pass imperceptibly, because my own sense of it was as distorted by the ingestion of the cancers as was that of the devilish creatures I was repulsing.

Now it had become night and the Hall was in darkness. I remembered my half-promise of an assignation with Patricia Stragg when I had completed my work, but there was no sign of her. She normally left the Abbey halfway through the after-noon, and today would probably not be prepared to face what might be a third rejection.

Thoughts of her were distracting me. The important matter was that the pit was secure again, or reasonably so, and would remain in that condition until the next day at least. If the new intestinal epithelial pellets were as powerful as I suspected, it was even possible that another visit to the squint might not be necessary until the day after.

I moved swiftly around the Great Hall, lighting more can-dles, pulling the blinds across the tall windows, blocking out the night, the glimpse of the moon and the stars, but most of all the white ground-mist that moved in across the valley at this time of the year, to lie like a winding sheet across the grounds of the Abbey.

After I had checked once more that the door to the hagioscope was sealed, I went through the gloomy corridors to the domestic wing of the house, returning my platter, glass and cutlery to the scullery. Of Mrs Stragg there was still no sign. I left everything by the sink, then ascended to my apartment on the second floor. I stripped off all my clothes (as usual at this time of day they were sodden with old sweat and the seams scuffed uncomfortably against my flesh), and immersed myself in a bath of hot water.

When I went into my chamber afterwards, Patricia Stragg was there. She had lit my paraffin lamps and was waiting by the side of my bed, naked but for the sheet she held against her body. I glared at her, resenting her persistence, but even so unable to deny the animal lusts she aroused in me. She lowered the sheet so that I might gaze at her body. I relished the sight of her tired face, her pale heavy thighs, her dimpled elbows and knees, the girdle of fat about her waist, her large drooping breasts, the pasture of black curling bristle at the junction of her legs where soon I would gladly graze. I placed my hands on her shoulders, then ran my tongue down her face and body, pausing to nuzzle on her heavy breasts with their tiny but tempting lumps of hard fibre buried deep within. I pushed her down on the bed and quickly serviced her, thrusting with greedy passion at her ample body.

I was exhausted afterwards, but my need to study was constant, so leaving Patricia Stragg to make her own way out of the house I pulled on my reading gown. With tremendous weariness of tread I went up to the next floor to the library. Here I took down several volumes of psychology: on the meaning of revenge, of fear, of repulsion. I glanced through them drowsily in the inadequate lamplight for half an hour. My books were the sole comfort of my life, but so drained was I by the encounter in the hagioscope, and by satisfying Patricia Stragg's agitated sexual needs, that I found it impossible to concentrate.

Later I returned to my chamber and slept.

In the morning I discovered a singular fact: part of one of the pellets from the day before had been packed between two of my lower back teeth and was still firmly in place. Neither pushing at it with my tongue nor scraping with a fingernail could dislodge it. When I had dressed I took a match, broke off the head to make a tiny jagged spear, and tried to pick out the compacted meat with that. Again, no success, but I did finally manage to shift it far enough to release some of the juices that by some marvel it still contained. They trickled across my taste buds.

Twelve minutes flashed by in a subjective moment! I checked the lapse of time, then returned the watch to my waistcoat pocket, still only half-believing that the act of consuming necrotic flesh could have such a potent effect on my mind. No matter how frequently the time distortion occurred, it invariably astonished me.

I realized I was entering a familiar state of mind, in which starkest gloom jostled with boundless optimism. I therefore decided to measure the effect of the pellets I had eaten the previous day. Since it had obtruded itself into my life, the German bomber had come to signify a kind of yardstick of temporal motion. Its advances and reverses were a guide to the progress of the main conflict. Now that I had realized this connection it made no sense to subject myself needlessly to the torments of the pit. I could gain the reassurance I sought with much less risk to my sanity.

It was raining when I left the house and the crisp frosts of the previous few days were no more. The sloping sward of the Long Lawn was already sodden in its lower reaches. I was glad to reach the cinder path that led into the trees.

The Slough, when I came to it, lay undisturbed, the surface calm and untrammelled, apart from the constant patterns of overlapping circles made by the rain on the few stretches of clear water. Above the muddy water, a precious few inches above it, lay the plummeting body of the doomed warplane. At once my spirits lifted! The latent power of the pellets now in my possession was beyond doubt.

In the latest manifestation, the aircraft was more or less physically intact, not counting the visible damage the machine-gun rounds had caused to the cockpit cover and engine cowling. Both wings were attached, and although the spilling fuel, the blazing fire and the black smoke streamed back from the engine, it was possible to see it as still a fighting plane, not a broken wreck.

The tip of the wing closer to me – the one that I knew within a second or two of real time would break off catastrophically as the plane ploughed into the mud – was only two or three inches from the solid ground on which I stood.

A single session in the hagioscope, and this! One meal of the new pellets! Many more such pieces still to come!

Was it at last the final stage of the bitter struggle against the chaos of the pit?

Then, immediately banishing the heady optimism, a voice said in my mind: 'Get me out of here!'

It was the same voice as that familiar, loathsome cry from the heart of the pit. My first thought: *It cannot be!* Had the monster found a way to track me beyond the hagioscope, away from the house, to here?

It came again, more urgently: 'I am about to perish! I implore you! The canopy is jammed! Can't you do something?'

I realized that it was the helmeted figure who stood in the cockpit. His face was pressed desperately against the perspex panes of the cockpit cover and both of his arms were reaching up, struggling to release the catches that held it in place. His movements were frenzied, panicky.

'I can't help you!' I shouted at him.

'Yes you can! Find something with which to release me. I beg you! Save me from this!'

'What are you?' I cried. 'Who are you? What do you want?'

'I am an emissary from the future.'

I am strong with mysticism, not with physical or muscular development. The predicament of the man on the aircraft wrenched at me, but it was not in my power to assist him. He wanted me to wrestle with the jammed cockpit cover? Or to try to cut my way through the metal side of the fuselage? I regarded him across the short distance that separated us. He was locked in a time and destiny of his own, an alien intruder, subject to the will of a universe fundamentally different from mine.

His voice came at me repeatedly, a sane but desperate plea for help. Wondering what if anything I could do, I stood there regarding him, playing at the soreness of my gum with the tip of my tongue, fretting at the piece of pellet that had become lodged in my teeth the day before. It seemed to have worked a little more loose since waking this morning, and when I sucked at it I distinctly felt it shift. Still watching the man in the aircraft I picked at the fragment of meat with the nail of my ring finger, and in a moment it was out. The familiar essence lifted like gas against my taste sensors.

The plane moved back.

'You are who I am seeking!' the voice cried in my mind. 'You are Owsley!'

'I am.'

I recoiled with shock from the discovery that he knew my name!

'And you are haruspical!' he called.

'I am.'

Now he stood erect, abandoning his panicky efforts to release the cockpit cover. His demeanour was strangely calm. 'You must release me if you can. You doubtless know why.'

'I believe I do,' I said, responding to the composure that had come over him and which was also now surrounding me. 'But there are questions—'

'None matters!'

'How did you—?'

'Owsley, be silent!' His mood had abruptly changed again. 'Release me from this aircraft! Then perhaps we might have reasons to converse.'

Disliking the authoritative tone, yet even so respecting it, I turned away from him and followed the long path back in the direction of the Abbey. I looked around me as I walked, hoping to spot something hard and heavy and made of metal. Nothing offered itself as suitable. When I entered the house I noticed at once from the clock in the stairwell that more time had fled while the pellet juices flowed in my mouth. It was already past noon and as I went along the ground floor corridors I glimpsed Mrs Stragg pacing impatiently in the short passage outside the kitchen. Fortunately, she happened to have her back towards me at that moment, so I was able to pass unseen beyond her.

In the utility room, after a search, I found a long steel spanner or wrench, I knew not which, apparently left behind by a workman at some time in the past. I assumed it would be sufficient for the task of breaking through the thick perspex, but my skills, as I say, are not those of the physical body. As I carried the heavy implement back down the lawns towards Beckon Wood I felt self-conscious with it and knew that it hung at an unnatural angle in my grasp. The weather was still cold and unpleasant: it was raining persistently and the damp twigs on the drooping branches of the trees brushed against my face and hair. As I followed the bend in the path and again saw Beckon Slough, I raised the spanner in my hand. Holding it before me I strode across the muddy ground to the site of the wreck.

The man remained standing within the cockpit, calm and poised, awaiting my return. I went to where the tip of the wing hovered a few inches above the muddy ground.

'While you were gone,' the man said, in my mind, 'I was trying to establish how best to force the canopy.'

'Don't you know already?' I said, facing him.

'Why should I?'

'You are a member of the Air Force, are you not? The German *Luftwaffe*?'

My mind seemed to laugh mockingly. 'I, an aviator? I have never before been inside such a thing. I am a man of learning and of the spirit, as you.'

'Who are you?'

'My name is Tomas Bauer. You, I know, are James Owsley.' Amazement stirred again in me, but at once the man added: 'Of course, you are the one I have travelled to find.'

Since the death of my father I had known that I was upholding a tradition, one that I had to honour, and one which eventually I should have to pass on to another. I had expected, though, that such release would not come for many years or decades. Tomas Bauer's words, and the mystical circumstances of his arrival, informed me that the moment had come. Waves of relief, excitement and a distinct tremor of fear passed through me.

However, the immediate problem remained of what to do to release Tomas Bauer from the aircraft. I was still holding the spanner aloft, but the feeling of foolish physical ineptitude was still paralysing me.

I heard in my mind: 'James Owsley, you must do as I direct. No more words!'

I tried to assent, but it was as if a sponge flooded with chloroform had been pressed irresistibly over my mind, making it insensible. I felt myself propelled forward, raising my right foot like an automaton to step on the very tip of the wing itself. It took my weight, without dipping. I stepped forward and walked across the curved upper surface of the wing towards the bullet-riven cockpit. When I reached the curved housing of the engine I had to scramble over the hot metal case, carefully not placing any part of my body in the dangerous stream of escaping fuel. The propeller, still turning slowly a few inches away from me as I passed, set up a torrent of forced air behind it, neither to my perception moving nor turbulent but somehow compressed by the rotation of the airscrew.

Then I was against the side of the cockpit cover itself, looking in at the man who had taken control of my mind. Tomas had removed his leather helmet and I could see his features clearly. He was a young man, tall and ruggedly built, with a shock of blond hair and a sturdily jutting jaw. He stared at me with an intent frown, exercising his mental will against mine.

There was a part of the transparent canopy where two panels of it overlaid each other, apparently the place where the two halves joined after the front part had been slid forward and locked in position. Tomas directed me towards it. I slipped the edge of the spanner against what crack I could see, then heaved at it with all my might, trying to use it as a lever.

When the thick perspex did not shift I felt my arms swing backwards, raising the spanner above my head. I brought it down with a tremendous blow, one far more heavy than anything I would have believed myself capable of before now. The cockpit cover shattered at once, a large star-shaped hole appearing in the flattened top. Three more blows forced an irregular aperture large enough for a man to escape through.

I reached down and held Tomas's arms as he found footholds in the cramped cockpit and pushed himself up and through to freedom. As he clambered around I could not help looking down and past him, to where I could see the bodies of the two German aviators. The one in the left-hand seat had clearly suffered a direct hit from a bullet, because a large part of his helmet and skull had been broken away. He was slumped against his dashboard of instruments. I could see a bulge of blood rising through the gap in his head and knew it soon to be a fountaining gout to join the soak of blood that already covered his flying suit. From this evidence of a pumping heart I realized that the pilot must be, to some small extent, still alive. The other aviator, who outwardly appeared uninjured, although my view of him was restricted, also was leaning forward with his face against the instruments. His body was broken in some horrible way I shrank from trying to imagine. I had to assume he was dead or unconscious, even though there were no apparent wounds on him.

While I was regarding this disagreeable sight with a sense of increasing horror, Tomas had climbed swiftly out of the cockpit and was standing on the wing beside me. He tugged at my arm, swinging me round.

'We leave,' he said peremptorily. These were the first words he had so far uttered while I had a clear sight of his face. As I hastened to follow him, down the wing and through the turbulent stream of compressed air behind the propeller, I realized that the words I was hearing in my mind were not the same as those forming in his mouth. The words did not move with his lips.

As I thought about this, he instantly replied: 'I speak in German. You will hear, I believe, English. It is the same for me, in reverse. It is best, I think.'

He jumped down from the wing. After a few uncertain steps on the muddy bank of the Slough he strode off along the cinder pathway. His long black coat swung in the air behind him. Now he was freed from the aircraft he was walking with easy, powerful grace, like an athlete. From his gait I would not have credited that he was haruspical: others of my calling that I had met were, like me, small in stature, bookish, introspective, timid in all matters that required strenuous activity. Tomas had implied that he was no better equipped to contend with problems of the physical world – otherwise, surely, he could have escaped from that plane without my help? – but even so nature had apparently blessed him with a strong and agile body.

When we reached the part of the path where I normally struck up the Long Lawn towards the house, Tomas Bauer came to a halt. He turned towards me as I caught up with him. The dark shape of the Abbey, squatting on the brow of Beckon Hill, loomed up behind him. He extended a hand of friendship towards me.

'I thank you, James Owsley,' he said, and now that I was only a few inches away from him I found distracting the dissonance there was between the words I heard and the movements of his lips. 'To you I owe my life.'

'Why were you on the aircraft?' I said. 'It makes no sense to me. Where was the aircraft going and who sent it? How was it shot down? How did you contrive it to crash on my property? What –?'

He held up the palms of his hands to silence me.

'Nor does it make sense to me,' he said. 'I was in Germany,

you are in England. The war was running its course and I could find no other way to reach England—'

'To which war do you refer?'

'The war between our two countries, of course.'

'There is no war,' I said. 'True, there are portents, but the German Chancellor would not be so insane—'

'He is mad enough,' said Tomas. 'You can be sure of that. In my time his madness has led to a war that is engulfing most of Europe. It is irrelevant to the greater struggle, the one in which you and I engage, but there is no avoiding it for practical matters. I was effectively trapped in my homeland, while my true work was here. The German army is poised to invade England—'

'But this is fantasy!' I cried.

'To you it might seem so. But I speak of what is a grim reality of the time in which I live. Four, maybe five years from this moment. Madness? Yes it is! Engines of war are turning, but they are not such deadly machineries as the ones you and I face. We confront a larger madness, a virulent incursion whose terrors would dwarf in significance a mere military conquest by one nation of another. You reside above the pit of hell and its denizens seek release. The portents have been written in texts since the dawn of time. I have studied many such texts and so, I know, have you. Our task is beyond history! War, pestilence, genocide, famine . . . these are trivial concerns, compared with what we confront! I had no alternative: I had to escape to England to be with you. After much doubt I came to the conclusion that the only way was to travel with one of the planes that was flying to bomb your English towns. I knew there would be risks, but in my desperation I saw no alternative.'

'You raise more questions than you answer,' I said.

'And I have told you they are of no account. I am here; that is sufficient. Are we at last to unite and engage together in our struggle against the creatures of the pit?'

'In my life there is no other concern,' I said.

'Nor in mine. So we must address ourselves to it.'

He turned from me and strode purposefully up the lawn towards the Abbey. Once again I found myself following in his wake. His manner was decisive, arrogant, imperious. He behaved as if I had been merely caretaking the house until the moment of his arrival. As I trotted behind him, already furious with myself for allowing him to dominate me, flashing memories of the years I had endured alone were shining in my mind, almost dazzling me. Was Tomas Bauer somehow projecting them at me?

No matter the source: I could not ignore them. I remembered the first time my father took me into the squint, so that I might experience the raw evil of the pit's emanations and truly learn what it would mean to follow him there. He thrust my face against the opening so that I had to stare down into the merciless darkness, and while he held me with his knee against the small of my back he began an endless braying sermon. His leg moved up and down against me, his yelling voice becoming a terrifying stridulation. It was a new and stunning insight into my father. When I managed to free myself and struggle round to face him in the confined space of the hagioscope, he was looming over me, lit from all sides by the candles that guttered from every crevice in the rock walls. He bellowed his ranting, maniacal entreaties into the pit, swaying horribly from side to side, a Bible held aloft in one hand, a glistering golden crucifix in the other.

I also could not forget the physical after-effect that the first experience had on me: the long hours that followed while I retched disconsolately into the pewter bowl beside my bed, a purging that was a making ready of my body for the fray that on some dark level it must have known would be coming. Then there were those few precious weeks when my father allowed me to work alongside him, and when I, in my naïveté, had believed he was encouraging me and that we would work together for years to come.

I did not realize straight away that his sudden interest in me was only a preliminary to a greater event: his resolution suddenly collapsed and he subsided into insanity. The disintegration of his will happened, so it seemed, overnight. Another glimpse of memory: a terrible confrontation with him in the Great Hall, when in the boiling rage of his madness he beset me with what he interpreted as my sacrilegious mystical leanings and physically threw at me the entrails on which I had been preparing the day's labours in the pit, challenging me to consume them while he watched. Impossible, of course. He desperately wanted me to follow him, but my calling stood like a barrier between us, blocking his sight of me.

After this confrontation, a hiatus. There was my father gibbering quietly and in solitude while nurses worked in relays to minister to his needs, while I stood alone at the gate of the pit, attempting for the first time to thwart the malignant ones below in the only way I knew, and not doing too well. My father's death came as a release for me. Mostly at first it was a release from the guilt that I felt about our relationship, but in more practical terms his death freed the financial fruits of the estate. These were now mine to enjoy. Before his decline, while he yet retained ambitions for me, my father had had the foresight to endow a family Trust to finance an independent pathology research laboratory in a London clinic. This act not only revealed to me that in his last months he had come to terms with what I might be capable of, but also ensured that our family's material wealth, otherwise so ineffectual against the denizens of the sunken world, could be applied to the production of a steady supply of scientifically reliable epitheliomata.

The first consignment of cancerous bowel growths and malignant intestinal tumours had arrived at Beckon Abbey within three weeks of my father's burial. Thereafter they were delivered at a rate of approximately one package every ten days. The supply was erratic, both in haruspical suitability and in time of delivery, but in recent weeks both matters had greatly improved.

All this was mine. My life, my sacrifice, my commitment and dedication. My father, his father, the generations of the family before us; we had all stood at the dreadful portal and resisted the earthly incursion of the Old Ones.

Now Tomas Bauer had entered our private hell. He arrived in a bizarre warping of time and space, stepping out of some unimaginable future, then arrogantly removed my sense of primacy. I watched him as he walked ahead of me. His able body took him in swift strides up the Long Lawn to the house, while I, the overweight and physically frail product of a lifetime of poring over books and of consuming protein-rich foods, was soon a considerable distance behind him and in a great deal of discomfort. I never ran or exercised, rarely took my body to its limits. My energies had to be conserved for my work. My only physical activity was the hasty, frenzied, irregular satisfaction of Patricia Stragg's sexual needs.

Tomas reached the door on this garden side of the house and passed within as if he had been accustomed to going in and out of my house for all his life. I was so far behind him that by the time I stumbled up to the door, winded and dishevelled, he had been inside for two or three minutes. I allowed the door to slam closed behind me. I leaned against the jamb, coughing helplessly while I tried unsuccessfully to steady my breathing. I looked feebly into the vestibule that opened out in this part of the building. Sweat was streaming down my temples and into my collar and every inhalation was a painful labour. I could feel my heart pounding like a fist within my chest cavity, beating to be released.

Tomas Bauer had already ascended the flight of steps that led to the upper hallway, from which, after passing along a wide corridor where most of my family's art treasures were displayed, he would eventually gain access to the Great Hall and the terrors within. He was standing on the top step of the flight and Patricia Stragg was with him. I could not hear his voice, but she was nodding compliantly. She heard my arrival and glanced down the stairs towards me. As our eyes briefly met I heard Tomas's mentally projected voice:

'—from now, if you please, Herr Owsley is no longer—'

The weirdly disembodied voice faded again as she turned away, like a lighthouse beam sweeping by. I heard her say, in English: 'Very well, sir. I understand.'

I called up to her: 'What is it you understand, Mrs Stragg?'

She made no answer, but the newcomer inclined his head more closely to hers, speaking softly and urgently. As he did so she turned again to look down the steps in my direction, a look of conspiratorial attention on her face. Although the lids of her eyes were suggestively half closed, the fact that she again turned towards me accidentally opened up his words through her consciousness.

He was saying: '—tonight it will change, for I have ransacked his mind and I know what he is to you, but now you are mine, if you come to me when I will, I shall take you as mine, for you are the ravishing prize I have sought in return for the sacrifice I make in this quest, but you will be rewarded with such pleasures as you cannot easily imagine, for I have the power—'

And on, glibly and pressingly, suggestions and innuendoes and flattering promises. I heard them all until the moment when at last she looked away from me and the torrent of intimations was silenced.

I was recovering my wind at last and I began to mount the stairs.

'Patricia,' I called. 'What is he saying to you?'

She glanced at me again (his oleaginous insinuations had temporarily ceased), and she said: 'Mr Owsley, I must ask you not to approach!'

'I am still the master of the house, Patricia,' I said. 'I want you to accord our visitor every courtesy, but you will continue to take instructions only from me.'

She spoke, but I knew at once that the words were not hers. She was mouthing them on behalf of Tomas Bauer. Her voice had taken on a deeper timbre than usual.

She said, (Tomas said): 'You have failed to stem the tide of evil that flows beneath this mound. Your efforts have been insufficient to the task. I shall assume responsibility. You may assist me if you wish, but I should prefer you to stay away. This is no longer a matter for your family, but concerns the world. It is my mission to seal the pit forever.'

'You don't know how!' I shouted. 'You have no experience!'

He stared directly at me.

'No experience? What then is this?' With both of his strong hands he ripped at the front of his tunic, pulling it open. The buttons on his shirt followed, and his broad, hairless chest was revealed. A misshapen, reddened mound disfigured the area around his left aureole and a grotesquely enlarged nipple drooped horribly. Brown traces of a stain from some bodily discharge lay on the pale skin beneath. 'You, haruspex, have

89

consumed many such tumours. But this one, I say, is upon me and within me and it is consuming me. What better way is there to know evil than to have it upon you? And you say I know nothing!'

I was, in truth, stunned by his revelation. Tears were welling in his eyes and his head was shaking uncontrollably, as if with a nervous tic. His chest rose and fell with his suddenly stertorous breathing. I knew beyond question that he was not deceiving me. His bared chest made him vulnerable, piteous, the red carcinomatous flare marking his flesh like the petals of a burgeoning flower. He was a man who already stood on the brink of his own hellish pit.

'Tomas,' I said after a long silence. 'Would we not be better co-operating?'

'I think not. I am here to take your place, Owsley.'

I detected, though, a softening of tone, a decrease in his arrogance.

'But surely—' I indicated his infected chest. 'How long can you survive?'

'Long enough. Or do you propose to eat my entrails too?'

I was shocked again, this time by the candour of his reply. It did mean, as he had claimed, that in addition to placing words in my mind he could listen back to what I was thinking. I had been unable to suppress my inner excitement when I saw the rich potential of the tumour he had revealed on his breast. Doubtless he had sensed that too.

'Eventually, I should have to,' I admitted. 'You must know that, Tomas. You are haruspical too.'

'Not as you.'

'You eat human flesh!'

Mrs Stragg gasped and turned away from us both. Tomas grabbed her arm, and spun her around.

'To your work, woman! Never mind what methods we use. I am hungry! I have not eaten in days.'

She looked imploringly at me. 'Mr Owsley, is this right?'

'Do as he instructs, Patricia.'

'You concede my mastery, then?' cried Tomas, looking directly at me. Triumph charged his eyes.

'Mrs Stragg, prepare the next meal,' I said. 'You may use the usual ingredients. Places should be laid for two. We shall dine in the Great Hall.'

I noticed she hesitated for a second or two longer. I recalled our usual conversations at this point when we discussed the way in which she was to prepare the pellets, but I nodded noncommittally at her and she left. Tonight of all nights I was prepared to let her cook in whatever way she felt best.

Feeling that a new understanding had been reached with Tomas Bauer, and even that some sympathy might be possible between us, I climbed the remainder of the steps to join him. He had lost interest in me, though, and was already striding away. Maddened again by his disdainful behaviour, first seemingly vulnerable, then almost without warning as overbearing as ever, I at first made to follow him but immediately decided against it.

Instead, I went downstairs, walked through to the kitchen to speak quietly to Patricia Stragg, then went to my library. I closed and locked the door, and with a dread feeling that Tomas Bauer would inevitably know what I was doing, took out the final volume of my father's irreplaceable set of haruspical grimoires, written in Latin.

The task of translation, started by his own grandfather and as yet only partly accomplished, was familiar and necessary, but also unfinishable. I sought only distraction. The abstruseness of the text never did help me concentrate at the best of times and on this evening my mind was racing with feelings of anxiety and conflict. I knew Tomas Bauer was somewhere in the Abbey, prowling around, investigating every corner of the old building. At odd moments I could detect his thoughts, and they came at me in distracting bursts of non-sequitur. Fear was coursing through me: it was almost as if one of the monsters below had at last broken out of the pit and invaded this continuum of reality. Tomas's intrusion was of that magnitude. Nothing was going to be the same again.

Unless he died. I could not rid myself of the memory of his horribly inflamed chest, the cancer bursting through the flesh and skin. It was surely a terminal ailment? If so, how long would it be before he became too ill to function?

Was his inexplicable arrival from 'the future' connected somehow with his illness? From what was he really trying to escape when he travelled to England? Did he have one final destiny to fulfil? Was it involved with my haruspical mysticism, so that, in effect, it was not he himself who was taking control but the cancer he bore?

Mrs Stragg came hesitantly to the door of the library, calling my name. I laid aside the precious tome with a sense of finality and eased open the door. The candle flames bent to the side of their wicks in the sudden draught from the corridor, and wax ran in floods down the guttered stems.

'The meal is ready, Mr Owsley,' she said. 'Do you still want me to serve it in the Great Hall?'

'Yes, I do. I shall have to unlock the door for you.'

'Sir, that's what concerns me. Our visitor has already found a way inside.'

'He is in the Hall *alone*?'

'I could do nothing about it. I knew you would be angry.'

'Very well, Patricia. I am not angry with you. Is the food ready to be eaten?'

'As I said.'

'And you have prepared two portions?' She nodded, and I regarded her thoughtfully. 'If the meal is still in the kitchen, let me come with you so that I might inspect it – '

A voice came: 'If you are thinking of tampering, Owsley . . .'

Mrs Stragg and I both started with surprise. I know not what was in her thoughts, but to me it was further proof that the end of my era as custodian must almost be upon me. Tomas Bauer had invaded everything and I could not function like that. The feelings that welled up in me were a confusion of relief, dismay and anger.

When we reached the kitchen, Mrs Stragg took up the large japanned tray bearing the dishes and we both set off towards the Great Hall. I scurried before her to push open and hold each of the doors along the corridors. When we reached the entrance to the Hall I saw that the reinforced locks had been burst asunder by main force. I immediately saw Tomas within, standing in an aggressive manner with his arms folded and his legs braced, staring at the place from where the hagioscope viewed the room.

I said quietly to Mrs Stragg: 'As soon as you have left the Hall, I want you to collect your personal belongings and depart the house. Do you understand?'

'Yes, Mr Owsley.'

'I suggest you do it as soon as possible. Do not delay for anything.'

'When should I return?'

I was about to reply that Tomas Bauer would surely let her know, when his supplanting voice burst into my mind.

'I'll call her when and if I'm ready! Bring the food!'

'Let me take the tray,' I said to Mrs Stragg. 'You should leave at once.'

Her gaze briefly met mine. I had never before seen such a frank, unguarded look from her.

'I shouldn't say it, sir, but the best of good fortune to you.'

'Fortune is not what I want, Patricia, but I thank you for that. I need strength, and the resolve to stand up to this man.'

Tomas Bauer was moving towards us, so I turned decisively away from her and walked into the main part of the Hall. Tomas indicated with his hand that I should carry the tray to the long oaken table, then he stepped close beside me as I walked nervously across the polished boards of the floor. I set down the tray and lifted away the chafing covers. I saw at once that Patricia had done us proud, and prepared all the most powerful of the pellets. She had cooked them by the simplest of means, boiling them up with a selection of garden vegetables into a stew which would be appetizing were it not for the main ingredient.

Tomas Bauer said in my mind: 'In spite of what you think, I am here to salute you, James Owsley. In your country, honour is for many people a matter of pride, and to others self-sacrifice is a privilege. Although I have come to replace you, it is not out of contempt. How may I best show my esteem?'

'Why can we not work together?' I said. 'This talk of replacing me is inappropriate. You have come at a moment when I am certain the course of the battle is about to turn. Look at what lies before us.' I gently waved the palm of my hand above the protein-rich stew that Patricia Stragg had cooked for us. 'To work beside me would be the greatest honour you could pay me.'

'That would not be possible,' Tomas said, and I sensed a trace of sadness in his tone. 'Your way is not the right way. You have to depart.'

'Can I not even show you of what I am capable?' I said. 'Let us take our meal into the hagioscope and partake of it together.

94

Then you will realize how the fiends' movements inside the pit will not only be reversed, but placed so far back that a final sealing of the pit might conceivably be possible, and soon.'

Tomas replaced the chafing lids on the plates.

'Let us indeed visit the hagioscope,' he said. 'But not for what you propose. I must inspect the pit for myself, try to comprehend it. I have to set about planning my defence against whatever it contains.'

Once again I found my own ideas and wishes swept aside by his imperious manner. He thrust one of the covered plates into my hands, then took the other and walked steadfastly towards the entrance to the squint. I followed, my heart already beating faster in anticipation of confronting again what I knew was beyond its narrow confines.

It turned out that although Tomas clearly knew of the existence of the hagioscope, and indeed its approximate position in the wall, he had not worked out how to gain entrance to it. He made me show him how to operate the concealed mechanism, then tried it for himself once or twice. With the main panel set to one side he glanced briefly into the space beyond, before stepping aside to allow me to enter first. I already knew that there was only enough comfortable space for one person at a time, so as Tomas squeezed in behind me I was already pressing myself against the cold stone wall at the back. The aperture that opened to the pit was at my shoulder and I could hear once again the familiar and disgusting movements of the beasts below. Inexplicably, they seemed much closer than ever before. I had spent too much time, too much energy, releasing this man from the crashing plane. How I regretted that!

'Sir, I request you to eat,' Tomas said in my mind.

I raised my arms awkwardly, trying to manoeuvre the plate around to a position in which I could take away the chafing cover again, but to do so meant I had to pass it directly in front of Tomas Bauer's face. To my amazement he jerked his forehead sharply forward, banging the plate in my hand, making it spin away in the confined space. The pellets, my precious and powerful tumours, burst out wetly in their gravy and spilled messily down my clothes and on the dark floor.

I smelt Tomas's breath, so close was his face to mine. In the wan light that seeped in from the Hall I could see his face, maniacally grinning.

'You will never have to taste your beloved pellets again, Owsley. Your purpose is more personal.' He was still holding his own plate and as he forced his body round in the cramped space he was able to place the dish on the narrow stone shelf I had myself been trying to reach. 'I shall come to those later, if they remain necessary. First, you must eat, sir, and do so until you are replete!'

'You have spilled my plate!' I cried.

'And deliberately!'

To my horror, Tomas once again ripped open the fastenings of his shirt and exposed his diseased chest to me. It was only six inches away from my face. The efflorescence of his cancerous breast gleamed in the dim light from the Hall. I madly glimpsed chasing patterns of conflict: life against death, blood pumping through diseased cells, grisly malignant tendrils reaching out like pollen-laden anthers to impregnate the as-yet normal flesh that surrounded the deathly bloom.

Neither of us moved, while I regarded this object of allure and repulsion. A thrill of anticipation was pouring through me like liquid fire.

Tomas raised both his hands and put them behind my head, a gesture that was partly a restraint, partly a caress. When he spoke next his words had a tender quality that until this moment I had never heard from him.

'I shall if you wish hold you, James. You may take what you will from what you see.'

'I have never divined with flesh that is still alive,' I said softly, and in awe of what he was offering me.

'Then do so now.'

Whether he drew my head forward with his hands or I moved of my own volition is something I shall never know, but next my teeth had sunk into the soft flesh of his swollen breast. His strong hands supported my head, while his fingers sensually stroked my hair. I used my tongue to explore the texture of the tumour, sensing its preternatural heat, its tenacious grip on its host, the way it spread like an unfolding corolla. Soon I had found its heart, the pistil, where lay the passive organs of love and reproduction, and final decay and death.

As Tomas Bauer's hands tightened on the back of my head I lunged forward, my jaw opened wide, my tongue guiding, my teeth easily piercing the thin wasted skin that still managed somehow to contain the tumour. I bit into the heart of the cancer. Tomas gasped with pain or passion, and I, sublimely, felt myself release wetly and sweetly. With the access of intoxicating pleasure, came the clarity of perception of the little death: Tomas had brought me to this!

His talk of working alone, without me, had never been true! My rôle was to release him from death. The thrill of the realization urged me on to abandonment: I buried my face ever deeper into his chest as the ecstasy coursed through me. The blackness of the malignancy surged forward to take me, seeming to open up around my eyes like a long dark cylinder, rotating, drawing me through the all-enveloping abyss of night.

I, haruspex, had entered the darkest entrail of all.

Time went past. Minutes, hours, days, years; none held meaning any longer. I had moved to a plane where the mere counting of time was irrelevant. I knew only the gushing flood of death, pumping out around my face, a warm nectar, blinding me, drawing me down, drowning me.

I could no longer see. I was in terminal darkness and I was leaning on, resting on, a slope that was nearly vertical. It was warm and fleshly, coated in slime, lacking anywhere I could obtain a good hold. I felt the terror of what might lie below me and yearned to climb away from it.

A vertical undulation rippled down the slope, shifting me out and back over the abyss below. Panic flooded through me. I was starting to slide, so I held on, paralysed by the abject terror of what would happen to me if my grip weakened. My hands had become claws, their long tines sinking ineffectually into the slimy membrane to which I clung. Oblivion was below. I reached forward and up, trying to gain purchase on the greasy slope. One of my claws felt as if it had found a firmer place, and, thus encouraged, I shifted my weight below, my doubly articulated legs stretching and pushing.

I clicked. I moved.

Another peristaltic undulation came heaving down. This time I was dislodged! I fell, my limbs waving in terror, my unwieldy body curling instinctively into a defensive hump. Only by great good fortune did one of my claws make fleeting contact with the membranous wall. I slashed in the claw and held on with all my strength, and as my body thrashed and collapsed against the scummy gradient I heard others of my kind clicking and clattering with their fright as they too struggled to hold on.

Their panicky sounds swelled around me, muted by the slime around us, but echoing brightly off our chitinous carapaces. The being closest to me, clinging on not far above in the darkness, turned a grotesquely swollen head towards me. Its two rear legs were raised, their horrid inverted knees braced against each other. With a violent spasm the legs rubbed together, setting off a shrieking stridulation.

Around us, the other arthropods took up the rasping chorus, the endless braying sermon; I too felt my rear legs twitching unstoppably against each other. My father, my ancestors, my damned destiny!

By the time the next peristaltic convulsion rolled down towards us I was ready for it, and rode the attack without losing any more ground. The stridulations changed pitch as the slimy wall rippled against us. I shuffled my legs, croaking and belching with the effort, determined never again to fall.

Soon, I started to climb. Beside me, above me, below, the other damned beings climbed too. Ahead was a glimmer of light, a suggestion of final release from the pit, an invitation to life. I knew only the urge to escape and climbed grimly on.

With the next surge of peristalsis a torrent of vile fluids washed down from above, a raging flood of slime and acidic liquid. I held on, while others fell. A violent contraction shook the wall and a great eructation of gases roared past me, carrying with it a fine spray of much of the slime. Again, others around me were dislodged. In my mind I heard their dying fall as at last they entered the abyss.

I resumed my climb, following my father.

If you have read this story and its short introduction you might be wondering what happened to the computer game it was intended to inspire. So am I.

I sent in the finished story, it was accepted, the fee was paid. I was dealing with an intermediary in the UK, whereas the software company turned out to be based in the USA. I never had any contact with them, direct or indirect. I later found out that the American company went through many financial convulsions, with voluntary bankruptcies, emergency share sales to the public, rescue packages from other corporations, mergers and dissolution.

I waited a long time for some kind of reaction to the story – had they read it? Was it fit for purpose? When will the software be released? And so on. No response came, then or later, so of course I drifted towards other things. In the end I exercised my right under the original agreement and sold the story to a British magazine, *The Third Alternative*. The fee from them was literally 1/150th of what the defunct computer corporation had paid. Unlike them, however, *The Third Alternative* – renamed *Black Static* – survives and continues to publish a range of unusual and challenging fiction.

From lack of reaction to the story when it was printed, I assumed either that its immense length (some 15,000 words) or its disgusting contents had put most people off. A later reprint in an anthology edited by Mike Ashley evinced the same silence. I can't and don't complain, but it means that its inclusion in this book is in effect its first real exposure.

I think of 'I, Haruspex' as a serious story, in spite of its heightened prose and the unpleasant material it contains, with several conscious links to my other work. The opening paragraphs, for instance, were a deliberate reference back to the beginning of 'The Head and The Hand'. There are also not immediately obvious connections to some of the stories in the Dream Archipelago sequence ('The Glass', 'The Seacaptain' and 'The Cremation' in particular), and the weird encounter with the crashed Heinkel bomber was a first attempt to grapple with the Second World War material I was researching during this period, for the novel *The Separation*.

Before – 'Palely Loitering'

After three stories dealing with the grimmest of subjects, 'Palely Loitering' should provide some light relief. It is a story about love, and in fact the purest and most innocent kind, that of teenage love. There is little more to it than that – unless you count the paradoxes of time travel.

I believe it was H. G. Wells who argued that any travel, any movement, involved the three physical dimensions: forward/back, up/down and side to side. But as he went on to point out, the movement also involved a fourth dimension – time. It takes a few seconds to cross from one side of a room to another, a few minutes to walk around a house, a few hours to stroll through countryside, and several days or weeks to cross, for example, the Siberian tundra.

'Palely Loitering' is a story I wrote without any kind of external prompting – that is, no one had commissioned me or invited me to send in a story. It was not long after I had written my Wells *hommage* novel, *The Space Machine*, and I still found the myth of the long, summery feeling of the Edwardian years attractive.

I was interested in the Wellsian simplicity of time travel, wondering if the time element of travel might become more powerful and more dominant than the physical, so that if there was some kind of time distortion one could walk or run along a certain path and not just use up time but advance through it. Or go back.

Palely Loitering

i

During the summers of my childhood the best treat of all was our annual picnic in Flux Channel Park, which lay some fifty miles from home. Because my father was set in his ways, and for him no picnic would be worthy of its name without a joint of freshly roasted cold ham, the first clue we children had was always, therefore, when Cook began her preparations. I made a point every day of slipping down unnoticed to the cellar to count the hams that hung from steel hooks in the ceiling, and as soon as I found one was missing I would hurry to my sisters and share the news. The next day, the house would fill with the rich aroma of ham roasting in cloves, and we three children would enter an elaborate charade: inside we would be brimming over with excitement at the thought of the adventure, but at the same time restraining ourselves to act normally, because Father's announcement of his plans at breakfast on the chosen day was an important part of the fun.

We grew up in awe and dread of our father, because he was a distant and strict man. Throughout the winter months, when his work made its greatest demands, we hardly saw him, and all we knew of him were the instructions passed on to us by

Mother or the governor. In the summer months he chose to maintain the distance, joining us only for meals, and spending the evenings alone in his study. However, once a year my father would mellow, and for this alone the excursions to the Park would have been cause for joy. He knew the excitement the trip held for us and he played up to it, revealing the instinct of showman and actor.

Sometimes he would start by pretending to scold or punish us for some imaginary misdemeanour, or would ask Mother a misleading question, such as whether it was that day the servants were taking a holiday, or he would affect absentmindedness. Through all this we would hug our knees under the table, knowing what was to come. Then at last he would utter the magic words 'Flux Channel Park', and, abandoning our charade with glee, we children would squeal with delight and run to Mother, the servants would bustle in and clear away the breakfast, there would be a clatter of dishes and the creak of the wicker hamper from the kitchen . . . and at long last the crunching of hooves and steel-rimmed wheels would sound on the gravel drive outside as the taxi carriage arrived to take us to the station.

ii

I believe that my parents went to the Park from the year they were married, but my own first clear memory of a picnic is when I was seven years old. We went as a family every year until I was fifteen. For nine summers that I can remember, then, the picnic was the happiest day of the year, fusing in memory into one composite day, each picnic much like all the others, so carefully did Father orchestrate the treat for us.

One day stands out from all the others because of a moment of disobedience and mischief, and after that those summery days in Flux Channel Park were never quite the same again.

It happened when I was ten years old. The day had started like any other picnic day, and by the time the taxi arrived the servants had gone on ahead to reserve a train compartment for us. As we clambered into the carriage, Cook ran out of the house to wave us away, and she gave each of us children a freshly peeled carrot to gnaw on. I took mine whole into my mouth, distending my cheeks, and sucking and nibbling at it slowly, mashing it gradually into a juicy pulp. As we rattled down to the station I saw Father glancing at me once or twice, as if to tell me not to make so much noise with my mouth . . . but it was a holiday from everything, and he said nothing.

My mother, sitting opposite us in the carriage, issued her usual instructions to my sisters. 'Salleen,' (my elder sister), 'you're to keep an eye on Mykle. You know how he runs around.' (I, sucking my carrot, made a face at Salleen, bulging a cheek with the carrot and squinting my eyes.) 'And you, Therese, you must stay by me. None of you is to go too close to the Channel.' Her instructions came too soon – the train ride was of second-order interest, but it came between us and the Park.

I enjoyed the train, smelling the sooty smoke and watching the steam curl past the compartment window like an attendant white wraith, but my sisters, especially Salleen, were unaccustomed to the motion and felt sick. While Mother fussed over the girls and summoned the servants from their compartment further down the train, Father and I sat gravely beside each other. When Salleen had been taken away down the train and Therese had quietened I started to fidget in my seat, craning my neck to peer forward, seeking that first magical glimpse of the silvery ribbon of the Channel.

'Father, which bridge shall we cross this time?' And: 'May we cross *two* bridges today, like last year?'

Always the same answer. 'We shall decide when we arrive. Keep still, Mykle.'

And so we arrived, tugging at our parents' hands to hurry them, waiting anxiously by the gate as the entrance fees were paid. The first dashing run down the sloping green sward of the Park grounds, dodging the trees and jumping high to see along the Channel, shouting disappointment because there were too many people there already, or not enough of them. Father beamed at us and lit his pipe, flicking back the flaps of his frock-coat and thrusting his thumbs into his waistcoat, then strolled beside Mother as she held his arm. My sisters and I walked or ran, depending on our constitutional state, heading towards the Channel, but slowing when awed by its closeness, not daring to approach. Looking back, we saw Father and Mother waving to us from the shade of the trees, needlessly warning us of the dangers.

As always, we hurried to the tollbooths for the time bridges that crossed the Channel, for it was these bridges that were the whole reason for the day's trip. A line of people was waiting at each booth, moving forward slowly to pay the entrance fee: families like ourselves with children dancing, young couples holding hands, single men and women glancing speculatively at each other. We counted the people in each queue, eager-ly checked the results with each other, then ran back to our parents.

'Father, there are only twenty-six people at the Tomorrow Bridge!'

'There's *no one* at the Yesterday Bridge!' Salleen, exaggerating as usual.

'Can we cross into Tomorrow, Mother?'

'We did that last year.' Salleen, still disgruntled from the train, kicked out feebly at me. 'Mykle *always* wants to go to Tomorrow!'

'No I don't. The queue is longer for Yesterday!'

Mother, soothingly: 'We'll decide after lunch. The queues will be shorter then.'

Father, watching the servants laying our cloth beneath a dark old cedar tree, said: 'Let us walk for a while, my dear. The children can come too. We will have luncheon in an hour or so.'

Our second exploration of the Park was more orderly, conducted, as it was, under Father's eye. We walked again to the nearest part of the Channel – it seemed less risky now, with parents there – and followed one of the paths that ran parallel to the bank. We stared at the people on the other side.

'Father, are they in Yesterday or Tomorrow?'

'I can't say, Mykle. It could be either.'

'They're nearer to the Yesterday Bridge, stupid!' Salleen, pushing me from behind.

'That doesn't mean anything, stupid!' Jabbing back at her with an elbow.

The sun reflecting from the silvery surface of the flux fluid (we sometimes called it water, to my father's despair) made it glitter and sparkle like rippling quicksilver. Mother would not look at it, saying the reflections hurt her eyes, but there was always something dreadful about its presence so that no one could look too long. In the still patches, where the mystifying currents below briefly let the surface settle, we sometimes saw upside-down reflections of the people on the other side.

Later: we edged around the tolls, where the lines of people were longer than before, and walked further along the bank towards the east.

Then later: we returned to the shade and the trees, and sat in a demure group while lunch was served. My father carved ham with the precision of the expert chef: one cut down at an angle towards the bone, another horizontally across to the bone, and the wedge of meat so produced taken away on a plate by one of the servants. Then the slow, meticulous carving beneath the notch. One slice after another, each one slightly wider and rounder than the one before.

As soon as lunch was finished we made our way to the toll-booths and queued with the other people. There were always fewer people waiting at this time of the afternoon, a fact that surprised us but which our parents took for granted. This day we had chosen the Tomorrow Bridge. Whatever the prefer-ences we children expressed, Father always had the last word. It did not, however, prevent Salleen from sulking, nor me from letting her see the joys of victory.

This particular day was the first time I had been to the Park with any understanding of the Flux Channel and its real pur-pose. Earlier in the summer, the governor had instructed us in the rudiments of spatio-temporal physics . . . although that was not the name he gave to it. My sisters were bored with the subject (it was boys' stuff, they declared), but to learn how and why the Channel had been built was fascinating to me.

I had grown up with a general understanding that we lived in a world where our ancestors had built many marvellous things that we no longer used or had need for. This awareness, gleaned from the few other children I knew, was of astonishing and mi-raculous achievements, and was, as might be expected, wildly inaccurate. I knew as a fact, for instance, that the Flux Channel had been built in a matter of days, that jet-propelled aircraft could circumnavigate the world in a matter of minutes, and that houses and automobiles and railway trains could be built in a matter of seconds. Of course the truth was quite different, and our education in the scientific age and its history was constantly interesting to me.

In the case of the Flux Channel, I knew by my tenth birthday that it had taken more than two decades to build, that its construction had cost many human lives, and that it had taxed the resources and intelligence of many different countries.

Furthermore, the principle on which it worked was well understood today, even though we had no use for it as it was intended.

We lived in the age of starflight, but by the time I was born mankind had long lost the desire to travel in space.

The governor showed us a slowed-down film of the launching of the craft that had flown to the stars: the surface of the Flux Channel undulating as the starship was propelled through its deeps like a huge whale trying to navigate a canal. Then the hump of its hull bursting through the surface in a shimmering spray of exploding foam, and the gushing wake sluicing over the banks of the Channel and vanishing instantaneously. Then the actual launch, with the starship soaring into the sky, leaving a trail of brilliant droplets in the air behind it.

All this had taken place in under one-tenth of a second. Anyone within twenty-five miles of the launch would have been killed by the shockwave, and it is said that the thunder of the starship's passage could be heard in every country of the Neuropean Union. Only the automatic high-speed cameras were there to witness the launching. The men and women who crewed the ship – their metabolic functions frozen for most of the flight – would not have felt the strain of such a tremendous acceleration even if they had been conscious. The flux field distorted time and space, changed the nature of matter. The launch was at such a high relative velocity that by the time the technicians returned to the Flux Channel the starship would have been outside the solar system. By the time I was born, seventy years after this, the starship would have been . . . who knows where?

Behind it, churning and eddying with temporal mystery, the Flux Channel lay across more than a hundred miles of the land, a scintillating, dazzling ribbon of light, like a slit in the world that looked towards another dimension.

There were no more starships after the first and that one had never returned. When the disturbance of the launching had calmed to a degree where the flux field was no longer a threat to human life, the stations that tapped the electricity had been built along part of its banks. A few years later, when the flux field had stabilized completely, an area of the countryside was landscaped to create the Park and the time bridges were built.

One of these traversed the Channel at an angle of exactly ninety degrees, and to walk across it was no different from crossing any bridge across any ordinary river.

One bridge was built slightly obtuse of the right angle, and to cross it was to climb the temporal gradient of the flux field; when one emerged on the other side of the Channel, twenty-four hours had elapsed.

The third bridge was built slightly acute of the right angle, and to cross to the other side was to walk twenty-four hours into the past. Yesterday, Today and Tomorrow existed on the far side of the Flux Channel, and one could walk at will among them.

iii

While we waited in line at the tollbooth we had another argument about Father's decision to cross into Tomorrow. The Park management had posted a board above the paydesk, describing the weather conditions on the other side. There was wind, low cloud, sudden showers. My mother said that she did not wish to get wet. Salleen, watching me, quietly repeated that we had been to Tomorrow last year. I stayed quiet, looking across the Channel to the other side.

(Over there the weather seemed to be as it was here: a high, bright sky, hot sunshine. But what I could see was Today: yesterday's Tomorrow, tomorrow's Yesterday, today's Today.)

Behind us the queue was thinning as other, less hardy people drifted away to the other bridges. I was content, because the only one that did not interest me was the Today Bridge, but to rub in my accidental victory I whispered to Salleen that the weather was good on the Yesterday side. She, in no mood for subtle perversity, kicked out at my shins and we squabbled stupidly as my father went to the toll.

He was an important man. I heard the attendant say: 'But you shouldn't have waited, sir. We are honoured by your visit.' He released the ratchet of the turnstile, and we filed through.

We entered the covered way of the bridge, a long dark tunnel of wood and metal, lit at intervals by dim incandescent lamps. I ran on ahead, feeling the familiar electric tingle over my body as I moved through the flux field.

'Mykle! Stay with us!' My father, calling from behind.

I slowed obediently and turned to wait. I saw the rest of the family coming towards me. The outlines of their bodies were strangely diffused, an effect of the field on all who entered it. As they reached me, and thus came into the zone I was in, their shapes became sharply focused once more.

I let them pass me, and followed behind. Salleen, walking beside me, kicked out at my ankles.

'Why did you do that?'

'Because you're a little pig!'

I ignored her. We could see the end of the covered way ahead. It had become dark soon after we started crossing the bridge – a presage of the evening of the day we were leaving – but now daylight shone again and I saw pale blue morning light, misty shapes of trees. I paused, seeing my parents and sisters silhouetted against the light. Therese, holding Mother's hand, took no notice of me, but Salleen, whom I secretly loved, strutted proudly behind Father, asserting her independence of me. Perhaps it was because of her, or perhaps it was that morning light shining down from the end of the tunnel, but I stayed still as the rest of the family went on.

I waved my hands, watching the fingertips blur as they moved across the flux field, and then I walked on slowly. Because of the blurring, my family were now almost invisible. Suddenly I was a little frightened, alone in the flux field, and I hastened after them. I saw their ghostly shapes move into daylight and out of sight (Salleen glanced back towards me), and I walked faster.

By the time I had reached the end of the covered way, the day had matured and the light was that of mid-afternoon. Low clouds were scudding before a stiff wind. As a squall of rain swept by I sheltered in the bridge, and looked across the Park for the family. I saw them a short distance away, hurrying towards one of the pagoda-shaped shelters the Park authorities had built. Glancing at the sky I saw there was a large patch of blue not far away, and I knew the shower would be a short one. It was not cold and I did not mind getting wet, but I hesitated before going out into the open. Why I stood there I do not now recall, but I had always had a childish delight in the sensation of the flux field, and at the place where the covered way ends the bridge is still over a part of the Channel.

I stood by the edge of the bridge and looked down at the flux fluid. Seen from directly above it closely resembled water, because it seemed to be clear (although the bottom could not be seen), and did not have the same metallic sheen or quicksilver property it had when viewed from the side. There were bright highlights on the surface, glinting as the fluid stirred, as if there were a film of oil across it.

My parents had reached the pagoda – whose colourful tiles and paintwork looked odd in this dismal rain – and they were squeezing in with the two girls, as other people made room for them. I could see my father's tall black hat bobbing behind the crowd.

Salleen was looking back at me, perhaps envying my solitary state, and so I stuck out my tongue at her. I was showing off. I went to the edge of the bridge, where there was no guard rail, and leaned precariously out above the fluid. The flux field prickled around me. I saw Salleen tugging at Mother's arm, and Father took a step forward into the rain. I poised myself and jumped towards the bank, flying above the few inches of the Channel between me and the ground. I heard a roaring in my ears, I was momentarily blinded, and the charge of the flux field enveloped me like an electric cocoon.

I landed feet first on the muddy bank, and looked around me as if nothing untoward had happened.

iv

Although I did not realize it at first, in leaping from the bridge and moving up through a part of the flux field, I had travelled forward in time. It happened that I landed on a day in the future when the weather was as grey and blustery as on the day I had left, and so my first real awareness, when I looked up, was that the pagoda had suddenly emptied. I stared in horror across the parkland, not believing that my family could have vanished in the blink of an eye.

I started to run, stumbling and sliding on the slippery ground, and I felt a panicky terror and a dread of being abandoned. All the cockiness in me had gone. I sobbed as I ran, and when I reached the pagoda I was crying aloud, snivelling and wiping my nose and eyes on the sleeve of my jacket.

I went back to where I had landed, and saw the muddy impressions of my feet on the bank. From there I looked at the bridge, so tantalizingly close, and it was then that I realized what I had done, even though it was a dim understanding.

Something like my former mood returned then and a spirit of exploration came over me. After all, it was the first time I had ever been alone in the Park. I started to walk away from the bridge, following a tree-lined path that went along the Channel.

The day I had arrived in must have been a weekday in winter or early spring because the trees were bare and there were very few people about. From this side of the Channel I could see that the tollbooths were open, but the only other people in the Park were a long way away.

For all this, it was still an adventure and the awful thoughts about where I had arrived, or how I was to return, were put aside.

I walked a long way, enjoying the freedom of being able to explore this side without my family. When they were present it was as if I could only see what they pointed out, and walk where they chose. Now it was like being in the Park for the first time.

This small pleasure soon palled. It was a cold day and my light summer shoes began to feel sodden and heavy, chafing against my toes. The Park was not at all how I liked it to be. Part of the fun on a normal day was the atmosphere of shared daring, and mixing with people you knew had not all come from the same day, the same time. Once, my father, in a mood of exceptional capriciousness, had led us to and fro across the Today and Yesterday Bridges, showing us time-slipped images of himself which he had made on a visit to the Park the day before. Visitors to the Park often did such things. During the holidays, when the big factories were closed, the Park would be full of shouting, laughing voices as carefully prepared practical jokes of this sort were played.

None of this was going on as I tramped along under the leaden sky. The future was for me as commonplace as a field.

I began to worry, wondering how I was to get back. I could imagine the wrath of my father, the tears of my mother, the endless jibes I would get from Salleen and Therese. I turned around and walked quickly back towards the bridges, forming a half-hearted plan to cross the Channel repeatedly, using the Tomorrow and Yesterday Bridges in turn, until I was back where I started.

I was running again, in danger of sobbing, when I saw a young man walking along the bank towards me. I would have paid no attention to him, but for the fact that when we were a short distance apart he sidestepped so that he was in front of me.

I slowed, regarded him incuriously, and went to walk around him . . . but much to my surprise he called after me.

'Mykle! It is Mykle, isn't it?'

'How do you know my name?' I said, pausing and looking at him warily.

'I was looking for you. You've jumped forward in time, and don't know how to get back.'

'Yes, but—'

'I'll show you how. It's easy.'

We were facing each other now. I was wondering who he was and how he knew me. There was something much too friendly about him. He was very tall and thin, and had the beginnings of a moustache darkening his lip. He seemed adult to me, but when he spoke it was with a hoarse, boyish falsetto.

I said: 'It's all right, thank you, sir. I can find my own way.'

'By running across the bridges?'

'How did you know?'

'You'll never manage it, Mykle. When you jumped from the bridge you went a long way into the future. About thirty-two years.'

'This is . . . ?' I looked around at the Park, disbelieving what he said. 'But it feels like—'

'Just like Tomorrow. But it isn't. You've come a long way. Look over there.' He pointed across the Channel, to the other side. 'Do you see those houses? You've never seen those before, have you?'

There was an estate of new houses, built beyond the trees on the Park's perimeter. True, I hadn't noticed them before, but it proved nothing. I didn't find this very interesting, and I began to sidle away from him, wanting to get on with the business of working out how to get back.

'Thank you, sir. It was nice to meet you.'

'Don't call me "sir",' he said, laughing. 'You've been taught to be polite to strangers, but you must know who *I* am.'

'N-no . . .'

Suddenly rather nervous of him I walked quickly away, but he ran over and caught me by the arm.

'There's something I must show you,' he said. 'This is very important. Then I'll get you back to the bridge.'

'Leave me alone!' I said loudly, quite frightened of him.

He took no notice of my protests, but walked me along the path beside the Channel. He was looking over my head, across the Channel, and I could not help noticing that whenever we passed a tree or a bush which cut off the view he would pause and look past it before going on. This continued until we were near the time bridges again, when he came to a halt beside a huge sprawling rhododendron bush.

'Now,' he said. 'I want you to look. But don't let yourself be seen.'

Crouching down with him, I peered around the edge of the bush. At first I could not imagine what it was I was supposed to be looking at, and thought it was more houses for my inspection. The estate did, in fact, continue all along the further edge of the Park, just visible beyond the trees.

'Do you see her?' He pointed, then ducked back. Following the direction, I saw a young woman sitting on a bench on the far side of the Channel.

'Who is she?' I said, although her small figure did not actually arouse much interest in me.

'The loveliest girl I have ever seen. She's always there, on that bench. She is waiting for her lover. She sits there every day, her heart filled with anguish and hope.'

As he said this the young man's voice broke, as if with emotion, and I glanced up at him. His eyes were moist.

I peered again around the edge of the bush and looked at the girl, wondering what it was about her that produced this reaction. I could hardly see her, because she was huddled against the wind and had a shawl drawn over her hair. She was sitting to one side, facing towards the Tomorrow Bridge. To me, she was approximately as interesting as the houses, which is not to say very much, but she seemed important to the young man.

'Is she a friend of yours?' I said, turning back to him.

'No, not a friend, Mykle. A symbol. A token of the love that is in us all.'

'What is her name?' I said, not following this interpretation.

'Estyll. The most beautiful name in the world.'

Estyll: I had never heard the name before, and I repeated it softly.

'How do you know this?' I said. 'You say you—'

'Wait, Mykle. She will turn in a moment. You will see her face.'

His hand was clasping my shoulder as if we were old friends, and although I was still shy of him it assured me of his good intent. He was sharing something with me, something so important that I was honoured to be included.

Together we leaned forward again and looked clandestinely at her. I heard my friend say her name, close to my ear, speaking so softly that it was almost a whisper. A few moments passed, then, as if the time vortex above the Channel had swept the word slowly across to her, she raised her head, shrugged back the shawl, and stood up. I was craning my neck to see her but she turned away. I watched her walk up the slope of the Park grounds, towards the houses beyond the trees.

'Isn't she a beauty, Mykle?'

I was too young to understand him fully, so I said nothing. At that age, my only awareness of the other sex was that my sisters were temperamentally and physically different from me. I had yet to discover more interesting matters. In any event, I had barely caught a glimpse of Estyll's face.

The young man was evidently enraptured by the girl, and as we watched her move through the distant trees my attention was half on her, half on him.

'I should like to be the man she loves,' he said at last.

'Do you . . . love her, sir?'

119

'Love? What I feel is too noble to be contained in such a word.' He looked down at me, and for an instant I was reminded of the haughty disdain that my father sometimes revealed when I did something stupid. 'Love is for lovers, Mykle. *I* am a romantic, which is a far grander thing to be.'

I was beginning to find my companion rather pompous and overbearing, trying to involve me in his passions. I was an argumentative child, though, and could not resist pointing out a contradiction.

'But you said she was waiting for her lover,' I said.

'Just a supposition.'

'I think you are her lover, and won't admit it.'

I used the word disparagingly, but it made him look at me thoughtfully. The drizzle was coming down again, a dank veil across the countryside. The young man stepped away suddenly. I think he had grown as tired of my company as I had of his.

'I was going to show you how to get back,' he said. 'Come with me.' He set off towards the bridge, and I went after him. 'You'll have to go back the way you came. You jumped, didn't you?'

'That's right,' I said, puffing a little. It was difficult keeping up with him.

As we reached the end of the bridge, the young man left the path and walked across the grass to the edge of the Channel. I held back, nervous of going too close again.

'Ah!' said the young man, peering down at the damp soil. 'Look, Mykle . . . these must be your footprints. This was where you landed.'

I went forward warily and stood just behind him.

'Put your feet in these marks and jump towards the bridge.'

Although the metal edge of the bridge was only an arm's length away from where we were standing it seemed a formidable jump, especially as the bridge was higher than the bank. I pointed this out.

'I'll be behind you,' the young man said. 'You won't slip. Now . . . look on the bridge. There's a scratch on the floor. Do you see it? You have to aim at that. Try to land with one foot on either side, and you'll be back where you started.'

It all seemed rather unlikely. The part of the bridge he was pointing out was wet with rain and looked slippery. If I landed badly I would fall – worse, I could slip backwards into the flux fluid. Although I sensed that my new friend was right – that I could only get back by the way I had come – it did not *feel* right.

'Mykle, I know what you're thinking. But I made that mark. I've done it myself. Trust me.'

I was thinking of my father and his wrath, so at last I stepped forward and put my feet in the squelching impressions I had made as I landed. Rainwater was oozing down the muddy bank towards the flux fluid, but I noticed that as it dripped down to touch the fluid it suddenly leaped back, just like the droplets of whisky on the side of the glass my father drank in the evenings.

The young man took a grip on my belt, holding on so that I should not slip down into the Channel.

'I'll count to three, then you jump. I'll give you a shove. Are you ready?'

'I think so.'

'You'll remember Estyll, won't you?'

I looked over my shoulder. His face was very close to mine.

'Yes, I'll remember her,' I said, not meaning it.

'Right . . . brace yourself. It's quite a hop from here. One . . .'

I saw the fluid of the Channel below me and to the side. It was glistening eerily in the grey light.

'. . . two . . . three . . .'

I jumped forward at the same instant as the young man gave me a hefty shove from behind. Instantly, I felt the electric crackle of the flux field, I heard again the loud roaring in my ears and there was a split second of impenetrable blackness. My feet touched the edge of the time bridge and I tripped, sprawling forward on the floor. I slithered awkwardly against the legs of a man standing just there, and my face fetched up against a pair of shoes polished to a brilliant shine. I looked up.

There was my father, staring down at me in great surprise. All I can now remember of that frightful moment is his face glaring down at me, topped by his black, curly brimmed, stovepipe hat. He seemed to be as tall as a mountain.

V

My father was not a man who saw the merit of short, sharp punishment. I lived under the cloud of my misdeed for several weeks.

I felt that I had done what I had done in all innocence, and that the price I had to pay for it was too high. In our house, however, there was only one kind of justice and that was Father's.

Although I had been in the future for only about an hour of my subjective time, five or six hours had passed for my family and it was twilight when I returned. This prolonged absence was the main reason for my father's anger, although if I had jumped thirty-two years, as my companion had informed me, an error of a few hours on the return journey was as nothing.

I was never called upon to explain myself. My father detested excuses.

Salleen and Therese were the only ones who asked what had happened, and I gave them a shortened account. I said that after I jumped into the future, and realized what I had done, I explored the Park on my own and then jumped back. This was enough for them. I said nothing of the youth with the lofty sentiments, nor of the young lady who sat on the bench. To myself, I had mixed feelings about the adventure. I spent a lot of time on my own – part of my punishment was that I could only go into the playroom one evening a week, and had to study more diligently instead – and tried to work out the meaning of what I had seen.

The girl, Estyll, meant very little to me. She certainly had a place in my memory of that hour in the future, but because she was so fascinating to my companion I remembered her only through him and she became of secondary interest.

I thought about the young man a great deal. He had gone to such pains to make a friend of me, and to include me in his private thoughts, and yet I remembered him as an intrusive and unwelcome presence. I often thought of his husky voice intoning those grand opinions, and even from the disadvantage of my junior years, his callow figure – all gangly limbs, slicked-back hair and downy moustache – was a comical one. For a long time I wondered who he could be. Although the answer seems obvious in retrospect it was some years before I realized it.

My penance came to an end about three months after the picnic. This parole was never formally stated but understood by all concerned. The occasion was a party our parents allowed us to have for some visiting cousins and after that my misbehaviour was never again directly mentioned.

The following summer, when the time came around for another picnic in Flux Channel Park, my father interrupted our excited outpourings to deliver a short speech, reminding us that we must all stay together. This was said to us all, although Father gave me a sharp and meaningful look. It was a small, passing cloud, and it threw no shadow on the day. I was obedient and sensible throughout the picnic. Even so, as we walked through the Park in the gentle heat of the day I did not forget to look out for my helpful friend, nor for his adored Estyll. I looked, and kept looking, but neither of them was there that day.

vi

When I was eleven I was sent to school for the first time. I had spent my formative years in a household where wealth and influence were taken for granted, and where the governor had taken a lenient view of my education. Thrown suddenly into the company of boys from all walks of life, I retreated behind a manner of arrogance and condescension. It took two years to be scorned and beaten out of this, but well before then I had developed a wholehearted loathing for education and all that went with it. I became, in short, a student who did not study, and a pupil whose dislike for his fellows was heartily reciprocated.

I became an accomplished malingerer, and with the occasional connivance of one of the servants I could readily feign a convincing though unaccountable stomach ailment, or develop rashes that looked infectious. Sometimes I would simply stay at home. More frequently I would set off into the countryside on my bicycle and spend the day in pleasant musings.

On days like this I pursued my own form of education by reading, although this was by choice and not by compulsion. I eagerly read whatever novels and poetry I could lay my hands on. My preference in fiction was for adventure, and in poetry I soon discovered the romantics of the early nineteenth century, and the then much despised desolationists of two hundred years later. The stirring combinations of valour and unrequited love, of moral virtue and nostalgic wistfulness, struck deep into my soul and made more pointed my dislike of the routines of school.

It was at this time, when my reading was arousing passions that my humdrum existence could not satisfy, that my thoughts turned to the girl called Estyll.

I needed an object for the stirrings within me. I envied the romantic poets their soulful yearnings, for they, it seemed to me, had at least had the emotional experience with which to focus their desires. The despairing desolationists, lamenting the waste around them, at least had known life. Perhaps I did not rationalize this need quite so neatly at the time, but whenever I was aroused by my reading it was the image of Estyll that came most readily to mind.

Remembering what my companion had told me, and with my own sight of that small, huddled figure, I saw her as a lonely, heartbroken waif, squandering her life in a hopeless vigil. That she was unspeakably beautiful, and utterly faithful, went without saying.

As I grew older, my restlessness advanced. I felt increasingly isolated, not only from the other boys at school, but also from my family. My father's work was making more demands on him than ever before and he was unapproachable. My sisters were going their own separate ways: Therese had developed an interest in ponies, Salleen in young men.

Nobody had time for me, no one tried to understand.

One autumn, some three or four years after I started school, I surrendered at last to the stirrings of soul and flesh, and attempted to allay them.

vii

I selected the day with care, one when there were several lessons at school where my absence would not be too obvious. I left home at the usual time in the morning, but instead of heading for school I rode to the city, bought a return ticket to the Park at the railway station, and settled down on the train.

During the summer there had been the usual family outing to the Park, but it had meant little to me. I had outgrown the immediate future. Tomorrow no longer concerned me.

I was vested with purpose. When I arrived at the Park on that stolen day I went directly to the Tomorrow Bridge, paid the toll, and set off through the covered way towards the other side. There were more people about than I had expected, but it was quiet enough for what I wanted to do. I waited until I was the only one on the bridge, then went to the end of the covered way and stood by the spot from which I had first jumped. I took a flint from my pocket and scratched a thin but deep line in the metal surface of the bridge.

I slipped the flint back in my pocket then looked appraisingly at the bank below. I had no way of knowing how far to jump, only an instinct and a vague memory of how I had done it before. The temptation was to jump as far as possible, but I managed to suppress it.

I placed my feet astride the line, took a deep breath and launched myself towards the bank.

A dizzying surge of electric tingling, momentary darkness, and I sprawled across the bank.

Before I took stock of my surroundings I marked the place where I had landed. First I scraped a deep line in the soil and grass with the flint, pointing back towards the mark on the bridge (which was still visible, though less bright), then I tore away several tufts of grass around my feet to make a second mark. Thirdly, I stared intently at the precise place, fixing it in memory, so there would be no possibility of not finding it again.

When satisfied, I stood up and looked around at this future.

viii

It was a holiday. The Park was crowded with people, all gay in summer clothes. The sun shone down from a cloudless sky, a breeze rippled the ladies' dresses, and from a distant pagoda a band played stirring marches.

It was all so familiar that my first instinct was that my parents and sisters must be somewhere about and my illicit visit would be discovered. I ducked down against the bank of the Channel, but then I laughed at myself and relaxed. In my painstaking anticipation of this exploit I had considered the possibility of meeting people I knew, and had decided that the chance was too slender to be taken seriously. Anyway, when I looked again at the people passing – who of course paid me no attention – I realized that there were subtle differences in their clothes and hairstyles, reminding me that for all the superficial similarities I had indeed travelled to the future.

I scrambled up to the tree-lined pathway and mingled with the throng, quickly catching the spirit of the day. I must have looked like any other schoolboy, but I felt very special indeed. After all, I had now leaped into the future twice.

This euphoria aside, I was there with a purpose and I did not forget it. I looked across to the other bank, searching for a sight of Estyll. She was not by the bench. I felt a crushing and illogical disappointment, as if she had deliberately betrayed me by not being there. All the frustration of the past months welled up in me, and I could have shouted with the agony of it. But then, miraculously it seemed, I saw her some distance away from the bench, wandering to and fro on the path on her side, glancing occasionally towards the Tomorrow Bridge. I recognized her at once, although I am not sure how. During that other day in the future I had barely seen her, and since then my imagination had run with a free rein, yet the moment I saw her I knew it was she.

Gone was the shawl and the arms that had been wrapped for warmth about her body were now folded casually across her chest. She was wearing a light summer frock, coloured in a number of pastel shades, and to my eager eyes it seemed that no lovelier clothes could have been worn by any woman in the world. Her short hair fell prettily about her face, and the way she held her head, and the way she stood, seemed delicate beyond words.

I watched her for several minutes, transfixed by the sight of her. People continued to mill past me, but for all I was aware of them they might not have been there.

At last I remembered my purpose, even though just seeing her was an experience whose joys I could not have anticipated. I walked back down the path, past the Tomorrow Bridge and beyond to the Today Bridge. I hastened across and let myself through the exit turnstile on the other side. Still in the same day, I went up the path towards where I had seen Estyll.

There were fewer people on this side of the Channel, of course, and the path was less crowded. I looked around as I walked, noticing that custom had not changed and that many people were sitting in the shade of the trees with the remains of picnic meals spread out around them. I did not look too closely at these groups – it was still at the back of my mind that I might see my own family here.

I passed the line of people waiting at the Tomorrow toll-booth and saw the path continuing beyond. A short distance away, walking slowly to and fro, was Estyll.

At the sight of her, now so near to me, I paused.

I walked on, less confidently than before. She glanced in my direction once, but she looked at me in the same uninterested way as she looked at everybody. I was only a few yards from her, and my heart was pounding and I was trembling. I realized that the little speech I had prepared – the one in which I introduced myself, then revealed myself as witty and mature, then proposed that she take a walk with me – had gone from my mind. She looked so grown-up, so sure of herself.

Unaware of my concentrated attention on her, she turned away when I was within touching distance of her. I walked on a few more paces, desperately unsure of myself. I turned and faced her.

For the first time in my life I felt the pangs of uncontrollable love. Until then the word had had no meaning for me but as I stood before her I felt a love so shocking that I could only flinch away from it. How I must have appeared to her I cannot say. I must have been shaking, I must have been bright with embarrassment. She looked at me with calm grey eyes and an enquiring expression, as if she detected that I had something of immense importance to say. She was so beautiful! I felt so clumsy!

Then she smiled, unexpectedly, and I had my cue to say something. Instead, I stared at her, not even thinking of what I could say, but simply immobilized by the unexpected struggle with my emotions. I had thought love would be so simple.

Moments passed and I could cope with the emotional

turbulence no more. I took a step back and then another. Estyll had continued to smile at me during those long seconds of my wordless stare, and as I moved away her smile broadened and she parted her lips as if to say something. It was too much for me. I turned away, burning with embarrassment, and started to run. After a few steps, I halted and looked back at her. She was still looking at me, still smiling.

I shouted: '*I love you!*'

It seemed to me that everyone in the Park had heard me. I did not wait to see Estyll's reaction. I ran away. I hurried along the path, then ran up a grassy bank and into the shelter of some trees. I ran and ran, crossing the concourse of the open-air restaurant, crossing a broad lawn, diving into the cover of more trees beyond.

It was as if the physical effort of running would stop me thinking, because the moment I rested the enormity of what I had done flooded in on me. It seemed that I had done nothing right and everything wrong. I had had a chance to meet her and I had let it slip through my fingers. Worst of all, I had shouted my love at her, revealing it to the world. To my adolescent mind it seemed there could have been no grosser mistake.

I stood under the trees, leaning my forehead against the trunk of an old oak, banging my fist in frustration and fury.

I was terrified that Estyll would find me and I never wanted to see her again. At the same time I wanted her and loved her with a renewed passion . . . and hoped, but hoped secretly, that she would be searching for me in the Park, and would come to me by my tree and put her arms around me.

A long time passed and gradually my restless and contradictory emotions subsided.

I still did not want to see Estyll, so when I walked down to the path I looked carefully ahead to be sure I would not meet her. When I stepped down to the path itself – where people still walked in casual enjoyment, unaware of the drama – I looked along it towards the bridges, but saw no sign of her. I could not be sure she had left so I hung around, torn between wincing shyness of her and profound devotion.

At last I decided to risk it and hurried along the path to the tollbooths. I did not look for her and I did not see her. I paid the toll at the Today Bridge and returned to the other side. I located the marks I had made on the bank beside the Tomorrow Bridge, aimed myself at the scratch on the bridge floor, and leaped across towards it.

I emerged in the day I had left. Once again, my rough-and-ready way of travelling through time did not return me to a moment precisely true to elapsed time, but it was close enough. When I checked my watch against the clock in the tollbooth, I discovered I had been gone for less than a quarter of an hour. Meanwhile, I had been in the future for more than three hours.

I caught an earlier train home and idled away the rest of the day on my bicycle in the countryside, reflecting on the passions of man, the glories of young womanhood, and the accursed weaknesses of the will.

ix

I should have learned from experience and never tried to see Estyll again, but there was no quieting the love I felt for her. Thoughts of her dominated every waking moment. It was the memory of her smile that was central. She had been encouraging me, inviting me to say the very things I had wanted to say, and I had missed the chance. So, with the obsession renewed and intensified, I returned to the Park and did so many times.

Whenever I could safely absent myself from school and could lay my hands on the necessary cash, I went to the Tomorrow Bridge and leapt across to the future. I was soon able to judge that dangerous leap with a marvellous instinctive skill. Naturally, there were mistakes. Once, terrifyingly, I landed in the night, and after that experience I always took a small pocket flashlight with me. On two or three occasions my return jump was inaccurate, and I had to use the time bridges to find the day I should have been in.

After a few more of my leaps into the future I felt sufficiently at home to approach a stranger in the Park and ask him the date. By telling me the year he confirmed that I was exactly twenty-seven years into the future . . . or, as it had been when I was ten, thirty-two years ahead. The stranger I spoke to was apparently a local man and by his appearance a man of some substance, and I took him sufficiently into my confidence to point out Estyll to him. I asked him if he knew her, which he said he did, but could only confirm her given name. It was enough for me, because by then it suited my purpose not to know too much about her.

I made no more attempts to speak to Estyll. Barred from approaching her by my painful shyness I fell back on fantasies, which were much more in keeping with my timid soul. As I grew older, and became more influenced by my favourite poets, it seemed not only more sad and splendid to glorify her from a distance, but appropriate that my role in her life should be passive.

To compensate for my nervousness about trying to meet her again, I constructed a fiction about her.

She was passionately in love with a disreputable young man, who had tempted her with elaborate promises and wicked lies. At the very moment she had declared her love for him, he had deserted her by crossing the Tomorrow Bridge into a future from which he had never returned. In spite of his shameful behaviour her love held true and every day she waited in vain by the Tomorrow Bridge, knowing that one day he would return. I would watch her covertly from the other side of the Channel, knowing that her patience was that of the lovelorn. Too proud for tears, too faithful for doubt, she was at ease with the knowledge that her long wait would be its own reward.

In the present, in my real life, I sometimes dallied with another fiction: that *I* was her lover, that it was for me she was waiting. This thought excited me, arousing responses of a physical kind that I did not fully understand.

I went to the Park repeatedly, gladly suffering the punishments at school for my frequent and badly excused truancies. So often did I leap across to that future that I soon grew accustomed to seeing other versions of myself, and realized that I had sometimes seen other young men before, who looked suspiciously like me, and who skulked near the trees and bushes beside the Channel and gazed across as wistfully as I did.

There was one day in particular – a lovely, sunny day, at the height of the holiday season – that I often lighted on, and here there were more than a dozen versions of myself, dispersed among the crowd.

One day, not long before my sixteenth birthday, I took one of my now customary leaps into the future and found a cold and windy day, almost deserted. As I walked along the path I saw a child, a small boy, plodding along with his head down against the wind and scuffing at the turf with the toes of his shoes.

The sight of him, with his muddy legs and tear-streaked face, reminded me of that very first time I had jumped accidentally to the future. I stared at him as we approached each other. He looked back at me and for an instant a shock of recognition went through me like a bolt of electricity. He turned his eyes aside at once and stumped on by, heading towards the bridges behind me. I stared at him, recalling in vivid detail how I had felt that day, and how I had been fomenting a desperate plan to return to the day I had left, and as I did so I realized – at long last – the identity of the friend I had made that day.

My head whirling with the recognition I called after him, hardly believing what was happening.

'Mykle!' I said, the sound of my own name tasting strange in my mouth. The boy turned to look at me and I said a little uncertainly: 'It is Mykle, isn't it?'

'How do you know my name?' His stance was truculent and he seemed unwilling to be spoken to.

'I . . . was looking for you,' I said, inventing a reason for why I should have recognized him. 'You've jumped forward in time, and don't know how to get back.'

'Yes, but—'

'I'll show you how. It's easy.'

As we were speaking a distracting thought came to me: so far I had, quite accidentally, duplicated the conversation of that day. But what if I were to change it consciously? Suppose I said something that my 'friend' had not; suppose young Mykle were not to respond in the way I had? The consequences seemed enormous and I could imagine this boy's life – my own life – going in entirely different directions. I saw the dangers of that and I knew I had to make an effort to repeat the dialogue, and my actions, precisely.

But just as it had when I tried to speak to Estyll, my mind went blank.

'It's all right, thank you, sir,' the boy was saying. 'I can find my own way.'

'By running across the bridges?' I wasn't sure if that was

what had been said to me before, but I knew that had been my intention.

'How did you know?'

I found I could not depend on that distant memory, and so, trusting to the inevitable sweep of destiny, I stopped trying to remember. I said whatever came to mind.

It was appalling to see myself through my own eyes. I had not imagined that I had been quite such a pathetic-looking child.

The younger me had every appearance of being a sullen and difficult boy. There was a stubbornness and a belligerence that I both recognized and disliked. And I knew there was a deeper weakness too. I could remember how I had seen myself, my older self, that is. I recalled my 'friend' from this day as callow and immature, and mannered with a loftiness that did not suit his years. That I (as child) had seen myself (as young man) in this light was condemnation of my then lack of percipience. I had learned a lot about myself since going to school and I was more adult in my outlook than the other boys at school. What is more, since falling in love with Estyll I had taken great care over my appearance and clothes and whenever I made one of these trips to the future I looked my best.

However, in spite of the shortcomings I saw in myself-as-boy, I felt sorry for young Mykle and there was certainly a feeling of great spirit between us. I showed him what I had noticed of the changes in the Park and then we walked together towards the Tomorrow Bridge. Estyll was there on the other side of the Channel. I told him what I knew of her. I could not convey what was in my heart, but knowing how important she was to become to him, I wanted him to see her and love her.

After she had left, I showed him the mark I had made in the surface of the bridge. After I had persuaded him to make the leap – with several sympathetic thoughts about his imminent reception – I wandered alone in the blustery evening, wondering if Estyll would return. There was no sign of her.

I waited almost until nightfall, resolving that the years of admiring her from afar had been long enough. Something that young Mykle said had deeply affected me.

Allowing him a glimpse of my fiction, I had told him: 'She is waiting for her lover.' My younger self had replied: 'I think you are her lover, and won't admit it.'

I had forgotten saying that. I would not admit it, for it was not strictly true, but I would admit to the wish that it were so.

Staring across the darkening Channel, I wondered if there were a way of making it come true. The Park was an eerie place in that light. The temporal stresses of the flux field seemed to take on a tangible presence. Who knew what tricks could be played by Time? I had already met myself – once, twice, and seen myself many times over – and who was to say that Estyll's lover could *not* be me?

In my younger self I had seen something about my older self that I could not see on my own. Mykle had said it, and I wanted it to be true. I would make myself Estyll's lover, and I would do it on my next visit to the Park.

x

There were larger forces at work than those of romantic destiny, because soon after I made this resolution my life was shaken out of its pleasant intrigues by the sudden death of my father.

I was shocked by this more profoundly than I could ever have imagined. In the last two or three years I had seen very little of him and thought about him even less. And yet, from the moment the maid ran into the drawing room, shrilling that my father had collapsed across the desk in his study, I was stricken with the most awful guilt. It was I who had caused the death! I had been obsessed with myself, with Estyll . . . if only I had thought more of him he would not be dead!

In those sad days before the funeral my reaction seemed less than wholly illogical. My father knew as much about the workings of the flux field as any man alive, and after my childhood adventure he must have had some inkling that I had not left matters there. The school would certainly have advised him of my frequent absences and yet he said nothing. It was almost as if he had been deliberately standing by, hoping something might come of it all.

In the days following his death, a period of emotional transition, it seemed to me that Estyll was inextricably bound up with the tragedy. However much it flew in the face of reason, I could not help feeling that if I had spoken to Estyll, if I had acted rather than hidden, then my father would still be alive.

I did not have long to dwell on this. When the first shock and grief had barely passed, it became clear that nothing would ever be quite the same again for me. My father had made a will, in which he bequeathed me the responsibility for his family, his work and his fortune.

I was still legally a child and one of my uncles took over the administration of the affairs until I reached my majority. This uncle, deeply resentful that none of the fortune had passed to him, made the most of his temporary control over our lives. I was removed from school and made to start in my father's work. The family house was sold, the governor and the other servants were discharged, and my mother was moved to a smaller household in the country. Salleen was quickly married off, and Therese was sent to boarding school. It was made plain that I should take a wife as soon as possible.

My love for Estyll – my deepest secret – was thrust away from me by forces I could not resist.

Until the day my father died I did not have much conception of what his work involved, except to know that he was one of the most powerful and influential men in the Neuropean Union. This was because he controlled the power stations which tapped energy from the temporal stresses of the flux field. On the day I inherited his position I assumed this meant he was fabulously wealthy, but I was soon relieved of this misapprehension. The power stations were state-controlled and the so-called fortune comprised a large number of debentures in the enterprise. In real terms these could not be cashed, thus explaining many of the extreme decisions taken by my uncle. Death duties were considerable, and in fact I was in debt because of them for many years afterwards.

The work was entirely foreign to me and I was psychologic- ally and academically unready for it, but because the family was now my responsibility, I applied myself as best I could. For a long time, shaken and confused by the abrupt change in our fortunes, I could do nothing but cope.

My adolescent adventures in Flux Channel Park became memories as elusive as dreams. It was as if I had become another person.

(But I had lived with the image of Estyll for so long that nothing could make me forget her. The flame of romanticism that had lighted my youth faded away, but it was never entirely extinguished. In time I lost my obsessive love for Estyll, but I could never forget her wan beauty, her tireless waiting.)

By the time I was twenty-two I was in command of myself. I had mastered my father's job. Although the position was here- ditary, as most employment was hereditary, I discharged my duties well and conscientiously. The electricity generated by the flux field provided roughly nine-tenths of all the energy consumed in the Neuropean Union, and much of my time was spent in dealing with the multitude of political demands for it. I travelled widely, to every state in Federal Neurop, and further abroad.

Of the family: my mother was settling into her long years of widowhood and the social esteem that naturally followed. Both my sisters were married. Of course I too married in the end, succumbing to the social pressures that every man of standing has to endure. When I was twenty-one I was introduced to Dorynne, a cousin of Salleen's husband, and within a few months we were wed. Dorynne, an intelligent and attractive young woman, proved to be a good wife, and I loved her. When I was twenty-five, she bore our first child: a girl. I needed an heir, for that was the custom of my country, but we rejoiced at her birth. We named her . . . well, we named her Therese, after my sister, but Dorynne had wanted to call her Estyll, a girl's name then very popular, and I had to argue against her. I never explained why.

Two years later my son Carl was born, and my position in society was secure.

xi

The years passed, and the glow of adolescent longing for Estyll dimmed still further. Because I was happy with my growing family, and fulfilled by the demands of my work, those strange experiences in Flux Channel Park seemed to be a minor aberration from a life that was solid, conventional and unadventurous. I was no longer romantic in outlook. I saw those noble sentiments as the product of immaturity and inexperience. Such was the change in me that Dorynne sometimes complained I was unimaginative.

But if the romance of Estyll faded with time, a certain residual curiosity about her did not. I wanted to know: what had become of her? Who was she? Was she as beautiful as I remembered her?

Setting out these questions has lent them an urgency they did not possess. They were the questions of idle moments, or when something happened to remind me of her. Sometimes, for instance, my work took me along the Flux Channel, and then I would think briefly of her. For a time a young woman worked in my office, and she had the same name. As I grew older, a year or more would sometimes pass without a thought of Estyll.

I should probably have gone for the rest of my life with these questions unanswered if it had not been for an event of global importance. When the news of it became known it seemed for a time to be the most exciting event of the century, as in some ways it was. The starship that had been launched a hundred years before was returning.

This news affected every aspect of my work. At once I was involved in strategic and political planning at the highest level.

What it meant was this: the starship could only return to Earth by the same means as it had left. The Flux Channel would have to be reconverted, if only temporarily, to its original use. The houses in its vicinity would have to be evacuated, the power stations would have to be disconnected, and the Park and its time bridges would have to be destroyed.

For me, the disconnection of the power stations – with the inevitable result of depriving the Neuropean Union of most of its electricity – created immense problems. Permission had to be sought from other countries to generate electricity from fossil deposits for the months the flux stations were inoperable, and permission of that sort could only be obtained after intricate political negotiation and bargaining. We had less than a year in which to achieve this.

But the coming destruction of the Park struck a deeper note in me, as it did in many people. The Park was a much loved playground, familiar to everyone, and for many people ineradicably linked with their memories of childhood. For me, it was strongly associated with the idealism of my youth and with a girl I had loved for a time. If the Park and its bridges were closed, I knew that my questions about Estyll would never be answered.

I had leapt into a future where the Park was still a playground, where the houses beyond the trees were still occupied. Through all my life I had thought of that future as an imaginary or ideal world, one unattainable except by a dangerous leap from a bridge. But that future was no longer imaginary. I was now forty-two years old. It was thirty-two years since I, as a ten-year-old boy, had leapt thirty-two years into the future.

Today and Tomorrow co-existed once more in Flux Channel Park.

If I did not act in the next few weeks, before the Park was closed, I should never see Estyll again. The memory of her flared into flame again, and I felt a deep sense of frustration. I was much too busy to go in search of a boyhood dream.

I delegated. I relieved two subordinates from work in which they would have been better employed, and told them what I wanted them to search for on my behalf. They were to locate a young woman or girl who lived, possibly alone, possibly not, in one of the houses that bordered the Park.

The estate consisted of some two hundred houses. In time, my subordinates gave me a list of over a hundred and fifty possible names, and I scanned it anxiously. There were twenty-seven women living on the estate who were called Estyll. It was a popular name.

I returned one employee to his proper work, but retained the other, a woman named Robyn. I took her partially into my confidence. I said that the girl was a distant relative and that I was anxious to locate her, but for family reasons I had to be discreet. I believed she was frequently to be found in the Park. Within a few days, Robyn confirmed that there was one such girl. She and her mother lived together in one of the houses. The mother was confined to the house by the conventions of mourning (her husband had died within the last two years), and the daughter, Estyll, spent almost every day alone in the Park. Robyn said she was unable to discover why she went there.

The date had been fixed when Flux Channel Park would be closed to the public, and it was some eight and a half months ahead. I knew that I would soon be signing the order that would authorize the closure. One day between now and then, if for no other reason, Estyll's patient waiting would have to end.

I took Robyn further into my confidence. I instructed her to go to the Park and, by repeated use of the Tomorrow Bridge, go into the future. All she was to report back to me was the date on which Estyll's vigil ended. Whether Robyn wondered at the glimpses of my obsession she was seeing, I cannot say, but she went without demur and did my work for me. When she returned, she had the date: it was just over six weeks away.

That interview with Robyn was fraught with undertones that neither side understood. I did not want to know too much, because with the return of my interest in Estyll had come something of that sense of romantic mystery. Robyn, for her part, clearly had seen something that intrigued her. I found it all most unsettling.

I rewarded Robyn with a handsome cash bonus and returned her to her duties. I marked the date in my private diary, then gave my full attention to the demands of my proper work.

xii

As the date approached I knew I could not be at the Park. On that day there was to be an energy conference in Geneva and there was no possibility of my missing it. I made a futile attempt to change the date, but who was I against fifty heads of state? Once more I was tempted to let the great preoccupation of my youth stay forever unresolved, but again I succumbed to it. I could not miss this one last chance.

I made my travel arrangements to Geneva with care and instructed my secretarial staff to reserve me a compartment on the one overnight train which would get me there in time.

It meant that I should have to visit the Park on the day before the vigil was to end, but by using the Tomorrow Bridge I could still be there to see it.

At last the day came. I had no one to answer to but myself. Shortly after midday I left my office and had my driver take me to the Park. I left him and the carriage in the yard beyond the gate, and with one glance towards the estate of houses I went into the Park.

I had not been in the Park itself since my last visit just before my father died. Knowing that one's childhood haunts often seem greatly changed when revisited years later I had been expecting to find the place smaller, less grand than I remembered it. But as I walked slowly down the gently sloping sward towards the tollbooths, it seemed that the magnificent trees, and the herbaceous borders, the fountains, the pathways, and all the various kinds of landscaping in the Park gardens were just as I recalled them.

But the smells! In my adolescent longing I had not responded to those. The sweet bark, the sweeping leaves, the clustered flowers. A man with a mowing machine clattered past, throwing up a moist green smell, and the shorn grass humped in the mower's hood like a sleeping furry animal. I watched the man as he reached the edge of the lawn he was cutting, turned the machine, then bent low over it to start it up the incline for his return. I had never pushed a mower, and as if this last day in the Park had restored my childhood I felt an urge to dash across to him and ask him if I might try my hand.

I smiled to myself as I walked on: I was a well-known public figure, and in my drape suit and tall silk hat I should certainly have cut a comic sight.

Then there were the sounds. I heard, as if for the first time (and yet also with a faint and distracting nostalgia), the metallic click of the turnstile ratchets, the sound of the breeze in the pines that surrounded the Park, and the almost continuous soprano of children's voices. Somewhere, a band was playing marches.

I saw a family at picnic beneath one of the weeping willows. The servants stood to one side, and the paterfamilias was carving a huge joint of cold beef. I watched them surreptitiously for a moment. It might have been my own family, a generation before; people's delights did not change.

So taken was I by all this that I had nearly reached the toll-booths before I remembered Estyll. Another private smile: my younger self would not have been able to understand this lapse. I was feeling more relaxed, welcoming the tranquil surroundings of the Park and remembering the past, but I had grown out of the obsessive associations the place once had for me.

I had come to the Park to see Estyll, though, so I went on past the tollbooths until I was on the path that ran beside the Channel. I walked a short way, looking ahead. Soon I saw her, and she was sitting on the bench, staring towards the Tomorrow Bridge.

It was as if a quarter of a century had been obliterated. All the calm and restful mood went from me as if it had never existed, to be replaced by a ferment of emotions that was the more shocking for being so unexpected.

I came to a halt, turned away, thinking that if I looked at her any more she would surely notice me.

The adolescent, the immature, the romantic child . . . I was still all of these, and the sight of Estyll awakened them as if from a short nap. I felt large and clumsy and ridiculous in my over-formal clothes, as if I were a child wearing a grandparent's wedding outfit. Her composure, her youthful beauty, the vital force of her vigil . . . they were enough to renew all those inadequacies I had felt as a teenager.

But at the same time there was a second image of her, one which lay above the other like an elusive ghost. I was seeing her as an adult sees a child.

She was so much younger than I remembered her! She was smaller. She was pretty, yes . . . but I had seen prettier women. She was dignified, but it was a precocious poise, as if she had been trained in it by a socially conscious parent. And she was young, so very young! My own daughter, Therese, would be the same age now, perhaps slightly older.

Thus torn, thus acutely conscious of the division in my seeing of her, I stood in confusion and distraction on the pathway, while the families and couples walked gaily past.

I backed away from her at last, unable to look at her any more. She was wearing clothes I remembered too well from the past: a narrow white skirt tight around her legs, a shiny black belt, and a dark-blue blouse embroidered with flowers across the bodice.

(I remembered – I remembered so much, too much. I wished she had not been there.)

She frightened me because of the power she had, the power to awaken and arouse my emotions. I did not know what it was. Everyone has adolescent passions, but how many people have the chance to revisit those passions in maturity?

It elated me, but also made me deeply melancholic. Inside I was dancing with love and joy, but she terrified me. She was so innocently, glowingly young, and I was now so old.

xiii

I decided to leave the Park at once . . . but changed my mind an instant later. I went towards her, then turned yet again and walked away.

I was thinking of Dorynne, but trying to put her out of my mind. I was thinking of Estyll, obsessed again.

I walked until I was out of sight of her, then took off my hat and wiped my brow. It was a warm day but I knew that the perspiration was not caused by the weather. I needed to calm myself, wanted somewhere to sit down and think about it . . . but the Park was for pleasure, and when I went towards the open-air restaurant to buy a glass of beer, the sight of all the heedless merriment was intrusive and unwelcome.

I stood on the uncut grass, watching the man with the mower, trying to control myself. I had come to the Park to satisfy an old curiosity, not to fall again into the traps of teenage infatuation. It was unthinkable that I should let a young girl of sixteen distract me from my stable life. It had been a mistake, a stupid mistake, to return to the Park.

But inevitably there was a deeper sense of destiny beneath my attempts to be sensible. I knew, without being able to say why, that Estyll was waiting there at her bench for me, and that we were destined at last to meet.

Her vigil was due to end tomorrow and that was just a short distance away. It lay on the far side of the Tomorrow Bridge.

xiv

I tried to pay at the tollbooth but the attendant recognized me at once. He released the ratchet of the turnstile with such a sharp jab of his foot that I thought he might break his ankle. I nodded to him and passed through into the covered way.

I walked across briskly, trying to think no more about what I was doing or why. The flux field prickled about my body.

I emerged into bright sunlight. The day I had left was warm and sunny, but here in the next day it was several degrees hotter. I felt stiff and overdressed in my formal clothes, not at all in keeping with the reawakened, desperate hope that was in my breast. Still trying to deny that hope I retreated into my daytime demeanour, opening the front of my coat and thrusting my thumbs into the slit-pockets of my waistcoat, as I sometimes did when addressing subordinates.

I walked along the path beside the Channel, looking across for a sight of Estyll on the other side.

Someone tugged at my arm from behind and I turned in surprise.

There was a young man standing there. He was nearly as tall as me but his jacket was too tight across his shoulders and his trousers were a fraction too short, revealing that he was still growing up. He had an obsessive look to him but when he spoke it was obvious he was from a good family.

'Sir, may I trouble you with a question?' he said, and at once I realized who he was.

The shock of recognition was profound. Had I not been so preoccupied with Estyll I am sure meeting him would have made me speechless. It was so many years since my time jumping that I had forgotten the jolting sense of recognition and sympathy.

I controlled myself with great difficulty. Trying not to reveal my knowledge of him, I said: 'What do you wish to know?'

'Would you tell me the date, sir?' I started to smile, and glanced away from him for a moment, to straighten my face. His earnest eyes, his protuberant ears, his pallid face and quiffed-up hair!

'Do you mean today's date, or do you mean the year?'

'Well . . . both actually, sir.'

I gave him the answer at once, although as soon as I had spoken I realized I had given him today's date, whereas I had stepped forward one day beyond that. No matter, though: what he, I, was interested in was the year.

He thanked me politely and made to step away. Then he paused, looked at me with a guileless stare (which I remembered had been an attempt to take the measure of this forbidding looking stranger in a frock coat), and said: 'Sir, do you happen to live in these parts?'

'I do,' I said, knowing what was coming. I had raised a hand to cover my mouth, and was stroking my upper lip.

'I wonder if you would happen to know the identity of a certain person, often to be seen in this Park?'

'Who—?'

I could not finish the sentence. His eager, pinkening earnest-
ness was extremely comical. I spluttered an explosive laugh. At
once I turned it into a simulated sneeze, and while I made a play
with my handkerchief I muttered something about hay fever.
Forcing myself to be serious, I returned my handkerchief to my
pocket and straightened my hat. 'Who do you mean?'

'A young lady, of about my own age.' Unaware of my
amusement he moved past me and went down the bank to
where there was a thick cluster of rosebushes. From behind
their cover he looked across at the other side. He made sure I
was looking too, then pointed.

I could not see Estyll at first, because of the crowds, but
then saw that she was standing quite near to the queue for the
Tomorrow Bridge. She was wearing her dress of pastel colours
– the clothes she had been wearing when I first loved her.

'Do you see her, sir?' His question was like a discordant note
in a piece of music.

I had become perfectly serious again. Just seeing her made
me want to fall into reflective silence. The way she held her
head, the innocent composure.

He was waiting for a reply, so I said: 'Yes . . . yes, a local girl.'

'Do you know her name, sir?'

'I believe she is called Estyll.'

An expression of surprised pleasure came over his face and his
flush deepened. 'Thank you, sir. Thank you.'

He backed away from me, but I said: 'Wait!' I had a sudden
instinct to help him, to cut short those months of agony. 'You
must go and talk to her, you know. She wants to meet you.
You mustn't be shy of her.'

He stared at me in horror, then turned and ran into the
crowd. Within a few seconds I could see him no more.

The enormity of what I had done struck me forcibly. Not

149

only had I touched him on his most vulnerable place, forcing him to confront the one matter he had to work out for himself in his own time, but impetuously I had interfered with the smooth progression of events. In *my* memory of the meeting, the stranger in the silk hat had not given unsolicited advice!

A few minutes later, as I walked slowly along the path, pondering on this, I saw my younger self again. He saw me and I nodded to him, as an introduction, perhaps, to telling him to ignore what I had said, but he glanced away uninterestedly as if he had never seen me before.

There was something odd about him: he had changed his clothes, and the new ones fitted better.

I mused over this for a while until I realized what had happened. He was not the same Mykle I had spoken to – he was still myself, but here, on this day, from another day in the past!

A little later I saw myself again. This time he (I) was wearing the same clothes as before. Was it the youth I had spoken to? Or was it myself from yet another day?

I was quite distracted by all this but never so much that I forgot the object of it all. Estyll was there on the other side of the Channel and while I paced along the pathway I made certain she was never out of my sight. She had waited beside the tollbooth queue for several minutes, but now she had walked back to the main path and was standing on the grassy bank, staring, as I had seen her do so many times before, towards the Tomorrow Bridge. I could see her much better there: her slight figure, her young beauty.

I was feeling calmer at last. I no longer saw a double image of her. Meeting myself as a youth, and seeing other versions of myself, had reminded me that Estyll and I, apparently divided by the flux field, were actually united by it. My presence here was inevitable.

Today was the last day of her vigil, although she might not know it, and I was here because I was supposed to be here. She was waiting, and I was waiting. I could resolve it, I could resolve it now!

She was looking directly across the Channel and seemed to be staring deliberately at me, as if the inspiration had struck her in the same instant. Without thinking, I waved my arm at her. Excitement ran through me. I turned quickly, and set off down the path towards the bridges. If I crossed the Today Bridge I should be with her in a matter of a few seconds. It was what I had to do.

When I reached the place where the Tomorrow Bridge opened on to this side I looked back across the Channel to make sure of where she was standing.

But she was no longer waiting. She too was hurrying across the grass, rushing towards the bridges. As she ran she was looking across the Channel, looking for me!

She reached the crowd of people waiting by the tollbooth and I saw her pushing past them. I lost sight of her as she went into the booth.

I stood at my end of the bridge, looking down the ill-lit covered way. Daylight was a bright square three hundred feet away.

A small figure in a long dress hurried up the steps at the far end and ran into the wooden tunnel. Estyll came towards me, raising the front of her skirt as she ran. I glimpsed trailing ribbons, white stockings.

With each step Estyll moved further into the flux field. With each frantic, eager step towards me, her figure became less substantial. She was less than a third of the way across before she had blurred and dissolved into nothing.

I saw her mistake! She was crossing the wrong bridge! When

she reached this side – when she stood where I stood now – she would be twenty-four hours too late.

I stared helplessly down the gloomy covered way, watching as two children slowly materialized before me. They pushed and squabbled, each trying to be the first to emerge into the new day.

XV

I acted without further delay. I left the Tomorrow Bridge and ran back up the slope to the path. The Today Bridge was about fifty yards away, and, clapping a hand on the top of my hat, I ran as fast as I could towards it. I thought only of the extreme urgency of catching Estyll before I lost her. If she realized her mistake and began to search for me, we might be forever crossing and recrossing the Channel on one bridge after another – forever in the same place, but forever separated in time.

I scrambled on to the end of the Today Bridge, and hurried across. I had to moderate my pace, as the bridge was narrow and several other people were crossing. This bridge, of the three, was the only one with windows to the outside. As I passed each one I paused to look anxiously towards each end of the Tomorrow Bridge, hoping for a glimpse of her.

At the end of the bridge I pushed quickly through the exit turnstile, leaving it rattling and clattering on its ratchet.

I set off at once towards the Tomorrow Bridge, reaching for the money to pay the toll. In my haste I bumped into someone. It was a woman and I murmured an apology as I passed, affording her only a momentary glance. We recognized each other in the same instant. It was Robyn, the woman I had sent to the Park. But why was she here now?

As I reached the tollbooth I looked back at her again. She was staring at me with an expression of intense curiosity but as soon as she saw me looking she turned away. Was this the conclusion of the vigil she had reported to me on? Was this what she had seen?

I could not delay. I pushed rudely past the people at the head of the queue and threw some coins on to the worn brass plate where the tickets were ejected mechanically. The attendant looked up at me, recognized me as I recognized him.

'Compliments of the Park again, sir,' he said, and slid the coins back to me.

I had seen him only a few minutes before – yesterday in his life. I scooped up the coins and returned them to my pocket. The turnstile clicked as I pushed through. I went up the steps and entered the covered way.

Far ahead: the glare of daylight of the day I was in. The bare interior of the covered way, with lights at intervals. No people.

I started to walk and when I had gone a few paces across the flux field, the daylight squared in the far end of the tunnel became night. It felt much colder.

Ahead of me: two small figures, solidifying, or so it seemed, out of the electrical haze of the field. They were standing to-gether under one of the lights, partly blocking the way.

I went nearer and saw that one of them was Estyll. The figure with her had his head turned away from me. I paused.

I had halted where no light fell on me, and although I was only a few feet away from them I would have seemed as they seemed to me – a ghostly, half-visible apparition. But they were occupied with each other and did not look towards me.

I heard him say: 'Do you live around here?'

'In one of the houses by the Park. What about you?'

'No. I have to come here by train.' The hands held nervously by his side, the fingers curling and uncurling.

'I've often seen you here,' she said. 'You stare a lot.'

'I wondered who you were.'

There was a silence then, while the youth looked shyly at the floor, apparently thinking of more to say. Estyll glanced beyond him to where I was standing, and for a moment we looked directly into each other's eyes.

She said to the young man: 'It's cold here. Shall we go back?'

'We could go for a walk. Or I could buy you a glass of orange.'

'I'd rather go for a walk.'

They turned and walked towards me. She glanced at me again, with a frank stare of hostility. I had been listening in and she well knew it. The young man was barely aware of my presence. As they passed me he was looking first at her, then nervously at his hands. I saw his too-tight clothes, his quiff of hair combed up, his pink ears and neck, his downy moustache. He walked clumsily as if he were about to trip over his own feet, and he did not know where to put his hands.

I loved him, I had loved her.

I followed them a little way, until light shone in again at the tollbooth end. I saw him stand aside to let her through the turnstile first. Out in the sunshine she danced across the grass, letting the colours of her dress shine out, and then she reached over and took his hand. They walked away together, across the newly cut lawns towards the trees.

xvi

I waited until Estyll and I had gone and then I too went out into the day. I crossed to the other side of the Channel on the

Yesterday Bridge, and returned on the Today Bridge.

It was the day I had arrived in the Park, the day before I was due in Geneva, the day before Estyll and I were finally to meet. Outside in the yard, my driver would be waiting with the carriage.

Before I left I went for one more walk along the path on this side of the Channel and headed for the bench where I knew Estyll would be waiting.

I saw her through the crowd: she was sitting quietly and watching the people, dressed neatly in her white skirt and dark-blue blouse.

I looked across the Channel. The sunshine was bright and hazy and there was a light breeze. I saw the promenading holidaymakers on the other side: the bright clothes, the festive hats, the balloons and the children. But not everyone blended with the crowd.

There was a rhododendron bush beside the Channel. Behind it I could just see the figure of a youth. He was staring across at Estyll. Behind him, walking along deep in thought, was another Mykle. Further along the bank, well away from the bridges, another Mykle sat in long grass overlooking the Channel. I waited, and before long another Mykle appeared.

A few minutes later yet another turned up, and took up position behind one of the trees over there. I did not doubt that there were many more, each unaware of all the others, each preoccupied with the girl who sat on the bench a few feet from me.

I wondered which one it was I had spoken to. None of them, perhaps, or all of them?

I turned towards Estyll at last and approached her. I went to stand directly in front of her and removed my hat.

'Good afternoon, miss,' I said. 'Pardon me for speaking to you like this.'

She looked up at me in sharp surprise. I had interrupted her reverie. She shook her head, but turned on a polite smile for me.

'Do you happen to know who I am?' I said.

'Of course, sir. You're very famous.' She bit her lower lip, as if wishing she had not answered so promptly. 'What I meant was—'

'Yes,' I said. 'Do you trust my word?' She frowned then, and it was a consciously pretty gesture – a child borrowing a mannerism from an adult. 'It will happen tomorrow,' I said.

'Sir?'

'Tomorrow,' I said again, trying to find some subtler way of putting it. 'What you're waiting for . . . it will happen then.'

'How do you—?'

'Never mind that,' I said. I stood erect, running my fingers across the brim of my hat. In spite of everything she had the uncanny facility of making me nervous and awkward. 'I'll be across there tomorrow,' I said, pointing to the other side of the Channel. 'Look out for me. I'll be wearing these clothes, this hat. You'll see me wave to you. That's when it will be.'

She said nothing to this, but looked steadily at me. I was standing against the light, and she could not have been able to see me properly. But I could see her with the sun on her face, and with light dancing in her hair and her eyes.

She was so young, so pretty. It was like pain to be near her.

'Wear your prettiest dress,' I said. 'Do you understand?'

She still did not answer, but I saw her eyes flicker towards the far side of the Channel. There was a pinkness in her cheeks and I knew I had said too much. I wished I had not spoken to her at all.

I made a courtly little bow and replaced my hat.

'Good day to you, miss,' I said.

'Good day, sir.'

I nodded to her again, then walked past her and turned on to the lawn behind the bench. I went a short way up the slope, and moved over to the side until I was hidden from Estyll by the trunk of a huge tree.

I could see that on the far side of the Channel one of the Mykles I spotted earlier had moved out from his hiding place. He stood on the bank in clear view. He had apparently been watching me as I spoke to Estyll, for now I could see him looking across at me, shading his eyes with his hand.

I was certain that it was him I had spoken to.

I could help him no more. If he now crossed the Channel twice, moving forward two days, he could be on the Tomorrow Bridge to meet Estyll as she answered my signal.

He stared across at me and I stared back. Then I heard a whoop of joy. He started running.

He hurried along the bank and went straight to the Today Bridge. I could almost hear the hollow clumping of his shoes as he ran through the narrow way, and moments later he emerged on this side. He walked, more sedately now, to the queue for the Tomorrow Bridge.

As he stood in line, he was looking at Estyll. She, staring thoughtfully at the ground, did not notice.

Mykle reached the tollbooth. As he went to the pay desk, he looked back at me and waved. I took off my hat and waved it. He grinned happily.

In a few seconds he had disappeared into the covered way, and I knew I would not see him again. I had seen happen what was to happen next.

I replaced my hat and walked away from the Channel, up through the stately trees of the Park, past where the gardener was still pushing his heavy mower against the grass, past where many families were sitting beneath the trees at their picnic luncheons.

I saw a place beneath a wide old cedar where I and my parents and sisters had often eaten our meals. A cloth was spread out across the grass, with several dishes set in readiness for the meal. An elderly couple was sitting there, well under the shade of the branches. The lady was sitting stiffly in a folding canvas chair, watching patiently as her husband prepared the meat. He was carving a ham joint, taking slices from beneath the notch with meticulous strokes of the long sharp knife. Two servants stood in the background, with white linen cloths draped over their forearms.

Like me, the gentleman was in formal wear. His frockcoat was stiff and perfectly ironed, and his shoes shone as if they had been polished for weeks. On the ground beside him, his silken stove-pipe hat had been laid on a scarf.

He noticed my uninvited regard and looked up at me. For a moment our gaze met and we nodded to each other like the gentlemen we were. I touched the brim of my hat, wished him and the lady good afternoon. Then I hurried towards the yard outside. I wanted to see Dorynne before I caught the train to Geneva.

In my experience most readers do not 'react' to the appearance of a new short story – by me or by anyone else. There are occasional exceptions to this, when a certain story will suddenly become newsworthy or celebrated for some other reason, but in most cases the events surrounding a short story are that it is written, it is submitted to an editor (or several, if it does not sell to the first), and finally it is published a few months later. The payment is never very large and because published short stories are always a part of something else – a magazine, an anthology, a website, etc. – the individual writers mostly have to settle for the satisfaction of having written the thing. Fame, wealth and literary recognition accrue from short stories only slowly, if ever.

Self-congratulation is not the point of this book, but 'Palely Loitering' did fairly well when it first appeared. I sold it to the first editor I submitted it to: Edward Ferman, who published *The Magazine of Fantasy & Science Fiction* every month in the USA. My story came out about a year later, in January 1979, and to my surprise it was illustrated on the cover with a painting executed by the artist Ron Walotsky. 'Palely Loitering' occupied the first forty pages or so of that issue. Also in 1979 I included it in a collection of short stories for Faber & Faber, titled *An Infinite Summer*. The following year the story was shortlisted for a Hugo Award, and won a BSFA Award.

The collection *An Infinite Summer* was more or less the last appearance of the story – it has therefore been unavailable for around four decades.

Postscript for bibliophiles. That particular issue of *Fantasy &*

Science Fiction – a magazine which has always interested itself in the more literary end of the genre spectrum – included the work of several writers, some of whom have become better known than they were in 1979. As well as myself they included Orson Scott Card, John Kessel, Robert Aickman and Stephen R. Donaldson. Isaac Asimov had one of his regular science columns, and there was a batch of reviews by the supreme book critic of the fantastic, John Clute.

Before – 'An Infinite Summer'

In the summer of 1974 I was deeply engaged with writing the first draft of my novel *The Space Machine*. It was the longest book I had written. Because it was set in the Wellsian ambience of the first years of the twentieth century, about which I had never tried to write before, and had a plot that required a lot of juggling, I was finding it challenging and absorbing. (This was before I wrote 'Palely Loitering', I should add.) Much of *The Space Machine* was set in Richmond, Surrey: in the present day, Richmond is a middle-class outer suburb of London, but at the end of the nineteenth century it was a small and rather select town for well-to-do businessmen and professionals. Richmond is set on a pretty position on the banks of the River Thames, with higher ground behind, leading to the expanse of Richmond Park, then and now a huge area of more or less unspoiled countryside.

Richmond was only a few miles from where I lived in Harrow on the Hill. I visited the town several times before I started the novel, walked the streets, enjoyed the views and took a great number of photographs. I came across a book of old photographs of Richmond, taken in Victorian and Edwardian times. When I compared the then-and-now images I developed an imprecise but alluring sense of time having frozen. Much of the old Richmond was still unchanged – although modern buildings, road markings, advertising signs, and so on, now intruded, it was possible to sense what the town had once been like. I was particularly interested in the area where the River Thames flowed through the town between wooded banks. That was more or less unchanged.

Little of this came into *The Space Machine*, but it gave me a grounding in imaginative plausibility, adding if not to the final product at least to my own feelings about it.

I was only a few chapters from the end of the first draft when an interruption occurred. Out of the blue an American editor called Harlan Ellison wrote to me to demand I drop everything and write him a story for an anthology he was in the process of completing. I wrote back and said no. I explained politely that my commitment to finishing the novel meant I did not want to break the flow, but thanks anyway for the suggestion.

Mr Ellison's reply a week or so later was insistent, even bullying. He claimed his unfinished book (which he described as a 'milestone', a 'landmark', a 'book of posterity') would not be complete without a 'taboo-busting' contribution from me, that he would hold the book open until I relented, making the dozens of other writers already signed up wait until I delivered. This attempt at persuasion seemed insincere and hectoring, not to say self-serving, and it had a negative effect on me, a feeling that intensified the more I thought about it.

In fact, I had heard of the project before this. The incomplete book was already a controversial matter, marked by seemingly endless bluster, a vanity project propped up by boastfulness. It had dragged on for years. The rights to the book when and if completed had been sold and resold to different American publishers as deadlines came and failed to be met. Many good writers who over the years had sent in stories as requested were discontented that their work had become stuck, apparently irretrievably, in a pointless limbo. They wanted to have their stories released back to them, but the few who tried were subjected to a peculiarly unpleasant kind of browbeating and emotional blackmail. Several authors had already died without seeing their stories in print.

I did not want to become yet another writer involved in

this imbroglio. Anyway, my unfinished novel mattered more to me. I said no again, but Mr Ellison would not give up. After another letter from him (this was, of course, long before texting or emails) saying that his project would be paralysed until I relented, I reluctantly gave way. I took my draft of the novel to a point in the story where I felt I could put it on hold, and tried to think of something else to write.

I was by this time so suffused in the Wellsian *fin de siècle* world that for a long time I felt creatively stymied. Having to step back from it, even temporarily, was disruptive and unsettling. I had already put in many months of work and was moving towards the climactic sequence. Also, I was bothered by the thought of having to bust taboos, whatever that meant. Possibly as a reaction against that I began to think about the stimulating experience of discovering the almost timeless atmosphere of the Richmond river front. An idea began to form. 'An Infinite Summer' was the result.

The story was gentle in nature, nostalgic, with a yearning tone. As things turned out, whatever my story was actually about became irrelevant. Although I finished the story in less than a month and sent it across by airmail, it wasn't even acknowledged and it certainly wasn't read. I sent an enquiry two months later, without getting a response. I left the story with Mr Ellison for more than four months while I returned to *The Space Machine* and completed it, but I heard nothing more from him about it. It was not the kind of sensational shocker he appeared to want, but he would never know that. Years later he revealed he had not read it, nor for that matter many of the other stories he was hoarding.

Towards the end of 1974 a new British anthology series called *Andromeda*, edited by Peter Weston, was announced. I sent 'An Infinite Summer', and it was published a few months later.

An Infinite Summer

August, 1940

There was a war on, but it made no difference to Thomas James Lloyd. The war was an inconvenience and it restricted his freedom, but on the whole it was the least of his preoccupations. Misfortune had brought him to this violent age, and its crises did not concern him. He was apart from it, shadowed by it.

He stood now on the Thames bridge at Richmond, resting his hands on the parapet and staring south along the river. The sun reflected up from it, and he took his sunglasses from a metal case in his pocket and put them on.

Night was the only relief from the tableaux of frozen time; during the days the dark glasses approximated the relief.

It seemed to Thomas Lloyd that it was not long since he had last stood untroubled on this bridge. The memory of the day was clear, itself a moment of frozen time, undiminished.

He remembered how he had stood here with his cousin, watching four young men from the town as they manhandled a punt upstream.

Richmond itself had changed from that time of his youth, but here by the river the view was much as he remembered it. Although there were more buildings along the banks, the meadows below Richmond Hill were untouched, and he could see the riverside walk disappearing around the bend in the river towards Twickenham.

For the moment the town was quiet. An air-raid alert had been sounded a few minutes before, and although there were still some vehicles moving through the streets, most pedestrians had taken temporary shelter inside shops and offices.

Lloyd had remained, to walk again through the past.

He was a tall, well-built man, apparently young in years. He had been taken for twenty-five several times by strangers, and Lloyd, a withdrawn, uncommunicative man, had allowed the mistake to go uncorrected. Behind the dark glasses his eyes were still bright with the hopes of youth, but many tiny lines at the corners of his eyes, and a sallowness to his skin, indicated that he was older. Even this, though, lent no clue to the truth. Thomas Lloyd had been born in 1881, and was now approaching sixty.

He took his watch from his waistcoat pocket, and saw that the time was a little after twelve. He turned to walk towards the pub on the Isleworth road, but then noticed a man standing alone on the path beside the river. Even wearing the sunglasses, which filtered away the more intrusive reminders of past and future, Lloyd could see that it was one of the men he called freezers. This was a young man, rather plump and with prematurely balding hair. He had seen Lloyd, because as Lloyd looked down at him the young man turned ostentatiously away. Lloyd had nothing now to fear from the freezers, but they were always about and their presence never failed to make him uneasy.

Far away, in the direction of Barnes, Lloyd could hear another air-raid siren droning out its warning.

June 1903

The world was at peace, and the weather was warm. Thomas James Lloyd, recently down from Cambridge, twenty-one years of age, moustachioed, light of tread, walked gaily through the trees that grew across the side of Richmond Hill.

It was a Sunday, and there were many people about. Earlier in the day Thomas had attended church with his father and mother and sister, sitting in the pew that was reserved tradition-ally for the Lloyds of Richmond. The house on the Hill had belonged to the family for more than two hundred years, and William Lloyd, the present head of the family, owned most of the houses on the Sheen side of town as well as administering one of the largest businesses in the whole of Surrey. A family of substance indeed, and Thomas James Lloyd lived in the know-ledge that one day the substance would be his by inheritance.

Worldly matters thus assured, Thomas felt free to divert his attention to activities of a more important nature: namely, Charlotte Carrington and her sister Sarah.

That one day he would marry one of the two sisters had been an inevitability long acknowledged by both families, although precisely which of the two it would be had been occupying his thoughts for many weeks.

There was much to choose between the two – or so Thomas himself considered – but if his choice had been free then his mind would have been at rest. Unfortunately for him, it had been made plain by their parents that it would be Charlotte who would make the better wife for a future industrialist and landowner, and in many ways this was so.

The difficulty arose because Thomas had fallen impetuously for her younger sister Sarah, a state of affairs of absolutely no moment to Mrs Carrington.

Charlotte, twenty years of age, was an undeniably handsome young woman, and Thomas much enjoyed her company. She appeared to be prepared to accept a proposal of marriage from him, and to be fair she was endowed with grace and intelligence, but whenever they had been together neither had had much of interest to say to the other. Charlotte was an ambitious and emancipated woman – for so she styled herself – and was constantly reading historical tracts. Her one consuming interest was in touring the various churches of Surrey to take brass-rubbings from the plates. Thomas, a liberal and understanding young man, was pleased she had found a hobby, but could not own to a sharing of the interest.

Sarah Carrington was an altogether different proposition. Two years younger than her sister, and thus, by her mother's estimation, not yet eligible for marriage (or not, at least, until a husband had been found for Charlotte), Sarah was at once a person to be coveted by virtue of her unavailability, and yet also a delightful personality in her own right. When Thomas had first started calling on Charlotte, Sarah was still being finished at school, but by astute questioning of Charlotte and his own sister, Thomas had discovered that Sarah liked to play tennis and croquet, was a keen bicyclist, and was acquainted with all the latest dance steps. A surreptitious glance into the family's photographic album had established that she was also astoundingly beautiful.

This last aspect of her he had confirmed for himself at their first meeting, and he had promptly fallen in love with her. Since then he had endeavoured to transfer his attentions, and with some success. Twice already he had spoken to her alone; no minor achievement when one considered the enthusiasm with which Mrs Carrington encouraged Thomas always to be with Charlotte. Once he had been left alone with Sarah for a few minutes in the Carringtons' drawing room, and on the second occasion he had managed a few words with her during a family picnic. Even on this brief acquaintance, Thomas had become convinced that he would settle for no less a wife than Sarah.

So it was that on this Sunday, Thomas's mood was full of light, because by a most agreeable contrivance he had ensured himself at least an hour alone with Sarah.

The instrument of this contrivance was one Waring Lloyd, a cousin of his. Waring had always seemed to Thomas a most unconscionable oaf, but remembering that Charlotte had once remarked favourably on him (and feeling that each would be eminently suited to the other), Thomas had proposed a riverside stroll for the afternoon. Waring, suitably confided in, would delay Charlotte while they walked, so allowing Thomas and Sarah to go on ahead.

Thomas was several minutes early for the rendezvous, and paced to and fro good-naturedly while waiting for his cousin. It was cooler by the river, for the trees grew right down to the water's edge, and several of the ladies walking along the path behind the boathouse had folded their sunshades and were clutching shawls about their shoulders.

When at last Waring arrived, the two cousins greeted each other amiably – more so than at any time in the recent past – and debated whether they should cross by the ferry, or walk the long way round by the bridge. There was still plenty of time in hand so they opted for the latter course.

Thomas reminded Waring of what was to happen during the stroll, and Waring confirmed that he understood. The arrangement suited him – he found Charlotte no less delightful than Sarah, and would doubtless find much to say to the older sister.

Later, as they crossed Richmond Bridge to the Middlesex side of the river, Thomas paused, resting his hands on the stone parapet. He was watching four young men struggling ineptly with a punt, trying to manoeuvre it against the stream towards the side, while on the bank two older men shouted conflicting instructions.

August, 1940

'You'd better take cover, sir. Just in case.'

Thomas Lloyd was startled by the voice at his side, and he turned. It was an air-raid warden, an elderly man in a dark uniform. On the shoulder of his jacket, and stencilled on his metal helmet, were the letters ARP. In spite of his polite tone of voice, he was looking suspiciously at Lloyd. The part-time work Lloyd had been doing in Richmond paid barely enough for food and lodgings, and what little spare there was usually went on drink. He was still wearing the same clothes as he had five years ago, and they were the worse for wear.

'Is there going to be a raid?' Lloyd said.

'Never can tell. Jerry's still bombing the ports, but he'll start on the towns any day now.'

They both glanced towards the sky in the south-east. There, high in the blue, were several curling white vapour trails, but no other sign of the German bombers everyone so feared.

'I'll be safe,' Lloyd said. 'I'm going for a walk. I'll be away from the houses if a raid starts.'

'That's all right, sir. If you meet anyone else out there, remind them there's an alert on.'

'I'll do that.'

The warden nodded to him, then walked away towards the town. Lloyd raised his sunglasses for a moment, and watched him.

A few yards from where they had been standing was one of the freezers' tableaux: two men and a woman.

When he had first noticed this tableau, Lloyd had inspected the people carefully and judged by their clothes that they must have been frozen at some time in the mid-nineteenth century. This tableau was the oldest he had so far discovered, and as such was of especial interest to him. He had learned that the moment of a tableau's erosion was unpredictable. Some tableaux lasted for several years, others only a day or two. The fact that this one had survived for at least ninety years indicated just how erratic the rate of erosion was.

The three frozen people were halted in their walk directly in front of the warden, who hobbled along the pavement towards them. As he reached them he showed no sign of awareness, and in a moment had passed right through them.

Lloyd lowered his sunglasses. The image of the three people became vague and ill-defined.

June, 1903

When Waring's prospects were compared with those of Thomas they seemed modest and unremarkable, but by ordinary standards they were none the less considerable. Accordingly, Mrs Carrington (who knew more about the distribution of the Lloyd wealth than anyone outside the immediate family circle) greeted Waring with civility.

The two young men were offered a glass of cold lemon tea, and then asked for their opinion on some matter concerning an herbaceous border. Thomas, well used to Mrs Carrington's small talk, couched his reply in a few words, but Waring, anxious to please, set forth into a detailed response. He was still speaking knowledgeably about replanting and bedding when the sisters appeared. They walked out through the French window and came towards them across the lawn.

Seen together, it was obvious that the two were closely related, but to Thomas's eager eye one young woman's beauty easily outshone the other's. Charlotte's expression was more earnest, and her bearing more practical. Sarah affected a modesty and timorousness (although Thomas knew it to be just an affection), and her smile when she approached him and shook his hand was enough to convince Thomas that from this moment his life would be an eternity of summer.

Twenty minutes passed while the four young people and the girls' mother walked about in the garden. Thomas, at first impatient to put his plan to the test, managed after a few minutes to control himself. He had noticed that both Mrs Carrington and Charlotte were amused by Waring's conversation, and this was an unexpected bonus. After all, the whole afternoon lay ahead, and these minutes were being well spent.

At last they were released from their courtesies, and the four set off on their planned stroll.

The girls each carried a parasol: Charlotte's was white, Sarah's was pink. As they went through the grounds towards the riverside walk, their dresses rustled on the long grass, although Charlotte raised her skirt a little, saying that grass did stain cotton so.

Approaching the river they heard the sounds of other people: children calling, a lass and a man from the town laughing together, and a rowing eight striking in unison to the cox's instructions. As they came to the riverside walk, and the two young men helped the sisters over a stile, a mongrel dog leaped out of the water some twenty yards away and shook itself in a cascade of droplets.

The path was not wide enough for them to walk abreast, and so Thomas and Sarah took the lead. Just once he was able to catch Waring's eye, and the other gave the slightest of nods.

A few minutes later, Waring detained Charlotte to show her a swan and some cygnets swimming by the reeds, and Thomas and Sarah walked slowly on ahead.

By now they were some distance from the town, and meadows lay on either side of the river.

August, 1940

The pub was set a short distance back from the road, with an area in front of it laid with paving stones. On these, before the war, there had been some circular metal tables where one could drink in the open air, but they had been removed for scrap iron during the previous winter. Apart from this, and the fact that the windows had been criss-crossed with tape as a precaution against blast, there was no outward sign of the war's austerities.

Inside, Lloyd ordered a pint of bitter, and took it with him to one of the tables.

He sipped the drink, then regarded the other occupants of the bar.

Apart from himself and the barmaid there were four people present. Two men sat morosely together at one table, half-empty glasses of stout before them. Another man sat alone at a table by the door. He had a newspaper in front of him, and he was staring at the crossword.

The fourth person, who stood against one of the walls, was a freezer. This one, Lloyd noted, was a woman. She, like the male freezers, wore a drab grey overall, and held one of the freeze instruments. This was shaped rather like a modern portable camera, and was carried on a lanyard strung around the neck, but it was much larger than a camera and was approximately cubical in shape. At the front, where on a camera would be a bellows and lens, there was a rectangular strip of white glass, apparently opaque or translucent, and it was through this that the freezing beam was projected.

Lloyd, still wearing his dark glasses, could only just see the woman. She did seem to be looking in his direction, but after a few seconds she stepped back through the wall and disappeared from his sight.

He noticed that the barmaid was watching him, and as soon as she saw him looking at her she spoke to him.

'D'you think they're coming this time?'

'I shouldn't care to speculate,' Lloyd said, not wishing to be drawn into conversation. He took several mouthfuls of the beer, wanting to finish it and be on his way.

'These sirens have ruined the trade,' the barmaid said. 'One after the other, all day and sometimes in the evenings too. And it's always a false alarm.'

'Yes,' Lloyd said.

She continued for a few more seconds, but then someone called her from the other bar and she went to serve. Lloyd was greatly relieved for he disliked speaking to people here.

He had felt isolated for too long, and had never mastered the modern way with conversation. Quite often he was misunderstood, for it was his way to speak in the more formal manner of his own contemporaries.

He was regretting having come in for a drink. This would have been a good time to go to the meadows, because while the air-raid alert was on there would be only a few people there. He wanted to be alone whenever he walked by the river.

He drank the rest of his beer, then stood up and walked towards the door.

As he did so he noticed for the first time that there was a recent tableau by the door. He did not search for the tableaux for he found them disturbing, but new ones were nevertheless of interest.

It seemed that there were two men and a woman sitting at the table; the image of them was indistinct, and so Lloyd took off his sunglasses. At once the brilliance of the tableau surprised him. It had been caught in sunlight, and was so bright that it overshadowed the real man, who still sat regarding his crossword at the far end of the same table.

One of the two frozen men was younger than the other two people, and he sat slightly apart. He was smoking, for a cigarette lay on the edge of the table, the end overhanging the wooden surface by half an inch. The older man and the woman were together, because they were holding hands and he was bending forward to kiss her wrist. His lips rested on her arm, and his eyes were closed. The woman, apparently well into her forties, was amused by this because she was smiling, but she was not watching her friend. Instead, she was looking across the table at the younger man, who, beer glass raised to his mouth, was watching the kiss with interest. On the table between them was the man's untouched glass of bitter, and the woman's glass of port. The smoke from the young man's cigarette, grey and curling, was sunlit and motionless in the air, and a piece of ash, falling towards the floor, hovered a few inches above the carpet.

'Do you want something, mate?' It was the man with the crossword.

Lloyd put on his sunglasses again in haste, realizing that for the last few seconds he had been seeming to stare at the man.

'I beg your pardon,' he said, and fell back on the excuse he often used. 'I thought for a moment I recognized you.'

The man peered myopically up at him. 'Never seen you before in my life.'

Lloyd affected a preoccupied nod and passed on towards the door. For a moment he caught a glimpse again of the three frozen victims. The young man with the beer glass, watching coolly; the man kissing, bent over so that his upper body was almost horizontal; the woman smiling, glancing towards the young man and enjoying all the attention that was being paid her; the sunlit, sinuous smoke.

Lloyd went out of the pub, and into the warm sunshine.

June, 1903

'Your mama wishes me to marry your sister,' Thomas said.

'I know. It is not what Charlotte desires.'

'Nor I. May I enquire as to your feelings on the matter?'

'I am in accord, Thomas.'

They were walking along slowly, a little way apart from each other. Both stared at the gravel of the path as they walked, not meeting the other's eyes. Sarah was turning her parasol in her fingers, causing the tassels to swirl and tangle. Now they were in the riverside meadows they were almost alone, although Waring and Charlotte were following about two hundred yards behind.

'Would you say that we were strangers, Sarah?'

'By what standards do you mean?' She had paused a little before answering.

'Well, for instance, this is the first occasion on which we have been allowed any degree of intimacy together.'

'And that by a contrivance,' Sarah said.

'What do you mean?'

'I saw you signal to your cousin.'

Thomas felt himself flush, but he considered that in the brightness and warmth of the afternoon it would go unnoticed. On the river the rowing-eight had turned and were passing them again.

After a few moments, Sarah said: 'I am not avoiding your question, Thomas. I am considering whether or not we are strangers.'

'Then what do you say?'

'I think we know each other a little.'

'I should be glad to see you again, Sarah. Without the need for contrivance, that is.'

'Charlotte and I will speak to Mama. You have already been much discussed, Thomas, although not as yet with Mama. You need not fear for hurting my sister's feelings for although she is fond of you she does not yet feel ready for marriage.'

Thomas, his pulse racing, felt a rush of confidence within him.

'And you, Sarah?' he said. 'May I continue to court you?'

She turned away from him then and stepped through the long grass beside the edge of the path. He saw the long sweep of her skirt, and the shining pink circle of her parasol. Her left hand dangled at her side, brushing lightly against her skirt.

She said: 'I find your advances most welcome, Thomas.'

Her voice was faint, but the words reached his ears as if she had pronounced them clearly in a silent room.

Thomas's response was immediate. He swept his boater from his head, and opened his arms wide.

'My dearest Sarah,' he cried. 'Will you marry me?'

She turned to face him and for a moment she was still, regarding him seriously. Her parasol rested on her shoulder, no longer turning. Then, seeing that he was in earnest, she smiled, and Thomas saw that she too had a blush of pink colouring her cheeks.

'Yes, of course I will,' Sarah said.

Happiness shone in her eyes. She stepped towards him extending her left hand, and Thomas, his straw hat still held high, reached forward with his right hand to take hers.

Neither Thomas nor Sarah could have seen that in that moment a man had stepped forward from beside the water's edge, and was levelling at them a small black instrument.

August, 1940

The all-clear had not sounded, but the town seemed to be returning to life. Traffic was crossing Richmond Bridge, and a short distance down the road towards Isleworth a queue was forming outside a grocer's shop while a delivery van was parked alongside the kerb. Now that he was at last setting off on his daily walk, Thomas Lloyd felt more at ease with the tableaux, and he took off his glasses for the last time and returned them to their case.

In the centre of the bridge was the overturning carriage. The driver, a gaunt middle-aged man in green livery and a shiny black top hat, had his left arm raised. In his hand he was holding the whip, and the lash snaked up over the bridge in a graceful curve. His right hand was already releasing the reins, and was reaching out towards the hard road-surface in a desperate attempt to soften the impact of his fall. In the open compartment at the rear was an elderly lady, much powdered and veiled, wearing a black velvet coat. She had been thrown sideways in her seat as the wheel axle broke, and was holding up her hands in fright. Of the two horses in harness, one was apparently unaware of the accident, and had been frozen in mid-stride.

The other, though, had tossed back its head and raised both its forelegs. Its nostrils were flaring, and behind the blinkers its eyes were rolled back.

As Lloyd crossed the road a red GPO van drove through the tableau, the driver unaware of its presence.

Two of the freezers were waiting at the top of the shallow ramp which led down to the riverside walk, and as Lloyd turned to follow the path towards the distant meadows, the two men walked a short distance behind him.

June, 1903 to January, 1935

The summer's day, with its two young lovers imprisoned, became a moment extended.

Thomas James Lloyd, straw hat raised in his left hand, his other hand reaching out. His right knee was slightly bent, as if he were about to kneel, and his face was full of happiness and expectation. A breeze seemed to be ruffling his hair, because three strands stood on end, but these had been dislodged when he removed his hat. A tiny winged insect, which had settled on his lapel, was frozen in its moment of flight, an instinct to escape too late.

A short distance away stood Sarah Carrington. The sun fell across her face, highlighting the locks of auburn hair that fell from beneath her bonnet. One foot, stepping towards Thomas, showed itself beneath the lace-sewn hem of her skirt, shod in a buttoned boot. Her right hand was lifting a pink parasol away from her shoulder, as if she were about to wave it in joy. She was laughing, and her eyes, soft and brown, gazed with affection at the young man before her.

Their hands were extended towards each other. Sarah's left

hand was an inch away from his, her fingers already curling in anticipation of clasping him.

Thomas's fingers, reaching out, revealed by irregular white patches that until an instant before his fists had been clenched in anxious tension.

The whole: the long grass moist after a shower a few hours before, the pale brown gravel of the path, the wild flowers that grew in the meadow, the adder that basked unnoticed not four feet from the couple, the clothes, their skin . . . all were rendered in colours bleached and saturated with preternatural brilliance.

August, 1940

There was a sound of aircraft engines.

Although aircraft were unknown in his time, Thomas Lloyd had now grown accustomed to them. He understood that before the war there had been civilian craft — great flying-boats that went to India, Africa, the Far East — but he had never seen any of these, and since the outbreak of war the only aircraft he had seen were military. Like everyone else of the time he was familiar with the sight of the high, black shapes, and with the curious droning, throbbing sound of the enemy bombers. Each day air battles were being fought over south-east England. Sometimes the bombers got through, sometimes not.

He glanced up at the sky. While he had been inside the pub, the vapour trails he noticed earlier had disappeared, but a new pattern of white had appeared, further to the north.

Lloyd walked down the Middlesex side of the river. Looking directly across the water he saw how the town had grown since his day: on the Surrey side, the trees which once had concealed the houses were mostly gone, and in their place were shops and offices. On this side, where houses had been set back from the river, more had been built close by the bank. Only the wooden boathouse was unchanged from his time, and that was badly in need of a coat of paint.

He was at the focus of past, present and future: only the boathouse and the river itself were as clearly defined as he. The freezers, from some unknown period of the future, as ethereal to ordinary men as their wishful dreams, moved like shadows through light, stealing sudden moments with their instruments. The tableaux themselves, frozen, isolated, insubstantial, waiting in an eternity of silence for those people of the future generation to see them.

Encompassing all was a turbulent present, obsessed with war.

Thomas Lloyd, of neither the past nor the present, saw himself as a product of both, and as a victim of the future.

Then, from high above the town, there came the sound of an explosion and a roar of engines, and the present impinged on Lloyd's consciousness. A British fighter plane banked away towards the south, and a German bomber fell burning towards the ground. After a few seconds, two men escaped from the aircraft, and their parachutes opened.

January, 1935

As if waking from a dream, Thomas experienced a moment of recall and recognition, but in an instant it was gone.

He saw Sarah before him, reaching towards him; he saw the bright garishness of the heightened colours; he saw the stillness of the frozen day. Sarah's laugh, her happy face, her acceptance of his proposal – they came from a moment before.

But they faded as he looked, and he cried out her name.

She made no move or reply, stayed immobile, and the light around her darkened.

Thomas pitched forward, a great weakness overcoming his limbs, and he fell to the ground.

It was night, and snow lay thickly on the meadows beside the Thames.

August, 1940

Until the moment of its final impact, the bomber fell in virtual silence. Both engines had stopped, although only one was on fire, and flame and smoke poured from the fuselage, leaving a thick black trail across the sky. The plane crashed by the bend in the river, and there was a huge explosion.

Meanwhile, the two German pilots who had escaped from the aircraft drifted down across Richmond Hill, swaying beneath their parachutes.

Lloyd shaded his eyes with his hand, and watched to see where they would land. One had been carried further by the aircraft before jumping, and he was much nearer, falling slowly towards the river.

The Civil Defence authorities in the town were evidently alert, because within a few moments of the parachutes appearing, Lloyd heard the sound of police and fire bells.

There was a movement a short distance from Lloyd, and he turned. The two freezers who had been following him had been joined by two others, one of whom was the woman he saw inside the pub. The freezer who seemed to be the youngest had already raised his device, and was pointing it across the river, but the other three were saying something to him. (Lloyd could see their lips moving, and the expressions on their faces, but as always he could not hear them.) The young man shrugged away the restraining hand of one of the others, and walked down the bank to the edge of the water.

One of the Germans came down near the edge of Richmond Park, and was lost to sight as he fell beyond the houses built near the crest of the Hill. The other, buoyed temporarily by a sudden updraught, drifted out across the river, and was now only some fifty feet in the air. Lloyd could see the German aviator pulling on the cords of his parachute, trying desperately to steer himself towards the bank. As air spilled from the white canopy, he fell more quickly.

The young freezer by the edge of the river was levelling his device, aiming it with the aid of a reflex sight built into the instrument. A moment later, the German's efforts to save himself from falling into the water were rewarded in a way he could have never anticipated: ten feet above the surface of the river, his knees raised to take the brunt of the impact, one arm clutching the cord above his head, the German was frozen in flight.

The freezer lowered his instrument, and Lloyd stared across the water at the hapless man suspended in the air.

January, 1935

The transformation of a summer's day into a winter's night was the least of the changes that Thomas Lloyd discovered on regaining consciousness. In what had been for him a few seconds he had moved from a world of stability, peace and prosperity to one where dynamic and violent ambitions threatened the whole of Europe. In that same short moment of time, he himself had lost the security of his assured future, and become a pauper. Most traumatically of all, he had not been allowed to take to its fruition the surge of love he felt for Sarah.

Night was the only relief from the tableaux, and Sarah was still locked in frozen time.

He recovered consciousness shortly before dawn, and, not understanding what had happened to him, walked slowly back towards Richmond town. The sun had risen soon after, and as light struck the tableaux that littered the paths and roads and as it struck the freezers who constantly moved in their half world of intrusive futurity, Lloyd realized neither that in these lay the cause of his own predicament, nor that his very perception of the images was a result of having been frozen himself.

In Richmond he was found by a policeman and was taken to hospital. Here, treated for the pneumonia he had contracted as he lay in the snow, and later for the amnesia that seemed the only explanation for his condition, Thomas Lloyd saw the freezers moving through the wards and corridors. The tableaux were here too: a dying man falling from his bed; a young nurse – dressed in the uniform of fifty years before – frozen as she walked from a ward, a deep frown creasing her brow; a child throwing a ball in the garden by the convalescent wing.

As he was nursed back to physical health, Lloyd became obsessed with a need to return to the riverside meadows, and before he was fully recovered he discharged himself and went directly there.

By then the snow had melted, but the weather was still cold and a white frost lay on the ground. Out by the river, where a bank of grass grew thickly by the path, was a frozen moment of summer, and in its midst was Sarah.

He could see her, but she could not see him. He could take the hand that was rightly his to take, but his fingers would pass through the illusion. He could walk around her, seeming to step through the green summer grasses and feel the cold of the winter soil penetrating the thin soles of his shoes . . .

And as night fell so the moment of the past became invisible, and Thomas was relieved of the agony of seeing her.

Time passed, but there was never a day when he did not walk along the riverside path, and stand again before the image of Sarah, and reach out to take her hand.

August, 1940

The German parachutist hung above the river, and Lloyd looked again at the freezers. They were apparently still criticizing the youngest for his action, and yet seemed fascinated with his result. It was certainly one of the most dramatic tableaux Lloyd himself had ever seen.

Now that the man had been frozen it was possible to see that his eyes were tightly closed, and that he was holding his nose with his fingers in anticipation of the plunge. But at the same time it was clear that he had been wounded in the aircraft, because blood was darkly staining his brown flying jacket. The tableau was at once amusing and poignant, a reminder to Lloyd that however unreal this present might be to him, it was no illusion to the people of the time.

In a moment, Lloyd understood the particular interest of the freezers in this unfortunate airman, for without warning the pocket of frozen time eroded, and the young German plunged into the river. The parachute billowed and folded in on top of him. As he surfaced he thrashed his arms, trying to free himself of the cords.

It was not the first time Lloyd had seen a tableau erode, but he had never before seen it happen so soon after freezing. His theory was that the duration of the tableau was dependent on how close the victim was to the freeze instrument. The German airman had been at least fifty yards away. In his own case, he had escaped from the tableau while Sarah had not, and the only explanation he could guess at was that she must have been nearer to the freezer.

In the centre of the river the German had succeeded in freeing himself of the parachute, and was swimming slowly towards the opposite bank. His descent had been observed by the authorities because even before he reached the sloping landing stage of the boathouse, four policemen appeared from the direction of the road and helped him out of the water. He made no attempt to resist them but lay weakly on the ground, awaiting the arrival of an ambulance.

Lloyd remembered the only other time he had seen a tableau erode quickly. A freezer had intervened to prevent a traffic accident: a man stepping carelessly into the path of a car was frozen in mid-stride. Although the driver of the car had stopped abruptly, and looked around in amazement for the man he thought he had been about to kill, he evidently assumed that he had imagined the incident, because he eventually drove off again. Only Lloyd, with his ability to see the tableaux, could still see the man stepping back, arms flailing in terror, seeing too late the oncoming vehicle. Three days later, when Lloyd returned to the place, the tableau had eroded and the man gone.

He, like Lloyd, and now like the German aviator, would be moving through a half world, one where past, present and future co-existed uneasily.

Lloyd watched the white canopy of the parachute drift along the river until at last it sank, and then he turned away to continue his walk to the meadows. As he did so he realized that even more of the freezers had appeared on this side of the river, and were walking behind him, following him.

As he reached the bend in the river, from which point he always gained his first sight of Sarah, he saw that the bomber had crashed in the meadows. The explosion of its impact had set fire to the grass, and the smoke from this, together with that from the burning wreckage, obscured his view.

January, 1935 to August, 1940

Thomas Lloyd never again left Richmond. He lived inexpensively, found occasional work, tried not to be outstanding in any way.

What of the past? He discovered that on 22 June 1903, his apparent disappearance with Sarah had led to the conclusion that he had absconded with her. His father, William Lloyd, head of the noted Richmond family, had disowned and disinherited him. Colonel and Mrs Carrington announced a reward for his arrest, but in 1910 they moved away from the area. Thomas also discovered that his cousin Waring never married Charlotte, and that he had emigrated to Australia. His own parents had died, there was no means of tracing his sister, and the family home had been sold and demolished.

(On the day he read the files of the local newspaper, he stood with Sarah, overcome with grief.)

What of the future? It was pervasive, intrusive. It existed on a plane where only those who were frozen and released could sense it. It existed in the form of men who came, for whatever purpose, to freeze the images of their past.

(On the day he first understood who the shadowy men he called freezers might be, he stood beside Sarah, staring around protectively. That day, as if sensing Lloyd's realization, one of the freezers walked along the riverbank, watching the young man and his time-locked sweetheart.)

What of the present? Lloyd neither cared for the present nor shared it with its people. It was alien, violent, frightening, but not in such a way that he felt threatened by it. To him, it was as vague a presence as the other two dimensions. Only the past and its frozen images were real.

(On the day he first saw a tableau erode, he ran all the way to the meadows, and stood long into the evening, trying ceaselessly for the first sign of substance in Sarah's outstretched hand.)

August, 1940

Only in the riverside meadows, where the town was distant and the houses were concealed by trees, did Thomas ever feel at one with the present. Here past and present fused, because little had changed since his day. Here he could stand before the image of Sarah, and fancy himself still on that summer's day in 1903, still the young man with raised straw hat and bended knee. Here too he rarely saw any of the freezers, and the few tableaux in sight could have come from the world he had left. (Further along the path was an elderly fisherman, time locked as he pulled a trout from a stream; a boy in a sailor suit walked sulkily with his nanny; a young servant girl, dressed in her day-off clothes, dimpled prettily as her beau tickled her chin.)

Today, though, the present had intruded violently. The exploding bomber had scattered fragments of itself across the meadows. Black smoke from the wreckage spread in an oily cloud across the river, and the smouldering grass poured white smoke to drift beside it. Much of the ground was already blackened by fire.

Sarah was invisible to him, lost somewhere in the smoke.

Thomas paused, and took a kerchief from his pocket. He stooped by the river's edge and soaked it in the water, then, after wringing it out, he held it over his nose and mouth.

He glanced behind him and saw that there were now eight of the freezers with him. They were paying no attention to him, and walked on while he prepared himself, insensible to the smoke. They passed through the burning grass, and walked towards the main concentration of wreckage. One of the freezers was already making some kind of adjustment to his device.

A breeze had sprung up in the last few minutes, and it caused the smoke to move away smartly from the fires, staying lower on the ground. As this happened, Thomas saw the image of Sarah above the smoke. He hurried towards her, alarmed by the proximity of the burning aircraft, even as he knew that neither fire, explosion nor smoke could harm her.

His feet threw up smouldering grasses as he went towards her, and at times the variable wind caused the smoke to swirl about his head. His eyes were watering, and although his wetted kerchief acted as a partial filter against the grass smoke, when the oily fumes from the aircraft gusted around him he choked and gagged on the acrid vapours.

At last he decided to wait; Sarah was safe inside her cocoon of frozen time, and there was no conceivable point to his suffocating simply to be with her, when in a few minutes the fire would burn itself out.

He retreated to the edge of the burning area, rinsed out his kerchief in the river, and sat down to wait.

The freezers were exploring the wreckage with the greatest interest, apparently drifting through the flames and smoke to enter the deepest parts of the conflagration.

There came the sound of a bell away to Thomas's right, and in a moment a fire tender halted in the narrow lane that ran along the distant edge of the meadows. Several firemen climbed down and stood looking across the field at the wreckage. At this Thomas's heart sank, for he realized what was to follow. He had sometimes seen photographs in the newspapers of crashed German planes – they were invariably placed under military guard until the pieces could be taken away for examination. If this were to happen here it would deny him access to Sarah for several days.

For the moment, though, he would still have a chance to be with her. He was too far away to hear what the firemen were saying, but it looked as if no attempt was going to be made to put out the fire. Smoke still poured from the fuselage, but the flames had died down and most of the smoke was coming from the grass. With no houses in the vicinity, and with the wind blowing towards the river, there was little likelihood the fire would spread.

He stood up again, and walked quickly towards Sarah.

In a few moments he had reached her and she stood before him: eyes shining in the sunlight, parasol lifting, arm extending. She was in a sphere of safety. Although smoke blew through her, the grasses on which she stood were green and moist and cool. As he had done every day for more than five years, Thomas stood facing her and waited for a sign of the erosion of her tableau. He stepped, as he had frequently done before, into the area of the time freeze.

Here, although his foot appeared to press on the grasses of 1903, a flame curled around his leg and he had to step back quickly.

Thomas saw some of the freezers coming towards him. They

had apparently inspected the wreckage to their satisfaction, and judged none of it worth preserving in a time freeze. Thomas tried to disregard them, but their sinister silence could not be forgotten easily.

The smoke poured about him, rich and heady with the smells of burning grass, and he looked again at Sarah. Just as time had frozen about her in that instant, so it had frozen about his love for her. Time had not diminished, it had preserved.

The freezers were watching them. Thomas saw the eight vague figures, standing not ten feet away from him, were looking at him with interest. Then, on the far side of the meadow, one of the firemen shouted something at him.

He would seem to be standing here alone; no one else could see the tableaux, no one else knew of the freezers. The fireman walked towards him, waving an arm, telling him to move away. It would take him a minute or more to reach them, and that was time enough for Thomas.

One of the freezers stepped forward and in the heart of the smoke Thomas saw the captured summer begin to dim.

Smoke curled up around Sarah's feet and flame licked through the moist, time-frozen grasses around her ankles. He saw the lace at the bottom of her skirt begin to scorch.

And her hand, extended towards him, lowered.

The parasol fell to the ground.

Sarah's head drooped forward, but immediately she was conscious and the step towards him, commenced thirty-seven years before, was concluded.

'Thomas?' Her voice was clear, untouched.

He rushed towards her.

'Thomas! The smoke! What is happening?'

'Sarah – my love!'

As she went into his arms he realized that her skirt had taken fire, but he placed his arms around her shoulders and hugged her intimately and tenderly. He could feel her cheek, still warm from the blush of so long ago, nestling against his. Her hair, falling loose beneath her bonnet, lay across his face, and the pressure of her arms around his waist was no less than that of his own.

Dimly, he saw a grey movement beyond them and in a moment the noises were stilled and the smoke ceased to swirl. The flame which had taken purchase on the lace of her skirt now died, and the summer sun which warmed them shone lightly in the tableau. Past and future became one, the present faded, life stilled, life forever.

After – 'An Infinite Summer'

As I mentioned in the notes on 'Palely Loitering', in 1979 I published a collection of stories with 'An Infinite Summer' providing the title. Like the other stories in that book it had its period in the sunlight, but has not been available since in any form.

The story clearly would not have been written if Mr Ellison had not barged into my novel and demanded I drop it in favour of his book. For that I suppose I should be grateful. However, he had no real interest in me or whatever I might write for him. He clearly lost whatever vestige of interest he might once have had as soon as I sent the manuscript.

All I know is that had I left the story with him as I was supposed to, it would be lost to the world. The anthology Mr Ellison was purportedly producing was not completed and published. After many more years, in which even more stories than mine were belatedly acquired, and other publishers came in on extravagant promises and left after discovering the true paralysis that afflicted the project, the whole thing was abandoned.

Many of the stories he acquired have never been published, and are now unlikely ever to see the light of day. The book itself was unpublishable in any conventional printed format because of its insane size. (At one point Mr Ellison claimed it was six times the length of *War and Peace*!) Ironically, by the time digitization of texts became widespread, and compact discs and DVDs and downloads were available to all, Mr Ellison had lost interest and abandoned all hope of ever finishing what he had started. I have gone into this unhappy story in some detail because on the whole readers are unaware of many of the unnecessary tensions created behind the scenes by people like him, and the time and energy they can waste – not just theirs, but other people's.

I have never regretted rescuing 'An Infinite Summer' from this hopeless mess – not for an instant. The story won no awards but it was re-anthologized a few times. It has been out of print for many years.

Before – 'The Ament'

'The Ament' was first published in 1985, in an anthology of new stories called *Seven Deadly Sins*. It was published in the UK in an attractive hardcover edition by Severn House, but I know of no other editions. Of the seven traditional sins on offer, I drew *Anger*.

The other authors published in the same book were Elizabeth Troop (*Pride*), Rose Tremain (*Envy*), Wendy Perriam (*Gluttony*), William Trevor (*Avarice*), Ronald Frame (*Lust*), and Helen Lucy Burke (*Sloth*). Although I assume the book sold at least some copies, I know of no one who has ever read my story, and for that matter the same may well be true of the other stories.

More grimness ensues, I fear.

The Ament

i

I had dreamed again in the night, and I awoke early in the morning with a feeling of exhilaration and fulfilment. I lay there in the filtered half-light from the curtained windows, waiting for my alarm radio to switch itself on. I usually liked to be awake in time to hear the news, so the clock was set for two minutes before the hour. While I waited for the music and commercials to begin, I lay with my hands folded contentedly across my stomach, dwelling pleasurably on the dream.

I had killed again. It was a dream, only a dream, but for me such night-time killings were a recurring, if infrequent, part of my inner life. Killing dreams were my feast, and after them I was sated. Last night had been a rape and a strangling, violent and dangerous and fast. My thumbs ached and my face was sore, and I could still feel or imagine the clamping grip of the woman's hands on my wrists.

The radio started to play and when the news began I listened to it, wondering if the local segment might contain anything that would interest me. I had been wearing my wristwatch in the night and as I listened to the newsreader's voice I lightly fingered the watch. It was tight against the skin. I eased it away,

196

feeling the tug of the metal back and the strap as they separated from the flesh. I remembered that the woman had gripped me over the watch and during the killing it had briefly crossed my mind that she might break it.

I shifted my position, heaving myself up and pushing the pillow against the headboard behind me. I found my spectacles and put them on, then examined my wrist under the light from the bedside lamp. Where the strap had been was a red, indented weal all around my wrist, each of the expanding metal slats marked out clearly on the skin. The wrist itself was swollen and puffy, and when I tried to flex my hand it felt sore. I rubbed my arm, knowing that in the warmth of a bed the limbs sometimes swell slightly. In any event I had been recently putting on weight and the strap was now too tight.

By the time the news ended I was fully awake, so I climbed out of bed and dressed. It continually irritated me that Mrs Adams would not bring the morning delivery of mail to my room, which meant that every day I had to dress and go downstairs before I did anything else. I was the only resident in the house who was an active correspondent – most of the mail that came to the house was mine. I had lost count of the number of times I had asked her to bring my letters to my door – she was always going up and down the stairs at this time of the morning, and it would not have inconvenienced her. It seemed there was nothing that would induce her to oblige me. In the old days, while Mr Adams was still alive, I had been able to pick up my mail outside my door and go back to read it in bed. Then, when I was ready, I would shave and bathe and dress, and the day would already have a comfortable shape to it.

But now my habit was that today's clothes were yesterday's clothes, and they were the day before's.

I glanced in the mirror beside the door and inspected the

sore area of my face. Two parallel scratches ran down from above one eye to the bottom of my cheek. In the dream, the woman had scratched me as she struggled, but I had not realized that I must have clawed at myself while I slept. It did sometimes happen, but never before in such direct correlation with a dream. I fingered the marks gently, wondering whether I should buy some ointment for them.

I went quietly down the staircase, found my letters still lying on the doormat, and started up the stairs to return to my room. Mrs Adams had heard me leave my room and was waiting for me on the half-landing at the turn of the stairs. I had not heard her footsteps.

'Oh, it's you, Mr Welbeck!' she said, in the voice that managed to convey surprise, pleasure and censure in one breathy note.

'Good morning, Gracie,' I said, trying to look preoccupied with the letters I was holding, flicking through them and sorting the larger envelopes to the back of the pile. I had to pass her on the landing, and she laid her hand briefly on my forearm.

'Mr Welbeck, I know you normally have to go out on Thursdays, but I thought I should mention the noise. You see, I'm expecting visitors—'

'I'll be out all day today. There won't be any noise.'

'You know I hate to interfere, but it's your typewriter. It makes so much noise that sometimes I can't hear myself think.'

'I'm going out in an hour's time.'

'Yes, but you see, if you should come home before my visitors leave—'

'I won't.'

'If only you would put down a thicker carpet, Mr Welbeck, or even a rug. Something to muffle the noise against the floorboards.'

'Yes, I'll do that,' I said. 'Now . . . you must excuse me. I have to do some work before I leave.'

She was still on the half-landing when I closed my door, her lips pursed and her brow creased petulantly.

Mrs Adams was nearly eighty, and the older she grew the more unreasonable she became. We had two pet topics of conversation: my typewriter noise, and my curtains. Both were insoluble problems. What I had never told Mrs Adams was that my typing table already stood on three thicknesses of carpet, and that the nuisance of the noise was enlarged only by her awareness of it, and by her belief that a man who stayed at home all day writing was somehow pursuing an unusual occupation. Unusual, that is, in her terms. I had never mentioned the carpets to her, mainly as a test to see if she ever entered my room in my absence. I reasoned that simply because her obsession with my noise nuisance, real or imagined, continued to be something she complained about, it was unlikely she went into my room.

The curtains were a different matter, but just as petty. I preferred to work by artificial light and kept my curtains closed all day. This somehow offended her sensibilities and she was always 'reminding' me that I had 'forgotten' to open them.

Although these were continual irritants to me, what really lay behind them was the fact that my presence in her house reminded her that her reduced circumstances had obliged her to take in lodgers. I had actually lived in the house for more than twenty years and considered it my permanent address. The noise of my daily work signalled my presence to her visitors, and my permanently closed curtains conveyed the same to her neighbours. These were presumably what she could not forgive.

When I had closed the door I filled my pipe, lit it, then sat down at the desk to go through my morning's mail.

This was the principal pleasure of the day and I took my time over it. I opened first what I sensed were the routine arrivals: bills and circulars and so on, leaving to last the envelopes I either recognized or which aroused my curiosity. Today there was one of the regular packages from the newspaper cuttings agency, with several dozen clippings from national and provincial papers, only a few of which I had found for myself earlier in the week. I read them through slowly, setting each one down into a number of small piles, for later filing. The irritation caused by Mrs Adams quickly receded as I began to find the usual patterns developing: old stories continuing, new ones reported from a variety of different viewpoints, fresh developments in cases long familiar to me. It was all here, superficially dealt with though it might be by the newspaper accounts: the raw material of the darker side of life, crimes against the person, the cruelties and sudden passions, acts of revenge and senselessness.

And somewhere, usually once or twice a month, the mysteries. The crimes unsolved, the paradoxes, the coincidences, the inexplicable outbreaks of violence.

Also in the pile of envelopes, which I came to eventually, were letters from three of my regular correspondents: other writers, other criminologists. I had an informal agreement with several colleagues under which we freely exchanged discoveries, theories or recently established evidence which we knew or suspected might be useful to each other. We each had our own areas of special interest. The problem we all encountered was the mass of material, so much, in fact, that it was generally impossible to keep an overview of our specialities. We were constantly sidetracked into irrelevancies, and so, gladly, we passed on as much of this surplus to each other as we could spare.

When I had opened all my mail I relit my pipe with a feeling of satisfaction, moderated only by the knowledge that I had no time to deal with any of it. On a normal day I would spend several contented hours working my way methodically through this material, filing, noting, updating my papers, writing some of it into an article or a chapter of a book. But it was Thursday, the one day of the week when I never even tried to settle down to serious work.

After checking the time on the clock radio I spent a few minutes glancing through the cuttings that dealt with two particular cases I had been following, then placed all the material that had arrived that morning in the various places set aside for it. I kept my files deliberately untidy, a discouragement to anyone who might enter my room in my absence, but even so, when I left I secured the door with the double lock I had installed myself, and for which I had the only keys.

ii

He stopped for breakfast on the way to the Gibbertson Institute. He was a large, dishevelled man, his clothes smelling of tobacco and unclean habits. He wore a plastic mackintosh over his jacket and trousers, and as he walked it swooped behind him like a semi-transparent cape. He had bought a newspaper on the way to the restaurant and he held this rolled up tightly in one fist. He appeared unaware of the movements in the street around him, his eyes directed towards the ground, and he brushed past other pedestrians without a glance. Andrew Welbeck, aged 61, born in London, still resident in the Tufnell Park area of Kentish Town, unmarried, unemployed or self-employed, a nuisance to his landlady, an object of minor curiosity to the others who rented rooms in the same house. An unlikely subject for a scientific experiment, yet his involvement with it was central to his life, providing him with a small but regular income and giving an external shape to his affairs.

The restaurant he went to was old-fashioned, privately run by a family of Turkish Cypriots. The two plate-glass windows on either side of the door were filmed with condensation, blurring the illuminated plastic menu-board that hung on chains behind. Welbeck did not even glance around as he went in, except to find an unoccupied table near one of the windows. When his order was brought he ate with one hand, slicing the food with his fork and shovelling it into his mouth while he read. (While he was eating, two women came in from the street and sat at the table next to his. After a muted conversation, and several sideways looks at Welbeck, they moved to another table; one of the women fanned her hand in front of her nose, a sour expression on her face.) Welbeck was a selective reader; he looked at few of the pictures, he ignored the sports pages, the radio and television listings, the feature articles, the foreign news. All he read were the news stories from Britain, and here too he discriminated about what he read. He passed the political news, union strife, pessimistic forecasts about the economy, the activities of the royal family. What he read was the news about ordinary people, their accidents and incidents, crimes, betrayals, surprises, good fortune and bad, and these he read several times, as if committing them to memory.

He finished his meal with a cup of tea, sipping at it a few times before draining the rest in two quick swallows. He paid his bill, then left, walking towards the nearest bus stop.

The bus deposited him near the junction of Euston Road with Tottenham Court Road. He walked briskly now, staring straight ahead, only looking up briefly at the lighted windows as he reached the Institute building itself.

Then, outside the main entrance to the building, in a place from which he could see into the lobby and the porter's desk, Welbeck came to a halt. He waited outside, staring in, until the porter happened to glance up and see him there.

iii

I entered the building, striding past the porter's desk without giving or receiving acknowledgement, and took the lift to the fifth floor.

To me this was still the new building, even though it had been in use since the early 1960s. My memories went much further back. The first building had been in Moorgate, in the City, but that had been destroyed during the Blitz. For the rest of the war years, and all through the 1950s, the Gibbertson had used temporary premises made available by University College, but it had taken them nearly twenty years to raise sufficient funds to buy the present building. I liked the Moorgate building best, probably because of childhood associations. Sometimes after our visits my parents would take me on little outings, to the Tower, to the Embankment, and always to the ABC for cakes and a cup of tea before the trolley-bus ride home.

Because I was a little late arriving, I went straight to the studio to make my presence known to the waiting technicians, then moved along to the changing room and took off all my clothes. I put on a white flannelette dressing gown and returned to the studio.

We were waiting for Annie. She had arrived before me, but had apparently gone down the corridor to use the bathroom. Everything was ready: the lights were set up, although not yet switched on, the camera was loaded, the rostra and the neutral backcloths were placed on their marks. Because filming took place only once a week, this makeshift studio was used at other times as a consultation room, and every Wednesday evening the staff had to remove everything and reinstall the film equipment. As soon as we had finished, it would all be changed back again.

I sat down on the edge of my own rostrum, waiting for Annie.

Ever since I had woken up, images from the dream had been hovering peripherally in my mind, but now, with nothing to do until Annie turned up, I concentrated on what I remembered of them.

Most of all it was loathing, although beyond this I had no idea of my motives. My killing dreams always lacked reason. I did not kill for gain, revenge, ideology, or even for lust, but out of simple blind hatred for the victim.

Women I always strangled, but that was because they were women, and after I had used their bodies it was natural to kill with my hands. I usually raped them first, but the killing was not for sexual reasons. I killed them because . . . well, because of the way they died. Women were smaller than me, they were weaker, the sound of their laboured breathing as I constricted their throats was shrill and agonized. Men grunted and kicked; women hissed and struggled. They died noisily, whereas men usually went in silence.

But I never strangled men. Those I killed by beating or knifing, or once, distastefully, by smothering. I did not smother a second time.

Last night I had loathed that woman and I was glad when she was dead. Other than this I did not know why I had killed her, but I *had* killed her. That at least was certain. My murders took place in dreams, in the security of non-reality, where I could not be interrupted or caught, where my victims' cries would

204

never be heard, where I could appear mysteriously and fade away afterwards. But although they were dreams they also had a kind of reality. I had been sure of this ever since the killing dream of the man I later knew was called Kent, Dixie Kent.

At the time I killed him I had no idea who he was. It was just a dream, a murder by beating: I had struck him repeatedly with a short section of heavy wood, slick with rain and mud, and studded all along one side with rusty nails. He had died noisily, but quickly. I had recalled the dream vividly the morning after, but no more than any of the other dreams that I had experienced at that time. The difference with Dixie Kent was that his death was widely reported in the press and on television.

Kent was a convict who had been serving a sentence for a number of violent crimes. He had escaped from prison some months before and was the subject of a major police search. When his body was found it was important news. His murder was a mystery and the culprit was never found. But I, and I alone, knew beyond doubt that I was responsible. As soon as I saw his face in the newspapers, when the scene of the crime was shown on television news, I remembered everything with a clarity that left me in no doubt.

If that murder was real, then so too were all the others.

Now I checked and rechecked, searching for news of my activities, but since the killing of Dixie Kent I had never made headline news. I was less sure about the others I had killed in my dreams. But I knew what I was doing and what I had done. I killed when I moved in the landscape of my dreams.

Annie arrived, smiling briefly at me, nodding to the technicians. She had her handbag over her arm and a plastic cup of coffee in the other hand. She put these down on a desk, then pulled her white dressing gown more tightly across her body.

'Is it cold in here this morning?' she said. 'Or am I imagining it?'

'It'll soon warm up when we get the lights on,' Geoff said. Geoff was the camera operator, new to the job. I had lost count of the cameramen who had slipped briefly into and out of this job. It wasn't real film work, and most of the operators were junior assistants, helping out from one of the other departments in the building.

'How are you, Annie?' I said.

'Same as usual, thanks. How about you?'

'All right.'

Sometimes we didn't speak on these occasions. At other times something would briefly make us interested in each other again and we would take lunch together afterwards. We had known each other all our lives, and yet in some respects we were still virtual strangers.

Still we met, once a week, on and on as the years went by. Like me she had never married, although unlike me she had a successful career and the fees she received from the Gibbertson were hardly more than pocket money. For me, the Gibbertson money was my only source of reliable income. It had made me lazy over the years, cushioning me from reality. I earned very little from the books and articles I wrote, because the market for the minutiae of criminology was a small, specialist one. I knew Annie had a pension with her job – the Gibbertson would have to provide that for me, just as it had provided most of my livelihood.

The lights were turned on, and Geoff declared the camera ready. Annie went first, removing her dressing gown, and then, rubbing the palms of her hands together, climbed on to the left-hand rostrum and took up her position. She waited patiently as the shot was lined up to precise measurements. I scarcely glanced at her naked body. I knew it almost as well as I knew my own.

Then it was my turn. I stood on the right-hand rostrum, waited for the camera to be lined up and the measurements taken. A few feet of film full-face, a few more of my left profile, and more of my right. Then the back of my head. Annie stood beside me in the glare of the lights, waiting for the next sequence.

When these solo shots were completed, we climbed down while the two rostra were pushed together on to the second mark, and then we went back up for the joint, full-length shots. We faced each other, faced away, stood side by side. The last shot was a close-up of our two heads, facing each other from a standing position, so that the difference in our heights would register. For this sequence alone we looked into each other's eyes, trying not to blink.

This shot was the only one that made me uncomfortable. It reminded me of how we had changed over the years. We both had grey hair now, and mine was thin on the crown. Annie's face was lined and she had put on a great deal of weight as she aged. But more than this: to look at her as closely as this was a weekly reminder of a brief involvement we had had when we were in our late teens.

The Second World War was still on then and we shared a feeling of impermanence known to many in those years, that at any moment something would happen to separate us. For a few weeks we had been the most chaste of lovers, holding hands, kissing, then very properly returning to our separate homes. The Gibbertson filming continued all through the war, as it had before and since, and in that short period, when we posed on the rostra and looked into each other's eyes as the camera turned, the moment had held a certain romantic significance.

But all that passed quickly. Annie and I were spoiled by the superficial familiarity we had with each other, and continued on into our own lives.

I tried not to dwell on the past.

The reminders, though, were all of the past. What else was there *but* the past in a film taken of our growing bodies, once a week, every week, from the time we had been born?

We had both been signed to it by our parents, a commitment to scientific study until the age of twenty-one. It was renewable, by consent only, of course, but the war had been continuing and the Institute had obtained me a deferment of the call-up. Money was tight. There were always reasons – Annie had had them too. Sixty-one years after we began, here we still were, standing once a week in a bleakly unfurnished room, having our physical growth and decay recorded for the benefit of science.

iv

This is how it might have been:

Every year Andrew Welbeck and Anne McDonald were offered the chance of viewing the film that had been shot. They usually declined, although Annie had seen it through from beginning to end about five times. Welbeck had watched it only once, when he was in his mid-thirties.

The first sequences were the least successful: the two new-born babies, curled and crying, never in the same relative position to the camera from one shot to the next, lent a discontinuous and erratic quality to the pictures. Only as the children grew a little older, and could be persuaded or restrained, was there continuity in the montage. Additionally, in the early days the camera and lights and film stock had been primitive, and there was a lack of subtlety in the monochrome images of the flesh tones, with stark shadows thrown behind. During the 1930s the Institute had obtained a supply of colour film, clearly intending to go on using it indefinitely, but not only were the colours garish and red-hued – and the film dyes had not lasted well over the years – but the supply had run out and all through the war years and into the 1950s the film returned to black and white. There had been talk recently of finding the money to transfer the entire film to videotape, and use modern techniques to clean up the images, either perhaps to render the whole sequence into a modified and graded form of black and white, or to use computer enhancement to adjust the colours and perhaps even add colour tones to the monochrome sequences.

In spite of the inconsistencies in the image, and all the practical difficulties, the films nevertheless had a striking quality. From the time the children had grown used to being photographed, a distinct and apparently steady physical continuity could be seen, and the growth and ageing of their bodies clearly observed.

Seen in one continuous sequence the edited films revealed the emphases in growth in childhood, the limbs and trunk developing far more quickly than the face and head. From the early teens the two bodies grew perceptibly towards adulthood, with the development of the sexual organs and, perhaps less predictably, the emergence of the adult expression, seeming to force its way through from behind the faces. Hair thickened, grew, receded, changed colour. In Welbeck's case incipient baldness had appeared by the time he was thirty.

Welbeck had chosen not to view the films after the first time – had he done so he would have seen his baldness advancing, his body thickening, his muscles starting to sag, his chest sinking slowly towards an ever more prominent abdominal bulge, his face becoming lined and his overall height gradually shrinking by about an inch. He would have seen Annie ageing at the same rate: the young body he had seen so often, yet never touched, steadily losing its youthful firmness, her breasts spreading out and drooping, her waist thickening, the dimples of cellulite appearing in the fleshier parts of her legs and arms. Her expression, too, changed with age. As a young woman Annie had a fresh, open expression, but this narrowed and hardened as she moved into middle age, changing yet again as she grew through her fifties.

Today, Annie had recaptured some of her attractive younger looks, and was pleasant-faced, a comfortable and contented woman now at ease with her years.

Welbeck's own face had shown similar changes. He was noticeably surly in his teens, replaced by self-confidence as he grew up, but as the years took him into the onset of old age his face developed a withdrawn, secretive expression, his eyes narrowed under the permanent creases in his forehead.

All of this was what Welbeck saw on the day the film was shown to him, and the rest of it was what he would have seen had he agreed to view the film in later years. But there was one other film, and Welbeck had inadvertently seen it as well.

That film began, like the others, in black and white. Two babies lay in the garish lighting, their tiny limbs moving fretfully. One was a boy, one was a girl. There was the same jerkiness to the montage here, but soon it settled down and the eerie sight of visible growth began. Watching it, Welbeck had believed he was looking at himself.

The film had been halted abruptly. Someone turned on the room lights. There were several moments of confusion, while the psychologist who at that time was the head of the department explained to him that the technician had by mistake projected the wrong piece of film. Following a short delay, the correct sequences were shown.

After it all, the explanation. There had been an earlier attempt to film the growth of children, they said, but one of them had fallen ill and subsequently died, bringing the project to a premature end. Inadvertently, it was this footage that they had shown that day.

On his next visit to the Gibbertson, Welbeck raised the subject again, asking for more details.

What he was told was that it was the little girl who had died. Her name was Marie, and she had contracted influenza. The male child's name was Duncan. Because the project required two babies of identical age it had been decided to start again from the beginning. Young Duncan was released from his weekly commitment, and in due course two replacement newborn babies were found. These were himself, and Annie.

It was after this incident, apparently so trivial, that Welbeck's attitude to the project changed. So far as the staff at the Institute were concerned he seemed more detached, less committed to the film. He turned up reliably once a week, he posed quietly for the camera, he spoke only briefly to the other people there, and when it was all over he dressed and went home.

v

I dressed and headed home. I wanted to get back to my work, to the pleasures of detail and cross reference and of debating the relative importance of circumstantial evidence. I had several letters I wanted to answer. But the portents were not good. I was usually distracted on Thursday afternoons, because the filming sessions interrupted my thoughts. I could never close my mind to what was going on. I had sworn to myself more times than I could remember that I would break my contract. There was, in fact, little pressure to continue, just the assumption from everyone involved that I had gone on so long I would never back out. Maybe it was true that it was only the momentum of habit, but on Thursday afternoons, when I was thinking of getting back to work, habit seemed the least important reason.

I was rarely able to concentrate on Thursday afternoons, and sometimes I lost the next day too. On occasions the mood continued through the weekend, breaking my routines and distracting my thoughts.

Today, the coincidence of a filming session with the killing dream in the night was enough to guarantee that work would be impossible. Yet I headed home, trying to deny the feeling, spurring myself with the thought of the letters and cuttings I had received in the morning mail. I dealt with problems by trying to ignore them.

I had never learned how to deal with what obsessed me.

My worlds were inner and outer, obsessive and problematical. I always tried to ignore what went on in the outside world. I could never stop thinking about the rest.

My interior life was an endless monologue, nagging me, urging me, pushing me towards some response to itself. This was how I interpreted the killing dreams – they were messages from my inner world. I tried to sublimate them by organizing them into files and correspondence and case notes, but this was just an excuse. The work to which I pretended was really my attempt to externalize, to convert obsession to problem.

As I walked towards the house I glanced up at the windows. I glimpsed a dark movement behind one of them and knew that Mrs Adams had been waiting for me. I generally returned at this time on a Thursday. Her life was empty but for me. I gave her an interest. I was for her some kind of intense and destructive hobby. She had no interior life of which I had ever been aware, nor, for that matter, any other kind of life. In her fantasies her days were filled with visitors and excursions, but in recent years her existence had been solitary, lonely. *I* was her interest, and she wanted to shape me like modelling clay.

I could not face even a brief session of bantering argument with her, so I turned my head away quickly and walked on. The glimpse of her forced me into a decision, an acknowledgement of the fact that my obsessions were aroused once more.

I paused at the end of the street. It had suddenly occurred to me that I could visit Lesley. I had not seen her for some years,

Going to her house would not only occupy the rest of the afternoon but might help salve some of the distractions. She was adjacent to my obsessions, and talking to her had often helped in the past. On the other hand, her house was in South London, a part of the capital I rarely visited and did not on the whole like. It meant taking a long journey on the Underground.

I looked back towards Mrs Adams's house, undecided what to do. As always the house looked unwelcoming: cold, hostile to me, personified by my feelings about its owner. Only when I was inside my room with the door closed, and only then if I was entirely wrapped up in my work, did I feel it was my home.

I decided after all to visit Lesley and walked towards the Underground station.

Lesley was the sister of Marie, the child being filmed by the Gibbertson before her premature death. Lesley was a few years younger than Marie, and was approximately my own age. I first met her a few years earlier, when I had started to try to trace Duncan Prentiss, the boy who had been Marie's partner.

If there was a focus to my obsessions it was Prentiss. If there was a purpose to my work and investigations, if there was a reason for my continued participation in the filming, it was Duncan Prentiss.

I began to procrastinate on my journey to visit Lesley, and when I reached Tufnell Park station I decided to have lunch before continuing. I went to one of the cheap cafés I often used. When the food was brought I ate it too hastily, wishing now that I had not delayed. After I paid the bill I walked quickly to the station, my belly churning with indigestion.

Once on the train I went into my familiar introspection, folding my hands over my stomach and staring at the wooden ribbed floor of the carriage.

Duncan Prentiss obsessed me because he had once usurped me, destroying something crucial to my own sense of identity.

I grew up believing that the Gibbertson film project was an integral part of my life. When I was old enough to realize that Annie and I were the *only* children who were being filmed I assumed I was unique. It was my experience – it could not be invaded by anyone. I was special, I had been picked out, I could not be replaced.

Indeed, I remember my parents often telling me such things when I was small, presumably as flattering inducements. By the time I was ten I accepted my uniqueness without a second thought.

As I grew through my teens and into adulthood, this arrogance slowly changed to a more internalized conviction. I realized that my uniqueness was simply the chance of selection, and that once the Gibbertson had started to work with me it was more in their interests to continue than it was in mine. But by then I had started to get interested in Annie.

The changes that were taking place in our bodies could not be ignored. Every week I was present when a pretty girl of my own age undressed in front of me, and stood close beside me as someone filmed us. Annie was too familiar to me, and the situation was too clinical, for anything to happen then. We could and did meet at other times, though. I had always been bashful with girls, but Annie was different. For a time we courted each other, shyly and conventionally, our weekly sessions naked together an undiscussed anomaly in what we saw as our real lives.

But that was the irony. For me, the filming had taken on a profound sense of identity, and I lived for the sessions in front of the camera. Annie did not exist for me except as a naked girl, her young breasts rising, the soft curve of her buttocks, the tantalizing triangle of dark hair. I could not equate this knowledge of her with the stiff and formal friendship we were experimenting with outside.

One night I tried to bring the two together, with an unpremeditated attempt to kiss her and touch her and rip her clothes away. She rejected me, instantly and finally, and that was the end of it all.

Except that once a week we continued to meet, stood naked together, and allowed strangers to film our bodies.

My way of coping with this was to act as if she and I did not exist outside the film. The feelings of hurt and rejection eventually faded and the tensions between us receded, but by then the transmutation of my childhood arrogance had been completed.

The change was this: because of Annie I had fallen into the habit of thinking that the film, and *only* the film, was my reality. It was proof that I had been, that I had lived, that I had grown and changed and continued to grow and change. My identity, my *self*, was contained in the Gibbertson film.

For several years after this the weekly visits to the makeshift studio became my rationale. I thrived on the knowledge that a copy of me was being created, that it was external evidence for myself. I became for a long period an enthusiastic collaborator, looking forward to the filming sessions as the high point of each week. The Institute was in financial and organizational difficulties as a result of the war, and also during the years of post-war reconstruction. At times it even seemed possible that the project might have been abandoned altogether were it not for my enthusiastic participation.

So for a long time I had been accustomed to the idea that not only was the filming important as a scientific project in itself, but that it was also crucial to the way I interpreted myself. I was in the film, and the film recorded me . . . but at the same time the film *was* me.

Then, during the 1950s, one of the project directors casually asked me if I would be interested in seeing the film so far. I agreed, and that was the day on which I discovered Duncan Prentiss had been there before me.

I am not rational about my reaction to this. I felt angry, humiliated, jealous. I felt he had intruded on something deeply personal and private. He roused in me possessive feelings about Annie. I wanted to kill him.

And all this from the sight of a helpless baby, growing into a child as I looked.

But I watched him, and this is the crux of the matter, I watched him *thinking I was looking at myself.*

During those first few moments, seeing the scratchy black-and-white film with its harsh contrasts and unflattering lighting, I had felt a sensation I find difficult to identify: a warm feeling of proprietorship, an indulgent glow of self-love, an intimate knowledge and a sense of privy insights. The fractious baby, squirming on the rostrum, its wrinkled face and down-like hair. Later, the sight of the body straightening and strengthening, the muscles shaping into a child's puppy fat, the hair darkening and thickening, the face acquiring the force of personality behind the eyes. All this awakened an interest in myself I had never known before. I started anticipating, looking at the filmed image for glimpses of the adult self I had become.

Then the mistake was discovered and they quickly turned off the projector. I sat in the semi-darkness, daylight glowing around the edges of the blinds that had been pulled across the windows, and tried to listen to a quiet, tense discussion between the technical assistant and the project director. How had this happened? Where was the correct film? And so on. I was too shocked to react properly. All I could think was: *I thought it was me. Who was I looking at?*

From the confusion and embarrassment I sensed in the others I was left to wonder why I had not been told. When the explanations eventually came – the feelings of the families, terrible tragedy, and so on – I was not satisfied.

Who was Duncan Prentiss, whom I had thought was myself?

Then the other realizations: I was no longer unique. He had been here before me, I was a substitute.

The reality of myself contained in the film was no longer real. By his existence, Duncan Prentiss denied me mine.

That night I had the first of my killing dreams. In it I saw myself confronting the adult Duncan Prentiss, and after an argument in dreamy silence I clubbed him to death.

I dreamed of killing him just that once, but other killing dreams had followed, sometimes two or three in a year, sometimes less frequently.

The knowledge of Duncan Prentiss changed everything. Any sexual interest between Annie and myself died for good, then with an intensity that astonished me transferred itself to the girl who had died, Marie. I saw her not as dead, but as growing up beside me in this camera reality, naked with me, her body provocative, soft, available, brushing against mine, moist and yielding to my touch.

Adjacent to the killing dreams were my dreams of sex, every bit as vivid and real.

In my dreams I repeatedly killed Duncan Prentiss, just as I repeatedly ravished Marie. My dream victims, people who were unknown to me, were substitutes for them just as I had been a substitute for Prentiss.

The dreams were mere dreams, coming to me unbidden, an outlet for the obsessions that drove me. Or so I had thought until the incident with Dixie Kent.

If I had in reality killed Kent, had I also killed Prentiss? Of that event I had only a dream as evidence, and it was long ago. I had never forgotten it but at the time I had given it little real significance, thinking it to be only a dream. Since the death of Dixie Kent I wanted that uncertainty solved. I wanted proof that Prentiss had died.

Then, maybe, the dreams of rape and killing would cease.

The train finally reached my station. I rode up to street level in the swaying, creaking lift, then tried to find my bearings. I always felt lost in South London. When I walked out of the station the streets looked unfamiliar and confusing to me. I went back to the station ticket hall to look at the map of the local streets, and after a detailed search I found Lesley's road and worked out a route to it from the station.

I walked quickly, feeling I had a purpose. I had always liked Lesley; she looked much as I imagined Marie would look now.

I found the house without too much trouble, and rang the doorbell. After a pause, Lesley was there. She looked stouter than I had remembered her, greyer of hair.

I said: 'Hello, Lesley. I wonder—'

She slammed the door abruptly, making the polished brass

knocker lift and fall with a sharp banging sound. I recoiled, feeling surprised and hurt. The last time I had been here, hadn't she invited me inside? We had spent a long time discussing Marie, and our lives. Perhaps she had not recognized me after all this time, or thought I was a salesman or some other unwanted caller.

I waited indecisively for a minute or so, not wishing to force myself on her. I too disliked people calling unexpectedly on me, but I had travelled a long way across London and it would be foolish to give up if she had simply mistaken me for someone else.

I rang the doorbell again, then, to be sure I had been heard, raised and released the knocker several times.

When the door opened again there was a man standing there. I had no idea who he might be.

'May I speak to Lesley, please?' I said. 'Mrs Llewellyn?'

'What do you want?'

'You probably don't know me,' I said. 'But I'm an old friend of Lesley's, and—'

'I know all about you, Welbeck. What do you want?'

'I'd simply like to talk to Lesley for a few minutes.'

'She's not here, and doesn't want to see you.'

'Then may I—?'

I could hear Lesley's voice in the background, shouting something, either to me or to the man. He had half closed the door so that all I could see of him now was his shaded face, one shoulder and a leg.

'Go away, Welbeck, or we'll call the police.'

'I hardly see that—'

'I'm warning you, Welbeck—'

He was not yielding an inch. He was a large man, with grey, wiry hair that stood up in crisp curls from his brow. His eyes protruded. He was breathing hard.

I retreated, feeling annoyed with him. Why had he said Lesley was not there, when he knew I had already seen her and she was shouting to us from inside the house? Why should he threaten me with the police?

My last visit had been civil enough. We had not only talked about Marie but also about Duncan Prentiss, and I had even shown her some of my files. That man had not been there then. Who could he be? Lesley's husband had been dead for many years. A brother? But she and Marie had had no brothers, which was something I knew for sure.

While I worried about this I lost my way and wandered in the streets for a long time before I managed to find the Underground station. It was late in the afternoon when I returned home.

vi

This is known to have happened:

It was 1927, and Andrew Welbeck was just approaching his fourth birthday. He knew where he was being taken, because he had been going there every week from the time he had been born.

In those days the Gibbertson film was shot on Saturday afternoons because most people could not get time off work during weekdays. Andrew had only the vaguest idea of the names of the days, but one he was already sure of was Saturday. He hated Saturdays, and cried and fought with his mother all through the mornings until his father came home for lunch. They forced Andrew to eat, but he clenched his lips together and spat dribble at them, then cried again when they slapped his face and arms. He would scream on the trolley-bus going down to Moorgate, and hold back and struggle, pulling against their arms as they led him through the streets.

Once inside the large building, though, he would go into an unresisting silence, almost as if tranquillized. There was a woman who usually met them. When she was there she gave him toys to play with or hold, but he hated her as much as all the others. Once she slapped him when his mother wasn't looking. She was the one who took away his clothes and stood over him while the men pointed the lights at him and took the film. He understood about the film in a childish way, and had a kind of understanding of what was going on, but nothing about it made him care. It seemed to him to be some kind of mysterious activity that went on among the adults, for their benefit and for their reasons, and of which he was merely the object of attention.

The little girl who was also there every week was a potential ally, but she showed no interest or friendship. They were sometimes made to sit together before or after the film was shot, but then they ignored each other or fretted to be reunited with their parents. While they were actually on the rostra the parents were within sight but not within reach, standing beyond the lights and behind the technicians.

Andrew could smell the smoke from his father's pipe, a familiar smell made alien by the surroundings.

On this day in 1927, though, his father was not present. There was some kind of argument. His father had come home late from work, and for the first time Andrew went down to the trolley-bus stop with just his mother. She too seemed especially angry, jerking at his arm whenever he made a noise.

When they were inside the building his fears mounted and he started to cry, struggling against his mother's hand. When the woman with the toys appeared he screamed, and as his clothes were taken away from him he tried to cling on to them, pulling ineffectually against the woman's superior strength. In the middle of this his bowels voided, and he was slapped again and taken away to be cleaned. His mother was nowhere near him, talking in a quiet, tense voice to the parents of the little girl.

He had to be dragged to the rostrum, and while the bulky camera was trundled towards him the woman held him flat against the stand.

The lens of the camera was brought to within about twelve inches from his face. There was a delay while the man operating the equipment made some adjustments. One of the lights was moved to the side. The woman was holding Andrew down against the bare wooden stand, one of her hands pressing his shoulder in place. Her scented arm crossed in front of his eyes, blocking his view of the camera.

'Hold still, Andy,' the woman said. 'If I let you go, will you be a good boy and keep very still?'

Andrew said nothing.

One of the men said: 'He's been crying again, Daisy. See if you can wipe his eyes dry.'

The woman said again: 'Will you hold still, Andy?'

'Where's my Daddy today?'

'Daddy's at home,' he heard his mother say, out of sight, out of reach. 'Do what the lady tells you.'

He felt the pressure of the woman's hand slacken as she moved back from him to reach for a swab of cotton wool. As soon as she did so Andrew saw the lens of the camera. It seemed closer to him than he had ever seen it before, black, round, shiny, looming over his face like a dark mirror.

Andrew leaned towards it, seeing movement in the reflected image. Something enlarged on the convex bulge of the glass, peering towards him as he peered towards it. He leaned further, supporting himself with an elbow. When he was two or three inches from the glass he saw the reflection of his face, distorted and curving backwards.

The woman returned to him, swab in hand. She held his head in the crook of her arm, and dabbed gently at the tears still moistening his cheeks and jaw.

Squirming in her hold, Andrew said earnestly: 'There's a face in there, I saw a face.'

'Don't wriggle so much, Andy. That's better.'

'But there's someone inside!'

The woman glanced back at the camera. 'That's a picture of you, Andy. There's nothing to worry about.'

'But I saw it!'

'Yes, yes. Now . . . I think that's all right.' She leaned away, looking towards the cameraman. 'He's ready now.'

'I don't want to see that face again –' His lower lip was trembling.

'Andy, it was only you. It's a reflection.'

But three-year-old Andrew said, 'There's a face in there.'

'It was you, Andy. Don't you understand?'

His tears forgotten, Andrew lay still against the stand, looking rigidly towards the lens. The reflected light that glinted on it now was too small to be clearly visible, but it was fixed in his mind that behind it lay a secret chamber, a closed box, a prison, and there inside it was a version of himself, hideously distorted, curving backwards, held forever inside the instrument. He listened to the whirring noise of the camera, understanding at last what it was doing. It was sucking himself out of himself and swallowing him inside.

Paralysed by this realization he waited until the camera clicked into silence, submitted quietly as his body was moved for the next shot, submitted again, waited while the little girl

223

was placed on the rostrum next to his, heard the camera whirring again, allowed himself to be moved to a new position.

And whenever he could he looked back at the lens, trying to see past the impassive glossy surface to what he now knew was the copy of himself imprisoned inside.

He went home quietly after this, but that day in 1927 held one more upheaval. They went home, he and his mother, but when they arrived they found that his father was no longer there.

vii

I was almost home after my trip to see Lesley but in the street next to the one I lived in I saw a crowd and a number of policemen in uniform. I walked down to investigate. Police cars were double-parked along the street, and orange tape had been tied across the pavement to restrict entry. Blue lights flashed on every vehicle. When I tried to get closer I was turned away by a police dog handler.

There was a derelict site just beyond, and I could see that dark-blue canvas screens had been erected around a part of it. Intrigued, I went to the local newsagent and bought a copy of the *Evening Standard*. The story was headlined on the front page: the sexually assaulted body of a young woman had been discovered among bushes on a piece of waste ground in Tufnell Park.

Excitement stirring, I deliberately read only the first two paragraphs to whet my interest, then carried the newspaper quickly home. As soon as I was safely inside my room with the door locked, I spread the paper on the table and stood over it to read the report.

The woman was thought to be a Filipino immigrant who worked as a waitress in a local pizzeria, who had not arrived home after work the previous night, and about whom the police had been making enquiries all day. The body had been found by children playing on a site where it was planned to build a small block of flats. The newspaper described the body as being 'partially naked', and that preliminary examination suggested she had been raped before being strangled. The body had been removed for forensic examination, and a police search was in progress. The newspaper warned that the killer might strike again, and advised all women in North London to be on their guard.

I felt giddy with excitement.

I thought not of the dead woman, but of Duncan Prentiss. I thought not of the struggling, frantic female body in my arms, her head jerking back against my face, her hands wrenching at my wrists, her torn dress and exposed flesh glinting at me in the light of the street lamps – I thought of Prentiss.

His had been the first killing, so long ago.

I thought of the place: a cinder path above a railway line, with a wire fence on one side and the bricks of the houses' yard walls on the other. Straight along the path in one direction was an electric light, attached to the wall of a footbridge that led across the tracks to the houses on the other side. Puddles glimmered darkly along the path, and it was raining lightly. A train must have recently gone through because a red lamp glowed dimly behind the semaphore signal close to the bridge.

A row, a noisy argument, was taking place inside one of the houses, and somebody somewhere was hammering on a large metal object. It was nowhere I had ever been in my life, except in my dreams, except in this dream.

Prentiss's appearance surprised me. I had been expecting

someone large, physically threatening. I had thought he would have a sardonic, mocking laugh, that he would affect superiority to me in every way. When I recognized him, walking along the path towards me, I saw that he was shorter than me, thinner, slightly older. He was soaked through by the rain, with dark patches spreading over the shoulders of his elderly mackintosh. He did not know who I was, and after a glance at me as we approached each other he looked away. I accosted him.

'It's you, Prentiss,' I said.

'Who the hell are you?'

'I'm Andrew Welbeck. You know who I am.'

He tried to shoulder his way past me, but I seized his arm and swung him around. I was shaking with fear.

'We've an old score to settle,' I said.

'You're crazy, whoever you are.'

He had a northern accent, which surprised me. I thought he was doing it as a taunt, and it angered me more. I jabbed him with my hand, the fingers pushing rigidly forward against his collarbone and the soft flesh around it. To feel his body gave me extra determination, and I pulled my hand back, tightening it into a fist.

He ducked, backed away, shoved past me, and with his head down began to hurry along the path in the direction he had been going. The sight of his nervous form, scuttling away from me, convinced me that he was the right man, and I ran after him. I caught up with him easily, grabbing him and swinging him around to face me. I was full of power, and knew that I held his life in my hands.

Then he shouted. 'Help me! Please *help me!*'

I bashed him hard, my fist slamming against his cheekbone and thrusting him back against the wire fence. He recoiled, shouting again for help. I knew no one could hear him, and took my time. I held him by the throat, looking around for a weapon. A few feet from us the gate to one of the backyards was open, and through it I could see a stack of old lumber piled there. I dragged Prentiss by his hair, then crouched down and took hold of a stout piece of wood.

I released Prentiss. As he backed away from me I slammed the club down on him. I missed his head. It glanced off his ear and crunched into his shoulder. I heard him gasp, and he let out a terrible yowling cry. The wood was splintering into my hand, but I swung it again, this time catching him on the side of his head. He staggered away and collapsed against the wire fence overlooking the railway cutting.

While he sprawled there I finished him off. Two hard blows against the top of his head crushed his skull, and he slumped in the puddles that lay around the bottom of the fence.

I stepped back from him to make sure no one was in sight, then using my feet I pushed him through the gap at the base of the fence until he was lying at the top of the railway cutting. I had to climb over the fence myself to make him roll down the slope. His body was loose and unwieldy and even after he had started slithering down through the long grass and weeds I had to kick him twice more to get his body under the cover of some bushes.

When it was done I scrambled back up the slope, and ran away.

As I awoke I was crossing the iron bridge to the other side, my boots making a dull echoing sound on the footway.

But then I was awake, in my own bed, in the room I called home, in Mrs Adams's house.

It was the first of my killings. A dream of death that came from my inner world, and for a long time I allowed myself to believe that that was all it was. But when other killings followed, and one at least had the conviction of reality, I began my quest for objective evidence of murder.

After solitary searching of newspaper files – inconclusive, because I hardly knew how to go about it – I eventually made contact with other criminological researchers. Most of them were amateurs like myself, but from them I learned how to sift through evidence, how to notice anomalies and inexplicable occurrences, and I began my files of the unexplained crimes, the unsolved murders, the sordid transactions of death.

Somewhere among them would be the crime that had killed Prentiss.

Now here was the Filipino waitress: a headline story, the first item in a new file.

How had that happened? All through the day the memories of my dream had been distracting me, but why had I attacked this woman? Where had it begun?

Still standing against the table, facing down towards the newspaper, I closed my eyes and tried to remember.

The dream had begun – where does any dream begin? You are just there, and it happens.

My dreams were part of a continuum, an alternative reality, parallel to my outer life, always there waiting for me to enter. There was no beginning, no end as such, simply a period in which I entered and briefly existed. Thus, my first contact with the dream was seeing the woman approach. I had been standing . . . standing in grass, a piece of corrugated iron sheeting lying rusty beside me. Beyond that, indistinct in the half-light from the street, a pile of rubble. Houses stood on one side, the road on the other. A car went by.

I saw and heard the woman in the same moment: her movement, and the distinctive clacking of metal-tipped high heels on the paving stones, made me turn my head. She was alone, wearing a dark coat and a headscarf. I moved towards her, stumbling slightly as my toe went under the sheet of iron. This attracted her attention, and after she had seen me she looked back over her shoulder as if planning to cross the road. I knew that unless I kept the initiative all would be lost, so I dashed across to her and grabbed her. She shouted something, which I did not understand.

My dreams had made me practised in my deeds. I clouted her hard across the head, then got my arm around her throat and dragged her backwards on to the patch of land. She was struggling and kicking, and so I hit her head again. I said nothing. When we were out of sight of the road I laid her on the ground and repeatedly hit her face with the flat and back of my hand. She was now only semi-conscious, so I ripped open her coat and tore at her clothes. Then I began.

There was no motive I was aware of. Do dreams have motive? There was excitement and pleasure, and a dizzying sense of power, a feeling of freedom and permissibility that I never knew in my outer world. Without motive, dreams release you from the inhibitions of life.

But this dream was different again, in a new way. It had occurred in a place I knew. It was one street away from where I lived, somewhere almost visible from my own window. Why had I killed so close to home?

I went to that window, pulled back the curtains and looked down into the road. It was all much as normal, except that at one end, partially blocking access to the street, a white police van had been parked.

I watched for several minutes, noticing that a number of men were moving from house to house, knocking on doors and speaking to the people inside. I stood back from the window, not wishing to be seen, but secure in the fantasies of my dreams.

viii

Four days after the woman's body was discovered in Tufnell Park, two plain-clothes officers from Scotland Yard's Murder Squad called at the Gibbertson Institute building in Euston Road. They interviewed the senior staff in charge of the Human Growth Observation Unit, enquiring about the participation in the project of Andrew Welbeck, currently being held for questioning about the murder. At their own request, the two officers were shown a short section of the film that was being made by the Unit.

Professor C. D. Latham, the head of the Unit, at first denied that the Institute had ever had any contact with Welbeck, but at the request of the officers he ordered a search of the records. This revealed that a child called Andrew Thomas Welbeck had been one of a number of children selected for the original project in 1923, had been photographed on a regular basis for a time, but in the end had been released because of what was described as unsuitable behaviour in front of the camera. The Institute no longer had any knowledge of the people whose contracts were cancelled while they were children.

As the project was still in progress, the police said they wished to interview the present participants, and asked for their names. Here Professor Latham refused to help, saying that unless the police could show that they had any material connection with the charges, all such information was maintained on a strictly confidential basis.

ix

When the doorbell rang I moved softly to my door and listened while Mrs Adams walked at her usual measured pace down the stairs. I was out on the landing by the time she had opened the door.

'Good evening, ma'am. We're police officers.'

'How may I help you?'

'We're making routine enquiries. You must have heard about the unfortunate young woman who was killed last night.'

'Yes, I did. How can I help?'

'It's just a formality. Could you give us the names of all the people who live in this house?'

I heard Mrs Adams give her nervous little laugh.

'Oh, that's easy,' she said. 'I live here alone. Ever since my husband died, let me see, seventeen years ago.'

'And you don't rent out any of your rooms?'

'Good heavens, no. I'm all alone here.'

There was a silence, and I waited.

Then the doorbell rang again, this time pressed for much longer. When it ceased, I heard fingers rattle the letter-box flap. From my position on the landing I could see dark shapes through the frosted-glass inlays in the door. One of them was shifting, as if impatiently.

Knowing I was safe, knowing I had nothing to fear, I went down the stairs and opened the door. I blocked the gap with my body, just as the man had done at Lesley's house. There were three people waiting: a man in civilian clothes, a uniformed constable and a policewoman.

'Yes?' I said.

'Police.' The plain-clothes man briefly held up a warrant card contained in a plastic wallet.

'Can I help you?'

'What's your name?'

I told him, and he looked at a printed list attached to a clipboard.

'You live here alone?'

'There's . . . the landlady, and four other tenants.'

'What are their names?'

'The landlady's called Mrs Adams, and – I'm afraid I don't know the names of the others.'

'They're not on the roll.' The detective turned the board away from me, as if to look at it in a better light. Then he lowered it. 'Mr Welbeck, I need to know your whereabouts last night, between the hours of eleven p.m. and three in the morning.'

'I was at home. Here.'

'Can you produce anyone to confirm that?'

'Do I have to?'

'If you can we will eliminate you from our enquiries.'

'I'm afraid I was on my own. I had an early night, and was reading in bed with the radio on.'

'Would you mind stepping out here, sir, where we can see you better?'

'Why?'

'Just do as I say.'

Taking care to pull the door to behind me, I went out on to the front step. Although the sun had set, the sky was still light and I could see all three of them clearly. I clasped my hand protectively over my wristwatch. The policewoman, who was closest to me, suddenly put her hand over her mouth and nose and turned away.

'Do you realize your face is heavily scratched, sir?' said the detective. 'How do you explain that?'

'No, I mean – I cut myself shaving this morning.'

'Open the door, Mr Welbeck. I think we'll have a look around inside.'

The uniformed constable had taken my arm, holding it firmly

in a grip I knew I could not escape from. With my free hand I passed over the keys of the house.

There, suddenly, it ended.

I was with them as they searched the house, and listened to them exclaim at what they found. I said nothing as they discovered where I had left Mrs Adams' body three years earlier.

I was impressed by the efficiency with which they radioed for assistance, and also by the speed with which more officers arrived. Soon after that I was taken away. I saw nothing of the search that followed, when my files were ransacked, the garden was dug up and the floors and partition walls of the house were dismantled. I saw the pictures in the single newspaper I was allowed, and carefully clipped out the news stories and started a file. Much of the reporting was inaccurate, in my view, and I wrote to all my correspondents, one by one, to list the discrepancies. But then, gradually, I lost interest in what was happening to me and what was being said about me.

I was elsewhere, content in my inner life, dreaming of my earlier state of innocence, trapped inside a box, looking out through a distorting lens at my outer self, naked and helpless, growing apace, thickening, ageing, decaying.

After – 'The Ament'

The word 'ament' has become archaic, as has the name of the condition suffered: amentia. Approximately comparable to dementia, amentia can be roughly defined as feeble-mindedness, or any general mental deficiency. Use of it to describe someone in the present day would almost certainly be considered to be prejudicial or negatively defining.

I came across the word when reading some of the works of F. Tennyson Jesse, the journalist, novelist and criminologist active during the middle years of the twentieth century. I found her description of a murderer as an 'ament' intriguing and unusual. I assumed what she was implying was that murder is an inherently aberrant, sociopathic act, and therefore anyone who commits murder must by definition be feeble-minded or socially deficient. Although I realized immediately that the term was outdated I stored it away mentally, as writers do, thinking it might be useful one day.

Ms Jesse's studies of crime are highly regarded, and still influential. In 1934 she wrote a fictionalized case study of the murderers Thompson and Bywaters, *A Pin To See the Peepshow*. In this she defined what she called the six categories into which murders fall: those who kill for *Gain*, *Revenge*, *Elimination*, *Jealousy*, *Conviction* or, simply, *Lust of killing*. These categories are of course not all that different from the seven deadly sins which were the subject of the book to which we were contributing.

This is probably an appropriate place to mention, if only in passing, that one of my own occasional secret pleasures, a minor deadly sin, is reading books which deal with true-life crime, especially unsolved murders or disputed guilty verdicts. There is a whole literature of speculation about the true identity of Jack the Ripper, probably the brand leader in this literary genre, but there are several other celebrated cases of wrongful conviction or apparently unsolvable mystery. (This was how I discovered Ms Jesse's remarkable work.) I graduated to the reading of these cases several years ago, after discovering and then moving on from the novels of Albert Camus and Jean-Paul Sartre. A well-argued forensic examination of faulty evidence is gripping stuff, tempting to any author who can locate an appropriate mystery, an interesting case of injustice. For these reasons I have long been interested in the fascinating case of Adolph Beck (mistaken identity), and might one day find a way of writing about him.

Before – 'The Invisible Men'

This story was written in 1973, shortly after I had completed my novel *Inverted World*. They are not alike. I was in transition as a writer, not yet established in either sense: of having any kind of reputation, or the more important one of trying to find an individual voice. This is clearer to me now than it was at the time, which I remember mostly for the long hours of work I was putting in every day. That sort of close focus removes the ability to see a perspective, a context. *Inverted World* was written to be a fairly traditional science-fiction adventure, whereas 'The Invisible Men' is a political story, speculative in nature.

It was written for an anthology called *Stopwatch*, edited by George Hay. Hay was an erratic, good-natured, idiosyncratic, infuriating, barmy, lovable genius: his ideas and words tumbled out so quickly it was hard to keep up with him. In the 1970s he seemed to be everywhere: giving interviews on commercial radio stations, trying to make scientists talk to writers, and vice versa, setting up an academic Foundation for the study and application of science fiction (the Science Fiction Foundation is still in existence, at the University of Liverpool), trying to get film producers to make more science-fiction movies, and from time to time putting together anthologies of short stories which he intended should contribute to or perhaps elucidate his maze of wonky ideas and initiatives.

His editorial brief for *Stopwatch* was subversion, which in some ways is a narrowing of possibility for a writer, but at the same time is an open field: all good literature subverts. In his idiosyncratic, erratic, barmy (etc.) introduction to the published book, George Hay said of my story that it 'kicks you in the political backside', and recommended 'escapologist readers' to give it a miss.

Stopwatch appeared in a hardcover edition from New English Library in 1974, and was reprinted as a paperback a year later.

The Invisible Men

While I was waiting for Charles Greystone to arrive, my attention was drawn by the sight of a man repainting the hull of a sailing yacht that was resting supported on its keel, close to the edge of the mudflats. He was about fifty yards from where I stood and was taking no notice of me. He stood with his back to me beside the rounded wooden hull, carefully applying a coat of sea-blue paint. What attracted my particular interest was the fact that whenever he leaned across to dip his brush in the pot his shirt was stretched tight across his back, revealing a sinister-looking bulge beneath the pit of his left arm.

Greystone had warned me he might be delayed, although there was no doubt he would keep the appointment. This meeting was of equal importance to us both and we had had to delay prior engagements in order to make the time for this. I assumed that he was on his way after having arranged for a car breakdown, or some similar excuse.

The mud flats at Blakeney – this village where we had agreed to meet – had once been a bird sanctuary. Here, on the Norfolk coast some miles to the east of the Wash, the sea was shallow and over the centuries silt from the rivers Ouse and Nene had built up along the coastline to form a maze of narrow waterways and lagoons running between banks of grass-topped mud. I had been told that not many years before this had been a regular sanctuary for migrating geese, but now there were few birds of any kind to be seen. There were dozens of drilling rigs in this part of the North Sea – although not visible from Blakeney quay – and the damage from a big spillage a few years earlier had poisoned the flats. The Department of the Environment had instigated a cleaning programme, but as yet there was no outward sign of any large-scale return of wildlife.

I paced to and fro on the quay, feeling conspicuous in the anorak and sailing cap I had borrowed from my son. I felt sure that someone would recognize me, even though Greystone had assured me that his staff would take care of security.

The man painting the yacht stood up and stretched. He clambered down from the hull and walked around to the other side, carrying his pot of paint. He bent down so that he was partly out of view, reaching through the doorway of the cabin. It was obviously some time since the boat had last been paid any attention. The metal rail around the edge of the upper deck had rusted and several of the cabin windows were broken. Some of the rigging was still in place and I noticed that a length of bright new wire had been stapled to the mast. This, and the still wet paint, was the only sign that anyone had been near the yacht in five years.

More yachts were parked further away, where a dirt path led out across the mud flats. These too were neglected, their rigging clacking in the stiff breeze from the sea.

In a few moments the man came round the hull again, climbed up to his former position, and continued with his painting. Although I was the only person standing on the quay, not once did he even glance in my direction.

I looked at my watch: we were ten minutes beyond the appointed time. No less than Greystone, my available time was short. I was due to address a political meeting at Sleaford in the evening and would have to return to the scientific research station at nearby Walsingham in under an hour to take the helicopter.

In spite of time being short, and the present circumstances that had made this meeting necessary, my mood was not grim. What had happened to me in the last ten days was – for the man who occupied the highest political office in Britain – possibly the worst imaginable disaster, and yet my mind was more untroubled than at any time I could ever remember. Perhaps it was because of the certainty, beyond doubt, that this was the end of my political career – in some respects a relief. Possibly there were other factors. The masquerade of putting on the casual clothes which Greystone had insisted on, the sequence of contrived accidents stage managed to give us both about an hour of stolen time, the prospect of what would happen to me after tomorrow: all these were contributing to my present feeling of a sort of heady unreality.

The village, too, seemed to be as starkly prepared as a stage-set. There were too few people about. Apart from the man working on the yacht I could see only two other people: one was a man standing with a glass of beer in the doorway of the local pub, and the other was stretched out along a ladder, apparently repairing the tiles of a roof. There were one or two parked cars on the quay, but none, as far as I could see, had anyone inside.

I stared out across the mud flats. The man continued with his painting.

A few minutes later I saw Charles Greystone walking along the quay towards me. He was wearing a Harris Tweed jacket, open-neck shirt and slacks. As he came up to me I heard a tile skid down the roof, and a second later it shattered on the pavement below.

'Harry! Good to see you!' Greystone pumped my hand.

'Shall we walk?' I said.

'This way.'

Where the main street of the village came down at a right angle to join the quay, a broad area of concrete had been laid, leading to the edge of the mud flats. From here the dirt path I had noticed earlier led alongside one of the narrow waterways towards the distant sea. It was cooler out here, and I zipped up the front of the anorak.

I noticed that the man with the paintbrush had once again moved around to the cabin and was standing with his head inside the doorway. As Greystone and I passed within ten yards of the upturned yacht, he straightened. He was holding a can of beer. He sat down and leaned against the hull, staring absently towards the village.

'It's going to be OK, Harry. I've cleared everything.'

'What do you mean?' I said.

'I've fixed it that we'll both give separate press conferences tomorrow. Later in the week we'll release written statements to the newspapers.'

I admired Charles Greystone more, I think, than any other man I had ever known. It was not only chance that had brought us to the present state of joint overall responsibility for the British government. His appointment as head of the American economic delegation was mostly as a result of my influence. We had worked well together in the five years I had been in office, and for four and a half of those years Greystone had been with me in London.

'What good would a statement do?' I said. 'We can't change what has already happened.'

'No, but it will bring it into the open.'

'And that would be an answer?'

We were now about five hundred yards from the village. I noticed another man. He was sitting in a small dinghy, holding a fishing rod. He had his back turned towards us, and did not look in our direction.

'We've broken the law, Charles,' I said. 'There's nothing to be done about that except take the consequences.'

'You want to go to jail?'

'Not particularly.'

'Then we have to bluff this thing out. The law was broken by us inadvertently, not by intent. The real culprits have been arrested and will be charged tomorrow. You and I are both honourable men.'

'You still believe that?' I said.

As we passed the man in the dinghy both of us had lowered our voices. He seemed, however, quite unaware of our presence. As we walked, I was keeping an eye open for other people. The only person I could see was a middle-aged woman with a dog, walking slowly towards us along the path.

'Listen, Harry, the frauds were organized and carried out by subordinates.'

'We're responsible for their actions.'

'But not to carry the can for them.'

'I think we are,' I said.

I glanced over my shoulder. We were now about a hundred yards beyond the man in the dinghy, but he had set aside his rod and was rowing slowly down the channel behind us. The woman approaching us along the path was less than two hundred yards away.

I noticed a second path, leading away from the channel and across the flats towards the next waterway.

'Let's walk this way, Charles,' I said.

'What the hell for?'

I didn't answer but took the other path. After a few moments' hesitation Charles followed.

I said: 'Did you know they've coined a new word?'

'Who have?'

'The tabloids. To "murdochize". If it means anything it describes putting economic expediency before political responsibility. In the left-wing press it also means to look to American finance for support. I've joined Charles Boycott and Thomas Bowdler, neither of whom I much admire.'

I was Harold Murdoch, Prime Minister of the United Kingdom.

'So that's a problem? Politicians have always been the whipping boys of the press. Back in the States I was known as the Pusher. It doesn't mean a thing.'

'It has done to me.'

There was a rise of ground ahead of us and we walked up the sloping path to its summit. We halted for a moment and I took the opportunity to look back. The man in the dinghy was standing up, staring in our direction.

As soon as he realized I had spotted him he bent over a small outboard motor in the stern and pulled the starting cable.

The engine fired at once and he sat down, steering the dinghy down the waterway towards a broader expanse of water which would take him, by a long route, to the other side of the mud flat we were crossing.

The woman with the dog had not changed direction and was still walking slowly towards the village.

Greystone said: 'You and I have to agree what to do.'

'You've made up your mind?'

'Yes I have. What about you?'

I nodded. 'I made up my mind even before this was brought to my attention.'

'What have you decided to do?'

'There's no alternative. I have to resign. I've already drafted my letter to the king.'

'For God's sake, Harry! There's no need for that!'

'Lower your voice,' I said.

As we walked down the further slope we came across a young couple who were sitting close together in the long grass. The young man was wearing a dark suit that seemed to me to be quite inappropriate for flirtatious activities here – I could see flecks of dried mud on his sharply tailored jacket – and the woman was wearing a dress of bright yellow material. To me it looked like the same shade of yellow used by one of the opposition parties. We had apparently surprised them because as soon as we appeared the woman reached over hastily to a radio, and turned a knob on its side. In a moment I heard snatches of music.

'Harry, don't quit now. You're by far the best man for the job.'

'Not any more, I'm afraid. There will always be a stain on my reputation.'

'But don't you see there needn't be? OK, if you like we're both morally responsible for what happened, but that's no reason to throw in every damned thing. Act positively . . . that's what has gotten you to where you are today. You have the power and the position to fight back. Go on TV, make a statement to the House. Deny all knowledge or responsibility and challenge your opponents to prove otherwise. Or, if you prefer, admit it was a mistake, apologize for the slip and drop a hint that you might have to resign. Come to think of it, that's probably the best way. The people will back you to the hilt.'

'Maybe so, Charles,' I said. 'You're probably right, but I couldn't do that. I would know I was obstructing justice.'

'It's the only way.'

'And that's what you intend to do?'

'Yes . . . with you or without you. I'd rather have you at my side but if I have to go it alone I'll fight for what I see as the truth.'

'Even as you admit to me you're guilty of a misdemeanour.'

'A technical misdemeanour,' he said.

We walked on.

As Greystone once more went over his attitude to the consequences of the fraud, my mind was occupied with other matters. I had been considering the possibility of resignation for a long time: I had no feeling of mandate any more, and only the sincere belief that I alone could retain some sense of independence for my country had delayed the decision thus far.

The Anglo-American Economic Recovery Program (AMERP) was my master, and Charles Greystone, as its Director, my superior. I knew, although precious few members of the Cabinet did, that within five years the last ties with Europe and the Commonwealth would be severed, and that from then it was only a matter of time before Britain became the fifty-first State of the Union.

'We have only to stand up and name names,' Charles was saying. 'Tell me why you can't do that.'

'There's no reason,' I said. 'Not now the *sub judice* rule has been suspended. There's always the risk of libel. That Act at least is still on the statute book.'

'You're old-fashioned, Harry. And you Brits have always been hung up on *sub judice*. What's wrong with an open court hearing?'

'Never mind.'

The path came to an end by the edge of the next waterway and we halted, looking along the bleak, ugly coastline towards Cley, the next village. In a few moments I heard the distant sound of a small engine and saw the dinghy sailing around the mud headland. The man steering it already held the fishing rod extended in his hand.

'Let's walk back,' I said, and without waiting for Charles I headed back in the direction we had just come.

The dinghy swung around sharply, and chugged back towards the headland.

'How are you fixed for time?'

'A few more minutes,' I said.

'What do you hope to achieve by resigning?'

I considered this for a moment. 'It would enable me to retain whatever personal honour I can put together from the wreck.'

'It would also be an admission of guilt.'

'Not necessarily,' I said. 'What about you? What would you achieve by making your position public?'

'I would clear my name.'

'Even though in private you admit technical culpability.'

There was no sign of the couple as we passed the spot in which we had seen them, but in a moment I caught a sight of the young woman in the yellow dress. She was the only flash of colour in sight. She was alone now and hurrying towards the village. I wondered what had become of her boyfriend.

'Harry, to resign now – at this point in time – would only make people wonder what else you were hiding. I suggest you come under public scrutiny with the palms of your hands spread wide.'

'And look people in the eye and admit I was an accessory to a billion-pound fraud? Then afterwards I go back to Downing Street and expect them to believe that I am still a responsible minister? Listen, Charles, you called me old-fashioned just now. Maybe you're right, but I'd rather think of myself as a traditionalist. It's British tradition for a public figure to resign his position if caught in the wrong.'

We had reached the original waterway and I went over to one of the beached sailing yachts and leaned against its side. Over my head the wind rattled through the taut rigging. Greystone stood near me, his hands thrust deep into his trouser pockets. I looked beyond him to where the waterway opened out.

In a minute or two the dinghy rounded the headland once more and chugged steadily towards the village. I watched it idly, wondering whether to suggest to Greystone that we should once more walk back across the flats. Suddenly, the young man jumped out from the side of the path. He crouched low and waved to the man in the dinghy. Immediately, the boat steered over to him. As the dinghy scraped its bottom in the shallows the young man shouted something, then clambered into the boat.

Once more it headed in our direction. By the time it passed us the two men had changed places. The young man was steering the dinghy and the other was preparing the fishing rod for his first cast. The expensive radio might or might not have been in the boat with them. I could not see it.

'Harry, you're a damnable hypocrite. Do you realize that? When the chips are down you won't face up to your responsibilities.'

'Most politicians are by nature hypocritical,' I said.

'Let me tell you about you British. You have some crazy idea of honour, that it and it alone is the right thing. If honour stands in the way of truth, or facts, then that's just too bad. You and I are in identical situations, but you won't face the facts and I will. That's the difference. You run away from them and I stand up to them. You retreat into smugness, whereas I'm prepared to stand under the lights and bare my soul that the people of your country and mine may decide whether or not I'm fit to do my job.'

'Some things are better left unknown.'

'You aren't in a position to decide that.'

'Who is?' I said. 'The gutter press?'

'If necessary, yes. At least they deal in facts.'

'That's a new idea,' I mused.

We stood in silence for a minute or two. In the background I was aware that the motor had cut out, and now the dinghy was drifting slowly a hundred yards from where we stood.

'What you mean,' I said in the end, 'is that if I resign you will lose credibility.'

'If you resign it will make the quest for the truth that much more difficult. But the truth can't be evaded. The people you govern have a constitutional right to the facts.'

'I'm afraid they haven't,' I said. 'This country doesn't have a legislated constitution.'

'Then the sooner we write one the better,' said Greystone.

'That's what I was afraid you would say.'

We started back towards the village.

I observed that the roof repairs were now complete, for although the ladder was still in place there was no sign of the man. It also appeared that the repainting of the yacht had been abandoned half-completed.

'So you're adamant,' said Greystone.

'Yes.'

'I go through this alone.'

'Yes.'

'Don't you have any regrets?'

'None whatsoever. I won't enjoy the audience with the

king and some of my colleagues will be disappointed, but I'm already looking forward to retirement. I don't see enough of my family.'

As we walked up the sloping concrete towards the quay, Greystone made one last attempt.

'Harry – think on what you're doing. No one can do your job better.'

'I know,' I said, knowing also who would step in to take my place.

'Have you considered the long-term consequences?'

'For myself?'

'For this country.'

'I don't see that my presence is going to make any difference one way or another. I don't envy you the problem of how you will depose the monarchy, but I'm sure you'll find a way. That's what you meant, wasn't it?'

'That's what I meant,' said Greystone. 'I don't want that any more than you do.'

'It's inevitable,' I said. 'America and Britain are both in economic ruin. America will recover first because its reserves are deeper. I think you should be able to pick up the old country rather cheaply. Bankrupt stock is usually sold off to the first bidder, not the highest.'

'You sound as if you are resigned to it.'

For the first time since Greystone had arrived my temper weakened.

'I've been having to live with the prospect for years,' I said. 'Gradually, I've seen my country being turned into a suburb of yours. I'm not going to say whether I think that's a good thing or a bad, but I will say this: No, I'm not resigned to it because it will not, in the end, be the answer. Your system of government works in America, not perfectly, but it does work. It will never work here. What's happened in the last few days has convinced me of that, and your reaction now only confirms that conviction. You can go in front of the cameras tomorrow with your palms spread wide, and maybe you'll convince a few people of your good faith. I'm not anti-American, Charles. You and I could never have worked so well together in the past if that were so. I have a deep and abiding respect for your country, but both Britain and America have changed since the time of George III. You can't introduce your country's methods here and hope for success. That's all.'

Greystone said: 'Maybe our methods would work a damned sight better than yours have done. Who is doing the bailing out?'

'Who is to say? I remember that a few years ago, when an earlier UK government tried to solve an Irish problem with British methods, that didn't work either.'

At the edge of the quay behind us, the dinghy scraped its side and the two men climbed out. Ignoring Greystone and myself they walked towards the pub on the corner. The young man was carrying the radio set.

I said to Greystone: 'Just one moment.'

I hurried over to the two men and caught the arm of the man I had first seen in the dinghy.

'Could you tell me the time, please?' I said.

He looked at me in surprise, then glanced at his wristwatch.

'Twenty minutes past four, sir,' he said, and made to move on after his companion.

'Thank you. Good fishing today?'

He shook his head, and walked on. I went back to Greystone.

'What was all that about?' he said.

'I wanted to find out if he was English or American.'

'Well?'

'English.' I looked at my own wristwatch. The man's had been ten minutes slow. 'Maybe I'm wrong in what I think, Charles. Only time will tell.'

'I've got to leave, Harry. You know where you can reach me tonight if you reconsider?'

'Yes . . . but I've made up my mind. I wish you well.'

'And I wish you well, Harry.'

We shook hands; Greystone's grip was firm and sincere.

'I'm sorry it came to this, Harry.'

'It was our own fault,' I said. 'The crime would not have happened if we'd been more alert.'

'Which crime do you mean?'

'The fraud, of course.'

Greystone released my hand, and I turned away. I headed for the main street of the village. My car would be waiting for me at the top of the hill. As I passed the pub I looked through the doorway.

The bar was closed: the blind had been put up over the counter and the lights were out. However, the people inside the pub had managed to get some drinks from somewhere, for they stood or sat inside the semi-darkened room with filled tankards. I recognized some of the people: the young man had been reunited with his girlfriend and they stood together with their backs against the counter blind. I saw the woman's dog, tied by its leash to the leg of one of the tables, but its owner was sitting at another table with the man who had been painting the yacht.

Just inside the door I saw the man who had been in the dinghy.

He was looking in Greystone's direction, speaking quietly into the radio communicator pressed to his lips.

He paid no attention to me as I stared at him and for a

moment I was tempted to go over to him and provoke some kind of petty incident. Instead, I turned on my heel and hurried after Greystone.

'One more thing, Charles!' I said to him as I caught him up.

'What?'

'From tomorrow afternoon I'll be a private citizen. Can I have your personal guarantee that your damned goons will not be hanging around me all the time?'

Greystone stared at me steadily. For a moment he said nothing and I wondered if he would have any reply at all to make.

Then he said: 'Maybe you should resign, Harry. Paranoia about imaginary enemies doesn't become you.'

The following day, in a private suite at Buckingham Palace, I watched Greystone's televised press conference. Even as he spoke openly and frankly to the newsmen jostling to place the next question, my mind held only the memory of him walking away past the looted shops and broken windows of Blakeney village, blind, or rendered blind, to the organization around him.

As often happens to an anthology of new stories, *Stopwatch* seems not to have made much of an impact. The reviews, as I recall, were few and far between – I have no idea how the sales of the hardcover or paperback editions actually fared. It was an interesting book, however. As well as my own story, there was new material from Robert Holdstock, John Brunner, Ian Watson, Ursula K. Le Guin, Josephine Saxton and David I. Masson. Even in 1974 that was a line-up of substantial and diverse talents. Most people seem to have missed it. Someone, as George Hay himself used to say characteristically, *someone ought to do something about it.*

Hindsight being the wonderful thing that it is, I can see in 'The Invisible Men' several strains of my own work, partly in stories I had already written to that date, but also in work to come. I have always been interested in what I call psychological invisibility – the person or thing that is there, physically existing and tangible, real and visible in every normal way, but which is not noticed or seen, or is not supposed to be noticed or seen.

An early story of mine called 'Transplant' was about a man who only saw what he wished to see – another from the same period, 'A Woman Naked', was about a woman punished by disallowing the rest of the world any sight of her. My novel, *The Glamour*, is about whole communities of psychologically invisible people, surviving unseen, eking a wraithlike existence on the edges of society. *The Affirmation* touches on this constantly, *The Prestige* has at one point an invisible narrator, and there are hints of psychological invisibility in parts of *The Islanders* and *The Adjacent*.

In fact, the direct and immediate stimulus for 'The Invisible

Men' came from my recent reading of a delicious short story by Graham Greene, 'The Invisible Japanese Gentlemen'. This was about a young writer blinding herself to the obvious.

Use of the name Murdoch as someone who 'placed economic expediency before political responsibility' was fortuitous. The verb 'murdochize' has not come into parlance.

Long after *Stopwatch*, George Hay and I ended up living in the same town, the seaside resort of Hastings in East Sussex. We were unaware of each other's presence for quite a while, and surprised when we eventually discovered it. George, I'm sorry to say, came prematurely to a tragic end. Hastings is threaded with 'twittens': traffic-free pathways or alleys that criss-cross behind the houses and main streets. George was walking in one of these when a car, illegally taking a short cut, collided with him at high speed. Rushed to hospital badly injured, George then suffered a heart attack – a long and difficult period of recovery began.

I went to visit him in hospital. I was amazed and gratified to discover that beneath the plaster cast and bandages, and behind the bottles and tubes and monitoring equipment, it was still the same George. Almost as soon as I arrived he was urging me to go out and put something right by *doing something about it*. He had plans, he had schemes for radicalizing the world, *if only enough people would listen!*

I urged him to relax, rest, let the doctors do their work. At first, George told me, they treated him for dementia. 'What on earth were you saying?' I said. George replied: 'I was only trying to explain why the government should set up a Ministry of Science Fiction.' He laughed at his own ridiculousness. Then he said: 'Now they're giving me Warfarin.' (Warfarin is an anti-coagulant, prescribed for heart attack patients.) 'That's used as rat poison, isn't it?' he added. We regarded each other seriously.

'Do you think they know something?' he said. 'They're talking about increasing the dose.' He laughed and laughed.

He was thought well enough to go home a few days later, but the damage was serious and he passed away not long after. Farewell, George!

Before – 'The Stooge'

'The Stooge' is another story written as a result of an unexpected commission, this time from one of the main clearing banks in the UK. Their risk management team was looking for some 'sci-fi' stories to illustrate certain important problems faced every day by main clearing banks. This is the kind of proposal that can make the heart of a writer sink like a lump of molten lead. Mine sank thus.

More details were revealed. The project involved the publication of a book containing the stories. It would be given to all members of staff, and used where appropriate as a training aid. My lump of molten lead began to solidify.

But then – the sort of problems the bank were concerned with were described. Security shredding of papers, data management, password leaks, viruses and malware, identity theft – none of them subjects that made the creative juices start pumping.

Wait a moment! I could do something with identity theft! After all, hadn't an American writer of comic books recently changed his name to mine, for reasons never made clear? I was unable to find out why he had chosen to pinch my name, out of all the possibilities. I felt I had been mugged in the street, robbed of the one thing that was inalienably mine: my name. I was the victim of perhaps the ultimate theft of identity.

I promptly signed up for the bank risk management deal, bagging the subject of identity theft before anyone else could get their hands on it.

Then came the period of contemplation: the working out of a story, the need to find a character whose story it would become, a situation, a time and a place, a point of view that was not just the airing of an old grievance.

For me identity theft had a vague but constant identification with stage magic, which of course was the subject of *The Prestige*. I did not want to go back to that, but most magicians' lives and careers are workaday affairs, unglamorous away from the bright lights, hard-working, underpaid, fraught with the possibility of things going wrong in every performance.

It's not typical of what I normally write (understatement), but 'The Stooge' is what resulted.

The Stooge

The audience was not a huge one that evening, which was reassuring. The seats closest to the stage were mostly filled, and the cheaper seats towards the back were also occupied. I was in the middle of the stalls with a handful of others. I was watching a ventriloquist trying hard to sing without moving his lips, while his unconvincing dummy stared woodenly around, opening and closing its idiotic mouth.

It was a cold November evening in 1963 and I was in the Queen's Theatre in St Albans. I had walked from the bus stop to the theatre through drizzling rain. My feet were still damp and I was stiff with nervousness.

The ventriloquist concluded his act with a song, a pathetic mock-duet with his dummy. A compere followed him on and told a few unfunny jokes, and then the next act was announced. It was *Splendido the Illusionist!* I clenched my fists, felt my heart start to race and all of a sudden I wished I could go to the lavatory.

Splendido appeared with a musical fanfare, a burst of flash-powder and a loud bang. He began his act with a flourish of brightly coloured flags and streamers, which he made to appear from nowhere. The three musicians making up the pit orchestra played noisily. Everything on the stage looked brightly lit, nowhere to hide. *Nowhere to hide!* I thought, suppressing a feeling of panic.

My fee was £10.10s.0d. I had been paid in cash, so that was all right. But now, soon, I would have to earn it. I sank a little lower in my seat.

It had begun a week earlier in a small suite of rooms above a bank in the high street of Stevenage, my home town. Along with half a dozen young men of about my age I was interviewed for a job I had seen advertised in our local paper: a magician's assistant! I had always loved magic, and saw this as a big chance.

I was the first to arrive and so I was the first to be interviewed. An attractive young woman wearing a subtle perfume led me into a separate room, where an ordinary-looking bloke with ginger hair sat at a table with some playing cards spread in a fan. The young woman left us, and the magician (I soon realized it was Splendido himself, in civvies and without make-up) performed a few basic sleight of hand tricks on me. He was good, I give him that – in fact he was very good. He did three tricks one after the other, watching me closely.

Then he said, glancing at a list at his side: 'Remind me of your name.'

'Barry Henson,' I said.

'All right, Mr Benson.' He fanned the cards across the table-top, face down. 'Choose a card, any card you like.'

I picked one and turned it over. It was the Three of Clubs. Written on it were the words: '*Harry Benson gets the job!*'

'Wow,' I said, thinking it probably wasn't the right time to point out he had got my name wrong. 'That's wonderful.'

'No,' said the magician. 'I need you to show some REAL surprise. Do it now.'

'*Wow!*' I said loudly.

'More.'

'*WOW! That's amazing!*' I shouted, leaping back from my chair with such alacrity I nearly knocked over the table.

'Perfect,' said the magician. 'Now you really do have the job. Congratulations. I want you to go with Angela, who will give you all the information you need.' The inner door opened at that moment, and the young lady appeared with a waft of her lovely scent. 'There are just two things you must remember at all times. Firstly, if I ever do any trick in front of you, you must react like that. Amazed, surprised, bowled over. Got that?'

'Yes, sir,' I said, because after all I was excited.

'Secondly, if I ask you your name, you will say "Milton". Is that clear? Your name is now Milton.'

'Yes, indeed.'

'So would you tell me your name, Mr Benson?'

'Actually, it's Barry Hen –' I saw the way he was looking at me. 'It's Milton.'

'Excellent.' He turned to the young woman. 'Angela, this is Mr Benson, whom you must now call Milton. Please tell him everything he will need to know.'

She led me through the connecting door and as she did so another applicant walked in behind me. The magician was already shuffling his cards.

The next few minutes with Angela sped by in a haze. She had wonderful brown eyes, long straight brunette hair, and a figure I would have swum the English Channel to see in a bathing suit. She kept smiling at me and narrowing her eyes when she spoke, leaning intimately towards me, sending out alluring signals I was eager to accept. Within about thirty seconds I would have worked for Mr Splendido for nothing at all, if it meant I could be close to this beautiful woman.

But she was businesslike too. She wrote down my name and address in a notebook – I told her my real name, but somehow she, like the magician, had got it irrevocably into her head that I was called Harry Benson. She smiled sweetly when I pointed it out to her, but she said: 'It doesn't matter, Harry. From now on you will be Milton.'

She gave me the fee in cash, and a ticket for a numbered seat in the stalls of the theatre in St Albans. I decided if becoming Milton or Mr Benson was what was required, then I would do it.

Just as I was about to leave, she murmured: 'Milton, I wonder if you would try something for me?'

I nearly shouted *Anything!*, but managed instead to say: 'OK. What is it?'

She led me across the room to where there was a vertical arrangement of three light planks, joined with hinges. As I followed her, there was an abrupt scraping noise of a chair from the next room, and someone shouted (feebly, I considered): 'GOSH!'

Angela asked me to stand next to the planks, then swung the outer ones across me, bringing the two edges together. In fact they clouted against my shoulders, and were prevented from closing.

'Would you turn to one side, Milton?'

I complied, and at once the two edges met neatly.

She released me and once again I saw that devastating combination of narrowed eyes and a secret smile, promising, or so it seemed, everything.

'Just wonderful,' she said. 'See you next week, then?'

From the next room I heard a crash of a table falling over, and a voice shouting: '*God Almighty, that's just BRILLIANT, Mr Splendido!*' There was a silence.

'He's overdoing it,' said Angela breathily. 'Most of them do.' Her warm hand lightly squeezed mine.

In St Albans, I huddled in my lonely stalls seat while Splendido performed magic. Angela was up there with him, wearing a skimpy stage costume: a glitter of sequins, a fragment of fabric here, two even more microscopic fragments there, no visible means of support anywhere else. She was in fact what I would have swum the Channel to see. I stared at her, absolutely and finally in love.

'Now I wonder,' boomed Splendido from the footlights. 'Would some brave young man care to step up on stage and assist me with my next illusion?'

The house lights came on. The audience started looking around, wondering who would be reckless enough to volunteer. A chap about three rows in front of me stood up, raising his hand. Splendido appeared not to notice. Another young man also stood up. I realized Angela had moved to the side of the stage and was looking directly at me.

Strewth! This was it!

I stood up, my knees suddenly shaking.

'Ah, a hero from among us!' said Splendido into his microphone. A spotlight found me, a glare of whiteness. I sidestepped along the row, then down the aisle. The pit orchestra played loudly. Angela hurried along the stage to the steps up from the auditorium. As I climbed them, she leaned forward suggestively with the spotlight on her, and I thought I would stop breathing.

She said softly through her stage smile: 'You look great, Harry. Do what he says, and we will meet later!'

Then she released me, and I was on my own.

'What's your name, sir?' said Splendido splendidly.

'Er – Milton.'

'Good! Let me show you something, Milton.'

From nowhere at all, he pulled a live dove from inside my shirt! ('*Wow!*' I shouted in amazement.) A rabbit came from my trouser pocket! ('*How did you do that?*' I yelled.) There was a trick with a flame, some razor blades, a billiard ball. I reacted with wonder and amazement each time.

Then he moved to a tall cabinet and trundled it forward on wheels. There was a door at the front and another at the back, so when they were both open it was possible for the audience to see through. He swivelled it around on its wheels.

'If you would be so kind, my dear . . . ?' He was holding the front door open and I saw a flash of sequins as Angela stepped inside, smiling broadly. 'Now you, Milton?'

I realized I was supposed to join her inside. The drummer in the pit set up a loud roll, and I crammed myself into the cabinet next to her.

For a few heavenly seconds I was pressed sensuously against Angela's voluptuous and almost naked body. A sequinned something, very soft, lay against my arm. I could feel her breath! Her hair tickled the side of my face! Splendido slammed the door at the back, slammed the door at the front and Angela and I were squeezed together in total darkness.

What then happened was so quick I hardly knew what was going on.

We were in complete darkness. The drum rolled ever more loudly. The cabinet was spun around. Angela was doing something to the wall behind me and there was a sliding sensation and a quick thud. I was suddenly contained inside a narrow triangular space, just the same as the one I had tried during the interview.

The band played a loud flourish, the front door opened, there was a burst of wild applause . . . and I was still trapped inside the secret compartment!

Angela was parading to and fro, across the stage.

I could barely move, but there were some tiny air holes close to my face. Peering through these I could not clearly see anything outside, but light from the stage was pouring into the now empty cabinet. The audience was still cheering and whistling and laughing. Mostly whistling!

I raised myself up, and peered down at the cabinet floor.

Lying there, lit by the theatre spotlights, were three tiny triangles of cloth, covered in sequins.

After the audience quietened down, and the band played the National Anthem, a lot happened at once. I saw nothing because I was still locked inside the cabinet. From time to time I made a series of pathetic crying noises ('Help!', 'I'm stuck inside here!', 'Let me out!', and again and again, 'Help!').

The stage lights went out. I was still trapped. ('Let me out!')

Two or three men moved the cabinet with me inside; it was dragged out of the theatre and after a lot more shifting, bumping and grunting they loaded it on the back of a van. I remained trapped. ('Help!') It was cold and dark and still raining. The van drove away, lurching horribly. I was still inside, banging from side to side. I was terrified the cabinet would fall over with me inside. ('Can anyone hear me?') I could hear other vehicles rushing by.

After a long time the van stopped, and two or three men moved the cabinet again. I was still there, and I wanted to go to the lavatory.

'Help!' I cried, but no one answered.

Eventually the cabinet stopped moving and something behind

me clicked. The hidden compartment came loose, and at last I could push my way out.

I had been deposited in someone's flat. As I stepped out of the cabinet the door to the flat slammed, and someone locked it from the outside. I was still trapped but at least now I was in a real place.

There was a toilet, food, drink, a shower, a sofa, a television, books, records. And a note. It was lying on the carpet in front of the cabinet.

It said: *Dear Milton (or may I call you Harry?). Make yourself at home! Don't worry about a thing. All you MUST do is climb inside the cabinet again at 6 p.m. tomorrow. It closes automatically. You will absolutely LOVE what you and I are going to do next! Angie. XXX.*

The 'O' in the word 'LOVE' was heart-shaped, and glued into the middle of it was a sequin. Beneath the note there was another £10.10s.0d.

I trapped myself inside the secret compartment well before 6 p.m., and waited. A similar sequence of events then followed, in which I was driven uncomfortably to another theatre. This time I hardly minded, already dreaming of what Angela, Angie, might be planning.

The evening did tend to drag by, because I had to stay inside the cabinet while the rest of the show went on, and I eventually realized that Splendido was top of the bill. It was a long wait in the cramped space.

Finally, though, Splendido's act began. Trapped as I was inside the cabinet I could see nothing but an occasional glint of light, but I heard everything: the bangs and the music and the applause.

Then he announced loudly: 'Would some brave young man care to step up on stage and assist me with my next illusion?'

There was a short delay, until I heard footsteps.

'What is your name, sir?'

'I'm Milton,' said a voice.

Milton! But that was me. My name had been pinched. If this chap was Milton, who was I?

Harry, Barry, Milton – all taken from me!

I waited, trying to imagine what was going on – I visualized doves and billiard balls and sudden flames. From time to time I heard a voice say, rather unconvincingly: 'Gosh!'

Then at last, at last! The moment I had been waiting for.

I felt the cabinet being trundled forward, heard the rising roll of a drum, felt the cabinet shaking as Splendido opened the doors at back and front. Then, just as I had been fantasizing all day, someone else clambered into the cabinet beside me. I detected the lovely, subtle perfume Angela always wore.

And she said quietly, just audible above the drum: 'Hi, Harry darling! You ready?'

'You bet,' I replied, delirious with anticipation.

'Ssh! Not too loud! Relax, and let me give you the time of your life.'

The back door slammed closed! The front door slammed closed! Splendido started rotating the cabinet for the audience to see . . . but inside a lot was suddenly happening.

In the total darkness I felt the hidden compartment click open. Instantly, I was released and pressing against Angela in the cramped interior. I felt her soft flesh, the rough scrape of sequins, her light breath, the brush of her hair against the side of my face.

She was touching me! Here, there, here again . . . all rather rudely. In fact, very rudely!

I couldn't tell what she was doing, except I liked it. There was no time to enjoy the press of her naughty hands, because –

I heard the secret compartment close, and in the same instant the main door of the cabinet burst open. I stumbled out, alone, blinking in the blaze of stage lights. The drums thundered, music burst forth.

I was aware of Splendido standing beside me, his arm raised theatrically. On the other side was a young man in everyday clothes.

He said, loudly, but rather unconvincingly: 'Oh gosh, that's *amazing!*'

But the trick was not over. The cabinet opened again, and now Angela burst out into the glare of lights. She was stark naked. She strode bravely across the stage. The audience roared its approval, laughing and clapping. Many of the men were whistling. The music was all around.

Angela came to me, took my hand and led me to the footlights to take a bow. The cheering redoubled.

I looked down at myself. I was wearing my normal clothes, but somehow, in some inexplicable way, I was now wearing extra garments on top of them.

Three tiny triangles of fabric, covered in sequins. Two were tied across my chest, one was around the front of my trousers.

I said, I couldn't help saying it: 'BLOODY HELL!'

The audience was roaring enthusiastically. Many of the men were standing up, waving their arms, shouting and whistling. Many others were laughing.

Angie strode past me in her glory – everything about her was dazzling, including her stage smile. As she swept past, inches away from me, she spoke without moving her lips.

'You're overdoing it, Harry!' she said. 'Bye now!'

She speeded up, taking two or three quick steps, then with athletic style leapt towards the new Milton. He caught her in a practised and elegant movement, cradling her in his arms.

(Practised? They had been *rehearsing*?) Angie pressed her face to his, planting a luscious kiss on his cheek.

He hurried past me, carrying Angie, moving quickly from the stage, into the wings, out of sight, away to somewhere I could not go.

Behind me Splendido took a bow.

The curtain came down, also behind me. I was alone.

After – 'The Stooge'

Uncertainty attends this story. I'm not sure about anything to do with it – what I and the bank understood as identity theft was probably not much the same. Come to that, I've never been entirely sure what the risk management team at the bank actually thought of my mildly racy version of identity theft. I don't think it was what they had in mind – but who knows? They accepted it quickly, without comment, and the book was duly published.

And another thing: I was not at all sure what a risk management team might be like in reality. The title made me nervous but they turned out to be convivial, amusing and generous people, who were good company and who took many of us contributors to a luxurious dinner one evening in Canary Wharf.

Not everyone who had written for the project turned up for that meeting, but among my fellow contributors to the book were Roger McGough, Ricky Gervais, Conrad Williams, Simon Tofield (*Simon's Cat*), and Alastair Reynolds. Because the book was published in-house it is almost certainly difficult to find or buy a copy – the title is *Consequences*, should anyone wish to try.

This is therefore the first time 'The Stooge' has been published in the mainstream.

The use of a stooge in a magical act is regarded as legitimate by most professional magicians, but in recent years it has fallen from favour. Members of an audience are frequently invited to step up to the stage and assist in an illusion, but in almost every case the volunteers will be genuinely unprepared, genuinely unknown previously to the performer.

It has happened to me – it's an unusual experience, to say the least, to have an apparently ordinary table fork placed in your hand by a magician, then to feel it bending and twisting itself into knots, the tines spreading themselves like a claw opening.

One of the aspects of magic I like most is the laughter it induces. People love to see magic, especially live magic, even more so if they are close up. They find it baffling and amusing, and some of the best magic acts are essentially comic turns. Verbal wit and manual dexterity seem to go together. Perhaps this was what 'Splendido' was doing wrong, and a clue to what was soon to precipitate his inevitable decline, even from the fading variety shows in provincial theatres that were his last hope. He used magic to baffle but not to amuse.

In the era in which the story is set, the early 1960s, British theatres still clung to the theory that the music halls might revive – I have depressing memories of going to a few of the tawdry shows myself at the time, when much of my working life was spent away from home, staying in second-rate hotels in provincial towns and cities. The evenings had to be filled with something. The regular fare included comedians, jugglers, dancers, ventriloquists, crooners, performing dogs . . . and illusionists. No doubt the performers were poorly paid, and for a touring magician like 'Splendido', a stooge would be an inexpensive way of working an illusion.

Before – 'futouristic.co.uk'

When as a teenager I first encountered American science fiction, I soon gravitated towards the work of writers like Robert Sheckley, William Tenn, Frederik Pohl, Richard Matheson. I had read the older 'classics' of SF (Asimov, Heinlein, etc.) but to a large extent those writers seemed to be interested in the wrong things: empires, armies, engineering, big business, and so on. I was more attracted to the writers who had emerged in the 1950s, influenced not so much by the terrible pulp magazines of the past, but by the sharper, laidback, more socially satirical modern markets like *Esquire, Bluebook* and *Playboy*.

When I began writing, still in my teens, Robert Sheckley's witty, surprising and plot-driven stories were my great inspiration. I wished to follow in his footsteps.

It was not to be. It's the work of every writer to find and develop his or her own voice, and much as I loved Sheckley and Tenn's mordant humour, Pohl's incisive satires, and Matheson's ingenious modern horror stories, they never came naturally to me. I wrote what I wrote, and have always done so.

The wish has never left me, though. Once or twice in this lifetime the opportunity to write a Sheckley-style social satire has arisen, at the same time as I have discovered an idea for a story that might fit. 'The Stooge' came fairly close, but 'futouristic.co.uk' came closer.

It came about from a BBC Radio 4 commission. They were planning a series of afternoon readings called *Perspectives*. The idea of the story came from thinking up the URL, which immediately became irresistible. The story was read aloud on the BBC one happy afternoon in the summer of 2009.

futouristic.co.uk

I finally gave in and opened the email. A copy of it had been arriving every day for the last two weeks. Everything about it warned me it was spam, probably carrying a deadly virus that would worm its way into my computer memory and trash everything it found. But in the end I thought a quick peek wouldn't matter.

Every day for those two weeks the same header had appeared in my inbox: *Lowest price Time Machine 4U?* Every day for two weeks I had deleted it, along with the offers of pills that would improve my sex life, the proposed deals with wealthy African businessmen and never-again opportunities to lose my money in an online casino.

But then I could stand it no more and gave in to temptation. I clicked 'Open' and read the email.

To my surprise, the message itself was addressed to me in person. My surname is Frogle. Most people can't spell it, let alone remember it. It was unusual for someone to get it right at the first attempt.

The email was from an outfit called futouristic.co.uk and it contained an image of an alleged time machine. The thing looked rather like a mobile phone, with four recessed wheels instead of a keypad.

The email began like this:

Dear Mr Frogle,
Let me assure you straight away that this is a genuine offer. The
time machine we sell really does work, and will carry you safely to
past or future, as you wish. If you want to see a live demonstra-
tion, all you have to do is click on this link now:
http://www.futouristic.co.uk/

Beneath the opening paragraph was a cartoon picture of a
clock, the hands drawn to look as if they were whizzing around.
The message continued below:

Please click on the clock logo whenever you wish. Try it NOW,
in FIVE MINUTES, in FIVE WEEKS . . . or even in
FIVE YEARS. We already know the exact moment when you
will try. No matter when you choose, you will IMMEDIATE-
LY receive the pleasant surprise of a lifetime.

Following this there was a long paragraph of technical information: I glimpsed incomprehensible details about nanoseconds,
displacements, paradox suppressors, temporal quantifiers, di-
mensional tolerance, and so on.

I looked back thoughtfully at the logo of the clock, wondering what might really happen if I clicked on it.

Resisting that new temptation I walked into the kitchen,
made myself some coffee, then sat again at my desk.

I stared at the logo in the email. The palms of my hands were
moist. A time machine? Seriously? It must be a confidence trick
of some kind . . . surely time travel is impossible? But then, the
more I thought about it the more I realized I was captured. I
did want to buy one!

My hand rested on the mouse, and I took the pointer to the clock. My finger itched to make a move.

I looked again at the email:

Witness the Battle of Agincourt! Watch the launch of Gagarin's rocket! Find out what really happened on 9/11! Be present at your own birth!

And finally:

Make yourself RICH – legally!

That was enough for me. Rich? I had never been rich. I clicked the mouse button and the clock cartoon changed instantly to a photo of a real clock.

At that exact moment my doorbell rang. A long, continuous ring . . . then again.

I tore myself away from the computer and went to the street door. A man was standing there, dressed entirely in white. He also had pale skin, white hair and the shiniest teeth I had ever seen. He was holding a little instrument that looked just like a mobile phone. Plastic-covered wires ran up from it and were clipped to his ear lobes.

He had a newspaper folded under his arm.

There was something familiar about his appearance, something haunting . . . and deeply worrying. We stared at each other, stared back. He seemed as surprised as me.

He seemed to be me. It was like staring into a mirror. We both opened our mouths to speak, then closed them again.

Then he said: 'Ah!'

'"Ah"?' I replied. Then I thought about it carefully, and after much consideration said: 'Ah!'

'This wasn't quite what I was expecting,' the man said. 'May I ask: is Gwendolyn Labelle available to come to the door?'

'Never heard of her,' I said.

'Does she live here?'

'Never heard of her,' I said stubbornly. I was starting to suspect this might be a joke, a stunt put on by a television show, or perhaps even an advertising campaign. I looked past the man into the street, but could see no sign of any cameras or microphones. 'Look . . . who are you, and what's going on?'

'I need to speak quite urgently to Gwendolyn Labelle. If she is here, please let me see her at once.'

'She is not here, has never been here, and therefore there is no way you can see her or speak to her, or anything.'

The man stepped back a little, glanced up at the walls and windows of my house, then frowned again. He reached into his pocket and took out a small plastic card, which he scrutinized intently. He returned it to his pocket, but for a few seconds continued to stare thoughtfully into the space where it had been.

'Is this the town of Sunderland, by any chance?' he said.

'Sunderland? No – that's at the other end of the country.'

'Oh dear.' He looked again at the card from his pocket. 'I think there might be a small problem.' He stared up at me, as if noticing me properly for the first time. Our faces were not far apart, and although his clothes and general appearance were exceedingly strange he looked so uncannily like me that I could hardly keep breathing. 'May I ask your name?' he said, after a moment.

'Frogle,' I said. 'Mitchell Frogle.'

He stepped back sharply, and took the newspaper from under his arm.

'My goodness, what a calamity! But never mind . . . I am paid by my company to use my own initiative, and this problem is not without a solution. I think I know exactly what to do. Kindly wait just a moment.'

He raised the electronic instrument that looked like a mobile phone, and jabbed his thumb against the touchscreen. I can hardly describe what happened then . . . but he seemed to *flicker*. He was there, he was not there, he was there again!

He still had the electronic instrument that looked like a mobile phone in one hand and a newspaper in the other, but this time I immediately realized that it was a copy of the *Gazette*, the local paper published in town. The one he had been holding before had apparently disappeared, or had been replaced.

'Ah!' he said again. 'Mitchell Frogle, I presume?'

'You know it is.'

'I do apologize for the little mix-up you had to endure just now. Most unfortunate. The only thing I must ask, to avoid any possible recurrence of such a problem, is that you forget everything that just happened. Please?'

'You mean forget about Gwendolyn Labelle who lives in Sunderland?'

'Yes! I mean – whatever it was. Never heard of her myself.' He flexed his shoulders, stood square to face me. The physical resemblance between him and myself was astonishing. 'Let's do this right at last,' he went on. 'It is wonderful to meet you in person, Mr Frogle! My name is Mitch and I am from a radical new corporation called futouristic.co.uk. I have brought you your new time machine.'

He held up the little electronic device that looked like a mobile phone.

★

I led Mitch into my kitchen and made him a cup of coffee. Like me he took it without milk, and with a tiny helping of sugar. Now we were out of the glare of sunlight and in the familiar surroundings of my own home, I was disconcerted by his pale appearance, his endless, flashing smile, but most of all by the way he looked.

He began a sales spiel: witnessing the Battle of Agincourt, and all that.

I interrupted him. 'Mitch,' I said. 'I am intrigued by the idea of having a time machine, but I'm concerned there's a catch.'

'OK,' said Mitch. 'Admittedly, you do have to buy the time machine from us. And it's not cheap. However, now that you are wealthy the price should not be a problem.'

'I'm not wealthy,' I said.

'Mr Frogle, after you win the lottery on Saturday you will be very rich indeed.'

'But I never buy tickets. Lotteries are against my principles –'

'Maybe your principles would be less strict if I told you the six numbers that are going to win the jackpot this week.'

Mitch unfolded the copy of our local newspaper and showed me the front page. The headline said, *Local man scoops the jackpot!* I looked at the text of the article with dazed eyes. The words 'Frogle' and 'lottery' and 'jackpot' and 'millions' leapt out at me.

'This is next week's issue, which I bought just now,' Mitch said. 'I popped into the future, next Friday, in fact, and picked it up for you to see. The jackpot this week will only be just over six million pounds, but that's not bad. The catch, as you describe it, is that we charge you a commission of ten per cent of your winnings. But the rest is yours to keep.' He tapped his finger significantly on his little electronic device. 'Do we have a deal, Mr Frogle?'

I admit that I did hesitate. Deep suspicions still lurked within.

'How can you guarantee a lottery win?' I said.

The smile appeared again, with a dazzle of teeth. 'Let's say practice makes perfect.'

'You've done it before?'

'Yes. Well, not every week. We have to find a suitable customer first and people like you don't come along all the time. But when they do –' He coughed modestly. 'You will be, let me see, our seventh jackpot winner this year. We are a business, and we do try to make a profit. And before you ask, I will certainly be paid a little personal bonus for making this deal. But the luck is all yours, and once you collect the winnings you may spend them however you like.'

'What did you say your firm was called?'

'Futouristic.co.uk.' He flashed a business card in my direction.

I stared at the newspaper on the table in front of me. It looked almost exactly like every other issue I had ever seen. I peered closely at the date on the top of the front page: sure enough, it carried the date of the following week. I turned to the back page – our local football team was going to lose again next week, three goals to nil. That had the ring of likelihood.

'I thought you said this was legal.'

'It is, Mr Frogle. But to make it legal you must actually buy the lottery ticket yourself, and pay for it. Otherwise –'

I stood up. I was convinced.

'Give me those six numbers,' I said.

Mitch was just a salesman, after all, so I got rid of him as soon as I could. Before he went I signed all the papers, among which was a cheque for more than six hundred thousand pounds. This was backed up with the deeds of my house.

'Don't worry about it,' Mitch said, turning the newspaper

around so I could see the headline again. 'We hold your deeds to make sure that you go through with your side of the deal, but you'll get them back immediately after the ceremony where you collect the money. You keep ninety per cent of everything.'

Mitch left me with a new box, sealed in shrink-wrap. It contained my own little time machine. After he had gone I opened it carefully, slid it out of its protective liner, fondled it lovingly, and tried clipping the leads to my ear lobes. The box also contained an installation CD, an instruction manual, batteries, mains charger and a car adaptor.

I slipped the batteries into the gadget and put them on to charge.

Then I walked down to our local newsagents and bought a lottery ticket. I filled in those six numbers extremely carefully.

When I was home again I read the time machine's manual, printed on thin paper and folded into a dozen vertical segments.

At first sight it looked comprehensive, but most of it was padded out by being translated into many other languages. I read through *Getting Started* in the English section.

After the instructions about charging the batteries, and so on, most of the manual consisted of a long list of historical events that could be visited, preprogrammed.

The Battle of Hastings, the launching of the *Titanic*, the Beatles playing at the Cavern Club, the first performance of *Romeo and Juliet* at the Globe Theatre, King Cnut holding back the sea, Björn Borg winning Wimbledon . . . and elsewhere in the world the storming of the Bastille, the attack on Pearl Harbor, the building of the Pyramids, Maria Callas singing *Tosca*, the assassination of President Lincoln, the fall of the Berlin Wall . . .

The list went on and on, a stunning compendium of our cultural and historical past.

The third section looked more technical, with details about programming my own destinations, past or future. I decided I should have to master all that later.

Something was nagging endlessly at me, and before I went to bed that night I decided I had to do something about it. I contacted the directory service, and with calm formality I was given the landline telephone number in Sunderland for Gwendolyn Labelle.

It rang a few times before it was answered, then a female voice.

'Hello?'

'May I speak to Ms Gwendolyn Labelle?' I said.

'Speaking.' Then I heard a sharp intake of breath. When she spoke next her voice was tense, excited. 'Is that you, Mitchell?'

'Er – yes.'

'Then you remembered! Oh, I am so pleased to hear from you again.'

'Again?'

'After last time. I know you had to hurry away, but it was so sudden and I thought I might have offended you. I wasn't sure what I should do. I can't tell you how happy I am you have called. I thought I had lost you. When can I see you again?'

'Again?' I said again.

'We can't leave it like that. After all those things you said, and after our delicious kisses . . .'

I knew my face was glowing red and was glad no one was with me to see it. I felt the perspiration popping from my brow. Her voice was low, confidential, knowing, the voice of a sensuous, eager woman, the voice of a passionate lover, but also the voice of a woman I had never met.

I said: 'Ms Labelle—'

'Gwendolyn,' she said.

'Gwendolyn, are you sure – I mean, do you know who I am?'

'How do you think I could ever forget you, Mitchell? Mitchell Frogle . . . but you insisted I should call you Mitch. Can you come back to Sunderland this weekend, Mitch? I am desperate to see you again.'

She let out a long-drawn breath, a quiet sound that seemed to reverberate with pent-up passion.

Suddenly I could picture Gwendolyn Labelle. A long, dark-red dress was draped about her, silver earrings dangled by her neck, her black hair was scooped up to reveal her lovely face. Her eyes were outlined in black, with tiny jewels glittering on the lids. She was reclining on a long velveteen draped couch, a glass of champagne stood on a low table beside her heavily ringed fingers . . .

In my wildly imagining mind's eye, I saw a glint of long, vampiric fangs resting lubriciously on her lower lip.

On an impulse I threw down the telephone receiver, and it clattered back into place. I leapt away from it, terrified it might call me back.

I took a cold shower, and went to bed.

When I woke up the next morning the charge light on the little time machine had turned green. I grabbed some breakfast and read the manual again. At last I was ready.

I chose an event more or less at random: the signing of the Magna Carta by King John in 1215. I attached the clips to my ear lobes, dialled in the code number as directed, and pressed *Go*.

There was a feeling of mild electric shock, almost pleasant, but so far as I could tell nothing else happened. Both ears briefly itched. Assuming I had done something wrong, I scoured the manual and tried again.

It failed, so I selected another event: the soccer World Cup Final, England vs West Germany, in 1966. Nothing.

The sacking of the White House by the British forces in 1812. Nothing.

I checked the batteries, checked the connections, read the *Troubleshooting* page in the manual.

Queen Victoria's Golden Jubilee. Nothing.

The storming of the Bastille. Nothing.

I logged on to the internet and tried to find futouristic.co.uk's website, thinking there might be technical support. After half an hour of trying I was still no closer either to locating them or being given an answer to my problems. I found a tiny screwdriver, and nervously removed the back of the plastic case: there were a few wires, several tiny printed boards, a memory chip – nothing that looked at all unusual.

I began to experience a sick feeling of dread.

I remembered the huge cheque I had written, the way I had handed over the rights to my property.

All I had to show for it was a single lottery ticket.

But at least I did have that and the guarantee of a big win. Already I was starting to make a mental list of what I would spend it on. I was beginning to suspect the worst, but even so I fantasized about moving to a bigger house, buying a luxury car, taking a round-the-world cruise, giving away presents to my best friends.

I put the problem out of my mind until after lunch, then went for a walk to clear my head. The dread that I was being cheated would not go away, but I clung to one undeniable fact. Mitch had shown me something that could only exist in the future – proof that I had won the lottery. How else could he have arranged that, without being able to travel in time?

And there was the name of his firm: futouristic.co.uk. They sounded like the sort of outfit that arranged trips to the future, perhaps booked tourists into hotels on the Moon or Mars, or took them swooping through the years ahead, watching their grandchildren grow up, seeing our cities grow and change, witnessing the terrifying effects of climate change, collecting prize after prize from the unlucky lotteries of the days to come . . .

Maybe I had just not used the thing correctly? When this thought occurred to me I was strolling through our local park and I paused beside the ornamental lake. Waterfowl ignored me.

I took out the alleged time machine, then switched it off and on, forcing a reboot. When it was ready I clipped the leads to my ear lobes and scoured through the manual yet again, slowly and carefully, checking everything was exactly as described.

This time I paid more attention to the final section, the one called *Roaming and Exploring*.

The section explained that the time machine allowed you to stray away from preset events and set your own coordinates, past or future. The manual warned new users to be careful. It was possible, the manual said, to traverse as little as one millionth of a second, or one million years. The manual said only experienced users should experiment with distant time periods, but that shorter periods within a recognizable time frame were always safe.

I checked to make sure there were no warnings against wearing any particular kind of clothes that might act as a barrier, or of being inside a building, or outside one, or in a time zone where the network, if there was one, could not be accessed, or recommendations not to try time travel without an assistant, or in fact anything I might have missed before.

I was not feeling adventurous. I only wanted to find out if

the thing was working. Five seconds into the past would be enough to establish that.

As I resumed my walk through the park I held up the little device where I could see it clearly, and spun the appropriate wheel to five seconds.

Then I pressed *Go.*

I couldn't have been looking where I was going, because I instantly realized there was someone walking slowly in front of me. I nearly bumped into him, and stumbled as I tried to avoid him.

'Sorry!' I called, and the man turned round to look at me. He looked horrified and amazed when he saw me. I reacted in the same way! It was me, myself, five seconds ahead of me!

I, the other Frogle, was holding a time machine and two plastic-coated wires ran up to his, to my, ear lobes.

He said loudly, in surprise: '*What?*'

At that instant I heard a voice behind me, someone stumbling, and saying: 'Sorry!'

I turned in horror and amazement and saw another Frogle behind me. I could not help myself. I said loudly: '*What?*'

He turned away. Behind him was another Frogle. 'Sorry!' '*What?*'

And behind him another. 'Sorry!' '*What?*'

Back and back and back, an endless line of Frogles, one after the other, stumbling, apologizing, turning back in surprise, finding myself behind myself, in front of myself. Right across the park, out into the street, down the hill, into the endless distance, out of my view.

Two words echoed around the town, around the world, around the infinite universe.

'Sorry!'

'*What?*'

In a panic I turned the time machine off. There was a sort of inward flash, a shock of electricity running from one ear to the other, and then sanity was restored. The Frogles all vanished. I was alone in the park, ignored again by waterfowl. Both of my ears were itching.

I took the little time machine home and put it away in its box. I never dared use it again.

When the lottery draw was announced at the weekend, the six winning numbers were displayed boldly on television. They were not my six numbers.

My cheque was cashed on the first day of the following week, but my bank queried it and telephoned me to make sure it was legitimate. I told them it was not an authorized payment, and they said they understood, told me these attempts at fraud were quite common these days, and promised they would not let the payment go through. That seemed to be all right, but I never saw the deeds of my house again.

That same Saturday evening a woman named Gwendolyn Labelle, who lived in Sunderland, won slightly more than six million pounds on the lottery. Shortly after her win she mysteriously vanished without trace, taking her money with her.

Within a couple of weeks someone who called himself Mitchell Frogle was living in her house. I discovered this when I called her number again. Mitch and I had a short and mysterious conversation, each accusing the other of something terrible, both of us denying it.

At the end, I said: 'Sorry!'

On the other phone, Mitchell Frogle said: '*What?*'

He threw down the phone receiver at his end. Then I hung up too.

The URL used in this story is, at the time of writing, still active. You may click on it if you wish, and you will see an invitation similar to the one received by Mitchell Frogle. However, you will not be sold or given or even lent a time machine.

Travel through time, at least in the way it is often depicted by writers of the fantastic, is not a possibility. Nor is it possible as it is depicted by myself, in this story. There is no future time – there is no historical past. Time is a continuous *now*, an infinitesimally small moment of perception, which has been preceded by a similar one, and which is followed by another.

It is, however, an attractive delusion that the physical circumstances of the world at any point in time might be revisited, or in the case of the future, that we might slip ahead to a physical world in which our own time exists as the historical past. Like many people I can quickly think of historical catastrophes which the world would be better off without – but then try to imagine the consequences of fixing them.

And who among us does not harbour a small personal catalogue of remembered errors, tactless remarks, lapses of taste, terrible decisions, hurt feelings, broken promises – how much better would it be to go back and avoid them, or correct them, or never make them? I regret to say that the wish is attractive, but in reality it is a delusion.

It will remain so, and on into the imaginable future. We live with the moment we have, because it is all we have.

Before – 'Shooting an Episode'

Writers are frequently asked about the authors they consider to be their influences. Literary influence is often misunderstood to mean that the influencee (so to speak) tries to write like the influencer, the admired author. In reality it doesn't work like that.

The writers I know have influenced me are ones who enabled or freed me creatively. Sometimes, when reading a book that was about to become influential, there would come a moment in which it was clear that some subject or method or approach I had never thought about before was not only possible but admirable. It could be anything – a way of describing a place, a plot development, an insight into character, an atmosphere, a writing style. A door in the imagination would suddenly fly open, a new challenge, a new possibility, something I could try to write in my own way.

I frequently cite the little known American author Guy Murchie as a literary influence on me. Murchie was several decades ahead of the modern fashion for 'psychogeography': ornately styled books with personal and detailed observations of the physical world and the ecological environment. Murchie's way of writing about these matters was more direct: his writing was evocative, personal, surprising, informed and above all lyrical. He was a professional aviation navigator: he read the stars, negotiated with winds. I was sixteen years old, head still stuffed with the dull facts of school Geography lessons, when I read his best book, *Song of the Sky* – Murchie changed the direction of my life. His descriptions of the world's storms, the cloud formations, the effect of gales on the oceans and their currents, the flight of birds, the beautiful names given to many local winds, the journeys of aircraft, the lives of trees, the drifting of gossamer spiders, instilled in me an enlightened and lasting awareness of the physical world. Guy Murchie loved language – his books were a marvellous discovery at an impressionable age, evoking a sense of wonder about the marvels of nature.

For entirely different reasons, the short stories of J. G. Ballard later had the profound impact of making me realize that fantastic writing could be about subjects other than military might, spaceships, empire building, exploring planets, and so on: Ballard wrote about art, music, sex, memory, poetry, movies, the environment – he admired Salvador Dalí, the Beat writers, Michelangelo Antonioni.

Then there was George Orwell. I discovered his work, as so many do, through his novel *Nineteen Eighty-Four*. It interested me, but I was in my mid teens and I was not sure I understood everything about it. I began looking around for more information about Orwell, and by this route I discovered his essays and journalism. Here I found what is in my view his best, most important work.

In one essay after another Orwell wrote simply but persuasively, objectively but with personal passion, factually but also inspirationally, about whatever subject he had chosen as his theme. His use of English was transparent and beautiful, free of stylistic flourishes, often conversational or informal, always clear not only about his subject matter but how he felt about it. I found it admirable and also exciting, a standing lesson in how to write well.

His subjects covered a wide range, from long essays about the state of Britain to intelligent literary discourse. Many of his book reviews defined the period he lived in: the thrillers of James Hadley Chase, the autobiography of Salvador Dalí. He also wrote about apparently trivial matters: the best way to make a cup of tea, seaside postcards, the price of books, and what he called good bad books. Some of his greatest pieces were autobiographical: his schooldays at Eton, working as a dishwasher in a Paris restaurant, a terrifying visit to the coalface of a deep colliery. And there were two pieces I found outstanding, both semi-autobiographical essays from the period when as a nineteen-year-old he went to Burma to serve as a colonial police officer. This was a part of his life that profoundly shaped his views of colonialism. The two essays are 'A Hanging', and my own favourite, 'Shooting an Elephant'.

For many years I would read Orwell's essays whenever I felt discouraged, or I was stuck in a novel or story I was writing, or I had been reading something I found turgid or florid or just plain poorly written. Taking a header into the cool, clear pool of Orwell's prose was always a tonic, a refreshment.

In 2016 I was invited to contribute to an anthology of new stories exploring the legacy of George Orwell's work in general, and *Nineteen Eighty-Four* in particular. The book was to be set a hundred years after that classic novel. Its title was to be *2084*. Because I still felt the shadows of my inadequacy about the original novel, and in particular the way it has so thoroughly penetrated modern political thinking and social understanding, I thought I would do better taking inspiration from what I personally saw as his most influential work.

My story was therefore called 'Shooting an Episode'.

Shooting an Episode

I was hated but respected. I accepted that.

I wanted neither but knew I deserved them both. It was the only time in my life when I was important enough to warrant these feelings, and then it was for only a brief period. Bad luck caused events to break around me while I was still there, still responsible, because if the episode had malfunctioned only a week or so before or after I would never have been involved.

It was partly my own fault: I already loathed the job. It was ludicrously well paid, as it seemed to me at the time, but I had already found out why so few people were willing to work there. By the day the episode happened I had decided that I would chuck it in as soon as I could. Money, respect, the freedom to instil fear and excitement in other people – none of these compensated for the hatred.

I already knew that the network would not want to replace me so soon – I had completed a training schedule, discovering as I did so that I was the only recent appointment going through the system. But I disliked the work. After only a couple of months I had texted in my resignation, so far without response. They were probably dragging it out to postpone my departure.

So I continued to go day by day to my office, fully aware of how the public around me felt about me. The network called

these people the players, and I saw them every day. The players knew who I was, and their feelings were obvious. Most of
them were obsessed with their gameplay, their digital handhelds
glowing, their fingers zapping against the screens, but whenever
I passed many of them would break off to stare at me – hostile
stares, intrusions, warnings, implied threats. No one ever struck
me but once or twice some of the women spat at me. I had
already established a routine: I went to my office early each
morning and did not return to the network flat where I was
living until the daytime crowds had dispersed, but before the
night drinkers emerged.

For the most part I was protected because the players were
obsessed with their gameplay. They loathed me for the power I
had over that, but the same power secured me.

From inside the comparative safety of the office I would watch
the players in the street through the thickly glassed windows.

Some, not all, wore VR masks attached to their brows –
these gave their wearers a characteristic stance, because as they
moved slowly along the street their heads were tipped back,
compensating for the strain on their necks caused by the slight
but extra weight of the device. It made them seem as if they
were searching for something, which in a sense they were. The
less practised of these players also lurched unsteadily as they
walked, because the VR blocked their real-time vision and they
were entirely dependent on the gameplay simulation of their
surroundings. This non-visual information was transmitted
directly to their optic nerves. Falls to the ground by these VR
players were frequent.

The majority of players, though, still preferred the handheld
displays, where the graphics were more reliably instant, because
of slightly lower resolution. These players wandered along,
staring down at their devices, tapping endlessly at the screens,

swiping and jabbing. The more advanced players had begun using the recently introduced psychic controls, with direct transmissions to and from their minds, but the majority still preferred the tactile response of fingers and hands, the universal dexterity.

I was working at what the network called a cell sub-station – after the training was completed I was promoted almost at once to the position of senior contracts producer, although the title was misleading. It made me sound as if I held a managerial position. The one-room sub-station staff consisted only of me, working alone.

While I had been training in the large hub office in the city things were not so bad. The high level of pay compensated for the daily problems, and of course there was the feeling of safety in numbers. Working in the large office was a heady experience, with a kind of nervy arrogance about our control of the players. The main offices were strong on teamwork – this spurious sense of unity mostly neutralized the feeling of personal risk. The building we worked from was anonymous, with many different unmarked entrances – we came and went to our jobs by carefully managed diversionary routes. And of course there was an armed security team on hand.

Two weeks ago, though, I had been posted away to this re-gional satellite station. A promotion of sorts. The town itself was for the most part a post-industrial wasteland, where numerous huge condominium towers were going up. There was country-side around, but much of it had been polluted, brown-fielded, turned to waste. It was a temporary assignment, the managers said, but even before I arrived I realized they had conned me.

One of the biggest ever reality productions was touring and heading by an indirect route towards the town. No one else in the network wanted the job because something always seemed to go wrong with the large tours. If this one came anywhere near the town I should have to deal with it.

After I arrived, took over the network apartment and established myself in the office, even the minimal feeling of independence evaporated when I realized how vulnerable I was. The players were endlessly critical of the way our productions depicted reality – they wanted more of it, or less, or something new. Always they wanted the new. For them reality was something that could be shaped, controlled, distorted into higher levels of real-seeming experience. The more the network gave them, the more they demanded.

The office was in a street not far from the centre of the town, but apart from the heavy locks on the main door, the closed-circuit monitors and the two thickly glassed windows, there were no special security measures. Although there were no signs or logos on the building, no clue as to what it was being used for, all the players clearly knew what it was. Armed security was available on the instant – the instant I sent the message for help. When the armed officers would actually arrive was a matter of conjecture. It would probably take an hour or two for them to reach me if trouble broke out.

Stress levels, I quickly found, were not confined to the cities – they were the same or worse here, in this small and depressing town.

Pay remained the main compensation. I was still being paid at the same rate as the city workers.

The first call came through soon after I had arrived in the office that morning. The caller's face was blanked – the screen showed an ideogram of featureless head and shoulders. I found that disturbing. It meant there was going to be something in the message I should not want to hear. Normal messages were texted, or came with live images. From my period in the main office I knew they put up avatars for inter-office comms when anonymity was required.

'We need all contracts maintained real-time today. Make the changeover now.'

It was a man's voice, presumably belonging to someone I had met or had at least worked with for a time, but I could tell from the flatness of tone that the voice was being synthesized. It could therefore as easily be a woman making the call, disguising herself. The neutrality of the voice, with the synthetic tone adapters I was familiar with, had a chilling authority. Annoying too – why did they do this to me?

'The contracts are up to date,' I said. 'I filed them last night, as usual.'

'Those don't count. The principals have decided they want the protocols ramped up. We are giving them a roll. You handle it.'

'Remind me,' I said, because while I had been waiting for them to accept my resignation I had let the memory of the training soften. I had never worked with a roll-up contract, but had heard about them. Roll-up contracts meant a slackening of the rules – the players (the watching public) and the principals (the main performers) could intermingle in some way. They could change places. I was hazy on the whys and hows.

The voice said: 'It doesn't matter. Enter the code.'

'What code?' I said, petulantly.

But the computer was already responding to an inflow of data. I could see the changes being monitored on the screen.

'Is that it?' I said, but the link had closed. I knew that it was possible for hackers to trace our microwave signals back to source, so at certain times network comms were kept short. This was presumably one of those times.

I stared at the activity on my monitor, gazing at the swift

changes without fully comprehending what was happening. Names of the players scrolled by unreadably quickly in four columns, but of course they were avatars, not real names. Many of them were asterisked or highlighted or coloured, the network's way of noting that certain avatars were nested or cross-purposed: an avatar of one group with another, and another, beyond them layer after layer, accumulating more highlights. These were the syndicates and punter blocs, the exchange groups, the fan cultivars with particular interests, the adapters, the backers, owners, sponsors, lobbyists.

The info was impossible to decipher, impossible for me to decipher. I could not read what was passing through in any event, such was the speed of change, so many hundreds of thousands of avatars, perhaps millions. New highlights were introduced: these indicated gender and age, relationships with other avatar players or syndicates, as well as coded levels of past and present consumer quotient, credit rating, history, vexatious litigant activity, aggravation, performance, commendation or recommendation, offending record and gaol sentences – and above all the financial records: fees paid, ancillary spending, non-gamer holdings, advertising exposure.

All this flashed past me on the monitor. I stopped looking after the first few seconds.

I thought of it as irrelevant, not only to my understanding of what was going on but also to the overall gameplay situation. The most direct impact it would have on my work was that I would have to issue revised contracts to every player and every principal – but even that was of course computerized.

I glanced at the CCTV monitor, where I could oversee the usual crowd of players sauntering past in the street. I could tell they had picked up the same information, because most of them looked pleased. That was not a good sign, as it would lead inevitably to an increase in activity. Several of the players could not resist glancing up at my monitoring cameras. That disturbed me.

Why should the network have done this? How were these decisions made? What, in particular, had brought on this particular shift in policy?

The morning passed with for me a growing sense of unease, a feeling that my problems were about to make themselves known. At lunchtime I took food from the office automat. Not long after that another call came in from the network, confirming my fears.

This time the transmitted image was of a woman, but stylized and impersonal, another graphic design. Her voice was synthesized once more – I suspected a man.

'Some of the principals have evaded security,' he or she said, without preamble. 'Several players have been killed. The equipment crew has stopped broadcasting – we suspect they have been evaded. Otherwise they might have had their equipment neutralized. Whatever happened to them, there is no longer any coverage. You must resolve it.'

'How?'

'The episode must be shot. You know how to do that. The equipment is there.'

'I don't know –' I said, but I was instantly interrupted.

'You will shoot it.'

'I don't know how. And why were the crew evaded?'

'We will monitor results. A security team has been despatched and will be in your activity zone soon.'

'Where are the principals now?'

'No information. Routine scans are in progress. Your equipment will vector you. This evasion must be ended.'

I knew that 'evasion' was the network euphemism for a

worst-case incident. The only evasions in the past I had heard about all involved violence – principals or players attacking the crews, with several deaths.

'I'm alone here, without backup.'

'You have all the equipment you need,' said the mellifluous, bland, calming voice of the electronically enciphered woman.

'Then what is in the script?'

'There is no script. This is roll-up, free format.'

'Can't the rules be changed back?'

But the line went dead. I glanced back at the CCTV monitors – on a normal day there would be a constant movement of players past the office, some of whom inevitably paused and looked towards the heavy windows. Today, though, a small crowd had gathered, waiting outside, looking expectantly towards the entrance.

I put up my contracts file on the computer, the summary. Money was pouring in because of the evasion, or the events behind it. For the network, presumably now to be faced with compensation claims from the families of the crew, this was a high-risk, high-earn situation. Payout now, payback soon.

I went to the real-time monitors, which normally I avoided. There were twenty screens, in four rows of five. The live action was shown here and archived – not by me or in this building, but shadowed elsewhere.

The network's leading attraction was a roving reality: twenty principals, preselected for their known earning power, their extreme psychological anomalies, their social antipathies, had been set loose. The crews followed them, sometimes covertly, often intrusively and interactively. There was no studio containment: they went out into the world.

I was in denial about the realities – after I made my final decision to leave I had closed my mind, merely performing minimal clerical functions. I knew all too well that there was a growing school of thought, expressed in some parts of the media, that accused the network of illegality. I did not want to walk out of the job only to be arrested. The bosses maintained that these claims only came from their competitors, but I was uneasy.

I issued contracts. I oversaw all the money that was paid out, most of the live money that came in. Money was the rationale of the whole enterprise. A lot of it went out, mostly to the principals, but there were other expenses too. Hush money, described as restitution expense, was frequently paid, but it was only a fraction of what the network hauled in every week. My outstation was one of dozens in this country, and this country was one of many that were networked, both with home-grown material but also with productions from affiliated countries. The money was a maze of wealth. I had nothing to do with individual deals – I saw only the totals. I passed everything on. I observed the rules, asked no questions, followed none of the scripts.

I had to do something about the current problem, the roving reality, the one that had caused an evasion.

The lack of clear rules gave the principals a straight path to wealth and celebrity, because within the vague parameters of the rules they could do whatever they wished. They could travel wherever they like, talk about any subject they wished, argue about everything, they could steal, burn, fornicate, attack each other, defecate, abuse or libel anyone they had a grudge against. Fornication was a constant, always performed for the cameras – everyone, players and principals alike, professed to be bored by it, but the ratings went up the more sex there was on screen. Libellous attacks happened too. The network fought every case where an aggrieved victim was bold enough to make a claim. The network sometimes lost and the payouts were immense, but every court case increased the audience, and with it the cashflow. The principals were under the protection of the crew that followed them: everything was permissible so nothing mattered, but because nothing was hidden everything was watched.

The principals were not allowed to kill each other, but that was simple to enforce because of the amounts of money paid to them. Sometimes the principals hated each other, the women were raped (the network euphemism was 'persuaded'), the men often beat each other up (network: 'disputed'), there were many other disgusting or violent actions (network: 'reminders required'). Hardly anyone tried to kill, though.

It was a show. Fame, wealth and celebrity attended every moment of reality. It was entertainment. The principals acted their roles, the players reacted in theirs. Money changed hands. Sometimes, as now, the players were encouraged to participate. More money, always that.

All the principals had to do to earn their money was remain in sight of the crew. It was a show. It was reality. Everyone was used to that. Reality was a commonplace. There was nothing beyond reality – no one believed in anything else, but once the crew was evaded the show was off.

I found the standby equipment, secured as usual behind strengthened panels and combination locks, then followed the intricate decoding procedure that let me take out the various components. I spread them on the bench.

In this I had been trained. The main problem was one I had encountered during the training sessions, which was that the various pieces had been designed and built for someone physically larger than me. I checked everything to the list, I tested all the contact points. I found the battery pack and the spare on the charging bench, connected the main one, made sure, made sure.

I removed my outer clothes, a jacket, jeans, and pulled on the armoured tunic, the strengthened leggings and boots, the accessories belt, tightened everything as firmly as possible. I pulled on the helmet, the weight resting unevenly on my head. I adjusted the straps. The device was still too loose, but there was nothing I could do about that. The heavy equipment was going to chafe against me. Finally I attached both batteries to the belt, connected the main one, checked the setting, checked it again, clamped the accessories' tote around both batteries.

I powered up. The head-up displays, the HUDs, booted into life – an array of adjacent images shining on the inside of the visor. They loaded, diagnosed their circuits, reported all were correct. If I moved my head quickly the images scattered and flashed. I was trained to move steadily, deliberately, to stabilize the perceived reality.

Steady movements were also unprovocative. They helped not to alarm anyone.

The image on the main computer monitor flashed up the comms from the network office. The stylized image of the woman was there again, but when 'she' spoke it was in an undisguised male voice.

'You have not followed orders. You must shoot now.'

'I am doing what I can. The equipment is the wrong size –'

'You must shoot now.'

'I am about to,' I said.

'Stand where I can look at you.'

I checked again the main harness of the helmet, then with everything – as I believed – correctly in place I stood so that I was in view of the cam.

'You are wearing clothes. You are supposed to have removed anything that identifies the network.'

'I have on my underclothes: a T-shirt, pants, nothing else.'

The man/woman said nothing but cut the contact. The screen blanked.

Dreading everything that might happen I released the locks on the main entrance and went into the street. Never before had I felt so exposed, so vulnerable. After the air con in the office, the outside felt suffocatingly hot and grimy. While I turned to secure the door many of the players who had been passing at that moment stopped. They stared at me.

I briefly had my back against them, but I observed their reaction on one of the HUDs.

I turned to face them, the full rig of the equipment in view. This had the expected but nevertheless chilling effect on most of them. They moved back from me, scanning their digital displays. Those with the VR hoods reared away, like alarmed horses.

Two or three of the men stayed put, holding out handhelds to try to take a shot of me, but this was ill advised, as they should have known. There were always a few chancers. The equipment instantly picks up imaging energy and before a shot can be taken it fires an incapacitating bolt back. Some of the more experienced players carried spare handhelds, or even jamming devices as a precaution against this, but even so the incapacitant was an effective deterrent.

The two or three chancers close to me reeled back, their hands and wrists inflamed from the destructive bolts. One of them fell to the ground, while the others stumbled away, hunched over the acute agony of their hands. The handhelds lay burned in the roadway, their touchscreens starred and fogged.

I moved on, trying to ignore the players around me, at least trying to look as if I was ignoring them. In practice it was difficult because so many of them were close around me, stepping in front.

Inside my helmet I was reading the directional satellite scan. I saw coordinates echoed to a HUD on one side, beneath them a ghostly, synoptic image of the street. On the main display I could see an image of devastation – apparently it was an older part of the town, one I had not been aware of before. We were still only two or three hundred metres from the office but I invariably approached from the other direction, in a hurry, head down. This area was unknown to me. I could not see it clearly. I found digital visuals distracting. They made me misstep, lose my way, because I preferred to look at the real world around me.

The players were following me. I could hear and sense them behind me, but of course the equipment was also logging them electronically. Numbers were reported on the HUDs, and the crowd following me was increasing in size. The growth was steady – not fast, but steady. Whether I wished it or not I was now leading a crowd. Crowds attract other people, crowds follow, crowds take on a collective identity, a seeming sentience.

This crowd was connected. Networked digital displays shone on all sides.

I was in the main street of the town, where immense building sites were fenced off, where cranes loomed over new condominium projects. Dust blew across the uneven road surface. Machinery hammered beyond the walls. The sun was high overhead, the metal parts of the equipment were beginning to burn against my unprotected skin.

We passed beyond the construction sites, came to a zone where smaller and older buildings lined both sides of the street. The imaging software reported that most of these places were unoccupied. When I angled my head so that I could see through the visor itself, past the HUDs, I noticed that many of the buildings were derelict. I saw gaping doorways, windows that had been boarded up, roofs that sagged or in many places had fallen through.

People, the sort of people who became players or principals, no longer inhabited individual buildings. It was more acceptable to cram into collective residences where relationships were quick to form, and re-form, where sexual and occupational preferences could be harmonized and explored. This was the modern society. Teams and syndicates were inevitably forged, investment interests hardened. I myself had lived in three different such condominium habitats before I incautiously took this job, and I yearned to go back to that lifestyle. I missed the playing, missed the gaming, missed the elaborate wagers, the sense of constant contact. I missed the instant gratification.

Feelings of rejection, of being a social pariah, had grown in me from my first days with the network. I had changed sides.

Being in the street of old dwellings gave me an unpleasant, dismaying feeling. Heat sensors reported the presence of humans concealed in several of the smaller places. They were not identified as being of special interest, so I carried on past. I imagined them to be non-gamers with lost lives seeking sanctuary, their tragic and pointless existence going on hidden from the world. Even so, I knew it was unlikely they would be allowed to remain permanently in the actual buildings. Many of the ruins were now owned by the various competing networks – they provided an occasional backdrop for action, places for principals to meet in secret, for players to gather and discuss strategy offline, for the cartels to lay off the more extravagant wagers. These places were regularly searched and the intruders ejected, especially if a roving reality came near.

I loathed the callous nature of the network that employed me, the economic priorities it pursued.

After walking for about ten minutes at the head of my

unwanted crowd – their numbers had increased to over one hundred – I noticed a similar knot of players ahead. They were clustered around something I could not make out from this distance, although the sensors were already registering it. The main display reported a 100 percentile reading, telling me that this was what I was seeking.

Then several more traces of material, organic but inactive, lower percentiles for now, were displayed from areas further away. On each of these the percentile score was slowly ticking upwards. I should have to visit them. I had to be ready to shoot. I would get to them in time.

My equipment was humming. I felt the battery pack growing warm, strapped against my waist. I was sweating in the hot sunshine, cursed by the heavy protective suit.

The crowd made a loud sound. I could not tell their voices apart – they noised in unison, all reacting at once to the same data. Most of what they were receiving was coming from my output.

The HUD reader which interpreted player intentions and motives, normally a soothing pale buff colour, sometimes with a few red highlights, now registered a mixture of fear, curiosity, revulsion and, of course, excited anticipation. The players nearest to me were pressing ahead, no longer willing to proceed so slowly, but by jostling me were trying to force the pace.

Most of them kept away from me. I was encircled – a few of them touched me, but all stayed close. They wanted me to get to the scene, shoot the scene, complete it, move on, finish the episode.

They parted in front of me, pulling to two sides – individuals acting in concert, a murmuration. The displays on their handsets flickered in unison. The way ahead was clear. My main lenses automatically zoomed, the HUDs giving me the sensation that I was swooping forward. In the same instant, the steadying gyros and servos kicked in, shifting the balance of the equipment so that it seemed to lose weight. I felt it urging forward, pulling me onwards.

The scene was a human body. At first the definition was not sharp enough for me to tell if it was a man or a woman. The body was in a heap, bent horribly, back arching, face down but still balancing somehow on its knees, a posture of obeisance, long hair spread across the stony ground. It was naked. On my sensors I saw the analytical reading for organic material, the scientific rationale – through the visor I saw naked buttocks, thrust grotesquely upwards at an unnatural angle, head pressed down into the dirt.

The crowd continued to separate, allowing me to progress alone so that I could concentrate on the shots. I stepped slowly forward, the equipment steadying and balancing itself, gauging the movements and reactions of the players. They were no longer crowding around me. They were standing with their handhelds, staring down at the screens, watching reality play before them.

Their fingertips dashed across the screens.

When I was close enough I could see that the body was a man's. I went as close as I dared, feeling the zoom lenses adjusting and reframing. The image remained steady, the colours were enhanced and naturalized, the focus remained sharp. There were deep cuts over the man's back and neck, and one of his arms had been pulled or cut away. The dark gap of the exposed armpit socket horrified me, but the limp, pallid limb, lying on the dusty road surface a few metres away, was even worse to contemplate. The fingers were clenched in a fist.

I was no longer guiding the equipment because the autos had taken control, the sensors responding to the smell of blood, the

307

presence of human flesh, the man's naked skin. The equipment felt lighter – the counterweights and gyros that held the sensors steady were alert, almost alive, compensating not just for the images they were collecting but for my movements too. The bulky weight of the equipment was no longer a problem for me – I felt I was able to soar, able to swoop.

The stabilized equipment began dragging me to one side, thrusting the lenses down, peering and peeking at the intimate details of the man's naked corpse. I was no longer in control. I let the equipment's AI do what it was programmed to do.

As the detailed examination went on the crowd became absorbed in what was coming through to them on their handsets. Their heads were bent over as they stared intently down at the screens. Many of them were tweaking the images: enlarging, inverting, saturating the colours. Their fingers and thumbs dashed across the touch-sensitive pressure points.

Some of the players were laughing – texts were going to and fro, images were being forwarded. Teams were in line, synching their mash-up animations, instantly generated from the base images I was transmitting.

The digital read-outs on my HUDs were steady, but on the players' displays closest to me I could see a dazzle of images, sliding, zooming, wiping, animating. Electronic noise rose around us: beeps and groans and jingles, swarming like a cloud of invisible flying insects. One man near me had mashed up an enlarged simulated animation of the man's corpse – somehow he had contrived the body to stand, to stagger forward, the remaining arm waving, the head sagging, a grotesque parody of life. Even as I watched, the detached arm was itself animated. It rose from the virtual ground, flew across the virtual space, made itself reunite with the floundering body.

I turned away. I took a step towards the corpse, a metre or

two away from me. This was a signal to the sensors that the sequence could be ended.

The crowd instantly picked up on the change and once again swerved away to the sides, leaving a space around me. They knew what I was about to do. Soon I was at the distance auto-specified as safe.

Most of the crowd had clustered behind me. A few seconds later the dead body was dematerialized by my deselector charge. I felt the blast in the same instant as the explosion occurred. My servos protected me from the pressure wave.

A shower of blood, small pieces of flesh and shards of bone spattered down. The players around me shielded their screens with their bodies, or wiped the glassy surface on their clothes. Filters protected me from the stench, the body armour saved me from the pieces forcibly expelled. The auto-wipers cleaned my visor and the exposed lenses.

We moved on, following the other traces. The next two bodies we came across were both female, clothed but horrific-ally wounded. Deep slashing cuts and dark contusions covered the parts of their bodies that had been exposed. As before, the steadying gyros kicked in, creating a stable platform for the shots I had to take.

'Too slow! Destroy now!' The words came through on the direct aural link, so I knew I was being monitored.

'There are players too close,' I said. 'I can't –'

'Get rid of the evidence now.'

I tried to wave my arms as a warning to the players closest to the two dead women, but their attention was locked on the digital displays. As the mess of bodily destruction explod-ed upwards in two balls of fire, with gore bursting out in all directions, I moved on and away. Blood and bone fragments rained down. Most of the players close to me were bloodied but unharmed, and many were thrown to the ground by the double blasts, but at least a score of those people closest to the bodies had taken direct hits from the explosions.

Their horrifying blast injuries, and deaths, marked me as a genuine enemy, worsening my position while simultaneously reinforcing it. I was more of a target, more of a threat, more to hate, more to fear.

Some of the players located digital devices dropped by those hit by the blasts, some of which were still working, and these were seized as loot. The players instantly synched them with their existing ones, carried on. Reality was doubled and tripled.

We trudged onwards.

We came upon the evaded crew not long after this. They were huddled against the side of one of the old buildings. There were six of them: two women and four men. They had been stripped of their protective armour and helmets, then ferocious-ly attacked. Their wounds were shocking, extensive – I looked at what was coming through the HUDs, rather than regard them for real. How many principals had gone for them? Why did the crew have no defence against these attackers? It was impossible to imagine it happening.

If I glanced directly at them, through the visor, I knew that the deaths were real, horrific, but on the digital displays there was a heightened unreality: too much colour, too much blood, too many swords and long blades and bludgeons left around the bodies. Reality was being trended into a new exaggerated version, worse but less real, more thrilling but also more con-scionable for the players.

Already the mash-ups were starting as the players seized on the images: the pictures came ghoulishly alive, less real became even less real, dead bodies rose. The players were making in-articulate, excited sounds I did not like.

It was not appropriate to destroy the bodies of evaded employees of the network, so I keyed in the code on the hand pad, marking the location of where I had found the crew. There was a team who dealt with the after-effects of evasion activity. To my surprise, one of my HUDs ran up confirmation of the names, avatars and photo IDs of the crew members. I glimpsed short biographies.

If the network had known this information all along, why had I been sent out to locate them?

The behaviour of the players was frightening me. They were clustering around the dreadful scene of death, pushing to the front, using their handhelds, reaching across. I glimpsed some of what they were channelling: images of cruelty and bizarre violence, reactivated, restarted, elevated to fantasy.

I pushed hard against the resistance of the stabilizing mechanism and forced myself away. For a few moments I left the crowd behind.

'I've no more traces,' I said into the direct link. 'Concluding now.'

'You are to continue,' said the voice in my head. 'The episode must be shot to the end.'

'It's finished. I found the crew. I'm going to close.'

'You have to continue.'

'Then direct me,' I said. 'What am I looking for?'

No answer.

I walked on, the equipment stabilizing but feeling heavy once again. A feeling of dread was growing in me. I was aware that the players were again moving towards me, as if they knew how the episode would end. Many of them had streaks of blood on their clothes and skin, their hair was matted with gore. They stumbled along, disregarding this, watching their handhelds.

They marched beside me, behind me, around me, my

attendant crowd of players. Although the sky was bright their digital displays shone and flickered, another reminder of the difference between reality and unreality. The players wanted closure on this episode – I had to deliver it. I too had been a player, so I understood their need. Somewhere ahead lay the conclusion.

I had no idea what I was looking for or what I would do when I found it, but I was being monitored. My network would guide me.

I had become the show, the centre of the action. Only I could shoot it and close it.

Even so, rational doubt remained. Whatever or whoever had caused the violent deaths of these people was no doubt the real focus of interest, and I, and my slow progress through the wasted landscape on this edge of the town, was merely a guide for the players. They were following, not to be my followers, but to discover what they believed I knew. They trusted me to lead them to it.

The only information I had that they did not was the info coming through the headset. Most of the read-outs had gone to standby, a flickering sequence of numerals moving too quickly for me to make any practical sense. I guessed they were counting or estimating the number of players. Also they were monitoring the comms between players, the mash-ups, the animations, the endless coded comments, the texts, the GIFs, the trade-offs, the wagers. Everything was recorded, open for reinterpretation, saved for future use, market research on the lam.

One of the HUDs on the furthest edge of my visor was echoing the output of these independent image makers. They moved too quickly for me to take them in, so I was not trying. Numerals were flickering there too – more than three hundred image and video streams were being generated and viewed, based on my shots, even while we continued to trudge across the broken, decaying ground.

The sheer activity of the numerals clearly implied the episode was not yet over.

I stumbled on a half-buried slab of concrete, jutting up through weeds. I lost my step and fell forward, but instantly the counterweights and gyros caught me, steadied me, held me in a semblance of verticality until I could regain my balance. My transmitted images remained steady.

I tried to use the direct link to restore contact with the network – I did not want to continue on into this sweltering, risky wilderness if I had already shot everything there was to be shot. The link to the network remained unanswered. I heard the white-noise hiss of no-signal, relayed in stereo to my earpieces.

With that collective intelligence mysteriously possessed by crowds – although less mysteriously in this age of digital linkage – the players around me suddenly came to a halt. It was my first awareness that I was approaching another target, but almost in the same instant my HUDs changed focus and brightness, and a percentile score appeared. Something, someone, was ahead.

I was more edgy than ever before. I was working without information or backup. I was entirely alone and in circumstances I barely understood and certainly could not control. All I had was the psychic armour of data: I possessed information that protected me, or at least the players' belief in the existence of that information was enough to protect me.

I presumed, I continued to presume.

An image swam into focus: it was another body, somewhere ahead, supine on the ground. I zoomed on it, resolved it, shed as much electronic noise as I could. I heard the response from the crowd – they appreciated my clarifying of the image. Looking past the displays, real-time vision, I could not see any sign of the actual body, but it was certainly there, some two hundred metres ahead of me, perhaps partly concealed by the uneven surface of the ground.

The image cohered again. Now I could see that the body was that of a young woman. She was lying on her back with legs apart, arms spread wide, head tilted back, almost a position of rest, or relaxation. She was naked. I dreaded having to look at her wounds.

The servos had already kicked in – I felt the heavy equipment taking up the mechanical balance, the equilibrium creating the illusion of comparative weightlessness. The images condensed into sharp focus, oversaturated colours.

Everything led me to that woman's body. The unyielding balance, the expectation of the crowd.

The players around me were of course reacting to the images I was transmitting. Several of them had sat down on the ground, others stood in team groups. All of them, everyone I could see with my eyes or pick up on the HUDs, were bending intently towards their digital handhelds. The green and red and blue LEDs on their earpieces glinted. Some of the players, clad in VR headsets, tipped their heads back as if scanning the sky, but I knew it was more to do with easing the headset than with gaining a visual angle. Already the first animations and mash-ups were being passed electronically to and fro – I heard sounds of satisfaction, amusement, anticipation.

The woman on the ground ahead of me suddenly sat up, resting herself casually on her elbows. She appeared to be un-injured. She said something, but she was still too far for me to hear her in realtime, and because of the constant sending that was going on around me the amplified pickup of her voice was electronically distorted.

I was being pulled by the counterweights towards her. Most

of the crowd remained where they had been, preferring now to view the outcome through their reality devices. Perhaps they were nervous that I might violently destroy her? Those who had been following at the rear of the crowd joined the others, forming a seated, half-prone gang of players. Behind me was a glittering array of digital screens. Heads remained bent down facing screens, VR users tipped blindly towards the sky.

The woman stood up as I came closer to her. She spread her arms, as if to prove she was helpless before me, carried no weapons, held no defences, had no supporters. She was in a field of stony ground and huge clumps of coarse grasses, long and yellow, swirling around her bare legs.

'You!' she shouted. 'I asked who you were!'

I had to wait for the diagnostics to complete. While they did I stared away from the electronic displays, through the visor. I realized that I knew who she was, or at least that I recognized her – she was one of the most famous principals, appearing regularly on reality shows. She was a star of the channels, had her own fan base, published many articles in the dedicated media. Her life, when off-reality, was constantly examined and envied and celebrated and criticized in the mass media. Everything she ate, visited, wore or bought was discussed endlessly.

While I was still groping through memory for her identity the diagnostics completed. Her real name was restricted, but her current avatar flashed up: it was *Catt@the@Great*. A massive trail of subsidiaries and principal associates and group members were affiliated to her – the fan base – but here she was alone.

There was a disparity between the electronic image of her and the reality I could see. Her body was painfully thin, as was her face. Her hair was a mess. Blood and mud streaked her unclad body.

'Turn a full circle with your arms raised!' I shouted on the amplifier.

'I want to know who you are first.'

'I've been sent. You killed those principals?'

'Probably. How many did you see?'

'Six of the network crew.'

'Yeah. Six was right.'

'I'm here to shoot you. The end of the episode.'

I pushed up the visor to expose my face – I was finding the constant dazzle of images and relayed sounds a maddening distraction. I could see her more clearly unaided – she was young, calm, but skeletally thin. She began walking towards me.

'Stay where you are!' I shouted, using the aural pickup to amplify my voice.

'OK.'

She leaned to one side, took a long shoot of grass and pulled it up. Holding it in one hand she stood placidly before me. Then she resumed walking slowly towards me.

'How did you kill them?'

I knew all this was not only being transmitted back to the company, it was also being recorded. The hum of the players' digital handsets heterodyned electronically behind the other signals. I glanced back. Not a single player was looking towards me. All worked their handhelds with frenetic energy. The VR users slowly wagged their shrouded heads to and fro.

'They give us weapons. We're not supposed to use them, but I did. It's all over now – I've had enough.'

'Enough of what?'

'This, that, every damned thing. Reality, what you call reality, what they think is reality. It's finished for me. I don't care any more. If you've come to arrest me, go ahead.'

'I'm not here to arrest you,' I said, my voice feeding back

in my earpieces. 'I have to shoot you. Show me where the weapons are. And don't move any closer.'

She spread her arms again and she did come to a halt. 'I don't have them any more. I don't know where they are. And I have a contract that allows me—'

'I know about the contract,' I said. 'It doesn't allow you to kill. What you did to those people in the crew. They wouldn't have hurt you.'

'They were going to shoot me, as you are. I feel better now. I only want the money I'm owed, and then I'll never hurt you.'

'You can't.'

'I don't care, don't care. It's over. Get me the money.'

She sat down again on the ground, a sudden movement but in spite of the stress in her voice it was a relaxed and graceful half-turn, her legs folding beneath her. As the long grass was crushed beneath her I heard a hum of response from the players' crowd. None of them moved. She turned her back on me, swirling the grass with her legs. I saw how ectomorphic her whole body had become: her spindly legs, her thin chest, the bony mounds of her vertebrae.

I was stricken with doubt about what to do. Her atrocities were beyond question – but now she was naked, defenceless, peaceable, harmless. The crowd was silent, waiting for me to act against her. I wanted to complete this, knew I had to, but also knew that every tiny movement or gesture or even decision I made was being monitored somehow by the network. I was not free to act in any way other than theirs, and yet I saw no way forward from this moment.

She and I were both at an end, a rejection of what had gone before. She said she no longer cared what happened. I was the same.

For a moment I tried to turn away, step back from her, but

as soon as I did I felt the full weight of the servos and balancing mechanism. The armour was preventing me from moving.

'I have to go through with this,' I said, allowing the steady armoured suit to hold me.

She said: 'At least tell me your name, lady. I should know who is doing this.'

'I am a gameplay coordinator,' I said. 'For this, I have no name.'

'Then what is your avatar?'

'I have none. You are Catt.'

'I am. I was. That's gone too. Nothing is real, there is no reality. This is what they have done to us.' She leaned earnestly forward, staring at me. 'Why don't you take off that armour, let me see you?'

There was a great silence in this arena of wasting scrubland. Even the players remained still. The sun was hotter than ever, beating down on us from high overhead. Warm air, trapped in the long grasses, drifted up and around my waist. Sweat was running down my back, over my face. My hands were slippery inside the gauntlets, where I gripped the controls.

The voice from the network said: 'How does she know you're a woman?' The voice was harsh, grating, an accusation. 'Did you tell her?'

'You know I didn't.'

'Shoot her now.'

White noise hissed again.

I wrenched my face away from the HUDs, looked through the visor at the woman. 'I have to take you in,' I said to her. 'That's the only way. Stand up again, so I can see you.'

'If I don't? I could walk away. I'm never going to do this again. If they give me the money—'

'I'd have to shoot you from behind.'

'Do what you normally do.' She climbed to her feet again, but this time her motion was not so fluid. I saw that one of her thin legs had a gash along the side of her thigh. She added quietly: 'Nothing matters any more.'

'Life matters,' I said, frightened for her. 'Don't throw it away.'

'This isn't life. This is reality. Shoot me now!'

The crowd suddenly came alive, and a deep, low, happy sigh spread away from them, breathed from innumerable throats. I glimpsed a dazzling movement on the handheld screens I could see to one side of me.

I released the deselector charge and the explosion tore her apart, throwing up a mess of annihilated flesh into the air, flames, heat, instant white steam, a ball of light.

Blood rained down.

I heard a roar of glee going up from the crowd, and in my earpieces the electronic interference from the hundreds of handhelds suddenly transmitting gave a repellent new note to the sound of no-signal.

As parts of the woman's body fell to the ground around me, a sad shower of blood and torn flesh, I saw the nearest players yank the phones from their ears, shake their heads to release their hair, look around, look anywhere but at their screens and displays and VR helmets. Most of them were grinning or laughing, tension purged by the shooting, looking around at each other with an unmistakable sense of triumph.

The crowd of players began to disperse at once, losing all interest in the scene of destruction I had made. The blood continued to drizzle down on me, tiny pieces of flesh and bone clotting the liquid streams that ran across the shell of my protective equipment.

I tore off the helmet, threw it aside. I eased the servo mechanism from my back, released it so that it fell behind me, crashing noisily on a patch of stones and pebbles. The gauntlets, the boots, the leg shields, the tunic that had protected my breasts, the thick belt that carried the battery packs, all fell away. Soon I was unprotected, wearing only my shirt and pants. I was now shoeless, bareheaded, exposed to the blistering heat of the sun.

I headed away from the place where the episode had ended, with most of the crowd ahead of me. They were walking in a relaxed manner, clearly relishing the reality they had all shared. I strode as quickly on the broken ground as my bare feet would let me, wanting only to return to the safety of the network building. I soon caught up with many of the stragglers from the dispersing crowd of players.

Some of them were already brushing their fingertips across the touchscreens, no doubt seeking the next experience of reality.

When they saw me many messages were instantly sent to and fro. I was observed, identified, I was unprotected. Fear rose in me, the fear of the crowd.

They parted in front of me, though, making way for me. No one touched me, spoke to me, threatened me. I was the only one without a handheld – they knew that about me.

A breeze sprang up as I passed the edge of the town, walking along the old street where the derelict buildings were. The slight wind moderated the sun's heat a little, passing across my face and legs and arms, lifting my thin shirt. I stared around as I walked, seeing the old and new buildings of the town for the first time since I arrived, smelling something in the air, hearing sounds that were not amplified or attenuated in some way.

The crowd had dispersed by the time I came into the part of the town where the network building was situated. I realized I was walking alone.

After – 'Shooting an Episode'

George Orwell wrote and completed his novel *Nineteen Eighty-Four* between the summer of 1946 and the early winter of 1948. Even on finishing it he was unsure of the title, suggesting to the publisher that it might be called *The Last Man on Earth*, or alternatively could use the year 1980 as a title. (It was later changed to 1982, then finally to 1984. The publisher said the date looked better in words rather than numerals, and that is how it was published, and that is how it is properly referred to today.) Some writers have theorized that Orwell merely took the year in which he was writing, and also arguably the social, political and moral background in which he was living, and transposed the last two digits: 1948 to 1984. Whatever the practical reason, it seems unlikely that Orwell saw the novel as a prediction of the future thirty-five years on.

The word 'prophecy' is a more useful word and concept for understanding the kind of book it was – a prophet is a teacher, and a prophecy is a revelation.

Then came an announcement of the new anthology to be called *2084*, numerals not words, and this was where 'Shooting an Episode' was first published. The editorial brief asked its contributors to predict what the world might be like six decades hence. To me, that's a difficult task, all but impossible. I have never been able to see into the future much beyond the next weekend. The request seemed to me to be harmlessly off-message, but tending to strike a wrong note. You can only ever write with conviction about the world in which you live, and any futuristic material can only be extrapolative ('if this goes on . . .') or metaphorical.

As all fiction is ultimately metaphorical, albeit with the use of artful and extended metaphors, this has been the way I normally prefer to work out my ideas.

I imagine the real world of 2084, some six decades away, will be as different from the present day, for instance, as was the world six decades or so in the past. Regard the 1960s, with The Beatles, miniskirts, the Cuban missile crisis, Richard Nixon as US president, the Apollo flights, student unrest, the appearance of the BASIC computer language. Mobile phones, the internet, social media, networking and reality TV programmes not only did not exist, their future existence was not even suspected. Perhaps six decades from now these icons of today will have returned to non-existence, or evolved into irrelevance, or been replaced by something better or worse, at least in the form we know them now. I can't anticipate what might replace them.

So 'Shooting an Episode' is an extended metaphor, a satire on the present day, an attempt at the true kind of prophecy. Orwell's essay was much the same: he saw his past role as a British police officer in what was then a part of India as oppressive and unjustified. The shooting of the rogue elephant was a metaphor for British imperialism. Becoming a tyrant destroys the freedom of both the oppressor and the oppressed, Orwell said.

Did he ever shoot such an elephant? No one knows for certain. Have I ever used virtual reality to blow someone to bits?

Not saying.

Before – 'The Sorting Out'

Here is another horror story, but this time it is based on dread, apprehension, a sense of menace, a fear of something irrational and inexplicable. That is a definition of pure horror, undisfigured by the supernatural or the grotesque, and it is a kind of horror most people will have experienced from time to time in the darker moments of their lives.

'The Sorting Out' is a story of quiet menace, and I believe it introduces a source of fear that has not been described before.

The editorial brief, from Ra Page, editor at Comma Press, one of the most innovative and successful of the new indie publishers in Britain, was a rare example of a genuinely inspiring idea. Mr Page wanted contemporary writers to explore and reinvigorate Sigmund Freud's famous list of the uncanny, *Das Unheimliche*. Freud's notion of the uncanny was based on certain objects, living beings, situations or phenomena which irrationally give us the creeps.

I assume, safely I hope, that most people reading this collection of short stories will have had a lifetime love of books. It is a unity among habitual readers, a natural sense of identity with the written and printed word, the sensual experience of opening a book, savouring the faint smell of clean paper and binding materials, touching the pages, turning them. (Readers of ebooks are easily forgiven for their temporary lapse into technology, and anyway they always come back.)

People who are not book lovers never quite grasp the sense of allure, because for them books have often been disagreeably associated with learning or business, or some other practical and involuntary need – however, these people too can and sometimes do mend their ways.

I have lived my whole life with books, and the worst hell for me would be incarceration in a cell without a shelf of paperbacks, renewed from time to time. I do not see myself as a collector, but as an accumulator, a gatherer of books. Gradually my books have increased in number, in spite of occasional but always traumatic visits to charity shops in desperate attempts to make space on shelves and keep a sense of reality.

One of the first short stories I ever wrote (never finished, never now to be finished) was a fantasy about someone whose collection of books silently passed a critical numerical point of no return, and thereafter increased in size entirely of its own reproductive abilities. The character in the story started writing fan letters to authors whose books he read, which they had not yet actually written.

That is not the source of fear in 'The Sorting Out', nor is it close.

The Sorting Out

She walked home in the warm night air, feeling the wind from the sea, sensing rather than hearing the movement of trees and bushes. Melvina was tired from her day in town, from the slow train journey home afterwards, but it had been a successful trip. Two commissions received, and a medium-sized cheque, as well as a general feeling that her life and career were back on track after recent upheavals.

The bag on her shoulder weighed her down, because she had celebrated in her own preferred way, in a bookshop close to the railway terminus. She thought about the weariness of her legs and back, and the prospect of a shower before falling into bed. She planned to sit up in bed browsing through her new books. Also, because thoughts are not linear or orderly, she was musing in disjointed fragments about an article she had just thought of writing, while she was on the train, inspired by watching some of the passengers as they dozed.

Thoughts of Hike intruded as well at random moments, the familiar aggravation, Hike the spoiler.

Now she was walking alone, almost home. It was a clear summer's night, with the stars brilliant above. It was a pleasant time to walk, although she would have enjoyed it more if she had not felt so weary. She passed the small park and war memorial on her left, where some of the houses that overlooked the open space still showed lights in their windows. Then at the end of that street came the flight of steps up to the loneliest part of the walk, a short passage across an area of open land. This was in fact the mound of one of the clifftops, with the sea away to her right and just a well-worn but unpaved path between the large bushes of gorse and tamarisk. Night scents briefly wafted by on the wind. At the end of this path was the terrace where her house was situated. She could see ahead the shape of the tall houses in their long darkened row, the single street lamp close to where she lived.

As she approached the short path that led through her over-grown front garden, she noticed there was something wrong. Her white-painted door was hanging ajar, an angle of the dark interior visible behind it.

Suddenly alert to danger, she felt her breath tightening. Had she left it open that morning? Had the door been open all day? Had someone broken in? Had Hike called round again while she was out? She hurried anxiously up the path to the door, pushed through.

Light from the streetlamp fell in from behind, casting her shadow at a steep angle across the floor, a shape of unexpected dread. She put her hand to the light switch, felt the sharp-edged plastic, the metal ring that held it in place, both so familiar to the touch. Her chest was heaving, her breath coming in uneven gasps. She felt as if she was suffocating. Terror of intrusion gripped her. The light came on: the familiar dim beginning, then the quick gain to full luminosity.

At first, nothing appeared to have been moved. Nothing she could see. The books on the shelf, the coats and scarves on the hooks, the two small paintings by the mirror. Hike's paintings, waiting for him to come and take them away.

Behind her, the door swung open with another gust of wind. Melvina went back and saw where some tool or heavy instrument had been bashed against the hasp, breaking it irretrievably, wrenching the lock out of the body of the door.

Frightened of the darkness outside, the darkness that so recently she had relished, Melvina pushed the door to. There was a pile of books on the door mat, apparently knocked to one side when the door opened. She had no memory of putting them there. She eased the door across them, then propped it closed by leaning her bag against the base of it.

She stacked the books neatly, out of the way.

Now. She took a deep, shuddering breath.

The house.

There were two rooms off the entrance hall, both on her right. She pushed a hand through the crack of the door to her study, reached around the door jamb to find the light switch and clicked it on. Dreading what might be in there, she kneed the door open and peered into the room. Her computer was there, her printer, her cluttered desk, the bookshelves, the filing cabinet. Nothing disarranged. A green LED flickered on her answering machine.

Familiar calm rested in the untidy room. There was no one in there, no one hiding. She walked across to the windows, feeling her knees tremble with the temporary relief. At least the intruder had not come in here, stolen or broken anything. She swayed, so she stepped back momentarily from the window and pressed down on the surface of the desk with a hand, steadying herself. She could see her own faint reflection in the rectangle of window and beyond it the light from the streetlamp.

She leaned close to the window and peered out into the night. There was a car parked in the road not far from the entrance to her house. It was unusual to see any car here after dark. She swished the floor-length curtains closed.

A book fell off the windowsill, landed on the carpet by her feet. She picked it up, closed it, laid it on the cupboard.

She had lived alone in this house from the start, when she bought it after Pieter's sudden death. Then it had been an escape, a new challenge and a fresh start. She became an unwilling widow, a single woman again, a role she had not expected.

Piet's death was something she had had no control over, but she had felt that a change of scene afterwards was necessary. As the months and the first two years went by, she grew comfortably into this place by the sea, always missing Piet, full of regrets about things they had never had the chance to do together, but getting by.

She had never felt threatened by her solitude, before this, but now aloneness was confronting her. There was no one to help her. The silence of the house surrounded her, enveloped her fears. Who had been in? Were they still there?

In the hallway again, she called: 'Hike? Is it you?'

So silent. She heard a familiar clicking sound from the kitchen, and the thump of the gas boiler igniting itself. Emboldened momentarily, she pushed open the second door, which led to the living room with the kitchen beyond, and stood in the doorway as she turned on the light.

For a moment she realized how exposed and vulnerable she was, should there in fact be anyone lurking in the darkness within, but the light came on and filled the room with comforting normality. Nothing appeared to have been disturbed. One of her books lay in the centre of the carpet, held open by one of her shoes. She walked past, went into the kitchen and turned on the light there. The fluorescent strip flashed noisily twice, then settled to its pink-white glare. In the corner was the boiler with its blue flame, visible through the inspection glass, the same as always. No one was there, no one concealed under the table, behind the open cupboard door. She looked everywhere. The door that led to the back of the house, the yard, the garden, finally to the open clifftop, was still securely locked and bolted.

She did not remember leaving the cupboard door open when she went out. She normally kept it closed because it jutted into the room. She looked inside – everything seemed to be in place. She looked in the fridge: no food had been taken.

She knew she had to go upstairs, search the rooms there.

She returned to the hall, looked at her bag holding the door closed. The lock hung away from its fitting. Bright scratches of exposed metal flared around it, where the paint had been scraped away. There was a deep groove where whatever had been used had dug in.

Why should someone be so desperate to break in? It had to be Hike – he was furious when she made him give his key back. But would Hike, even Hike, attack the door so violently?

She stood still, holding her breath, trying to detect the slightest sound from the upper floors. She had to search upstairs. That was next, unavoidably next. She was shaking with fear. She had not known such a reaction was possible, but when she looked at her hands she could not keep them still. Both her kneecaps were twitching and aching. She wanted to sit down, lie down, stop all this, return to the fear-free sanity she had known until three or four minutes before.

At the bottom of the stairs she laid a hand on the banisters, looked up at the familiar carpet, the old one that had been here when she bought the house and which she had been meaning to replace ever since. Every worn patch, every strand of exposed canvas, was reassuringly familiar. She took another breath, then changed her mind. She hurried back into her office, leaving the door in the hallway wide open so that she could see into the hall, and pulled her mobile from her pocket. She pressed the numbers that unlocked the keypad, but she fumbled it. She could not make her fingers go where she wanted.

She tried again, muffed it again. She remembered Hike had an instant-dial number. *Numero Uno*, he said, when he had set it up for her five weeks earlier, just before he drove away.

She pressed the speed dial key, then the '1' on the keypad. The ringing tone sounded in her ear.

She moved the handset briefly away from her ear, to listen for sounds from upstairs. She went back to the door, peered out at the bottom of the stairs, the part of the wall where one of Hike's old paintings still hung. Something else to go. The ringing tone continued.

How late was it? She glanced at her wristwatch: it was just after midnight. Hike was sometimes asleep by this time. She felt the back of the handset growing slippery, where she held it so anxiously. Then at last he answered.

'Hullo?' He sounded curt, muffled, annoyed at being woken.

She started to say: 'Hike . . .' but as she tried to speak the only noise she could make came out as a single gasping syllable. '*Ha-a-a-a!*' That uncontrollable sound amazed and appalled her. She sucked in air, tried again. This time she managed a high-pitched squeak: '*Hi-i-i-i!*' Silence at the other end. Humiliated by her own terror, she tried to control herself. Finally, she got his name out, nearly an octave too high: '*Hike?*'

'Yeah, it's me. Is that you, Mel?'

'*Hi—!*' She swallowed, took another shuddering intake of breath, concentrated on the words she had to say. 'Hike! Help me! *Please?*'

'It's the middle of the night. What's up?'

'Someone – there's someone in the *house*!' Too quick, too

high. She breathed, swallowed. 'Here, when I came in. I found the door –'

Again she remembered what had happened at the start, just those few minutes earlier. That dread feeling when she found the door open in the night, the darkness within, the silence. She almost let go of the handset at the memory. She sat down, lowering her backside against the edge of her desk, but immediately stood up again. Trying to keep her voice low, but hearing the stress make it harsh, she added: 'I think someone's still here.'

'Have you looked?'

'Yes. No! I haven't been upstairs. I'm too frightened. They might still be in the *house*!'

'Is this what it takes to get you to call me?'

'Hike, please . . .'

'How long has it been? Five or six weeks?' Melvina could not answer, cross-currents of Hike and the fear of an intruder flooding together. 'Is anything missing?' he said.

'I don't know. I don't think so.' The cross-currents gave her thoughts sudden freedom. 'Was it you, Hike? Have you been over here while I was out?'

He said nothing.

'Maybe it was just local kids,' he said after a moment. 'Kicking the door in for fun.'

'No . . . it's been forced. A chisel, a hammer, something heavy.'

'Are you asking me to drive over?'

Hike lived more than an hour away, by car. She had never seen his new place, nor even knew exactly where it was. He had always said he disliked driving at night. She had kept him away all this time, five blessed weeks without him.

'No, I'm OK,' Melvina said. 'I've just had a fright, that's all. I don't think there's anyone still here. I'll be all right.'

'Look, Mel – I think I'll drive over and see you anyway. You want me to pick up my stuff, and this might be an opportunity to do that.'

'No,' she said. 'It's after midnight. I told you and you agreed, you bloody well *agreed*, that you would send a friend to get your stuff. I want that room cleared out, all the paintings you left, everything.'

'I know. But you need me, otherwise you wouldn't have called me in the middle of the night.'

'No,' she said. 'I'll call the police. That's what I ought to do.'

Suddenly the phone went dead at the other end. Hike had cut off the call.

She put down the phone, laid it on her desk next to her keyboard. A mistake! A mistake to call him . . . but there was no one else. The flashing LED on the answering machine radiated normality, and for a moment she reached over and rested her finger on the *play* button. Then she remembered what had happened to the house. Talking to Hike had changed nothing. Just delayed things, just as always.

In the hallway she returned to the front door, looked again at the broken lock. She tried pressing the door into its frame and discovered that if she let the hanging lock be pushed back she could hold the door closed long enough to shoot the bolt at the top. As soon as she had done this she felt safer.

She picked up the pile of books that had been on the doormat when she came in, and without examining them stacked them roughly on the end of the lowest bookshelf.

Looking anxiously ahead of her, Melvina began to climb the stairs, pausing for a few seconds on each step. She was straining to hear any sound from above. The silence was absolute: no apparent movement, nothing being moved about, no footsteps. No one breathing.

The mobile handset suddenly rang, behind her in the study where she had put it down. She went rigid for a moment. Then, relieved, she ran down the four or five steps she had climbed and hurried back into her study.

'Mel, did you call me because you wanted me to drive over tonight?'

'No, I –'

No, I just wanted to be sure it wasn't you, Hike, she added silently, looking over her shoulder at the light coming in from the hall.

'I'm a bit more awake now,' he said. 'Have you noticed anything stolen? Has anything been moved? Is there any damage?'

'It's OK, Hike. I've searched the house. There's no one here and nothing's gone.'

'Couldn't you ask one of the neighbours if they saw anything?'

'Hike, you know I'm alone here. The other houses are still empty.'

Some of them were used as summer lets and visitors would probably start arriving in the next few days, but because of the recession most of the houses in this terrace were permanently vacant. Hike knew this, he knew the collapse in property values was why she had been able to afford the house on her intermittent earnings.

'Where did you go today?' he said suddenly.

'*What?*'

'You've been out of the house all day, and I've been trying to call you. Are you seeing someone?'

'It's none of your damned business! Is that all you're thinking about? What I've been doing all day? Someone's broken into my house and for all I know is still in here somewhere.'

'I thought you said no one was there.'

'I was still looking when you called again.'

333

'Are you seeing someone, Mel?'

She tried to think of some answer, but she was obsessed with thoughts of the house, the open door, that darkness and the silence. She felt the paralysis of her throat again, the mysterious seizing up of breath and vocal chords, the dominance of fear, the dumbness it caused. She gasped involuntarily, then moved the phone away from her ear. No more Hike. She pressed the main switch on the top of the handset, watched the Sony logo spinning back into oblivion, then darkness.

There were fourteen messages waiting on the landline answering machine – most of them would be from Hike, just as they were every other day. She flicked it off. Her hands shook.

Something moved upstairs, scraping on the floorboards.

Involuntarily, she glanced at the ceiling. The room above, the spare room, the one where Hike's stuff was still piled up awaiting the day when he or one of his friends would collect it. She strained to hear more, thinking, hoping, she had misheard some other sound, perhaps from outside. Then again: a muffled scraping noise, apparently on the bare boards above.

She emitted another involuntary, inarticulate noise: a sob, a croak, a cry of fear. Propelled by the fright that was coiled inside her, but at the same time managing to suppress it somehow, adrenaline-charged, she ran two steps at a time up the stairs. She went straight to the door of the spare room, threw it open and pressed her hand hard against the light switch inside. She went in.

Familiar chaos filled the room, the remaining debris of Hike's departure. His uncollected stuff was still where she had pushed it against one of the walls: piles of paper, canvases, pots, boxes with things in them, his easel, some of his horrible old clothes. His broken computer scanner and a tangle of cables. Three large crates of vinyl records and CDs. That bloody music he played so loud when she had been trying to work. Two suit-cases she had never opened, but which she assumed contained some of his clothes. Shelves where he had stacked his stuff, but not books – these were the only shelves in the house that were not crammed with books. This was in fact the only *room* in the house without books. Hike was not a reader, and had never understood why she was. He said the image was king, books were over. The only things he read were American comics, which he threw away or left on the floor.

There were other traces of him everywhere, reminders of him, his endless presence in the house, the upset he had caused her almost from the first week, later the resentment, finally the anger, the days and weeks of pointlessly wasted time, all the early curiosity about him lost, the endless regrets about letting him move in and set up a studio in this room, the feeling of invasion, of trying to make the relationship work, even at the end. Even, for a while, after the end.

Nothing in the room had been moved or interfered with and nothing had apparently been taken. The window was wide open as she had left it that morning, but the wind was blowing in from the sea. She pushed it closed and secured it. There was a cupboard door hanging open, a glimpse of the dim interior beyond. Still fired up by anger and fear, she strode across the room, stepped past Hike's cases and pulled the door fully open.

The cupboard was empty. The rack where his clothes had hung, the shelves where he had crammed his messy things, were all vacant. Nothing in there. Just a paperback book, tossed down so that its cover was curled beneath the weight of the pages.

She picked it up: it was Douglas Dunn's *Elegies*. It was one of hers – Hike and poetry were polar opposites. How had it come to be here in this room? She straightened the cover and gently riffled the pages of the book, as if comforting a pet animal that had been hurt. Holding it in her hand she left the room, but deliberately did not switch off the light. For now, she had an aversion to unlighted rooms, dark corners.

The light on the landing had gone out while she was in Hike's room. She turned it on again, only half-remembering if she had switched it off herself as she dashed upstairs to this floor. Why should she have done that? It made no sense.

The room next to Hike's was her own sitting room, a room set aside for reading, with more books, hundreds more books. There were shelves on three of the walls, floor to ceiling, a large and comfy armchair which she had bought as a treat for herself after Piet died, a reading lamp, a footstool, a small side table. A desk with papers and a portable typewriter she sometimes used if she didn't want to break off and go downstairs to the computer. The room had a closed, concentrated, comfortable feeling. She remembered Hike's derision when he saw the room the day he moved in. He said it was middle class, bourgeois. *No, it's just where I like to sit.* The room had become a sort of battleground after that, a minor but constant aggravation to Hike. After he left, she realized that she had frequently found herself making excuses to be in here, to explain that which could not be explained to someone who would never understand.

She was glad he was gone, glad beyond words, glad a hundred times, now a hundred and one. She never wanted him back, no matter what.

She glanced around the room: it was lit only by her reading lamp, but everything seemed to be untouched. Just books everywhere, as she liked them to be, in their familiar but comprehensible jumbles. She pressed the Dunn into a space on a shelf beside the door, preoccupied still with her worries, not noticing or caring which books she placed it beside.

She went next to the bathroom. Three of her books lay on the floor beneath where the glass cubicle door overhung the rim of the shower cubicle. They were three recently published hardback novels she had reviewed for a magazine a month before, and which she expected would have a resale value to a dealer. How had they come into the bathroom, though? She never took books in there.

She picked them up, examined them for damage. As far as she could see no harm had been done by water dripping on them. She opened the top one, and immediately discovered that it was upside down. The paper dust wrapper had been removed and put back on the wrong way round.

The other two books were the same.

Melvina stood on the landing outside her reading room, putting the dust wrappers back as they should be.

She felt her throat constricting again – her hands were shaking. She could not look around, fearful of everything now in the house.

She took a step into her reading room and placed the books on the shelf near *Elegies*. She backed out of the room without looking around too closely, horribly aware that something in there had been changed and she did not like to think what, nor look too closely in case she found out.

Hairs on her arms were standing upright. She was sweating – her blouse was sticking to her body under her armpits, against her back. But she was now determined to finish this. She climbed the final flight of stairs to the top floor of the house. She went to her sewing room first, under the eaves, with a dormer window looking out towards the road. The blue-white glare fell on the car parked close to her house. It looked like Hike's car, but in the dark most cars did.

She checked the room for any sign of intrusion. It was here

she kept her sewing table with the machine, the needlepoint she had been working on for a year or more, the various garments she had been meaning to get around to repairing. There was a wardrobe, and in that she kept the old clothes she was planning to take one day to a charity shop. Some of those clothes were Hike's.

The unshaded lightbulb threw its familiar light across everything – there was no one in the room, nowhere that anyone could be hiding.

Finally, quickly, she went to her bedroom. This was the room with the best view of the sea. She had originally planned it to be her office, but once she moved in she realized she would be distracted by staring out all day.

She turned on the central light, went straight in, saw her pale reflection in the largest pane of the window. She paused just inside the door, remembering. Hike had tried to change this room, said it was too feminine. He hated lace, frills, cushions, things he deemed to be womanly. He never discovered that there was no trace in her life of the frills he hated, never had been. It had not stopped him criticizing, and he slept there every night he was in the house. He did move the bed away from the wall where she had initially placed it, because, he said, he did not want to fall over her stuff if he had to get up in the night.

Melvina planned to move the bed back soon, but she wanted to put up more bookshelves before she did. She had been de-laying, because of the expense.

Everything she remembered of Hike was negative, unpleas-ant, rancorous. How had it happened? Since he left she had grown so accustomed to being weary of him that she had to make a conscious effort to remember that Hike Tommas had once been eagerly welcome in her life. The early days had been exciting, certainly because they brought an end to the long aftermath of Piet's death.

Hike had intrigued her. His wispy beard, his hard, slim body, and his abrasive sense of humour, all were so unlike genial Piet. Hike changed everything in her life, or tried to. His opinions – they soon became a regular feature, his attitude to life, his harsh judgments on others, a constant undercurrent of ill-feelings, but at first she found his reckless views on other artists and writers stimulating and entertaining. Hike did not care what he said or thought, which was refreshing at first but increasingly tiresome later. Then there were the paintings he executed, the photographs he took, the objects he made. He was good. He won awards, had held an exhibition at a leading contemporary art gallery, was discussed on the arts pages of broadsheet newspapers.

And the physical thing of course, the need she had, the enjoyment of it. They had done that well together. They made it work, but the more it worked the more it came to define what it was she disliked about him. She hated the noises he made, the obscene words he uttered when he climaxed, the way he held her head to press her face against him. Once she gagged and nearly suffocated as he forced himself deep into her mouth, but it did not stop him doing it again the next time. Hike was always in a hurry about sex. Get it over with, he said, then do it again as soon as possible.

Well, it was no longer a problem.

There was a pile of her books balanced on the end of the bed, placed exactly at the corner, leaning slightly to one side. Ten books, a dozen? They were paperbacks. She recognized them all, but they belonged in her study or reading room. She could not remember bringing them up here.

On the top was another by Douglas Dunn: *Europa's Lover*.

Then Nell Dunn's *Poor Cow*, J. W. Dunne's *An Experiment with Time*, Dorothy Dunnet's *The Unicorn Hunt*, George du Maurier's *The Martian*.

She never alphabetized her books by author. She either stacked her books by type, or sometimes left them in neat but unsorted heaps that she would get around to shelving one day. She always knew where her books were, or could find them quickly using the magic radar that most habitual readers had. The poetry came from her study, the other books from her reading room.

She felt her fingernails biting into the palms of her hands, the cold press of her perspiration-soaked blouse against her back.

Trying to stay calm she went to the books but the slight pressure and vibration of her feet on the floorboards was enough to cause the pile to topple. She lunged forward to catch them but they thudded down on the floor, some of them landing with pages open and the spines bent. She knelt to pick them up.

On that level, face close to the floor, she paused. She was next to the bed, close beside the dark area beneath.

Melvina bit her lip, leaned forward and down, so that she could look under the bed.

No one there. As she straightened with some of the paperbacks in her hand she felt exposed and vulnerable, moving backwards and getting to her feet without looking, not being able to see behind her, or to turn quickly enough.

But she stood up, looked around the room, then placed the books on the floor so that they would not fall again. She headed for the stairs.

Still feeling her knees quivering as she walked, Melvina went through every room in the house one more time, feeling that perhaps the worst was over. Both doors to the outside were secure, and everything was as she expected it to be.

Just the books. Why had the intruder moved her books around?

She went to the kitchen, closed the Venetian blinds and made herself a cup of hot chocolate. She was wide awake and still jittery.

She returned to her study and switched on her computer. Her mailbox would be full of Hike but tonight she would just delete everything from him without reading. She stared at the monitor, sipping her chocolate drink, while the computer booted.

She browsed through her emails, skipping over Hike's or simply deleting them unread. For a while he had been sending his messages from an email address that did not contain his name, apparently trying to get under her guard, but he had quit doing that last week. She stared at the screen, only half-seeing, half-reading the other notes from her friends. None of them ever mentioned Hike. To all her friends, he was a figure of the past.

She knew Hike was stalking her, and that one of a stalker's intentions was to make the victim think constantly about him. She also knew Hike was succeeding. It must have been him who came to the house. Who else would it have been? But then why had he taken back none of his property, which he knew she had repeatedly asked him to take away, or have taken away, but which he constantly used as one of his excuses for keeping in close contact with her? Perhaps he had said something about coming to the house in one of the emails she had already deleted?

Changing her mind, she found the trash folder of previously deleted emails and opened every one of his messages from the last three days. She skimmed through them, deliberately not reacting to his familiar entreaties, threats, reminders of promises

341

imaginary and real, his endless emotional blackmail about lone-liness and abandonment, his pleas for forgiveness, etc. Nothing new, nothing that explained what had happened today.

All she had to do was wait him out. Give it time.

She clicked away the trash folder, but a new message had arrived in her inbox, from Hike. The date stamp showed it had been sent a few seconds before.

Melvina closed her eyes, wondering how much time it would really need. When would he leave her alone?

Behind her there was a sound, heavy fabric moving.

Immediately, she stiffened, was braced against fear. She strained to hear. There was a slight sense of movement, then a quiet noise that sounded like a breath.

In the room with her. Someone was behind her, while she sat at her desk.

She froze, one hand still resting on the computer mouse, the other with her fingers beside the keyboard. The computer's cooling fan was making a noise that masked most of the quiet noises around her. Noises like the sound of someone breathing.

She waited, her own breath caught somewhere between her chest and her throat. She hardly dared move.

Her desk was about a metre away from the bay window, so there was space for someone to stand behind her. She turned in a hurry, accidentally knocking some pencils from her desk with her hand. As they clattered to the floor she looked behind her.

She stood.

Every light in the room was on. She could see plainly. There was a figure standing by the window, concealed by one of the full-length curtains.

She could make out the bulge, the approximate shape of the body hidden behind. She stepped back in alarm but her chair was there and she knocked against it. She stared in horror at the figure. The bulge in the curtains, the sound of breathing, the source of every dread.

Whoever was concealed there had taken hold of another of her books, because she could see it, a black hardcover without a paper jacket, held at waist height in front of the curtain. It was the only clue to the actual presence of the person hidden there. She was so close she could reach out and touch the book. It was being held somehow at an angle, an irregular diamond halfway up the curtain, in front of the bulge, gripped from behind . . . by someone breathing as they stood behind the curtain.

The curtain moved slightly, as if lifted by a breeze. A breath.

Another involuntary sound broke fearfully from her. She pushed back, shoving her chair to one side until she was pressing hard against the edge of her desk. She groped behind and her hand touched some pens, her notepad, the mouse, her mobile phone . . . and a ruler. A wooden ruler, a solid stick, the sort that could be rolled.

She grabbed it and without a thought of what she was doing she struck with revulsion at the book, like someone trying to kill a snake or a rat. The wooden ruler thumped hard against the book, dashing it to the ground. It fell in a violent flurry of pages, spine upwards, pages curled beneath it.

The curtain shook, swung, fell back against the window. She had expected a cry of pain as the book was dashed away.

Using the ruler, she parted the curtain.

No one was there. Just the black oblong of night-darkened window. She saw her reflection dimly in the pane. Her hair was wild, disarrayed, as if in fright. She smoothed it down without thinking why. The half-light window at the top of the frame was open, admitting a breeze, a breath of night air. She felt the cooling flow, but now she wanted the house to be secure, sealed. She balanced herself precariously on her office chair and closed the window.

The solitary car was still parked outside, under the street-lamp. It looked like Hike's, but he was more than an hour away. It could not be him – although mobile phones, wireless broadband, could be accessed from a car. Because of the light shining down from above, the car's interior was shadowed and she could not make out details – was someone inside?

She stared, but nothing moved.

Stepping down from her chair she picked up the book that had given her such a fright. It was John Donne's *Collected Poetry*, a hardback she had owned since she was at university. She clutched it with the relief of recognition, the old companionship, closed the pages, checked that none of them had been folded back when she knocked it to the floor. There was a dent at the top of the front cover where she had brought down the ruler. The spine, the rest of the binding, the pages, looked none the worse for the incident, but as she turned to put the book on the shelf where it belonged she discovered that there was a large patch of sticky stuff on the back board. She tapped her finger against it and was surprised at the strength of the glue that had been smeared there. This must have been used to hold it against the curtain.

She sat at her desk, despairing, and holding the damaged book. Why this one? She dabbed at the sticky stuff with a paper tissue, but it only made a mess, made the problem worse.

She put the book aside and closed down the computer. She wanted no more incoming emails. At last the room was silent – no whirring sound of the cooling fan, or of the wind from outside, or of anyone or anything moving inside the house. No footsteps or moving objects, no one breathing around her, no suggestion there was anyone near her, or hidden somewhere in a corner she had forgotten to search.

Tiredness was finally sweeping over her, as the physical exertion of the day's travels and the trauma of arriving home combined against her. But still she could not end the day, without being sure.

She moved swiftly from her study, walked straight to the damaged front door, pulled back the bolt and went outside. At once she was in the wind, the sound of trees and foliage moving, the night-time cleansing of the air.

She headed directly for the car parked beneath the streetlamp.

No one was inside, or appeared to be inside. She went forward, suddenly alarmed that there might in fact be someone hiding, who had ducked down as she left her house. In her haste she had not thought to bring a torch. She reached the passenger door of the car, braced herself, leaned forward, looked in through the window.

A parallelogram of light fell in from the streetlamp. There was a laptop computer on the front passenger seat, its screen opened up, and lying next to it was a mobile phone. Both revealed by their tiny green LED signals that they were in use, or at least were on standby. There was no sign of anyone hiding in the car. She tried the door, but it was locked. She went to the other side, tried the door there too.

When she turned to go back to her house she realized she had made no attempt to close the front door behind her. In a disturbing reprise of the first sign she had seen of the intrusion, it was swinging to and fro in the wind, a seeming invitation. She hurried back, rushed inside, pushed the door into place and slid the bolt closed.

She stood at the bottom of the stairs, looking up, listening for sounds from any of the rooms downstairs. The books beside the door, which she had not examined closely before, were still on the shelf where she had thrust them in haste.

Melvina picked them up with a feeling of dread certainty, and looked at the authors' names: Disraeli, Dickinson, Dickens, Dick, DeLillo, De La Mare . . .

Once again, full of fear, she toured the house. She checked all the doors and windows, she looked in every room and made sure that no one could be in any conceivable place of conceal-ment. Then, at last, she began to relax.

It was past one o'clock, and although she felt tired she was not yet sleepy. She went back to her cup of drinking chocolate, now lukewarm, and finished it. Then she climbed up the stairs to the bathroom, brushed her teeth and took a shower.

For the first time since she had bought the house, she found being inside the shower frightening: the closing of the cubicle door and the noise of the rushing water cut her off from the rest of the house and made her feel isolated and vulnerable. She wanted to extend sensors throughout the house, detect the first sign of intrusion at the earliest opportunity. She turned off the water almost as soon as she had started, even before it had become warm enough, and stepped out of the shower feeling wet but unwashed. She towelled herself down, still on edge, nervous again.

In the bedroom, she collected the books that had been stacked on the end of her bed, took them down to her reading room. Most of them belonged there, and she would put the others back in her study in the morning. She went downstairs, found the other books, all with authors whose names began with 'D'. Why? What was the significance of that?

She turned on the central light in her reading room, and once again she had the unmistakable feeling that something was different, something had changed.

The books on the shelves looked tidier than usual: no books rested face up on the tops of others. No books leaned to one side. None stuck out.

She looked at the shelf nearest her. Rossetti, Rosenberg, Roberts, Reynolds, Remarque, Rand, Rabelais, Quiller-Couch, Pudney, Proust ... All sorted into alphabetical order. By author. In reverse, Z to A.

She put down the pile of 'D' authors she was carrying, and turned to the shelves by the window. On the top shelf, at the left, were *Thérèse Raquin, Nana, Germinal, La Débâcle,* a volume of letters, all by Émile Zola. Next to him, Israel Zangwill's play *The Melting Pot* and his novel *Children of the Ghetto.* Next –

She went to the other end of the shelves, by the door. Here was the copy of Douglas Dunn's *Elegies,* where she had hurriedly stacked it with the three review copies, after she found it in the spare room cupboard. She now realized she had pressed it in beside Le Guin and Kundera.

She took it down, added it to the pile of 'D' authors.

One of the hardcovers close at hand was her treasured copy of Le Guin's *The Dispossessed.* She removed it from the shelf carefully, with her hand shaking again.

When she opened the book she found that it was upside down inside its paper dust jacket.

Carrying the 'D' authors, Melvina went downstairs again to her study. The first book at the top left-hand end of the main shelf was Jerzy Kosinski's *The Painted Bird,* and several more of his novels. Next to those, Koestler. Next to him –

Immediately beside her desk was a long gap in the sequence, which began after Dunstan and resumed with Defoe. The books she was carrying in both hands, a tall heap of mixed paperbacks and hardcovers, fitted loosely in the space.

She put them back, instinctively sorting them into the reverse sequence – she could not help it.

At the far end of her study, where there was another kind of gap, a space for new acquisitions, the last title was *Inter Ice Age IV*, by Kobo Abe.

The book was upside down inside its paper wrapper. Further back, Amis was upside down. Barstow was upside down. Fitzgerald was upside down. Greene was upside down.

Melvina went around the house one last time. She double-checked that every window was closed and curtained, that the front and back doors were securely closed, and that every light in the house was on. At last, she went to bed.

She read for a while, she listened to music on her MP3 player and she turned on the 2:00 a.m. BBC news. She lay in the half-dark, with a reading lamp on but turned away towards the wall, and with light spilling into the room from the hall. She turned, she fluffed pillows, she tried to cool down and then to warm up. Eventually she drifted into a state of half-sleep: lying still with her eyes closed, but with her thoughts circling and repeating. Time passed slowly.

She must eventually have fallen into a light sleep, because she was awakened suddenly by a blow to her face. Something hard and heavy, and with a sharp corner, landed painfully on her cheekbone and temple. It rested there inexplicably. Instantly she was awake, and moving. Whatever it was slid off her face, landed on the mattress beside her and fell to the floor.

She sat up, and swung her legs out of the bed so that she could sit upright. She swivelled her reading lamp around, and in its glare she picked up the book that had fallen on her. It was Charles Darwin's *Origin of Species*. It was her old paperback annotated edition, purchased years before, one of those many titles she was intending to read all the way through. One of these days.

From outside the house she heard the starter motor of a car, followed by an engine being revved. Still naked from the bed she went quickly to her sewing room next door, pulled aside the curtain, and looked down at the street. The car that had been parked outside her house was accelerating away. She could not see who was driving.

Melvina waited at the window, resting her hands on the sill, leaning her forehead against the cool glass. She watched until the car had driven away, out of sight, and could no longer be heard.

Predawn quietude began to spread around her – in the east there was a grey lightening of the sky, a mottled paleness, un-spectacular but steady. The trees across the road from her house gradually took on clarity and shape. She returned briefly to her bedroom, pulled on her robe, then she went back to the window.

Almost imperceptibly, the world was sliding into visibility and colour around her – the trees, the curving road, the closed sheds of the council cleaning depot at the end of her street, the roofs of her nearest neighbours' houses down the hill, the flowers in her overgrown garden. Melvina opened the window fully, leaned out into the air, relishing the cool atmosphere. She had not been awake at sunrise for many years. Now she could hear the sea, away behind her on the far side of the house, making a constant shushing on the shingle beach. Calmness spread through her. She waited until the sun had fully risen, but almost as soon as it became visible it disappeared behind a bank of grey cloud. A bird, hidden somewhere, began to sing. The daylight spread inexorably but gently.

Fully awake, Melvina returned to her bedroom and dressed in her oldest work clothes.

She went to the spare room and began to carry Hike's stuff downstairs. It took her an hour to collect up and move everything, and at the end of that time she was sweaty, tired and in need of a bath, but when she had finished Hike's belongings, all his photographs and paintings, including the two that had been hung in her entrance hall and the one on the stairs, all his art materials, his photo equipment, his easel and brushes, his papers, magazines, records, broken scanner, bags of cables and clothes in need of recycling lay in a heap outside. But not anywhere near her own house. Two of the houses a short way from hers were due to be let to visitors in two days' time, and she knew someone would clear away all the junk that had inexplicably appeared outside them.

It was going to be another warm day. Melvina opened every window, and settled down to work.

After – 'The Sorting Out'

'The Sorting Out' was published in 2006 in an anthology called *The New Uncanny*, which is of course a terrific title for this kind of story. Other contributors included A. S. Byatt, Jane Rogers, Hanif Kureishi, Nicholas Royle, Etgar Beret, Frank Cottrell Boyce and Ramsey Campbell.

'The Sorting Out' was later made into a rather good short film, written and directed by Caleb D. Shaffer, and with Elizabeth Bassham playing Melvina.

Unusually (for me) the idea of the story came from a dream. I entered a room where full-length curtains were closed across a window, but a book was suspended in front of the curtains. When I moved closer I realized that the book was being held in someone's hand, through the material of the curtain. There was somebody concealed behind the curtain. I woke up in terror.

From that small, inexplicable image, the entire story grew.

On a recent house move, my partner and I had to employ a local carpenter to build and fit new bookshelves for us. There were already several shelves available in the house, and of course we had two or three freestanding bookshelves of our own from the previous address, but we still needed more, many more. After the carpenter finished I measured the extra space we had: the total new shelves exceeded 350 feet, or about 110 metres. They were soon filled.

The gathering of books is a kind of quiet madness, but I always feel uneasy if I go to someone's house and do not see an abundance of them. To me, an absence of books is the opposite state: a calm, controlled sanity, tidy and unchallenging, allowing space and the movement of air, but it's a way of life that chooses a view of wallpaper over constant company, a warm environment, hundreds of friends on hand and dozens of old lovers instantly available.

'The Sorting Out' is of course essentially about the rift that exists between someone who cannot live without the encircle-ment of bookshelves and the volumes standing in rows upon them, and someone who can.

Last

Acknowledgements

Many thanks to the various editors who, over the years, have supported these stories. For this collection, special thanks to Nina Allan, for egging me on.

Previous appearances

'The Head and the Hand' – first published in *New Worlds 3*, 1972, copyright © Christopher Priest 1971, 2019 (Collected in *Real-Time World*, New English Library, 1974.)

'A Dying Fall' – first published in *Asimov's Science Fiction*, 2006, copyright © Christopher Priest 2006, 2019

'I, Haruspex' – first published in *The Third Alternative*, 1998, copyright © Christopher Priest 1998, 2019

'Palely Loitering' – first published in *The Magazine of Fantasy and Science Fiction*, 1979, copyright © Christopher Priest 1979, 2019. (Collected in *An Infinite Summer*, Faber & Faber, 1979.)